SUNDOWN

Engineering Gives the Devil a Sunburn

Carl H. Mitchell

ISBN 978-1-64003-204-0 (Paperback)
ISBN 978-1-64003-205-7 (Digital)

Covenant Books, Inc.
11661 Hwy 707
Murrells Inlet, SC 29576
www.covenantbooks.com

For my wife, Maryann, for our grown children,
Laura and Thomas, and for
grandchildren, A.J., Jaclyn, and Jacob.

A warm, caring, and loving nest never becomes empty.

ACKNOWLEDGMENTS

◆

In addition to my primary beta reader, my wife Maryann, who pointed out several tedious and too-long sections, this book benefitted from the guidance of several professionals in the literary field. Foremost, William Greenleaf, who provided critiquing and copyedit support that greatly improved point-of-view continuity, heightened suspense, and encouraged more detailed character and environmental descriptions. Barbara Kyle, who earlier had employed Skype with me to review the manuscript and point out several areas needing strengthening. Patricia Blaha, who brought proofreader experience to bear on the final draft. Finally, Denice Hunter, who interfaced with and focused Covenant Books' super team of copy editors, page designers, and cover artists. All had a hand in improving this book.

CHAPTER 1

◆

Thursday, August 9, 2057

NYC detective Nick Garvey and his partner, Detective Tim Branson, received a cell call at 5:47 a.m. to abort their stakeout of a kidnapping gang.

Captain Kevin Gilmore, their superior, originated the call. "Drop everything," he said. "Five male bodies were dumped on the steps of city hall just after five this morning. A half hour ago exactly, the mayor received a phone call suggesting he 'check outside your city hall front door.' I need you here now. City hall. Second floor. Cafeteria."

Nick and Tim arrived at 6:12 and were escorted down the hallway to the entrance to the cafeteria. Nick noted about a dozen men in suits, milling about on the other side of the closed doors. He glanced at Tim and shrugged as they waited for their captain, whom they were told was in the subbasement, conferring with the mayor.

Nick tried to picture the mayor, slight and no more than five foot six, giving orders to Captain Gilmore, six foot one and built like a bald linebacker wearing two sets of shoulder pads under his uniform. The "giving orders" part of the picture never computed for Nick.

Captain Kevin Gilmore appeared less than a minute later. "Gentlemen," he said, directing his greeting to just his two detectives.

"What have you got, Captain?" Nick asked. "Must be super important to call us away from—"

Captain Gilmore glanced toward the others in the hall and leaned in. "The vice president and four of his Secret Service agents. All dead."

Tim's eyes bugged wide open. "Holy shit!"

"Jesus," Nick said. The news, even to a cop of his tenure, came as a shock. He couldn't imagine a less-visible and less-powerful politician. Who would gain anything by putting Jerome Wellsley six feet under? And the four agents? He shook his head.

"The ME's already inside." Captain Gilmore thumbed at the cafeteria doors.

"Why here?" Nick asked. "Why not in our morgue? Last I heard, we still have one."

"The mayor doesn't want any news of this leaking out."

"Why us?" Nick asked.

Captain Gilmore shot Nick a look. "He called me. I'm calling you."

"You coming in with us?" Nick asked.

The captain shook his head. "The ME only wants those who will be working the case to question him. He doesn't even want these other agents from the Secret Service coming in." He put on his jacket. "I'm heading back to the precinct."

After the captain hurried off down the hall, the other agents stayed put while Nick and Tim stepped inside the cafeteria.

Directly ahead, about forty feet or so, the main serving area was bathed in bright lights. A man in a blue hospital-type gown was arms and elbows busy working on a table in front of him.

To Nick and Tim's immediate left was the self-serve buffet area. The lighting, normal. Four movable food carts were lined in front of the food bins. Stretched out atop each cart was a dead body. Nick scanned the tags. Four Secret Service agents, each with a single bullet hole in his forehead.

On the way from the stakeout, Nick's stomach had been rumbling for some food, but seeing the four corpses displayed "cafeteria style" next to tubs of coleslaw and macaroni salad silenced his stomach. Adding to his discomfort was the heavy odor of ammonia and other medical cleansers intermixed with the leftover smells of hamburgers, cabbage, and breakfast bacon.

Nick and Tim approached the medical examiner, who was hunched over the fifth body, presumably the vice president's.

The ME looked up. "Dr. Byron Adams," he said, raising the magnifiers hinged to his bifocals. "I don't like talking to higher-ups that may add to or subtract from the findings."

Nick nodded. "Understood. I'm Detective Nick Garvey, and this is my partner, Tim Branson." He paused, allowing the medical examiner to return his attention to the lifeless body of Jerome Wellsley. "And the findings here are . . ."

"The bodies were dumped shortly before 5:17," Dr. Adams said. "I was called in and arrived at 5:35. I believe you just saw that the four agents were shot. Not the case with the vice president."

Nick stepped to the end of the cart and bent down to read it.

Name: Jerome Wellsley
DOD: Thursday, 8/9/2057
TOD: est. 2:00 a.m. to 3:00 a.m.
Cause: Strangulation
File: NY-20570809-01

"It's pretty obvious you've determined how the vice president was murdered," Nick said. He looked up from the body on the makeshift gurney and turned to the ME. "But my captain will want your official statement."

"As well as any unofficial guesses you might offer," Tim added.

The doctor, his blue autopsy gown heavily soiled, placed his clipboard back on the table and took a deep breath. "Vice President Jerome Wellsley was strangled— obviously, as you say—but strangled by someone with extraordinary upper-arm strength." He rolled the body far enough onto its left side to expose the back of the neck. "The cervical column has been crushed—*snapped* may be a better description—between the C6 and C5 vertebrae," he said, pointing to the break with a gloved forefinger. "The perpetrator made a single wrap with either a plastic or rubber cord a bit less than a quarter inch in diameter. The cord interspersing the column between C6 and C5 indicates that the perpetrator was above the vice president. Death would have been extremely painful for at most ten seconds."

"Have you been able to narrow the time of death?" Nick asked.

"No."

The two detectives thanked the doctor and left for their precinct.

They were called straight into Captain Gilmore's office.

"Bottom line?" the captain said.

"The vice president was strangled," Nick replied. "Strangled from above by someone with super arm strength. He was killed sometime between two and three a.m."

"The four Secret Service agents?"

"Each shot in the forehead," Tim said. "Close range. Powder burns."

"Hand off all your current cases. This is your priority. Your *only* priority. Find who took out the vice president." Captain Gilmore exhaled slowly and shook his head. "Mayor Banner is antsy as hell. He's forgotten his usual priorities. Forgotten about babies being kidnapped right and left, about the World Council's meddling in city affairs, about the neighborhoods frequently thwarting our policing efforts, or his ultimate—about ice in January covering his sidewalk. He's panicked that the president will be next and that it will happen in New York City. I agree with his concerns in this case. He's calling the president now to get her to postpone the grid-lighting ceremony scheduled for two weeks from today."

"Will the mayor authorize overtime?" Nick asked, his tone almost serious.

"I won't even ask him."

Nick and Tim smiled at each other. The overhead grid, covering most of Manhattan, was supposed to capture sun energy beamed down from a thirty-year-old Japanese satellite and convert it to electrical power to light the city. The mayor had been opposed to the grid from day one. Ergo, no grid overtime. Ever.

"The first thing I want you two to do is—" The captain's cell phone rang. "Hello, Mr. Mayor. I was just—"

Captain Gilmore frowned and then waved Nick and Tim out of his office.

"I get the impression overtime is the least of the mayor's concerns," Nick said as he and Tim left the captain's windowless office and walked straight to their shared partners' desk in the middle of a room that had once held a crowded arrangement of twenty or more desks but now, with desk attrition matching police retirements and layoffs, boasted a total of just six.

They both sat and started shuffling through the several reports and papers in front of them, keeping an ear out for the captain calling them back to his office.

Nick was busy separating wheat from chaff when Tim extended an envelope across the desk. "It's addressed to you. Department of Custodial Affairs."

Nick picked up his opener and ripped open the top. He unfolded the insert. "Ah, shit." He slapped the letter down.

Tim blinked. "Sandra again?"

Nick nodded. "My daughter is intent on taking me to court for the fifth time this year. Wants me to relinquish all visitation rights with my granddaughter." He slumped back in his chair. "I wish she could understand that I don't want to inflict any pain on her or Nicole. I know I haven't been—"

"Stop beating yourself up. You haven't been the devil your daughter shouts you are. You've branded yourself Mr. Unworthy. You go out of your way to stay out of everyone's way. You have done nothing—"

Captain Gilmore stuck his head out of his office. "My office, guys. Now! The mayor struck out," the captain said before they could close the door. "President Allison told him that in no way would she cancel the grid-lighting ceremony."

Nick glanced at Tim. They would have some very long days and nights ahead.

"The mayor . . ." Captain Gilmore searched for the right word. "The mayor assured me that all our jobs depend on us protecting President Lenora Allison 100 percent."

"What did he say about the vice president?" Nick asked. "Do we follow up on his murder?"

The captain shook his head. "I was ordered to pass that assignment down. The mayor instructed me to assure that my best detectives have, in his words, 'sole responsibility and only that responsibility in preventing any harm, physical or otherwise, to the president.' You guys are my best. Welcome to unlimited, unpaid overtime."

Tim cleared his throat. "The vice president's demise may have been captured on some video surveillance. I don't think we should pass that work down because we might miss a possible connection to any attempt on the president."

The captain nodded. "My thought too. I'll have the videos downloaded from a ten-block radius, for a start."

"Fine," Tim said. "We have a time-of-death time frame. I'll set up a team to review them. Probably less than a hundred videos. One day is probably all we'll need."

The captain grimaced. "You're going to have help. Don't know if it will speed things up or slow them down. The mayor agreed to allow the Secret Service to work with us." The captain then turned to Nick. "The mayor didn't say anything about the World Council, but I'll worry for him. I believe you have a contact inside?"

"I do. I'll get on it."

"Good. Immediately, if not sooner. Sorry, but no car's available."

As Tim made a beeline for the two-man computer group, Nick made a quick phone call and then headed off on foot to the agreed meeting place.

Heading south to Saint Vartan Park, Nick tried out one argument after another aimed at persuading his decade-ago partner to put scruples and, possibly, his own safety aside in order to spy on his boss's boss: Jason Beck.

Captain Gilmore had little respect for Jason Beck, supreme director of the World Council. Nick, however, having worked on the streets, had a lot of respect for the man, the kind of respect given to a boa constrictor—an ageless boa constrictor with lacquered, wavy black hair ending in a pronounced widow's peak above an always-confident smile. A smile, Nick felt, never to be characterized as benevolent. He thought of Beck as the modern equivalent of the Wizard of Oz, with the only things behind the curtain being Beck's nefarious motives. While working the streets, Nick had come to realize that Beck's much-heralded yellow brick road was decorated with blood.

CHAPTER 2

◆

Nick reclined against the bench and took another bite of
his salami sandwich. He had made it yesterday, figuring it
would be his after-midnight lunch. *So much for meal schedules,* he thought.

The breeze wafting in from the East River brought a much-wel-
comed cool relief to a typically hot August day. It also brought the
overwhelming stench of garbage floating down the river, whose giant
defensive nets constructed all the way from Hoboken down to and
beyond Sandy Hook kept all refuse away from New Jersey and Staten
Island.

He knew that the murder of the vice president, coupled with
the president's refusal to reschedule the grid ceremony, was a recipe
for disaster. All it would take was some minor attention lapse. His
mission in the next few minutes was to get some help in sizing up
one potential crisis.

He was waiting to make contact and to make his pitch. He
knew it would take some wheedling but was confident he could get
his old partner to help. After that, he was expected to return to the
precinct. He slowed his chewing. He would damn well take his time.
It was a nice, warm August day, and he was not about to get indigestion. But then, all that ever waited for him back at the precinct was
indigestion, courtesy of Captain Gilmore, who probably had his own
bouts of indigestion, courtesy of the commissioner, who got his from
the mayor, who . . .

The hell with it. There wasn't much of an NYPD force left these
days, but he was still on it and still a team player.

Nick never completely pulled in his sensory antenna, especially when just coming off a stakeout of a baby-kidnapping gang. He let his gaze trail over to the gaggle of children busily demonstrating their skills on the swings and on the monkey bars. None of them were young enough to bring much on the black market.

Three little girls and one boy continued pumping their swings in sweeping arcs while two boys climbed all over the monkey bars, all a little over sixty feet from where he sat. Halfway between, their mothers watched their every move. The women, ten in all, one obviously pregnant and sitting on a bench, alternately observed and surveyed. Observed the children scampering about the playground hardware and surveyed the benches and grassy areas in all directions beyond the children for suspicious strangers. Barely an instant passed when one of the women, as if an insect with a multifaceted eye, was not sweeping an uneasy, appraising glance in his direction. Nick turned back to his sandwich.

From the corner of his eye, he continued to watch the children clambering over, under, and about the steel bars and swings. The sight took him back almost four months to when he had brought his own granddaughter Nicole, then just six years old, to this very park. No mothers had screened him then because he was so obviously a guardian like them. Nicole had pumped her swing up higher than any of the others did. She had climbed all over the monkey bars for at least ten minutes before she had pulled free of her madcap surroundings and dashed to his side.

She had opened her fist, thrust a silver barrette into his hand, spun around, and asked him to fix it in her hair. "It keeps coming loose, Grandpa," she had complained.

Nick had turned the clip over in his callused hand. He had seen where the wire loop on the underside had become bent to one side and wouldn't catch. Thumbing it straight, he had caught a handful of her hair the color of orange rinds, slipped on the barrette, and snapped it shut, satisfied by the feel and by the sound of its click, that it would perform for at least another ten minutes.

"There you are, Nicole. All fixed," he had announced, throwing his hands up and out as if calling for a spotlight.

"Thanks, Grandpa!" She had grabbed his hands, clapped them over her head, and trotted off.

The memory of that day warmed Nick. Nicole had been so full of a six-year-old's innocent enjoyment of life she had almost convinced Nicholas that life was meant to be good. At least in his granddaughter's presence, he wasn't Tim's Mr. Unworthy. He kept most others locked out of his life, but not Nicole. A smile stopped just short of reaching his lips. He had enjoyed the few hours spent with Nicole. Infrequent hours granted to him by his estranged daughter. His daughter, who yet again wanted to drive him out of his granddaughter's life.

Sandra. What haunted him day in and day out was how he would ever be able to melt his daughter's hatred of him. If it could be melted, he'd be at her side, helping her raise Nicole. She shouldn't be alone in that task.

Nick took another bite and swallowed it without chewing. How, he wondered, could he convince Sandra that he was not the devil, not the evil monster she had once shouted he was right to his face?

He was about to take another bite when he spotted his old partner, Gerry Martin, approaching the park, walking west along Thirty-Fifth Street.

Nick was about to wave when, just behind Gerry, he saw an inexperienced bikeshaw driver peddle himself smack into a recently erected grid stanchion. There was a loud clang as the bike's front end nose-dived, leaving its pilot peddling air for the better part of a second before making foot contact with the road. Nick watched as the cyclist returned both frame and empty two-wheeled freight section to an upright position and checked everything twice. Nick was surprised these grid stanchions supporting the citywide grid—he called it an overhead waffle—didn't cause more such encounters.

He finally managed to wave as Gerry entered the park. Nick bit his lip, still undecided about what argument would convince his old buddy to become a snitch. Whether or not he could make the case, Nick hoped they could at least remain friends.

CHAPTER 3

◆

Half-Penny, the first stalker, drifted into Saint Vartan Park's playground unnoticed. He suppressed a smile. The pre-planned distraction was most helpful. Everyone gave the crashing cyclist a long and dragged-out once-over.

Half-Penny looked for the best location to do his job while remaining part of the background. In the Manhattan of 2057, each baby-kidnapping team needed a lookout, an inconspicuous individual who could, over several days, unearth an infant that met certain profit-making requirements; who could isolate the best location for abduction; and who could size up various escape routes, determine the optimal moment, and signal initiation. Limber and lean sixteen-year-old Half-Penny was that lookout. He also had the added responsibility of "grab and run."

Half-Penny, scooping his basketball from hand to hand, sagged down onto an empty bench. Pretending to be winded, he allowed his head to sag slightly, all the while checking his surroundings.

His first visual target was the ancient set of rusted monkey bars a good thirty feet out and to his right. Nine boys and girls were making full, noisy use of the equipment: the monkey bars and four swings. None were old enough to present any problem to the operation, nor were any young enough to be the target. Children over eighteen months were too hard to "place," so they were seldom targeted. The children hanging from the monkey bars and those pumping their swings in ever-higher arcs were, however, just young enough to bring their mothers running were they to be suddenly in danger.

The mothers, owners of searching eyes watching each child's every move, were not more than twenty feet to the left of the children, almost fifteen feet in front of Half-Penny. Five women stood, surrounding a sixth sitting on a bench. Three other women stood together two or three steps toward the playing children. The last woman—nine children, there had to be nine mothers—was just a couple of steps removed from the playing children. None of these mothers would give him any problem; each would be either racing to rescue her child or tearing her focus away from the sitting woman for two or three seconds. He would need no more.

He hoped that, when he snatched the baby, he didn't have to hurt the mother—physically, that was. Half-Penny had been doing this for three years, ever since he was thirteen, and he always tried for a gentle snatch. A gentle snatch was always the result of surprise and was key to a clean escape. He didn't mind being a little rough, but if he had to wrestle with the mother, it would cost time—and possibly his freedom. After the snatch and handoff, the baby would be well on its way to a better life. His team captain, Herm, often told him about a baby's new parents: so happy to get the child, so able to provide a super life, so determined to love the baby a hundred times more than it had ever been loved before.

Actually, Half-Penny didn't mind the snatch itself. He was quick on his feet. Hell, his damn nickname told everyone that. A few hotshots could slam the brakes on a full run and stop on a dime; the street claimed he could do that and scoop up nine and a half cents of that dime. Herm claimed that, if you even blinked, Half-Penny could spin around, snatch up the remainder, and be off in a totally different direction. Half-Penny shook his head ever so slightly. No, he didn't mind the actual snatch as much as making the go/no-go call.

That was the part he hated. It was an extra responsibility: the checking of everyone and every exit at the scene. It was a responsibility that he remain still and observe. Observe and, even worse, *judge.* Judge when the mothers would best be distracted so that each would rush to their children's side, judge when there were no major obstructions to his escape, judge when conditions were right for all to go as planned.

He'd lost count how many times he'd told Herm that making the final call upset him, scared him, and made him tentative—all at the same time. For some reason, Herm never paid attention. Half-Penny bit his lower lip. Maybe Herm would pay attention when his fastest stalker skipped to New Jersey. Little John getting caught and killed during a snatch in a different neighborhood two weeks ago had prompted Half-Penny to figure he'd live longer if he could make it across the Hudson to New Jersey. Little John, speeding by on his bicycle, had taken another baby from Half-Penny and had pedaled maybe thirty yards before catching his tire in an open sewer grate. The bruised baby was rescued, and a whimpering Little John beaten to death by three mother she-devils.

Half-Penny didn't know who it would be on the bicycle this time, but he was sure that whoever it was would steer clear of sewer grates. He wasn't old enough to remember when there were thousands upon thousands of automobiles in Manhattan, but now with a gallon of gas costing almost as much as the car itself, there were less than two hundred cars in the city, making any getaway in a car stand out like . . . like . . . Half-Penny just hoped it would be a clean hand-off. Little John had been a master at the transfer—over forty babies during Half-Penny's three years, including fifteen from Half-Penny himself. Almost a year ago, one of the other cyclists had pulled in a baby, whipped around a corner, and slammed into a grid pillar that hadn't been there two days before when the route was cased.

The grid! Another reason Half-Penny was planning to escape to New Jersey. It covered Manhattan and was soon supposed to bring electric power to the city and lights at night. He didn't believe either the mayor or the president when they assured New Yorkers that the microwaves beamed down from space wouldn't harm anyone, not even someone sunbathing atop the grid. His grandmother had a microwave, and she used it to cook stuff during one of the three ninety-minute windows when the city supplied electricity. A neighbor's kid had put a cat in their microwave. The cat was all shriveled, and its eyes popped after the five minutes was up. He wasn't taking any chances with the grid.

Time to check the park once more, he thought. There'd be no Jersey without this snatch and just a couple more. The hardest part of leaving Manhattan would be getting his grandmother to go with him. For the past three months, well before the Little John incident, he had periodically been talking to his grandmother about leaving Manhattan. He could tell she was listening but not buying.

He shifted his attention from the six women to the last bench to the right of the play area, the bench near the far gate where Herm would enter, start the sequence, and then immediately exit. Two men sat half turned toward each other, a checkerboard on the seat between them. They were all gray hair and suspenders. Judging from the size of their stomachs, they would have trouble getting out of their own way, much less in his.

Half-Penny checked the park gate twenty feet to his left, his exit route.

Another man, middle-aged with slightly darker hair, weathered face, and no suspenders, was sitting on a bench on the opposite side of the pavement. He looked a bit unkempt and overinvolved with his sandwich. Although he appeared muscular with no belly bulk, he didn't strike Half-Penny as a serious threat. When Half-Penny made his move, if the man was still chomping his lunch, he'd be too busy to interfere.

Half-Penny, still feigning being winded, checked to his right. All the women were still double-checking every person in the park, including himself. It was obvious to him they didn't consider him a threat since none of their sweeping gazes stopped on him. Further on, the two old checker players were still pressed stomach to table.

He checked his exit route for the second time. Two men were now sharing the bench just inside the gate. The newcomer, closer to Half-Penny, was a bit younger than the other man. Half-Penny decided he was some kind of big shot, all spruced up in new, well-cut clothes. He named him Mr. Dandy. Mr. Dandy was listening to his bench mate, the worn-looking man in the rumpled suit who didn't look too many years younger than the checker players. From the looks of them, the older man, the one facing Half-Penny, was sort of lecturing Mr. Dandy, waving his sandwich in short, back-and-forth arcs with each point made. The older man earned the nickname Professor. From the way Mr. Dandy frequently turned away from the professor, Half-Penny could tell the younger man was not happy with most of the points being made.

These two could present a minor obstacle to his clearing the park after the snatch and before the transfer. He studied the younger man. The overall impression, even across forty feet, was of a strong chin backed up—in spite of the expensive suit—by a firmly muscled body. Dandy's countering motions of disagreement were firm at first but slowly became tentative and, finally, turned to those of surrender. He was being pressed to do something—pressed hard—and was struggling to find a way to press back.

The older man, the professor? Again, no problem for a world-class speedster like Half-Penny. The professor was finally taking a bite out of his sandwich. He'd be too busy either eating or pressuring Mr. Dandy. The professor probably even lectured students with food in his mouth. Again, no threat to Half-Penny's escape from the park.

Half-Penny took time to congratulate himself on his skill at judging people. Mr. Dandy would be the only problem. Half-Penny would have to figure some way to neutralize him before giving the all-clear signal.

CHAPTER 4

◆

Nick tried to conceal his exasperation. Gerry Martin had always been tough to dissuade from what he considered proper protocol. Now that he was part of the World Council, proper protocol apparently meant not revealing any council secrets.

Nick had spent the last two minutes trying to enlist Gerry's support for a joint NYC Police and World Council Task Force. They had been beat cops together, nine-plus years ago, well after New York City and the world had turned inside out. Nick hadn't expected a quick acceptance and now decided the direct approach was probably best.

He exhaled and leaned toward Gerry. "I need your help. The vice president of the somewhat United States was murdered this morning, as were four of his Secret Service detail." He paused, allowing the information to sink in, searching for any flickering reaction. "I know you are privy to some of the inner workings of the World Council. I need—"

"I heard about the VP," Gerry said, keeping his voice low. "And privy or not, there's been no hint the council was responsible."

Nick studied Gerry, trying to glean something from his complete lack of reaction, trying to decide whether the direct approach was counterproductive. Gerry seemed determined to stay out of the matter—at least until Nick could bring him around. "I need you to pass along any council plans targeting the president."

Gerry leaned forward, resting his arms on his knees and running a hand through his graying hair. He glanced up sideways at Nick.

"I can't just up and spy on my superiors. And for what? Because your paranoid mayor is convinced the World Council is planning to embarrass President Allison? Embarrass her? Come on, Nick, even you can't think—"

"I don't."

"You don't?" Gerry straightened, his eyes narrowing. "Then what?"

"I don't think they can afford to just embarrass her."

Gerry's lips tightened. "What are you suggesting? They want to destroy her?"

"At the minimum." Nick mustered his best piercing glare.

"The minimum?" Gerry repeated.

Nick leaned back, satisfied he'd finally gotten his former partner's attention. "The minimum. Of course, I'm sure Vice President Wellsley would have been happy with just 'the minimum.' Don't you think?"

Gerry's eyes locked on to Nick's. For a long moment, neither said a word.

Gerry looked away first, his gaze moving toward the playground. "The World Council had nothing to do with what happened to the vice president."

Nick arched an eyebrow. "You sound quite positive."

"It's not their style."

Nick watched as his ex-partner sucked his lower lip inward ever so slightly. It was an old habit, an indication that possibilities were being weighed and options considered. Buy-in could be near.

"Forget hard evidence." Gerry's eyes narrowed. "You don't even have soft evidence that the World Council is planning the assassination of President Allison. You can't even—"

"Can it, Gerry. You're starting to sound like one of the desk jockeys you used to hate." Nick caught his ex-partner's fleeting wince. "Have you forgotten what it feels like in your gut when you know something just isn't right?"

"I still have a gut, Nick, and I'd like to keep it."

"Afraid of your bosses?"

"You know better, Nick." He glared. "Just make your case."

Nick nodded. "President Allison has been a thorn in the council's side for the past five years. They tried to defeat her at the last election but couldn't. She's the strongest opponent to their . . . their—"

"Domination?" Gerry offered.

Nick nodded again. "In two weeks, she's going to throw the switch on the grid overhead. If she's right, all the lights in the city will flash to life. And when that happens—"

"*If.*"

"*If* that happens, the council's lamp of leadership sputters. And if it sputters . . ." Nick shook his head.

Gerry pounced. "And what if the grid itself sputters? She's the one done then. No creditability. They laugh, pity her, and move on. They win. Without lifting a finger."

Nick shook his head. "Oh, they'll have to lift more than just a finger. Remember Carter Johnson? He thought Allison was finished, figured he was just five days from winning the presidency. Before he could lift even a finger, the queen of bounce back rose from the dead and cleaned his electoral clock." Nick watched Gerry's face as last year's final presidential debate replayed in his mind.

"Fine. She's the Olympic champion of rising from one's own ashes. I'll give you that, but what about the rumor that some Arab terrorists are going to blow themselves up while giving the president a big hug?" Gerry tilted his head, puckering up with his best I-rest-my-case expression.

"A rumor," Nick repeated, pushing back. "I don't believe it for a minute. It's been almost thirty years since any Arabs were able to give us anything more than their middle finger." Nick shuddered in mock terror. "The only organization that would have the capability to carry off such an assassination is your World Council. The capability and, for the reason I mentioned, the motive."

Gerry's eyes narrowed again. "The mayor is on board with this? He shares your view?"

"He doesn't know what to get on board with."

"The commissioner?"

Nick tore another bite from his sandwich. He shook his head. "Just you."

Nick swallowed. "Just me. And my captain."

"Just you, your captain, and perhaps that old, infernal itch of yours that digs at the back of your neck every time you're left with a round peg and not even one hole, square or otherwise, to put it into, making you fly off into all kinds of strange orbits."

Nick put his sandwich down. It was make-or-break time. "Look, the commissioner doesn't want to have to tell the mayor he has to cancel the president's trip. He wants to separate fact from fantasy and, if there is such a plan, to cut it down at the source. I'm only one of a dozen tracking down the rumor. A rumor that I—look, my money's on your World Council. It's on your supreme leader, Jason Beck."

"They're not just *my* World Council. They're *everybody's* World Council. What makes you think they would feel they have to run up against the president? The council's the one with the power now. They own all the oil in the world. What do you think they've been doing the past twenty years? When they corner markets, they corner power. Do you really believe that turning the lights on in one big city will give them pause?"

"Damn right I do! For years power and control have been their middle names. You know that." He glared at Gerry. "We all know that. I wouldn't doubt they would like to control everything and everybody. Hell, they must have over a hundred laws controlling populations in any one country. World Council may be your organization's official name, but you know as well as I do that everyone calls your boys the Population Police—Pops for short. One mother, one child."

Gerry's blink rate doubled. When they'd been partners, Nick had come to realize that rapid blinking meant Gerry was trying to think of some path to middle ground.

Nick decided it was time to take one step back to softer ground and close the deal. "Then again, assassination might be too extreme," he suggested. "The council must have the world see that the president's plan is a fantastic failure. If it were to be viewed as a success, the president would immediately become the new gravitational center of world power. Again, they can't let that happen. Maybe sabotage is the more appropriate concept.

"I'm not asking you to sleep with your bosses. Just stay alert to any words or actions of theirs that might indicate—"

"That might indicate murder or mayhem." Gerry gave one last, slow blink and straightened in the bench.

"That might indicate such—if it falls in your lap."

"If it falls in my lap." Gerry nodded. His head shivered like a dog shaking off water. He mumbled something to himself, gave a drawn-out sigh, and stood. "If it falls," he repeated, and then nodded and turned to leave the park. But he turned back before taking even one step. "Just so the information favors are not all one-sided—" He nibbled at his lower lip, obviously unsure of continuing. He finally nodded, more to himself than to Nick. "You mentioned population control. If you have any information on one shadowy character calling himself El Camino, shoot me the details."

Nick chuckled. "El Camino? Isn't that the name of a car model a century or so ago?"

Gerry gave a didn't-say-he-was-smart shrug and started to turn toward the street. But again he turned back and pointed to Nick's jacket, where he no doubt knew an ancient but still deadly Glock was holstered inside. "Don't rely on that old thing 100 percent. Remember, cops don't own the streets anymore." He turned again and finally left the park.

Nick shook his head and chuckled. Gerry would be good to his word even if there was little chance anything helpful would just fall on his ex-partner's lap. What amused Nick was that Gerry could never leave a scene or a conversation without making some smartass remark that usually cut close to the truth. Cops didn't own the streets anymore in Manhattan. Not by a long shot. Twenty-plus years of decay had withered the "Long Blue Line," reducing it to just a few anemic traces of its former strength and glory. Many cops had been "let go" for lack of funding, many had just become fed up and retired, while a few, like Gerry, had hung on for a long while before getting a better job elsewhere. Then there were the hapless and almost helpless few like Nick and Tim, his current partner, Captain Kevin Gilmore, and others, each an exhausted "old guard" silently assuring one another that the city needed them.

Gerry was right, though. The police didn't own the streets. The paracops were the landlords now: groups of neighborhood men who monitored the ten, fifteen, or twenty square blocks they could control—"safeguard" was their preferred description. The city tolerated the groups mainly because they had no choice. A few groups had agreed to work in concert with the official police—the pro cops— whenever a severe problem arose in their neighborhood. The groups could be very helpful when they wanted to be but most hurtful when they felt someone was against them. The only force that could always neutralize them was the World Council Police, Jason Beck's storm troopers.

Nick recalled yesterday's front-page picture of Jason Beck. There hadn't been much change from twenty years ago. Sixty-one was the new forty-one, Nick figured, when a man had enough black dye for the hair atop his head, along his eyebrows, and across his chest.

Nick made another check of the park. Only one girl remained on the swings. All the rest were subjecting the monkey bars to severe tests. The children's every shout, grunt, and giggle was noted by their mothers.

The cluster of women was closer to him than were their whirling-dervish children. The women all seemed to wear the same dark clothes, typical for an era when fashion was barely remembered to have existed thirty years ago. Given the similar dress, it was difficult to distinguish one woman from the other, but Nick was certain of one thing: for each child, one mother was keeping tabs.

Feeling the uneasiness of their frequent, appraising glances in his direction, Nick returned to what remained of his salami sandwich. He picked at a hard section of the stale bread, musing that all the children would go home with their mothers. They were all over five years of age—unlikely targets, except for the rare pervert.

Nick finished his sandwich and decided to gift himself a couple more minutes on the bench before heading back to the precinct. The children were still engaged in the animated cackle of shouts, entreaties, commands, and laughter. Two of the little girls, their starched skirts of faded orange-and-yellow prints scrunched in at the knees, whispered secrets and then alternately laughed and giggled. The two boys on the monkey bars slipped down to the pavement and began kicking a soccer ball back and forth. Twice the ball bounced and rolled beyond their reach, only to be retrieved by an alert, quick-footed mother.

Nick's gaze drifted back to the mother-to-be sitting on the bench. Watching her cradle her belly reminded him of how, long ago, his wife, Judith, had stroked her swollen abdomen. With each perceived kick, she would smile and motion him to come over to feel "little Sandra" performing her morning exercises. Those were the days Nick found difficult to recall: the days when Judith had still been alive. Later he would hold "little Sandra" in his arms, and later still he would hold Sandra by the hand as they skipped along a wet, sandy beach.

Nick smiled. It was a full, warm day. A pleasant mid-August afternoon in Manhattan awaited the children and their moms, and they were, respectively, charged up and wary.

Too wary! Much too wary, Nick thought, suddenly feeling like a tightrope walker who was an inch off balance because he'd missed something soon to be important. The mothers were too wary, protecting a group of children too old to be prime kidnapping targets.

Only vaguely conscious of the tune he was quietly whistling, Nick trailed his gaze along the perimeter of the park, along each bench, across each path, beyond each gate in the chain-link fence. Only once did he let his attention wander—and then for little more than a second—as, beyond the swings and the monkey bars, beyond the faraway gate facing First Avenue, an elderly man wearing a tweed overcoat grappled with the leash to a majestic Irish setter busily sniffing the remains of a disemboweled water hydrant. Nick chuckled to himself as he pictured not the man taking the dog for a walk but the golden setter deciding when, where, and for how long the two of them would linger at any one of an infinite succession of hydrants. The old man looked to be in command no more than 10 percent of the time.

The ten women were as before: the pregnant one sitting and the other nine still playing the role of determined guardian, each watching alternately their own child and then all the others. Nick felt a sudden itch prickle the back of his neck as he crumpled the sandwich wrapper. The sitting woman wasn't looking up at any of the children. Nick couldn't remember her looking up once. The prickling became intense. The sitting woman was looking at her lap. She never looked up from her lap.

She wasn't pregnant. She was holding an infant! An infant wrapped in material identical to the mother's woolen coat.

He had missed it. He shook his head at how he'd let himself be distracted. An infant was prime stuff. An infant in a population-conscious world would bring an uncaring, determined king's ransom. An infant could be sold on the black market for ten times a police detective's annual salary. An infant was a form of currency, readily convertible at a moment's notice. An infant was difficult to trace and would have few if any memories of its real parents.

Nick studied the group of women again. Six were spread out radially from the infant and mother, like wagons circled around settlers before an attack. The remaining three were positioned closer to the active children. A stalker would find penetration of the shield around the mother with the baby almost impossible. The baby was well disguised, the only giveaway being the mother's woolen coat being worn in mid-August.

The neck prickling was replaced by an icy calm. The old man with the Irish setter was also wearing a heavy coat in mid-August. Standing, Nick turned toward the gate. Just the man was there—no Irish setter. A series of barks spun Nick back to the group of women. Twenty-five yards to their right, fifteen yards to the right of the children on the swings and the monkey bars, the setter had broken free of its owner and, snarling and barking, was loping toward the children.

"The dog!" a mother screamed.

"My god!"

The six standing women lurched forward to protect their children at the exact instant a young man jumped up from his bench and made for the sitting woman.

Missing only half a beat, Nick pulled his revolver and sent one bullet into the setter's skull, dropping the dog half-stretched at a forty-five-degree angle against the monkey bars.

A woman's scream turned Nick back to the mother on the bench. The young basketball bouncer was grabbing for the infant.

Nick was about to put a bullet in him when a blurred motion on his right told him the old man was making a move. Nick saw a shotgun being pulled out from under the tweed coat and pointed in his direction.

Nick squeezed a second shot. The man fell quickly, silently.

He turned back to the young man, who was standing with his empty hands in the air. He was staring at Nick, the light in his dark brown eyes coming on now that he knew his game was up. Before he could move, the nearest six women threw him to the ground and started beating and kicking him. One woman pulled a section of metal pipe from her oversized purse and made several swiping motions at the fallen man's head. She was unable to connect because the other five women thrashing about frustrated any attempt at a clear shot.

"Okay, ladies, enough," Nick said as he waded in, showing his badge. "Enough!" He pulled the women off one by one, three for a second time. He grabbed the pipe just as its owner discovered a clear path between pipe and skull.

"Kill the bastard!"

"Step on his face!"

"Give me a knife, and I'll cut his balls off!"

"Get outta here, cop! This is our neighborhood!"

"We run this park, not you!"

Nick held his ground as the women turned to vent their venom on him. He knew he had only a few seconds before group dynamics took over and they decided they could kill the stalker after they killed themselves a pro cop.

He shook his head. He should have just walked away. He had an assignment, and this was counterproductive. Too late now.

CHAPTER 5

◆

Nick wagged his Glock at the six women. "Okay, ladies, back off."

When no backward movement was forthcoming, he mustered his most steely-eyed, intimidating glare and focused on the former pipe swinger. "I'm taking this stalker in, and he'll spend the rest of his life behind bars."

"Big deal." She glared back. "A long life behind bars is nowhere near as just as a short life ending right here, right now." She stomped her right foot on the pavement, less than two inches from the stalker's bleeding head.

Nick waved the pipe back and forth this time, motioning for her to move back. She took two backward steps. The other five women paused for a moment, unsure of what to do next. One pulled back from the group and bent over the mother holding the baby.

Nick reached down with his pipe-free hand and pulled the bleeding stalker to his feet. It was then that he noticed the stalker was a mere teenager, midteen at best. The boy's legs were rubbery, barely able to support him.

Nick whispered into a torn ear, "You better learn to walk in the next five seconds, or I'm dropping you here for these women to have their way with you."

The boy's eyes widened at the same time his legs tried locking him upright. On the second try, they were successful.

Nick switched the pipe and his pistol, holding his gun in his left hand with the barrel stuck in the stalker's ribs. "We move, turkey. Now!"

Nick waved the pipe at the women. They held back and did not advance.

Jabbing the stalker's ribs with each step, Nick got them both out of the park and through the exit onto First Avenue, where he pitched the pipe over the fence into some bushes. Their path uptown was clear and their progress from Thirty-Fifth Street to Thirty-Sixth unimpeded.

Halfway to Thirty-Seventh, Nick saw the first paracop stepping out of a doorway across the street and keeping pace. In the sixty seconds it took to reach Thirty-Seventh, Nick spied four more paracops, each keeping both distance and pace. He knew there would soon be more.

He tried turning left at the corner but discovered a pack of at least ten paracops marching along Thirty-Seventh toward them. The time for keeping distance and pace was apparently over.

While jabbing furiously into his captive's ribs, Nick steered them both back onto First Avenue, where he again headed uptown. The nearest precinct, his own, Grand Central Hub Number 1, was at Forty-Fourth and Lexington. If he didn't reach a call box soon, he doubted he'd make it anywhere with his stalker intact. If the paracops did a proper job, he'd never make it closer than twenty feet from a call box. He shoved his suddenly aware prisoner ahead of him.

"Don't sweat it, little man," Nick said, pulling the boy around to face him. "I'll make sure I get out alive." Nick chuckled as the stalker's eyes widened. "You, of course, I'm not so sure." He winked at the suddenly shaking boy. "Just think: it's the risk of this very thing happening that makes yours such a high-paying profession. Makes you warm all over, doesn't it?" Nick winked again and nudged him with the Glock. "Keep moving. We stop, you're dead."

Nick suddenly longed for the old days, days twenty years ago when there were only professional cops and citizens.

By the time they had reached Thirty-Ninth, there were at least twenty-five paracops visible, some leading, some trailing. Nick figured they would make their stand and confront him at Forty-Second. Beads of perspiration broke out on his forehead.

As he was about to shove his prisoner across Fortieth Street, Nick remembered the grid construction warehouse. An escape plan flashed fully formed in his mind. He smiled and spun his prisoner facing right toward the East River and the warehouse tower jerry-rigged atop the lead-in roads to the abandoned Queens Midtown Tunnel.

Glancing back, he saw the paracops falter and stop. Reason and his own safety, if not that of his captive, dictated that Nick continue his drive toward the Grand Central Hub precinct. Reason and safety demanded that Nick continue up to Forty-Fourth, turn left, and make the three-block dash to his fellow officers. Reason and safety did not lie along the East River, where the two of them could be cornered and, at least one of them, served up for slaughter.

Confident their minds would need several seconds to adjust, to assimilate this new data, Nick pushed his stalker with increasing urgency. The boy stumbled once, but Nick caught him under the arms and kept him upright.

Nick, letting the visibility of his Glock pressed against the stalker's ribs substitute for flashing his badge, pushed past the three grid workers at the entrance to the tower. He shoved his captive into the elevator, whipped the gate shut, and slammed the button that would whisk them up to the grid maintenance level.

As the elevator started its climb, he saw the paracops suddenly slip into high gear. They stormed past the three workers and into the tower's ground floor. They were too late, and without the elevator, the only way to the top required a 250-foot climb up a rusted ladder. He had a sudden impulse to adroitly flip the young stalker's arm upward, miming an obscene gesture, but managed to resist.

The elevator gate opened onto a long, eight-foot-wide expanse of concrete littered with cans, newspapers, and wadded lunch bags. Nick shoved the stalker out ahead of him. Confident of only a forty-second lead at best, he silently prayed to whatever god was on call that the maintenance vehicles he had seen eight weeks ago were still parked next to the platform. Nick propelled the stalker forward and to the edge.

Two grid tractors were farther along to their right.

Although only six feet below, the transparent plastic grid work did little to counter the impression they were stepping out onto open space almost eighteen floors above the street.

"C'mon, little buddy. Move your ass!" Nick shoved his prisoner out over the grid.

The stalker screamed once briefly and landed with an insignificant thud. Nick landed on his feet and immediately pulled the kid to his feet and toward the two vehicles.

He kept telling himself that he didn't have to walk as if on eggshells. The waffle-like grid was an endless repetition of eight-inch open squares, each bounded on all four sides by two inches of fantastically clear, high-strength plastic. Allowing only a 45 percent open area, the four inches of plastic between cutouts was slightly convex, shedding more than 95 percent of rainwater while still allowing movement by foot. Starting just three inches below the grid and running parallel were the multitude of wires making up what the installing engineers called the "microwave rectenna."

Nick shoved the stalker into the back of the second tractor and then, after making sure it started up, cuffed both of the stalker's wrists to an exposed roll tube. Nick stepped back to the first tractor, raised the Glock, and shot all four tires, which immediately collapsed.

"We're off," Nick said, vaulting into the driver's seat. "Our friends won't catch us without that tractor."

He popped the clutch, and the tractor lurched forward, attaining in seven seconds its top speed of twelve miles per hour.

The grid slope near the World Council building—the old United Nations—was against them, rising from the 250 feet above street level at the tower to 350 feet at Second Avenue. The grid would be level from that point all the way to the Grand Central Hub. As it climbed the slope, the tractor slowed to a steady seven miles per hour.

Although he expected no pursuit, Nick glanced back to see if any paracops had set out on foot. There were none.

The breeze atop the grid was brisk, making it feel more like October than August.

After cresting Second Avenue, the tractor regained its top speed, twelve miles per hour, its oversized tires leveling the dips as each one-foot-square opening was encountered.

Nick smiled as he imagined Nicole at the controls of the tractor. She would love it. Then again, if Sandra had her way this time in court, there would be no more Nicole for him.

Nick shook his head to clear his thoughts.

He shot a quick glance back at his young stalker. "Hey there, passenger. I hope you're enjoying this rare excursion atop the Manhattan Rectenna, more commonly known as the grid. Very few civilians have had the privilege of a guided tour. I'm not an official guide, but with your late booking—double meaning intended—you'll have to settle for me." He glanced back again and chuckled at the stalker's deflated look. "Construction of this massive grid was started just over two years ago by a presidential commission, with activation scheduled for two weeks from now. Should be exciting: sunlight converted to microwave energy streaming down from a previously idle Japanese satellite to be caught by a special grouping of wires then bounced sideways to some small, adjacent, three-inch-diameter circular microstrip antennas. The grid itself covers pretty well all of Manhattan, stretching north to south some fifteen miles and from the Hudson to East River about ten miles."

Another quick check. The boy didn't seem to be paying attention.

"There just might be a quiz later, young stalker." Nick chuckled. "Once the old microwaves get captured, they're converted and sent out to turn on all the lights in the city. You're too young to remember how a city looks at night, all lit up. Beautiful sight. Beautiful."

Nick glanced back at his prisoner. The kid was looking down 350 feet to the street, his eyes wide with terror. Today there were maybe two hundred cars and limousines, not counting less than a hundred NYC Police cars. Nick remembered when there had been thousands of cars moving down there, crossing his lovely island every which way. It had been an awesome experience at night: headlights lit up like tiny pearls on a swirling necklace and the sound of hundreds of horns honking, tooting, and beeping. And all the cars with all their headlights had been nowhere near as bright as the hundreds of huge billboards, lit up and animated. They'd even had humongous television screens. Now Times Square was all dark with no TV, and at home, citizens were reduced to watching one station, which broadcast from six to nine every evening.

A barely audible moan prompted Nick to give his passenger a quick check. The boy had his head pressed against the roll tube between his handcuffs.

Nick shook his head and smiled. "We'll be arriving soon. Last call for refreshments."

The boxy precinct building, perched atop the old Grand Central Terminal, came into view as Nick steered them past Third Avenue. A tiny sigh of relief escaped Nick's lips.

"Let's go," Nick commanded, unlocking the handcuffs and then relocking them onto the stalker's wrists after he had pulled them behind his back. "You've got a semiprivate room waiting for you in the basement." His captive offered no resistance against Nick's grip. "Be cool, my little stalker. Twenty-five years will go by in a flash. Almost."

Tim Branson met them in the booking room. Together they processed the stalker. Street name: Half-Penny.

"Hey," Nick offered, "Half-Penny. That means you're not even worth a dime a dozen." Nick was unwinding and didn't have the energy to smile as the stalker sadly wagged his head.

Captain Gilmore opened the door to his office and motioned Nick to come inside.

"What is it, Captain?" Nick asked as he closed the door behind him.

"Before you brought in Mr. Quick Foot, did you get a sit-down with your executive from the World Council?"

"Not an executive. More an executive assistant. I asked him to keep his eyes open regarding anything resembling a plot against the president."

"He hadn't run across anything before you met?"

"No."

"I trust your judgment, but are you sure you can trust he won't alert anyone at the World Council?"

"I trust him completely. You know he's my old partner. Until ten years ago, we had each other's back for almost seven years before that. He knows how to keep his eyes open and his mouth shut."

"Shut and, hopefully, locked. You know how the World Council bigwigs feel about their not-quite bigwigs meeting with the NYPD."

Nick shrugged. "Only when authorized. We met for only three or four minutes. Probably not enough for them to notice."

"Fine. Tim's group will be getting the videos in about an hour. I want you to check them out as well. Until they get here, you and Tim can process your stalker."

CHAPTER 6

◆

Afeter forty-five minutes of fingerprinting, mug shooting, voice recording, DNA scalp scraping, retinal scanning, and comparison of all current Half-Penny data to the priors database, he was taken into the interrogation room. Nick was already at the table, looking through the booking documents that had been sent ahead. He made a show of shaking his head as he did.

He looked up at the sweating prisoner. He tapped the folder in his hand against the tabletop. "And here I thought Half-Penny was your christened name. How silly of me, Julian Ramirez."

A guard dumped Half-Penny into the chair opposite Nick and cuffed him to the underside of the table. The two guards then backed away and left.

Nick looked up with an amused grin. "Your grandmother is quite a woman. I see here when you were arrested seventeen months ago for . . ." He looked down at the folder now open on the table in front of him. "Stealing five tomatoes from a street vendor, she came to the Twenty-Third and, before officers could restrain her, slapped you twice for each tomato."

Half-Penny winced, the memory written across his face.

Nick chuckled aloud. "Just think what she will do to you for kidnapping babies."

Half-Penny clamped his eyes shut and started rocking back and forth in the chair. It was an obvious—and unsuccessful—attempt to disguise the tremors starting to take over his body: his hands first, then his neck muscles, followed by his pulsating cheeks.

Nick riffled through the papers in the folder and looked up at Half-Penny, waiting for the boy's eyes to open. When they did, Nick offered him his best almost-a-compliment look. "I must confess, I'm impressed as hell." He gave Half-Penny his best mock look of awe. "No doubt in my mind, you're better at stealing babies than ripping off tomatoes. I could tell right away when you made your move in the park that you were experienced—super experienced—but . . ." Nick stabbed his fingers at the sheaf of papers sticking from atop the folder. "But *wow!* Not one arrest." Nick smiled at the still-rocking Half-Penny. "Till today."

The rocking slowed.

"Even so, I gotta believe you're good. What's the service life span of a stalker? How many snatches before the paracops catch and kill you? I don't really know. None of us here knows, 'cause we usually only come across your breed when you're horizontal, bloody, and dead—and unable to respond to questions. Did I mention dead?

"Gotta admit, I saved your ass today." Nick gave Half-Penny a slow, self-satisfied smile. "Yup, gotta admit. Of course, don't know if I can save it twice in one day. I mean, when your grandma gets here, I may be out getting a coffee, and who knows what she—"

The rocking picked up speed. An almost-inaudible moan told Nick he was making headway.

He leaned forward. "Tell me, Julian 'Half-Penny' Ramirez, how long have you been snatching babies?" Nick's tone suggested that, if Half-Penny wasn't forthcoming, Grandma would be brought in to complete the interrogation.

Half-Penny slowed the rocking. "Almost three years. Please don't bring my grandmother in."

Nick made a mental note to let that last request go unanswered until the end of the interrogation. "Three years," he marveled. "Wow! Best we've encountered to date is thirteen months. Of course, our data is based only on family interviews conducted in the morgue." Nick wasn't even sure where the permanent NYC morgue was anymore. Still, the image was obviously having an effect on Half-Penny.

"I'm fast. I can outrun anybody."

"Anybody except six mothers. Three years." He looked Half-Penny straight in the eyes. "How many babies?"

The rocking stopped. Nick could see there was no resistance left in the young man. No need to mention Grandma again.

"How many babies?" Nick repeated.

"Twenty-three. Seventeen by myself. Each of the twenty-three will have a better life with their new parents."

"Who in hell told you that?"

Half-Penny's blink rate doubled.

Nick kept pushing. "Who'd you hand them to?" He knew the usual routine: party number 1 distracts; party 2 snatches; party 3, in mobile transportation, receives the handoff. But Julian here had been operational for "almost three years." Maybe he'd learned more than just how to outrun mothers and paracops.

"Jackson. I handed them to Jackson. Until this last one. He was killed. I was shown where the new geared-up bicycle was parked so I'd know exactly what it looked like, since the rider was new and not yet available."

"Address!" Nick demanded, shoving a small notebook and pen across the table toward Half-Penny. Nick knew that a quarter of the kids on the street couldn't read or write, but stalkers had to be able to read street signs and read and write passed notes. Nick stood, walked around the table, and undid the cuffs. "Address," he repeated. "Address of where the bicycle was parked."

Half-Penny slowly and neatly wrote one line and replaced the pen atop the pad.

Nick read the address and was about to wring a lot more information from Grandma's little darling when the room's steel door opened.

It was Tim Branson.

Tim stepped to Nick's right side and whispered into his ear. "Grandma was just brought in."

"Fun time," Nick whispered back. He turned to Half-Penny. "Detective Branson will ask you for more details on the address. I have to excuse myself for a few minutes while I get some more background on you."

Half-Penny's grandmother was in the third interrogation room. The file Nick had picked up just before entering said her name was Julia Ramirez. He glanced through the window to see a thin but not frail lady with thinning brown-not-yet-gray hair much like his own.

"Good afternoon, Mrs. Ramirez," Nick said. He pulled a chair around to sit next to the nervous woman, deciding it would look too confrontational sitting across the table from her.

"The policeman said Julian was arrested for stalking." Grandma Julia wrung her hands in fits and starts, her voice on the verge of cracking. She was old school, still using the term *policeman*.

Nick decided to play it soft and understanding. "True, but there may be some confusion."

"Can I see Julian?"

"Not yet. Maybe later." Nick twisted his chair sideways so he could face Julia Ramirez, who was now breathing in rapid, shallow breaths. He placed a hand atop hers on the table and pulled out his notebook. "Julian said something about kidnapped children having a better life with their new parents. Does that sound like him?"

Grandma Julia's shoulders sagged. "Oh god! He *did* take them. Both of his parents—my son and his girlfriend—abused him as a child. Physically and emotionally. Whenever I was present, he and I would chat on the sofa, and he would be almost fine, but when either of them came into the room, he would cower against the far end of the sofa, clutching a cushion. When he reached six, he asked to come live with me. When he reached seven, even *I* couldn't stand it anymore. I took him home with me and dared the two of them to take me to court. They didn't."

"And you've kept him ever since?"

"Yes. A year later, my son was murdered on the streets by some thug, and his girlfriend, who never wanted a child in the first place, was never seen in our neighborhood again. I can't say I've watched over Julian's every move or his every acquaintance, but I've tried my best."

Nick nodded. "I can see—"

The interrogation room door flew open. It was Captain Gilmore. "Nick," he said, leaning in from the door, "it's important."

The captain's concerned look gave Nick pause. He stood and followed him out of the room, pulling the door shut behind him.

Captain Gilmore took a deep breath and let it out. "Your daughter's in the hospital. They said she's in bad shape. No details. I've got a car waiting downstairs for you. I'll take care of Grandma. Tim will finish with your Half-Penny and put him in a cell by himself."

The captain gave him the few additional details he had and handed him a car pass.

Nick stood immobile for several seconds, unable to think, and then took the pass and raced toward the exit.

CHAPTER 7

◆

Nick wanted to push the accelerator to the floor but knew the response would add little speed beyond his current—he glanced at the speedometer—twenty miles per hour.

The NYPD had only forty-seven cars, three of which were high-speed, gasoline-driven pursuit vehicles. This had to be one of the slowest of the remaining forty-four. The saving grace was that there were few other cars on the road, restrictions having been in place for the past twenty-odd years. The restrictions weren't of the legal variety. The cost to buy a car—any car—was sky-high. Gasoline was unavailable to the ordinary citizen, and considering the cost of electricity, charging a car like the one he was currently driving pushed "sky-high" to the stratosphere.

Most worrisome to Nick was the poor state of medical care. Over the past twenty-five years, the number of doctors and nurses had drifted lower, the number of effective drugs had plummeted due to restrictions on replacement DNA research, and life expectancy had fallen from the mid-eighties for women to the low seventies. As a result, the population over those years had fallen off the statistical cliff. The fear that gripped Nick was that Sandra would be pushed over that edge.

He did have to weave through and around a swarm of bicycles, pedestrians, rickshaws, and skateboards. Nick's safety net was his siren. At least all forty-seven cruisers had sirens that provided a clear path ahead, even for the slowest of the slow, which he was now driving.

Nick knew worry was counterproductive, but he couldn't help turning over in his mind the words that Captain Gilmore had passed along: "She's in bad shape." How bad? Was she awake? Beaten? "Bad shape" had to mean she was alive, didn't it?

The captain had told him that Henry Braddock had called the ambulance and that he and his wife, Louise, had insisted on riding along with Nick's daughter to the hospital. The Braddocks were the closest Sandra had to grandparents, offering help, advice, and the occasional dinner recipe—only when asked. Understanding both sides of the strained father-daughter relationship, they kept Nick apprised of the many lows and the rare highs in Sandra's life. They had agreed to never let Sandra know that they even knew what her father looked like, let alone that they kept him up-to-date on her life.

Nick had known Henry Braddock years before Sandra had moved into the Braddocks' same apartment building, a mission accomplished by Nick offering his strong opinion that that building was one of the few she should *not* consider. Nicole was just two when Sandra had figured her life would be supremely better after severing all ties with her father. Henry and Louise, both in their early seventies, were aware of the dynamics and were glad to help. Nick never failed to thank them. Louise was a retired pharmacist, and Henry, a retired master welder and unable-to-ever-retire philosopher with a persistent back problem. Henry was the only atheist Nick knew who kept a Bible near at hand and who could quote pretty well any scripture if challenged. Louise had several times recounted the good-humored debates between Henry and their best-friend neighbors, two elderly retired nuns, Edna and Judy Patrick, over the existence of God.

Even Nicole had recounted one day how the two "sister nuns"— her term—had told Mr. Braddock that God created people, after which Mr. Braddock had said, "No, people created God." Nicole said they all smiled, laughed, and went back to their tea.

Nick remembered Henry and the nuns once playfully asking him which side he was on. "If someone throws a brick through a window, I arrest them," he had replied. "I make no distinction between a church window and a bar window." Henry and the two nuns had laughed and raised their tea mugs in a mock toast.

Since Henry didn't follow organized sports and both nuns rooted for the same teams, all now semipro, the only other thing he'd ever heard the two nuns and Henry debate was who had led the best big-band jazz group in history. The nuns were split between Count Basie and Duke Ellington; Henry's choice was Woody Herman. Again, many tea mugs were filled and emptied during untold fruitless hours, trying to reach a consensus.

Nick marveled at how quickly Nicole had taken to the two nuns. One had taught in a school for the deaf. Hearing that, Nicole had asked that nun to teach her how to read lips. He chuckled, remembering how she had learned so well he couldn't even whisper a secret without covering his mouth when she was in the same room.

His siren still wailing, Nick had to zig between two cyclists and then zag back around a woman pushing a baby carriage before yanking a sharp left onto East 101st Street and then slamming to a stop just before the Mount Sinai emergency ramp. He activated the NYPD theft alert transmitter, jumped out, locked the vehicle, and dashed up the ramp.

The triage desk was staffed by a lone nurse who didn't look as if she had been on this planet any less than 220 years.

Nick didn't care if she should have been in one of the beds herself. He flashed his badge, loudly demanding to know, "Sandra Blanding! What room?"

Less than two minutes later, he was at the door of her room, which, like most, stood open. He entered and was relieved to see Louise and Henry sitting in chairs on the other side of the bed.

Louise stood, and Henry started to rise, stopping when Louise placed a hand on his shoulder.

"She's out of danger, Nick" were Louise's first words.

Nick looked down at his daughter. Her face was covered with crisscrossed bandages. Except for the rise and fall of her chest with each breath, she was still. He suspected the tube traveling to the clear plastic covering over her nose was a precaution, since he didn't hear any respirator hiss.

Only a force of will prevented Nick from hyperventilating. "What—"

"Nick." Louise cupped the trembling top of his hand with hers. "It was Delmar."

Nick felt his neck tighten. They had told him about Delmar more than a year ago—about how uncomfortable they felt about him. Nick had hung around his daughter's apartment long enough to spot this Delmar and to trail him back to where he lived. Depending on what Louise and Henry had to say, Delmar was a dead man walking.

Louise waved her hand as if reading Nick's thoughts. "I was in the kitchen, but Henry heard everything. At the end, we both heard Delmar's threat." She turned to her husband. "You tell him, dear."

Henry nodded. "I heard shouting. Both from Sandra and from Delmar. It lasted about fifteen seconds or so—enough for me to get halfway to the door. I called out for Louise. Then Sandra screamed. She screamed twice. Then silence. As I touched the knob, I heard Sandra's door open. When I opened our door, there he was, looking at Louise and me, Sandra's door not yet closed behind him."

Louise brushed her hand across the footboard of the hospital bed. "She was on the floor—poor dear—moaning."

"Delmar scowled at us," Henry said. "'One peep, and you get the same,' he said. I'm one atheist who'll pray that there really is a hell. At least for that bastard."

"Then he just left," Louise finished. "Without closing the door."

"Did Nicole see anything?"

"No," Louise assured him. She was in school in the community room. "We left her with the Patricks."

Nick nodded his thanks.

"We'll stay with Sandra," Louise said and, as if reading Nick's mind, added, "You have someone to find."

CHAPTER 8

◆

ason Beck never had to use a gavel when calling the weekly one o'clock executive meeting. His glare was enough to call any meeting to order. It was 12:59, and his target for today, he was confident, would be on time.

He swept a casual gaze past each of the six others already seated around the glass-topped conference table, a table often used to seat more than thirty people comfortably—or, when he chose, quite uncomfortably, when some mere head of state came, hat in hand, pleading for some form of relief. Relief he granted only at the highest of costs.

Just seconds before one o'clock, Jason saw his second-in-command, associate director Christopher Price, enter the conference room, pull the massive mahogany door closed behind him, and take his chair at the opposite end of the table.

"Chris," Jason acknowledged, waving the room into quarter light.

The glass table in front of each seat sprang to life. Two illuminated video squares appeared in front of each participant.

"Let's get to it," Beck said as a bullet list of reports to be given appeared on the left screen of each set.

There were seven reports listed with their presenters:

* South and Central America & Pacific   Chet Bolling
* Europe, Africa, & AsiaBart   Collinsworth
* Technology & Energy Balance   Harvey Lauter
* Population Balance   Maria Garcia
* United States & US Associations   Chris Price
* New York City & Grid   Duane Evers

47

"Chet, you're up," Jason announced as the screens flipped to the first presentation. He felt it best to get the most insecure presenter up first and out of the way. Chet Bolling had the least-difficult area to cover. Definitely the easiest, Jason thought, although Chris clearly felt sorry for Chet and had suggested several times his responsibilities were too much for him and had recommended a reassignment to a much-easier task. Chris wasn't good at hiding his soft spot for those who couldn't cut the mustard. He had other faults, as well.

Jason watched Chet Bolling struggle to push his chair back and then apparently realized that the statement "You're up" didn't mean he had to stand. Chet pulled his chair back in, his three-hundred-plus pounds making it appear somewhat difficult. This "You're up" routine of Chet's was repeated at least three times a year, and Jason fully enjoyed each one. He was always amazed that, inside a neck as thick as Chet's, he could still see an Adam's apple bobbing up and down whenever Chet was nervous, which was nearly always.

Jason waved a hand at Chet to get in gear.

Having cleared his throat several times, Bolling started his presentation. "The conflict between Brazil and Argentina has almost stabilized. Bolivia has declared neutrality. Ecuador, the only South American country not bordering either combatant, has sued the World Court for relief of the continental blockade. Chile has—"

"Whoa," Jason commanded, raising a hand in mock defense. "That doesn't sound anywhere near 'almost stabilized.' In fact, the situation appears to have worsened. Significantly."

Fresh beads of perspiration formed on Bolling's forehead as he made nervous circles with a thick forefinger, first atop the map of Brazil and then over Argentina. The finger circles appeared briefly on the map, fading away within three seconds. "Well . . ." He stopped and took a deep breath. "When I say 'almost stabilized,' I mean that Brazil and Argentina have agreed to . . ." He paused for several moments to finger through his left square, his personal prompter. "Have agreed to 'neither attack nor support' others attacking the cosigner to this agreement."

From the look of relief on his face, Bolling apparently felt he was off the hook. He was forgetting one of the cardinal principals of the World Council: direct treaties or agreements between countries were to be disallowed. The World Council insisted on being used as sole intermediary with the sole power of assurance and enforcement.

"Enough," Jason said quietly. "Inform the presidents of Brazil and Argentina respectively that the 'agreement' must be reviewed by the council before we will consider supporting it. If they want our energy, they'll need our concurrence." He glowered at Bolling. "Have their ambassadors here tomorrow. Noon. Have them cool their asses in this room until one thirty."

"Yes, sir." Bolling kept his head slightly bowed while his eyeballs shifted left to right.

Both images in front of all members suddenly froze and then collapsed to black.

All eyes turned to Jason Beck.

"Change of plan," Jason announced. "I have all your reports and will distribute them as usual. Today, however, we have a problem that needs to be resolved." He studied Chris for a second. After noticing no unease, Jason turned toward Duane Evers. "Duane, I have a couple of questions for you."

Duane turned toward Jason, nodded, and glanced at Chris. "Yes, sir."

"I've heard that some of the paracop groups are starting to work at odds with the NYC Police. I've also been apprised that the NYC Police may be trying to infiltrate our own World Council inner circle."

Duane nodded again.

"Do you have any evidence?" Jason could see Chris's lack of concern as Duane gave a slight smile and reached toward his image screens.

"Two vid cams at Saint Vartan Park plus another several blocks away caught a most interesting sequence of events just"—Duane glanced down at his wristwatch—"shy of three hours ago." He tapped the frozen image on his right, and it sprang to video life on everyone's screens.

The view was from above the park and from the downtown side, with the East River on the right.

"This is the second in a sequence of two video captures but not as important as the first sequence," Duane announced. "None of these videos has sound."

At first, the scene at the park was peaceful: a group of children playing on swings and monkey bars near a dozen mothers, one sitting, the others standing and watching the children. Several men, two of them old, one middle-aged, and one young man bouncing a basketball, rested on benches. The impression of peacefulness was heightened by the absence of sound.

Suddenly, the close-to-old man at the extreme left of the screen view sprang to his feet as a large dog appeared from the right of the screen, charging at the children. While all the standing mothers raced to protect their children, the old man who had jumped up drew a revolver, shot the dog, and seconds later, also shot a man raising a shotgun as he entered the far right of the video frame. The screen also showed the young man drop his basketball and race to the only mother sitting on the bench and grab for something. It took everyone in the room a couple of seconds to notice that the "something" was a baby. The man with the shotgun was shot and fell to the ground. In the boardroom, they all watched six women race back, grab the baby snatcher, and start to beat him. They saw the old man wave his revolver back and forth at the women, rescue the bloody young man while showing a badge, exit the park, and head uptown with his captive.

The camera view shifted as the two left the first camera's range. They changed course when a group of men appeared from two side streets. The two men moved deliberately to the Fortieth Street grid elevator. From a third camera a street away, they were seen attaining the grid level and moving away in one of two grid crawlers. A group of men tried to follow but couldn't keep their footing.

"I've verified the identity of the man with the pistol," Duane concluded. "He's Detective Nicholas Garvey, NYPD, sixty-one years of age. The group of men chasing them is one of the many paracop brigades in the city."

"And the identity of the stalker?" Jason asked.

"In process."

Chris wore a confused expression on his face, and Jason knew why. This confrontation was no more and no less serious than the several incidents captured each week by the city's vid cams. The council had long ago linked into the video network and could pull up almost the complete flight path of a drunk pigeon, if it were important. Jason concluded that Chris was still in the dark over what had happened and over what was still to come. Time for enlightenment.

"You mentioned," Jason said to Duane while continuing to focus on Chris, "there was another video preceding this incident. Something even more interesting."

Duane tapped another image of the park, and everyone's right screen snapped into motion. From left to right, it was the same image of the park before all the excitement.

"Again, no sound," he said as he made some spreading motions with his fingers.

The view on each right screen zoomed in on the old man on the bench, the very detective who would later, as shown in the first video capture, shoot a dog, shoot a man, and rescue a stalker. He was eating a sandwich. Jason studied Chris, who raised an eyebrow in question when his executive assistant, Gerry Martin, came into view and sat next to the sandwich-eating policeman. They immediately started talking. Within less than a minute, they were making heated points at each other, head bobs, grimaces, and hand gestures, all while the detective continued to hold his half-eaten sandwich. After about three minutes, Gerry stood, made a couple of comments, and left.

Duane tapped his screen again, and all images froze. "Another ninety-seven seconds passed before the kid tried to snatch the baby."

All eyes in the room were on Chris.

"Chris," Jason said firmly, "could you get back to us with what transpired? As we all know, none of the council's officers are allowed to interface with the local police unless a crime has been committed. As we can see here, a crime had not yet been committed."

As Chris nodded, Jason surmised Chris surely knew there were land mines ahead but was wondering for the moment how many there were and for whom they were being set.

Chris nodded again. "I'll get back by the end of the day."

CHAPTER 9

◆

"Find everything there is to find about that detective," Jason commanded. "And find out who set up that 'accidental' meeting in that park on that bench. Did the detective request it, or did Gerry Martin?"

Duane nodded and turned to leave the room.

"A moment," Jason said, holding up a hand. "We've had Gerry Martin on periodic surveillance since he started here seven years ago." Jason softened his tone as he refreshed his memory.

Duane nodded. "Immediately before and after every public appearance. There are thousands of surveillance cameras in Manhattan; we could try pulling together his activity for the past three months, possibly six."

Jason shook his head. "I don't think we'll need that. However, put him on the full-time watch list as of now, stitching in anything you find since this morning's encounter."

After Duane left the conference room, Jason followed and went immediately to his office. He pulled a small hand phone from his desk and keyed in the full number.

"Fire up your lip-reading program," he said. "I have a video I'll bring first thing in the morning. It's from a distance. I'll need a quick analysis. Quick and thorough."

Jason received no argument. He opened a skinny door on the left side of his desk, reached in, and dropped the phone into a special metal container. Upon closing the door, he activated a switch. A muffled grinding sound came from within the desk. Time, he guessed, to buy another dozen throwaways.

He reached over to the right top drawer, opened it, and threw a switch that activated a recording bug in Christopher Price's office. Once he had inserted an earbud, he eased back in his chair, waiting to formulate, real-time, any needed plans.

He had learned how to motivate people to do exactly what he wanted them to do long before he'd met Chris during their under-graduate years at Dartmouth. They'd had two classes together during their freshman year: Greek and Roman history three days a week and economics, also three days a week. Less than halfway through that first semester, he recognized young Christopher Price as possessing an intellect equal to his own. The main difference, other than Chris's light red hair compared to his own dark brown, was that Chris had a "the world is beautiful as is so we should all live and let live" phi-losophy, a philosophy unlike his own: the world was waiting to be molded, molded by whoever stepped up to the task.

Jason chuckled. He'd been stepping up to the task since he was five years old.

He looked at the framed photograph of himself and his parents taken on his fifth birthday. Even by that young age, he'd formed a rudimentary understanding of their psyches and of where their irrita-tion buttons were. His parents, usually caring toward each other, did have the occasional confrontations. Jason remembered finding those incidents of confrontation most interesting—so interesting that, well before his next birthday, he found ways to provoke them into such exchanges while keeping himself blameless. As he grew older, he became more proficient in manipulating each against the other, con-vinced, just after his twelfth birthday, that he was the prime driver that pushed them into divorce court.

Still gazing at the photograph, Jason sent it a quick wink. The divorce was just a way station in all their lives. By the time they went to court, the irritation had grown from annoyance, to animosity, to finally, hatred. Each parent wanted guardianship, which revealed how invisible he had managed to keep his involvement.

Another chuckle. The judge had initially been convinced the mother should have sole custody, but his twelve-year-old self had convinced the judge that he cared equally for each parent and that the young boy of twelve wanted desperately to bring them back together. The judge finally ruled there would be joint custody, time to be split fifty-fifty. Jason was able to keep them at each other's legal throats until past his eighteenth birthday, when he attended Dartmouth on scholarship, leaving both parents to their own sour, hateful lives.

The sound in his earbud of an office door being closed brought Jason back to the present—a present in which he would soon hear what he guessed would be a self-serving description of what had supposedly happened between an NYPD detective and the suddenly suspicious Mr. Gerry Martin. Tomorrow morning he would know what had actually transpired, and after comparing it to what was claimed to have happened, he would discover if one or more of his inner circle could not be trusted.

CHAPTER 10

◆

Chris Price went straight from the meeting to his office. He stood in front of his desk and mentally debated how he should contact Gerry. The hair on the back of his neck still hadn't settled down from Jason's look as the park footage ended; instinct told him his next steps should be most careful. Too careless, and someone could get hurt; too secretive, and thirty years of trust could vaporize.

He sat behind his desk, picked up the phone, and said, "Gerry Martin, cell." He left a message for Gerry to come to his office as soon as possible.

Gerry arrived less than a minute later. "Saw Jason go into his office and draw the blinds," he said.

"No doubt," Chris said with no particular emphasis. "I have some questions, Gerry." Chris motioned to the chair across the desk. "Take a seat."

Chris saw Gerry's eyes narrow at the obvious formality of his words and demeanor. Hopefully, he would get the unspoken message that something was up.

Chris arched his left eyebrow ever so slightly.

Gerry sat.

"There's a video of you meeting with Detective Nicholas Garvey on a bench in Saint Vartan Park. Evers showed it earlier during the executive meeting."

Chris's second ever-so-slightly raised eyebrow hopefully told Gerry to wait until there was a question. Below the now normal eyebrow, he made sure his eyes projected a "be careful what you say and how you say it" look.

"You two appeared to have quite an animated conversation," he said. "Sufficiently animated that it was obvious to all of us that it was not a chance encounter."

Gerry nodded.

"Who called the meeting?"

"Detective Garvey."

"Why?"

"Information."

"Giving or asking?"

"Asking, primarily."

"Primarily?"

"He wanted to know if I had any information. He had to tell me what kind."

"And?"

"He told me that the vice president had been assassinated and that there were threats against the president that would be carried out during the lighting ceremony in two weeks. He felt an assassination attempt was likely."

"Did he suggest"—Chris squinted—"who might be responsible?"

"The council was his choice of several."

"Your response?"

"Told him he was way off base."

"Did he ask you for anything?" Again, the squint.

"To check around and, if I found anything pertinent, to get back with him. I told him he's got his job, and I've got mine. I got tired of talking with him, got up, and left."

Chris paused for several moments, debating with himself. "This is the police detective you partnered with sixteen years ago?"

Gerry nodded. "Yup, just shy of that. That's when we started. Worked as a team for many years."

"What is he liable to do? Is he the type to stick his nose—"

"Where it doesn't belong?" Gerry asked. "Only for a day or two."

Chris relaxed just a bit. He remembered the several times over the years when Gerry had described his old partner as a cop who, if he sensed something amiss, would stick his nose anywhere and every-where for as long as it took.

Gerry continued, his own eyebrows arched. "He'll follow up on his various imagined leads for a couple of days before his captain assigns him a new task. You know how understaffed the ol' NYPD is. For the past ten years, they've had to farm out more and more responsibility to neighborhood groups. That's why I left the force. I wanted a group that was strong, not weak."

"Strong, not weak." Chris pondered the words. "Did you see anything happen in the park after you left?"

"No."

Chris noticed a quick flash of mild alarm cross Gerry's face. He was obviously concerned that something had happened to Nick. Chris said nothing further, and Gerry didn't push the issue. The exchange of arched eyebrows could work wonders in an environment where no conversation was guaranteed private.

"Thank you, Gerry," Chris finally said.

Gerry stood, nodded, and left.

CHAPTER 11

◆

Nick checked his watch for what must have been the hundredth time: 11:27 p.m.

He arrived at the intersection of Forty-Ninth Street and Ninth Avenue in a little more than twenty minutes. On the opposite corner stood Delmar's apartment building. Nick parked behind a dumpster and checked his Glock. After he was satisfied that Delmar was nowhere in sight, he eased out of the sedan, locked it, and then, reaching under the front driver's wheel well, activated the alarm.

Nick hoped to catch Delmar flat-footed with a beer in his hand. Second best, he would be in his bed, asleep, and would wake to the barrel of cold steel pressed against his temple. Third best, he would be on the toilet. First best, wherever he was whenever Nick found him, Delmar would try to take him down and Nick would empty nine bullets into him.

"Yup, that would be first best," Nick muttered to himself as he opened the unlocked rusty gate at the rear of the apartment building.

Almost a year ago, the Braddocks had alerted him that they were concerned about the back-and-forth yelling and screaming they heard coming from Sandra's apartment. Henry, particularly, had sported a worried expression. "It's an escalating pattern I've seen for too many years."

When Nick had asked where, the answer had surprised him.

"More than nine years helping at Saint Lucy's Shelter," Henry had explained. "Providing protection and advice to abused and bruised women as well as to the occasional mangled man."

Nick had decided two things at that moment. One: he wouldn't ask atheist Henry if he had received any blessings from Bishop Morgan for his service. Two: it was time to introduce himself to Delmar Pillsbury.

He had confronted Delmar as he swaggered down the steps from Sandra's apartment. Nick, slouched against the trunk of the oak tree opposite the steps, had raised his left hand in a "Halt!" motion as Delmar's feet reached the pavement. Nick's gesture was one of a command, not an invitation. Delmar had stopped, a quizzical tough-guy expression and stance announcing he was king of the sidewalk and some old man in a rumpled suit had better move out of his way. Hanging from his neck, a gold chain sporting a five-or-six-inch gold disk with his initials in bright blue had swayed side to side.

Nick remembered their confrontation almost verbatim.

"A few words," Nick said.

"Very few, old man." Delmar shoved his hands into his pants pockets as if to show he was afraid of nothing.

"Fine." Nick pulled out his Glock and pointed it at Delmar's groin.

The tough-guy expression vanished, replaced by wide eyes and mouth agape.

"Relax, asshole. I'm not going to shoot your balls off."

"What . . . what do you want? Money? I can—"

"Forget money. I'm not after your money. I'm here to make a deal."

"Deal? What kind of deal?"

"A deal that will keep these bullets . . ." Nick gave the Glock a slight side-to-side wave. "In here and not in your pants."

The cockiness wavered. Delmar, off balance, was obviously assessing Nick to be a threat but was confused as to what kind.

"I'm Sandra's father. You hurt her; I hurt you."

Delmar took a deep breath and slowly exhaled, a sign to Nick the younger man was regaining control of himself, if not the situation. "Sandra's father. The cop. The one she hates."

"The very one," Nick assured him.

"Doesn't it bother you that she hates you?"

"Not your problem, scumbag." Nick motioned for Delmar to sit on the bottom step. "Your problem is if you become *my* problem.

Physically hurt my daughter just a little bit, and you'll lose one of those balls. A lot, you'll lose both. Involve her in one of your rackets, and I'll shoot out all four balls."

Delmar chuckled derisively. "You can't count, cop. Your lecturing has screwed up your arithmetic. I'm not some sort of freak. I don't have four balls."

Nick returned the chuckle. "I was including your eyeballs, moron." Nick saw the new math add up in Delmar's brain. "That's right. I won't be able to guarantee shooting out your eyeballs won't cause other damage."

"You want me to stay away from a daughter who hates your guts?"

"Not at all. I don't have the right to tell her who she can see or sleep with. I *can* tell you what I'll do to you if you go against my warning."

"Message received, old man."

"Fine. One more thing: I'll be keeping at least one eye on you every day. You will be seeing me now and then—but not nearly as much as I'll be seeing you." Motioning with the Glock, Nick waved him on his way.

During the intervening eleven months, Nick had made sure that Delmar noticed him. As a detective, he had arrest privileges throughout Manhattan. During those eleven months, he made sure he was seen outside Delmar's own apartment building, making several arrests of street scum, visibly strong-arming a few while apprehending them. During those eleven months, he had turned a blind eye to Delmar's frequent misdemeanors. Nick had justified to himself that, as long as Delmar didn't physically harm anyone, intervention was not warranted.

Now as he entered the rear of the apartment building, Nick shook his head in regret.

Delmar lived on the third floor. There were two stairwells: one in the front, and the other, which he was taking now, immediately inside the rear outside door.

Nick reached the third floor and started to open the hallway door when he saw Delmar leave his room with two large knapsacks and head for the front stairs. Nick was about to rip open the door and shoot when a couple with a young boy emerged from their apartment, obscuring his view of Delmar, who was already entering the front stairwell.

He'd never catch up with Delmar, but Nick had a good idea where he was headed: the Lincoln Tunnel. *If it were me,* Nick assured himself, *rather than stay and have my balls shot off, I would bribe passage out of Manhattan.* All Delmar would need was ten thousand dollars to get past the NYC Tunnel Security Force, plus another ten thousand at the far end of the tunnel to grease the palms of the Jersey-Penn Enforcement Police. Twenty thousand total! Nick was a well-paid NYPD detective, but his gross was not even five thousand a year. No wonder only flush felons could buy their way across the Hudson River. Underground river runners were always cheaper, but they didn't always care about protecting their business reputations. The tunnel and bridge security police were official groups that were awarded their positions because of political favors and well-known to have high integrity, given the right price—a reputation not easy for any corrupt group to come by.

Yup, Nick assured himself, Delmar was on the run to the Jersey-Penn Association. More opportunities for a scumbag asshole—and less chance of being cornered in Long Island by the New England Association, known for shooting assholes once they made themselves known.

Nick caught sight of Delmar turning left at the corner onto Tenth Avenue toward the tunnel. With one exception, all the old entrances to the Lincoln Tunnel had been sealed twelve years ago. The exception was the entrance branching off Thirty-Ninth Street. Nick decided to follow on foot. If he used the car and was noticed, there were too many alleys and fences that Mr. Scumbag could use to permanently disappear.

Delmar started to jog. Nick followed suit. He knew he wouldn't catch Delmar before he made contact with Tunnel Security. As he visualized the obstacles and hurdles ahead of them both, Nick calculated he'd get to the tunnel control barriers well before any negotiations were concluded.

After deciding to give himself more of an arrival edge, Nick picked up the pace to something resembling a trot. Years of experience chasing suspects assured him that he could keep the pace right up to the tunnel.

Within four minutes of turning south on Tenth Avenue, Nick had to zigzag around an anchored green-and-yellow truck, which was parked just before Forty-Third Street and had an elevated cherry-picker bucket. The large 48 on the cab's door made him think of Nicole. He had measured her height just three days ago, and she was forty-eight inches on the nose. He had bought her an ice cream to celebrate.

He glanced up and noticed the absence of work lighting just below the grid. Why were grid workers, wherever they were at the moment, working so late, especially in an area he thought had been completed months ago? He shook his head and continued his measured gait.

After another three minutes, he turned right off Tenth Avenue onto Thirty-Ninth Street, where he spotted Delmar drifting right onto the tunnel entrance ramp.

Delmar slowed his jog down to a walk, hefting the two knapsacks tight to his shoulders as he descended toward the amber-lit interior of the Lincoln Tunnel. Unless the control station had been moved, Delmar had two hundred yards once inside the tunnel. Nick was confident he had more than enough time. He slowed to a light jog and then a walk and proceeded to catch his breath.

Delmar entered the tunnel.

Nick kept his pace constant, Delmar's progress not being worthy of a second glance. He counted off ninety seconds until he also entered the tunnel. The evening light behind him was giving way to the amber floods in the tunnel. The artificial lighting was quite pronounced as the tunnel curved slightly to the right. Nick had been here over two years ago, and the control station was probably still just beyond the curve. He and the station would be visible to each other for at least a hundred yards.

As the distant barricades came into view, he could see Delmar just coming to a stop. Muffled voices began to echo back to him. Delmar had started the negotiations.

Nick continued his steady pace as he strode along the faded center line. About a minute passed before the echoed conversations became intelligible.

Delmar was shrugging off one of the knapsacks. "This should cover this end of the deal." He handed the knapsack to the uniformed man with the most shoulder braids.

It was that man who first looked up with an appraising glance at Nick as he approached.

When he was about ten yards away, Nick stopped and held up his badge.

The uniform with braids frowned. "And you would be wanting what?"

"Him," Nick said evenly, pointing at Delmar, who was just now beginning to turn around.

CHAPTER 12

◆

Delmar's eyes apparently didn't register Nick's image for several seconds.

Nick was tempted to wave.

"He wants to kill me!" Delmar finally shouted. He turned to run deeper into the tunnel but managed only three steps before two uniforms without any shoulder braids each grabbed an arm, lifting him aloft.

The obvious leader of the Security Force looked from Nick to the elevated Delmar and then back to Nick. "And you think you have jurisdiction why?"

Good question, Nick thought, introducing himself. Tunnel Security personnel were neither affiliated with the NYC Police or with any paracop group or any private company. They were paid directly by the city and had a few specific accountabilities but were otherwise free to exercise their own discretion. The mayor's office wanted to keep the tunnel flow controlled but, as was always the case, on the cheap. Turning back fugitives was not a source of "discretionary" income; charging them for an escort out of the city was. Most city officials were aware of the traffic but feigned ignorance, calculating that fewer bad guys in the city was for the good and the money split coming their way welcome. Nick had to convince them that, although there was no price on Delmar's head, keeping him would certainly be trouble for them. It was definitely time to make up a backstory, a most vile one.

"Are you a family man . . ." Nick moved closer and squinted at the man's name tag. "Captain Charles Reynolds?"

A slight nod was given, followed by a return squint at Nick's own tag and a hand gesture for him to come no closer.

"You have a kid?" Nick asked, obeying Reynolds's command.

A second nod as the man took off his Security Force hat. "And that has to do with your jurisdiction how?"

Nick took a deep breath and mentally crossed his fingers. "This creep," he said, cupping his badge under his extended forefinger aimed at Delmar, "can provide you with another—hell, another *two* kids if you like. Tell him what sex, hair color, eye color, nationality, and he'll fill your request within forty-eight hours." Nick could see from the widening brown eyes that he had Reynolds's attention. "If you have any"—Nick made a face that hinted at disgust but a refusal to judge—"special proclivities."

"He's lying!" Delmar shouted. "I don't buy and sell kids. I have never grabbed any kid. Not a one. That bastard has been chasing me—"

Reynolds raised a hand to stave off the building torrent of screaming words.

Delmar choked off his words midthroat.

Reynolds studied Delmar for several seconds. "So for a living you do what?"

"I don't . . . I *never*—"

Reynolds cupped Delmar's chin in his left hand and whipped his face around to face his own. "I didn't ask what you don't do. I asked what you *do* do."

Delmar's eyes widened in obvious panic. He raised a shaking hand and pointed at Nick. "He's blaming me for hurting his daughter."

"He blamed you when? From what I can see, you didn't know he was after you until you turned and saw him."

Nick said nothing. Time for Delmar to sink his own ship.

"He told me—no, he warned me that—"

"Told you? Warned you?" Reynolds shook his head. "There's a difference?"

"You have to protect me!"

"And I should do that why?"

"He wants to kill me. He told me a year ago he'd kill me, told me he'd shoot my balls off, told me—"

Reynolds held up a hand, commanding Delmar to stop. "He told you a lot of things a year ago. And he didn't kill you then. Why?"

Delmar was having trouble breathing. "I hadn't . . . I hadn't hurt his . . . his daughter a year ago."

"But now, a year later, he changed his mind. Why?"

Delmar's lower lip quivered and then curled into a snarl. "The bitch told me to get the hell out. No bitch tells me that. So I beat some—" Delmar realized he was digging his hole deeper.

Nick raised his hands and took just one step forward. "So tonight he beat my daughter into a coma. She's in Mount Sinai with tubes and monitors all over her body."

Reynolds locked eyes with Nick for several seconds. "My guess is your quarry here doesn't buy and sell children."

"I believe he does not."

"Interesting way for you to get a confession."

Nick offered a confirming nod.

"You have cuffs?" Reynolds asked.

Nick nodded again.

"He wants to kill me!" Delmar shouted.

"Be quiet. Detective Garvey doesn't strike me as the killing kind. I just think he wants to kick your ass—"

"All the way to the precinct," Nick said, completing the thought.

"Detective Garvey will be taking you into custody," Reynolds said, lifting both knapsacks, "while I maintain custody of these."

"Sounds fair to me," Nick concluded.

Before Delmar could be handed over to Nick, a convoy of trucks rumbled up to the control station. The number of vehicles—at least ten—and their green-and-yellow colors announced before any paperwork was handed over that the grid was getting more workers.

It took just over an hour to clear the eleven trucks, four with cherry pickers. It caught Nick's attention that all truck cabs bore three digits. The cherry pickers had the two hundreds, while the others, a mixture of wire and beam haulers and worker transports, had the three and four hundreds. The majority of the hour was taken up verifying each worker's credentials. Reynolds apparently didn't mind when Nick ambled to his side and watched him record each truck number and then count its contents.

Nowhere did Nick see any truck with just two digits. Nowhere was there a truck 48.

Reynolds confirmed that every truck's number included three digits. No more, no less.

It was 5:17 a.m. when Delmar was cuffed and handed over to Nick, who accepted Reynolds's offer to have one of his officers drive Nick and Delmar back to Nick's car.

CHAPTER 13

◆

J ason checked his watch: 6:21 a.m. After twenty minutes, he was getting a little impatient. He had handed the video block to Bert Freed, an obese, bald, smelly genius of a techno wizard in a wheelchair. Whenever Jason required some special computer analysis, he came here. Bert could untie and retie any digital Gordian knot, no sword required. Jason always got impatient, but Bert always delivered what was needed—just not at the snap of a finger. Bert was his man. His man in more ways than one. Bert had what some might call "peculiar" tastes in "pleasure" activities. Jason provided Bert with protection as well as live, healthy candidates for his "pet friend" Salazar, although Jason often mused that the "friend" part might be a significant understatement. Whatever.

In turn, Bert worked his magic whenever Jason called. Jason had provided Bert with the electronic keys to all but a specific subset of the council's worldwide computers. With Bert and his off-grid access, Jason had no worries that any other computer-literate eyes would stumble upon any unauthorized activity. Jason, of course, was at the top of the authorization food chain, but prudence and secrecy practiced continuously made his plans and surveillance private and perfect.

Jason had briefed Bert as to what he needed. "Run this through your voice thingamajig. I want to hear every word spoken by each of the two men on the bench." Jason always referred to Bert's various hardware miracles as thingamabobs or thingamajigs or, every once in a while, light-thingy flashers, since he could see it allowed Bert to picture himself in a somewhat superior position and to motivate him to impress the world's most powerful man, a man who only pretended to be technically illiterate.

Bert picked up the cube and then spun his chair and himself about 130 degrees counterclockwise. He belched as the chair turned. The room was filled with screens, keypads, metal racks with rippling lights, and the smell of last week's burgers.

Jason was always conscious that less than thirty feet away, in a circular pit, was Salazar, Bert's almost full-grown eight-foot-long Komodo dragon. Jason shot another glance in the creature's direction. It appeared to be sleeping. Probably fed recently. Whether it was sleeping or not, Jason always checked for the chain around the creature's neck. Damn lizards, unlike alligators, could lift their bodies about a foot off the ground to chase down a panicked deer and kill it. When not asleep, its ribbonlike tongue, forked at the end, darted out every eight to ten seconds.

After only twenty seconds of viewing, Bert announced, "It'll take about twenty minutes. This video faces the younger man. I can synthesize his words, but the older man will require I pull video from a pole cam a block away on the far side. It'll require several passes, but it'll work out unless he covers his mouth."

"He doesn't," Jason assured him.

Jason watched the wide screen in front of Bert spin away from the park and then, after several studied keystrokes, yield to a long-distance view from the traffic pole cam. He decided a single awestruck utterance would again assure Bert of the singularity of his own technical superiority. "Amazing," he mumbled just loud and just distinct enough. He caught the slight smirk turn the corner of Bert's mouth.

Bert still flipped several switches and adjusted a couple of black-and-silver knobs before swiveling his chair partway around to Jason. "This is the park where you had your first run-in with the future President Allison." It was a nonquestion. He swiveled back to the screens.

Jason, hiding his irritation, agreed that it was.

Bert was now zooming the image, framing the two men on the park bench. The older man was indeed facing the camera, but his image was blurred from the enlarged pixels. The older man's mouth could be seen to move but in barely recognizable fashion. Jason had no doubt Bert would solve the problem.

Jason turned his attention to the overall image of Saint Vartan Park. He remembered it well from the clash to which Bert had just referred.

Long before the well-publicized jousting match with Allison and company, he had joined the reelection campaign staff of New York's junior US senator, Henry Wells. Senator Wells was elected, and Jason was bitten by the political bug. He remained on the senator's staff and was one of the key advisors when he ran for a second term. It was then the senator ran into the buzz-saw campaign of upstart businessman Victor Goldman. Wells lost big. Jason spent six months analyzing the winner's methods. After those six months, he was most impressed. Most impressed with two of Goldman's young advisors: Lenora Allison and Carter Johnson.

It was during that Wells versus Goldman campaign battle that two separate rallies had been scheduled for the same time at Saint Vartan Park. His was the first. He'd had fifty-plus hired supporters holding placards and marching. Lenora's group had entered the park ten minutes later with over three hundred. Broadcast videos of the event tended to refer to the encounter as a whale swallowing a minnow.

It was after those broadcasts that Jason had vowed he would make sure in the future that he was the whale and that he alone did any and all required swallowing.

"I got it all!" Bert announced, spinning around to face Jason.

"Let's hear it," Jason commanded quietly.

Bert positioned the playback to where Gerry Martin walked into the park and stood beside the older man. Before any conversation began, they both glanced outside the park.

"There's a bozo on a bicycle who crashed into a grid pole," Bert pointed out.

There were greetings and pleasantries exchanged. No interfering street noises were present, since the conversation was simulated purely from mouth movements. At Jason's request, Bert cranked up the playback volume. The older man was requesting Gerry Martin to report any unusual actions of the World Council aimed at President Lenora Allison.

The video conversation picked back up with Gerry Martin protesting he couldn't "spy on my superiors."

The dialog continued back and forth, with the older man suggesting the World Council had some diabolical plan to destroy President Allison and with Gerry Martin challenging each argument put forth. Jason conceded that Mr. Martin had done a credible job in minimizing each of his bench mate's conspiracy theories.

The simulated voices Bert had hooked into his lip-reading program were exaggerated but clear. Sometimes, when one of the men spoke over the other, the differences in timber were . . . unexpected.

"I'm not asking you to sleep with your bosses," Detective Garvey said. "Just stay alert to any words or actions of theirs that might indicate—"

"That might indicate murder or mayhem," Gerry said, finishing the sentence.

"That might indicate such, if it falls in your lap."

"If it falls in my lap." Gerry nodded warily. "Like an eater on a metal box."

"Stop!" Jason commanded. "That doesn't make sense: an eater on a metal box? Was that what he actually said?"

Bert replayed the section and noted aloud that Mr. Martin's lips were hardly moving with each word as they had before. "He said that sentence to himself, not aloud."

"But your software made some sense of the rest of the words."

"Apparently."

Jason's eyes narrowed. "Rather than eater could the word have been *eagle*?"

"Maybe."

"Can you do a close-up on Gerry Martin's mouth as he says that sentence?"

Bert spread the screen until only Gerry's nose down to his chin was visible. He replayed the segment.

Bert shook his head. "Can't tell."

Jason had noticed the tongue press against the inside of the upper front teeth at the end of the word in question. He had no doubt Gerry had mouthed *eagle*. "Continue," he said.

The scene picked up with Gerry standing up. "If it falls," he repeated. Gerry paused and turned back to Nick. "Just so all the information favors are not all one-sided . . ." Gerry paused for a second or two, apparently deciding whether to continue. "You mentioned population control. If you have any information on one shadowy character calling himself El Camino, shoot me the details."

Detective Garvey replied, "El Camino? Isn't that the name of a car model a century or so ago?"

It was at this point Jason decided he had a major problem on his hands.

"Do you want to replay it?" Bert asked.

"No," Jason said, pausing to sort out from the conversation who knew what about anything. Anything relating to his plans for the president was of no value to him. Whatever might happen to the president would never be traced back to him. Over the next few weeks, he and the World Council would be models of cooperation and support. Part of being untraceable included Bert not having any clue.

As to the "eagle on a metal box," that problem was long gone, and any mention of it would only amount to hearsay. However, one of his earliest rules, even as a second-grader, was "silenced is safe."

"I'll have someone bring in dinner for Salazar," Jason promised.

"What about the ruckus after Gerry left?" Bert suggested.

"Not important," Jason said. "Put this cop, Nicholas Garvey, on twenty-four-hour video and, wherever and whenever possible, audio trace."

Bert nodded as Jason rose and left. Jason didn't have to tell him to keep the same surveillance level on Gerry. All management and assistants in the World Council were tracked. Always.

As he left Bert's apartment and before he got behind the wheel, Jason sent a simple numeric text: 2.05. An acknowledgment came back within thirty seconds. Jason nodded to himself and turned the key in the ignition. He'd have just enough time to get to Meeting Place No. Two in one-half hour.

CHAPTER 14

◆

Jason arrived at his second meeting place exactly one minute before the communicated half hour.

The other man, lean and one inch shorter than Jason's six-foot-two frame, arrived one minute later, on foot.

Jason got out of his car and motioned the other to join him for a stroll.

"There's someone in the organization who may well be on track to alter our recipe for success," Jason said. "He has recognized one of the ingredients in the recipe. I need you to disabuse him, permanently, of any modifications." Jason relied on the other man being comfortable with nonspecific instructions. He handed him a dossier with pictures of Gerry Martin.

"And the proof you'll be wanting how?"

"The usual."

"Time frame?"

"Today's Friday." Jason thought for a moment. "Have it done by Monday morning."

An accepting nod was given.

Jason turned to head back to his car.

The other man stopped him. "Executives of the seven associations are meeting in Philly over the next ten days. All four of our informants are keeping tabs on anything—positive *or* negative—that might impact the grid lighting. The executives, concerned President Allison might sway public sentiment against them, are scratching their collective heads to come up with plan B, or plan C, or all the way to plan Z, forgetting they don't even have a plan A."

"Anything credible?"

"Credible? No. Extreme? Yes. One of the associations, Carter Johnson's own Penn-Jersey Association, proposed exploding the Lincoln Tunnel to halt the completion of the grid. I feel we can steer the vote either way. From what you've said in the past, I assume you want to see the grid completed and its lighting attempted."

Jason nodded. "*Attempted* being the key word."

"I'll send word through to keep that proposal squashed."

Jason thought for a moment about Carter Johnson. His plan B in this case was plan Stupid, akin to shooting himself in the foot. Jason shook his head. This was easier than manipulating his own dad into giving his mom any one of a dozen ultimatums. Letting Carter Johnson keep his gun locked, loaded, and pointed at his own foot might prove helpful in the long term.

"Not squashed," Jason said. "Just tabled. Keep some interest in it going."

"Will do. And I'll make sure our fingerprints never show up on either side of the proposal."

Jason confirmed and returned to his car.

The other man also turned and walked away in the direction of the Lincoln Tunnel.

Jason pulled out his phone and pressed the screen once.

The line clicked open after three rings. "Yes, Director?"

"Jeremiah, I have an apartment to be searched after Monday morning."

Jason was 100 percent sure Gerry Martin would be out of the picture come Monday. He was also 100 percent confident of Jeremiah's loyalty. He passed along a description of the metal box with its embossed eagle. "It will probably be well hidden. Unhide it and bring it to me."

"Monday morning, Director. Consider it done."

CHAPTER 15

◆

It had taken almost fifteen minutes for the Tunnel Security officer and Nick to stuff the struggling, shouting Delmar into the back of Nick's patrol car.

"Maybe we should tape his mouth," the officer said, further suggesting that Nick's eardrums might not survive the trip.

Nick waved off the offer with a chuckle. "If he keeps going, he'll make it, but his voice won't."

On the way back to the precinct, Nick detoured past where he had seen utility truck no. 48. The street was empty. He continued on, reaching the precinct at about 9:00 a.m.

As he parked in front of the building, six unfamiliar uniformed men marched out the front door, piled into a black limousine, and drove off.

Nick ushered Delmar into the building and into a cell by himself.

Captain Gilmore motioned him to his office. Inside he relayed a message from Sandra's doctor that she was undergoing several tests and would be out of her room for at least the next few hours.

Tim waved to Nick to join him at the computer terminals.

"You got something on the videos?" Nick asked.

"Not yet. The Secret Service was here 'helping out' and just left. I may have a lead."

"Saw six of them when I drove up. What's the lead you may have?"

"They were here for all but yesterday's first half hour of checking the videos. They asked what we had already reviewed. I showed them our projected viewing log listed by time and location with check marks for those already reviewed. They studied the listing of six reviewed videos, several times having discussions among themselves. They struck me as somewhat too interested in the list and somewhat intentionally excluding myself and our two computer analysts, Glen and Fred, in any reaction. We and they worked through the night, and about two hours before you arrived, we all—the three of us and five of their six agents—took a coffee break for about twenty minutes. When—"

"When you got back, what happened?" Nick asked.

"When we returned to view the remaining twelve videos, we found two of them had no content. Only two blank ones out of a hundred and sixteen videos."

"Did the sixth agent who stayed behind say anything?"

"Yes. Claimed he never drinks coffee and just sat back and rested after a full night."

"Believe him?"

"We'll soon find out," Tim said, sitting down beside the two technicians and telling them to proceed. "When they seemed so very interested in those first six videos, I signaled Glen and Fred to set up each subsequent video to be automatically copied to our backup server as soon as it was keyed up."

Nick chuckled. "You guys are real sneaky SOBs."

"That we are," Tim said.

Glen and Fred nodded, smirking in agreement.

Nick rubbed his hands together in anticipation. "What did you find?"

"Sit down. We'll find out together."

Glen checked his log and read aloud the time of the coffee break. The technicians skimmed through the captured videos until they came to the start of the break. Glen ran the captured videos while Fred replayed the matching originals. Figuring they could follow the video playback when set at double speed, they waited only four minutes to reach the first blank on Fred's display. That ten-minute segment and the one after it were the ones blanked out. Intentionally, obviously.

The captured video runs were replayed at normal speed. A normal street scene in late afternoon was displayed. Very little activity was shown.

After several seconds, Nick recognized the scene as one he had passed while chasing Delmar. The only difference was the absence of truck no. 48. Another minute into that first video, truck no. 27 appeared and parked on Forty-Third Street about fifty feet back from Tenth Avenue. The truck remained parked in the same location for two-thirds of the second video.

"Twelve and a half minutes," Fred reported.

Nick and Tim looked at each other and shook their heads. The Secret Service wanted to hide something.

"I saw a similar truck parked next to the same building when I was chasing Delmar. When I saw it last night, it was parked on Tenth Avenue and not Forty-Third Street. From what I found out, that truck is not part of the grid build team. It's a phony."

The next five hours were spent downloading another hundred-plus videos covering the previous twenty-four hours across Manhattan, each scanned at triple speed for signs of any grid trucks. Six different trucks were noted, only one having three digits painted on its sides.

"That's a legit truck. The others, the phonies, have only two digits."

Captain Gilmore stepped out of his office and gave Nick a "Come here" tilt of his head. "I just got a call from the hospital," he said. "Sandra's okay. The doctors say her vital signs are all positive but that she's still in a coma. They said they need some additional history from you. You gotta go. Tim and the boys will keep going for a couple more hours. Then everyone breaks for the night. It's been over forty hours for you and Tim. Go to the hospital. Then get some rest. I need you both fresh tomorrow."

"Okay, but there's something fishy going on in more than one area. When I was chasing Delmar, I passed what I thought was a federally contracted grid construction vehicle. It had the number 48 on its side. I found out while in the Lincoln Tunnel that all contracted vehicles have three-digit numbers, not two."

The captain pursed his lips for a moment. "I'll have Glen and Fred follow up. You gotta get—"

"They're aware. The other fishy thing is that the group of Secret Service agents erased footage of several other trucks with just two digits. I don't trust them. We shouldn't give them free access to anything."

"Done. Now get going. You can follow up in detail after the hospital. *Well* after."

CHAPTER 16

◆

Jason decided not to make the two ambassadors wait beyond 12:15. He had too much on his plate to make them stew for the usual ninety minutes. He pulled Bolling into the conference room with him.

Both ambassadors rose as they entered the room.

"Sit, gentlemen," Jason said, his voice sharp and impatient. "My executive, Mr. Chet Bolling here, tells me your countries have signed a mutual nonaggression treaty without involvement of the World Council."

Like ruffians sent to the principal, both ambassadors dropped their gaze to the table.

Jason saw Chet smile at being called "executive" in front of the ambassadors. Two entities had been put in separate boxes where Jason wanted them.

"You ambassadors will return to your countries and inform your leaders that your 'treaty' no longer exists and that energy allotments for your governments will be cut in half for the next three months."

The ambassador from Brazil started to object. "We cannot survive three months of such draconian punishment." He started to rise.

"Sit!" Jason snapped. "At least you recognize punishment when you see it. The three months stands. During those three months, the World Council will assure no other countries in your political vicinity will attack either Brazil or Argentina in any way nor interfere with the deliveries of your reduced allotments. Your respective governments will submit to Council Executive Bolling drafts of proposed accords to be brought back for review and approval. Should

80

approval not be granted within three months, the reduced allotments will continue until Council Executive Mr. Chet Bolling signs off."

Both ambassadors swallowed and nodded.

Chet beamed.

Jason stared at the two ambassadors. "Am I clear? The World Council is not just a title."

"Clear," both ambassadors mumbled.

"You may leave now."

Jason motioned to Chet to stay behind. "I know I've been tough on you, Chet, but—"

"Not really, Supreme Direct—"

"Yes, Chet. Really. I see you growing in the position. Your executive area of responsibility is one of the more difficult ones. I've kept after you because I see your growth. Keep your eyes on the future. You have one here. A significant one. There will be big assignments, and there will continue to be small ones."

Chet tapped his first two fingers against his left thumb. "Would one of those small assignments be that you need six more puppies delivered?"

Jason nodded.

"On it, Supreme Director."

After Chet left, Jason reflected on Bert's reminder of his first "run-in" with Lenora Allison. She as president—and Carter Johnson as chief executive of the Penn-Jersey Association and elected leader of the seven associations—always warranted his attention. That attention had been earned in their early years and was warranted by continued successes later.

Politically speaking, Allison and Johnson were polar opposites: Allison was a free-market conservative bordering on libertarian; Johnson, a center-left liberal. How Victor Goldman ever kept them on the same team had always intrigued Jason. Intrigued *and* concerned him. He had concluded that the road to real power depended, among other things, on keeping political opposites . . . opposite. His guiding principle was to keep the body politic's left hand and its right hand giving each other the finger. With each side firmly rooted in its ideology, he could climb to the top, his agenda invisible.

He kept the occasional eye on Allison and Johnson while he, Jason Beck, was busy building his own political career, always hewing to the middle ground, always providing evidence—real or, when needed, fabricated—that any opponent of his who disagreed with him on any given issue was an extreme, incorrigible, intransigent Neanderthal.

His style brought success: one term as a US representative, followed by a successful election to the US Senate. His Allison-and-Johnson "occasional eye" became more focused on them two years later when they too were each elected to the US Senate: Allison, from Texas, and Johnson, from Michigan. Each was extremely vocal within their respective base's caucus. They each fought hard against the proposals put forth by the other's camp. Jason's concern about the political poles gravitating toward the middle dropped almost to zero. *Almost to zero,* he now mused, *for only a year and a little bit.*

In discharging his Senate duties, he gained extensive access to the United Nations and to its financial arm. The ties between that part of the UN and foreign nations so intrigued him that halfway through his Senate term, he resigned his office on July 24, 2023, accepting a key position with United Nation Finance. On September 18, 2024, he was appointed director of UN Finance when the previous director died in a plane crash.

He was quick to get his sea legs in his new position. He did notice, though, that both Senator Allison and Senator Johnson found their sea legs almost as quickly.

Two years after their own elections, they were rapidly rising stars and were each assigned to what must have been at least the thirty-seventh Social Security Preservation Task Force. SSPTF—he remembered the silly acronym that sounded to him like someone spitting out a lemon seed. Jason's "occasional eye" renewed focus when, after only nine weeks, Allison and Johnson revealed a jointly sponsored bill and got their respective bases to accept total revision of Social Security.

They agreed upon a system that remained coercive: if you worked, you had to pay in. They agreed that each worker would *own* their policy and upon their deaths could leave any balance to their heirs. They agreed that since the current "locked box" contained only IOUs, the government would henceforth not be allowed to ever touch the payments within. They agreed that the government's 2 percent interest rate was both paltry and was seldom paid. They agreed the marketplace over any twenty-year period would match the market's two-hundred-year history of at least 7.5 percent, almost four times better than the government's.

They agreed the new Social Security would be best. So did both the House and the Senate. So did the president. It took five years for 80 percent of the American electorate to agree. By that time, both Allison and Johnson had attained top posts in their respective parties.

During those five years, Jason missed no chance to maneuver either Allison or Johnson into the corner opposite the other. Jason's antenna worked overtime whenever any Senate proposal, bill, or investigation involved either one or both of them. His experience told him to keep the two up-and-coming party leaders, if not at each other's throats, at least locked in good dueling stances with political muskets at the ready. Political stalemate was not what Jason was hoping for. He wanted a pendulum swinging back and forth, benefitting first one party, then the other, awarding neither the top of the mountain. His method to political power was to climb the back of the mountain, unnoticed, until he reached the peak.

His maneuvering of one senator against the other reminded him of how he had manipulated his parents. He didn't, however, want to drive Allison and Johnson to some kind of political divorce court—just keep them focused on each other and fighting.

Jason relaxed for almost a minute. He had taken care of one immediate problem earlier today and was confident that his magic hand would win any and all days. The grid lighting would cement his domination.

Cement. He liked that image, especially if it included President Allison's feet stuck inside. One way or another, her feet would be encased in just thirteen days. Disposal after that could be quick or drawn out. His choice.

Jason allowed himself one brief, satisfied smile.

CHAPTER 17

◆

Nick eased into the padded armchair next to the hospital bed. Sandra seemed peaceful, her breathing easy and regular. The night nurse had told him his daughter was under an induced coma to help her heal. Since the hospital hadn't been able to meet with him when Sandra was first brought in, she had sat him down for twenty minutes and asked him a multitude of questions. Family history, more on her addictions, her allergies—Nick was surprised by the number of questions. He had finished the last several questions just after 8:00 p.m.

Nick gazed at Sandra and wished they were on speaking terms. The only time she would say anything to him was every other week, when he came to pick up Nicole for the weekend.

10:30 p.m. Nick struggled to keep his eyes open.

10:32 p.m. Surrender. He sank back into the armchair as his eyes closed.

Bit by bit, the darkness of sleep gave way: first to clouds and rainbows, then to just clouds, slowly swirling first clockwise and then counterclockwise. When they returned to curling clockwise, Sandra coalesced in front of the clouds, now pulsing as they began to whirl.

Sandra's image stayed immobile, floating in front of the clouds as she pointed a finger at Nick. "You killed Uncle Joey!" Sandra's eyes flared, her blond hair splayed out. This time her finger stabbed at Nick. "You killed Mama!"

The clouds pulsed more violently and began to overtake the floating Sandra. Before she disappeared, she thrust her finger at Nick one last time. "You're worse than garbage!"

Nick jerked upright in the hospital armchair, his face covered in perspiration. He shivered and checked his watch: 2:17 a.m.

He shook his head. He hadn't had a nightmare like that in more than six years, ever since Nicole had become a part of his life. Somehow she had kept the vengeful spirits at bay. Somehow she had brought sunshine piercing through the clouds.

That he hadn't had nightmares for so long didn't mean he wasn't haunted. Nick thought back to when his dimwitted brother-in-law got involved with what he, Joey, called "the last great drug run." On July 11, 2033, both houses of Congress had passed, via veto-proof majorities, a bill legalizing across-the-board recreational-drug usage. The president was letting it sit on his desk, refusing either to veto or to approve. In five more days, the bill would become law, and the drug cartels would be on their way out. A few last runs were being set up before old lines of business were closed down; hundreds of thousands of dollars could still be made—*would* still be made—until subsidized supply met street demand. The NYPD was gearing up to meet these thrusts head-on. Informants were squeezed for every drop of information. The cartels intended to go out with a bang; the NYPD planned an exit voiced in whimpers.

When rumors had reached Nick that Joey was probably involved, he came down hard on his wife's younger and only sibling.

Joey shook his head. "You've got both your Senate and your House of Reps saying all drugs are now okay. Soon the government itself is going to purchase what yesterday brought millions on the street. They hope the drug cartels will fold up peacefully—and they will, given half a chance and a little 'adjustment capital.' I'm just helping a friend make some last-minute adjustments. Last-minute *peaceful* adjustments."

"That's bullshit, and you know it." Nick stood and advanced menacingly.

"No, It would already be a law if the president would've signed one shitty little sheet of paper. No, not him. He wants to keep his cake and eat it, too. Is the world supposed to stand still while he plays both sides against the middle? The wire heads will get their ultra-cheap fixes soon enough. In the meantime, we have to help everyone through the start-up."

"Nothing but bullshit. The boys downtown are on to you. Well, not you specifically. You're too small a piece of shit to have a dossier, but they know what and they know when. They just don't know who and where. The word is out, Joey. If you run that money, you'll be a dead man."

"And what would my dear brother-in-law have me do?"

"Stay home. Stay clean."

"How touching. My brother-in-law is really concerned."

"I don't give a damn about you. Your sister and your niece, however, love you. I'd hate to have to tell them that, in addition to your being an asshole, you're also a dead one."

"Ah. Judith and dear little Sandra. No need to tell them, because I won't be dead and I won't be an asshole. I'll be part of the last great run."

Twenty-two hours later, Nick was in the morgue, looking down at his brother-in-law's body. A single bullet hole filled the gap between Joey's eyebrows. A gift from Joey's "buddies."

Nick had arranged to have the rest of his shift covered so he could race home and tell Judith. He had found her in the kitchen, dicing something, her large knife chopping a quick rhythm against the cutting board. Nick moved to her side. He had been about to clear his throat and deliver his news when he noticed there was nothing on the board: Judith was cutting air! He looked closely at her eyes. They were unfocused, almost glazed. She knew.

Nick covered her hand with his and slowed the movement of her hand. Six more sweeps of the knife, and her hand was still. He took the knife from her hand, placed it on the countertop, turned her to him, and put his arms around her. Her eyes were worse than unfocused; they were blank. He tried to pull her close, but her back was rigid, her whole body unyielding.

Over Judith's taut shoulder, he saw Sandra come into the kitchen. Before she could ask what was for dinner, Nick ushered her back into the living room, telling her dinner would be a little late because Mom wasn't feeling well.

He prepared dinner the best he could, got Sandra started, and then took Judith, still nearly comatose, upstairs and got her into bed.

He sat in the straight-back chair at the foot of the bed for almost an hour, waiting—*hoping*—for a flicker of emotion on Judith's blank face.

Finally, he went back down and helped Sandra set out her clothes for next morning's Sunday school. He didn't tell Sandra about Uncle Joey. He told himself he'd probably screw it up and push Sandra into the same state as Judith was in. They were alike in many ways, particularly in their devotion to Uncle Joey. He read Sandra a story from one of her many books about talking bears or elephants or crocodiles—he couldn't remember. He kissed her good night, a kiss he'd remember for the rest of his life.

Judith was still in bed, still staring at some point halfway to the ceiling. He undressed and climbed into bed. He kissed her on the cheek and then, when she did not respond, held her hand until he fell asleep.

He was pouring Sandra some cereal the next morning, wondering when he should try to get Judith out of her trance, when she appeared in the doorway, her face blotched and chalky.

"Judith!" he said, almost dropping the box as he moved toward her.

Judith raised her arms straight out in front of her. Nick caught himself up short and reached out to touch her hands. She whisked her hands down to her sides, avoiding his touch.

"No!" Judith moaned.

The tone, as if from the grave itself, caused the back of Nick's neck to prickle.

"You!" Judith said, eyes suddenly wide. She rushed at him. "You killed Joey! You knew what he was doing—he told me you knew—and you set him up. You killed him! You murdered him!" Sandra's bowl fell, clattering on the floor, as Judith pounded his chest with her fists. "You bastard! You murdered my brother. You goddamned bastard!"

Nick took the full fury of Judith's pummeling as he glanced toward Sandra's chair. It was empty. She had pushed it back and was running upstairs. Judith continued beating on his chest, and he continued trying to pretend that it didn't hurt and that it was necessary if she were to feel better.

It was near the end of the third month that Judith started to drink—something she rarely did. After a year passed, she was imbibing heavily. Within another six months, she had become an accomplished lush. Another six months, a full-time, seven-days-a-week alcoholic.

Sandra tried to keep him from attending Judith's funeral. She was closing in on twelve when her mother spent a weekend drinking vodka until she drowned in its poison. Sandra told the funeral director that Judith's last wishes were that Nick be kept away. The poor man, confused and uncertain, asked Nick what he should do.

Nick suggested she be "awarded" both sides of the viewing chapel while he kept quietly to the back, just inside the door. A similar arrangement would be observed at the actual burial. Their plan was executed without incident.

Time passed. Sandra came neither to her senses nor back home. Nick attended her grade school and high school graduations, each time unobserved in the back row. Three months after she left high school, he heard she was living with a low-echelon punk from the mob who had himself graduated to high-echelon punk in a street gang. Nick decided his best course was the appearance of a total hands-off approach. Behind the scenes, he pulled strings and promised favors to keep Sandra's king punk safely out of jail—as long as his offenses were small-time.

After five years and two different punks had come and gone, Nicole was born. Born in the nick of time. Three weeks early, but just minutes before Sandra would have died.

She had been rushed to the hospital, suffering from multiple contusions to the head, face, and neck. Abuse. Working quickly, the doctors brought Nicole into the world via cesarean. Sandra was then placed into an induced coma and was kept under careful watch for five days.

The maternity nurses kept asking Nick what the baby's name should be on the birth certificate. After he said several times it was not his place to name the baby, the nurses chose the first name of Nicole on the third day.

The coma protocol was lifted on the fifth day. Sandra started to respond to stimulus on the sixth day.

Standing at the foot of her bed, waiting for her to ascend to full coherence, he realized he hadn't been in her presence for more than a total of twenty minutes in the twelve years since the funeral. He regretted those twenty minutes and those twelve years, but he didn't know what he could have done differently. A distant but uneasy feeling told him that perhaps he hadn't cared to do anything differently.

When Sandra awoke and saw him, he said, "It's a girl. Healthy top to bottom. Can I stay?"

The permission, granted in a groggy state, was only partially retracted the next day. Nick was allowed to stay when Nicole was brought in. There was no way he was going to allow Sandra to drive him away from his new granddaughter. He guessed she could see he was ready to make an issue of staying and that she hadn't the strength to resist. That was one time he was only too eager to take advantage of another person's weakness.

Beachhead established, Nick made sure he ceded no ground, visiting with Nicole each weekend, informing Sandra days in advance of the few occasions when official business would take him out of the city and away from his time with Nicole. Nicole seemed aware of the tension between the two people closest to her, but somehow she didn't let it affect her. She hugged him with as much gusto as she did her mother. She became the most important person in Nick's life. He loved her like he wished he could have loved Judith at the end—and Sandra even now.

Even now, as he looked down at Sandra breathing evenly, sedated into her second induced coma.

Nick struggled to stay awake most of the night, nodding off only three or four times. At 8:00 a.m., two nurses wheeled in a tray of towels and sponges.

"You should go home. We're going to be almost an hour, and after us, she's got a bunch of tests and readings. She'll be lucky if she gets back before noon. The doctors project at least another two days before they'll bring her up and out."

Nick, remembering he had some unfinished business, nodded and left.

CHAPTER 18

◆

Nick drove to where he had seen truck no. 48 parked the night before. He got out and positioned himself on the sidewalk between the building and the supporting girder just at curbside. He eyed the girder, looking for any new maintenance activity. After pulling out his binoculars, he repeated his scan, much slower and with more attention to detail. He didn't know what should be catching his attention: scratches, new paint, new wiring, or everything.

He chuckled to himself. He wouldn't know new wiring from old. It just bothered him that the truck seemed out of place. He was sure it also bothered the Secret Service. The truck hadn't stopped for just a minute. It had stopped long enough to be up to something. Maybe it didn't have anything to do with the president's visit in two weeks, but it had something to do with something. Was that something the murder of the vice president? No itching at the back of his neck yet, but a thorough investigation just might keep the itching at bay.

Nick turned and studied the building next to him. When he had passed by, the truck had been parked in front. Visualizing his movements from the previous night, he moved to the spot where he remembered the truck had been parked. There was an old, rusted manhole cover about five feet to his right. He bent down and ran his hand across its embossed surface. He wouldn't be able to lift it without tools; it seemed welded shut like at least 80 percent of Manhattan's manhole covers. The cover had been at least two feet in front of the truck. He would check things out now and later return with workable tools.

Maybe the reason for the truck was inside the building.

The building was six stories in the center, five otherwise. The grid was low in this neighborhood. This building had five floors below the grid and only the building top above it. All the street-level windows in the front were boarded up. Not unusual. Nick moved back to the street to check the higher windows. Second and third floor, all boarded up. The fourth floor had one of its six windows partially boarded. Again, not unusual. Nick moved to the opposite sidewalk for a better viewing angle.

The fifth-floor windows had curtains. Very unusual.

Nick decided to investigate the inside. While looking both ways before stepping off the curb—an old habit from long ago when cars had been common—Nick caught a glimpse on his right of a figure darting back behind the far corner of the building behind him. He was being watched. Well, he'd just have to watch back.

Nick crossed to the boarded-up building. He stood in front of the center door for almost a minute, checking for any reflective surface, any unclouded pane of glass with which to see behind himself. There were none.

He drifted off to his left, again checking for reflective glass. Upon finding none, he turned the left corner of the building. The building next to it had been demolished long ago, with dozens of bricks and chunks of rusting steel facing littering the empty lot and attachment scars visible on his building of interest. He walked to the rear of the building and found every door and window boarded. He waited another two minutes to test his observer's patience before reappearing at the front. A young boy was clearly visible now, leaning against the building across Forty-Third Street in front of the corner he had hidden behind.

Nick started to turn back to his own building of interest when the boy pushed away from his building and started walking toward him. The young boy's gait struck Nick as casual, unafraid.

The boy, black, stopped in the middle of the street, not thirty feet from Nick. "What you lookin' for, mister? That building's locked up tight."

"But someone lives in there." Nick raised his arm and pointed. "Curtains."

"Just one old man. Has a garden on the roof."

"The old man have a name?"

"Probably. Don't know it, though."

"A garden, you say?"

The boy nodded.

"What does he grow?"

The boy shrugged. "You could see for yourself. Building behind me is open. Most of its windows are broken and not boarded up. With your glasses there, you can look across from one of its apartments and see the garden."

"Can you show me?"

The boy gave Nick an incredulous look.

"I know," Nick said. "Never with strangers."

The boy shook his head. "Strangers, maybe. Cops, no way."

"You're a smart kid."

"I learn from my dad."

"Your dad give you a name?"

The boy grinned. "Probably."

Nick shook his head and then decided he'd give the boy a chance to move back. "I'm going to take you up on your offer. I'm going to go partway up your building and check out the garden."

"Not my building." The boy held his ground but did turn sideways to facilitate Nick's passage. "Nathan."

Nick paused and looked back at the boy, who was grinning even wider. "Nathan?"

"Name my dad gave me."

Nick nodded and grinned back.

By the time Nick opened the door to the hallway—after climbing nine floors—he was not quite out of breath. Not quite but close.

The second apartment door he tried was open. He stepped in and went straight to the window and found that it offered a good view of the garden. It occupied all the flat space of the roof across the street.

Nick peered through the binoculars, focusing first on the concrete cube centered at the very back of the roof. He focused on its door and then moved forward and to the left until he found a path going from the front to the rear of the roof. Nick was not a gardener by any means, but he figured, in a rooftop covered with green plants, one had to have pathways to allow watering. He counted five paths running from left to right across the approximate ninety feet of the roof. Front to back, there were three on each side of the concrete cube, plus a center one running straight out from the door. These seven paths intersected the left-to-right five. A wide avenue ran along the very front, another at the very back.

He finally located the gardener. At the extreme right of the middle side-to-side path was a man moving slowly leftward, leaning on the cane in his left hand. The man paused every few steps, leaning further over his cane, stroking a leaf or a stem with his right hand, and then pulling open a small notebook hanging from a cord around his neck and, while resting his left elbow on his cane, making some writing motions with its attached pen. The man moved slowly toward the far-left edge of the roof. Repeating his stop-write-start movements, the gardener reached the left edge, paused for at least ten seconds, and then started walking in Nick's direction. He was a man at least in his seventies, stocky, balding, and for some reason, vaguely familiar to Nick.

Nick tried to recall where he recognized the man, and a blurred memory of a photograph on the front page of the *New York Times* flickered for a moment in the tangle of his memories. When he tried to bring it into focus, it vanished just as quickly. The man turned to his left, moved slowly to the center aisle, turned toward the door, and after about a minute, went inside.

Nick couldn't see any munitions or unusual machinery. There weren't even any vats of any size that could be used to store fertilizer or poisonous bacteria. He could see nothing out of the ordinary that would require a construction truck to park in front. Nothing.

He was about to go back to the stairs and to the street when the gardener and three other men, each wearing denim pants and shirts, emerged from the door. The four of them began at the leftmost back-to-front row and moved in unison toward the roof side closest to Nick. They moved quickly past the first and the second left-to-right paths. Halfway along the next group of plants, they stopped. The gardener showed them a page from his notebook, pointed to a plant, and moved on. They crossed to the center aisle, turned to the right, and then proceeded to the corner of the next crossing path. Again, they paused. Again, the notebook was shown. Again, they moved on, this time to one of the points on the far right where the gardener had made one of his first stops. This time the notebook was handed across to one of the three men. The man reviewed some details being pointed out by the gardener. The man nodded several times, after which he returned the notebook and they headed for the concrete stairwell cube.

As Nick started to turn, he looked down to the right and found the boy staring up at him. Nick was about to wave to him when the boy suddenly darted around to where Nick had first spotted him.

The quick move startled Nick. He looked a little farther up the street and saw the reason for the boy's vanishing act. An armored truck carrying at least eight World Council Pop Police in full uniform was just braking to a stop where the boy had been standing. Nick wasn't sure what the boy had done, if anything. He decided he had to intervene quickly before the officer thugs flooded the neighborhood, looking for a "runaway."

He took the steps three and four at a time and broke through the front door just as two of the "officers" were dragging the kicking boy from around the corner of the building. The boy was punching the two men with his fists almost as furiously as he was kicking them with his feet. Nick knew he obviously couldn't claim blood relationship with the black youth, so . . .

"What the hell you doing with my CI?" he hollered, flashing his NYPD badge.

The two officers stopped struggling with the boy and looked in the direction of an older man just then stepping down from the truck, obviously their commander.

"Kinda young to be a confidential informant, isn't he?" the commander said, frowning at Nick.

Nick knew he had to come up with something quick. Something believable and something in their interest so they would feel he and the boy were on their side.

"He's not really a CI. He likes that term better than *bait*, which is what he really is."

"Bait?" The commander frowned in confusion.

"One of your charters, I believe, is to *track down* and *shut down* any and all kidnapper gangs. True?"

The commander nodded slowly, as if trying to anticipate where Nick was going.

"Well, I have the same charter: track down, shut down. I've discovered the best way to do that is with bait." Nick pointed to the boy still being held aloft. "I caught one stalker just two days ago."

"Saint Vartan Park?"

Nick waved the badge in his left hand. "Ol' badge number 5278. One stalker behind bars being grilled, thanks to the invaluable help of young Nathan here." Nick again pointed to the boy.

Acceptance was beginning to wash across the commander's face. "I don't remember any mention of a young black . . ." He looked at the boy. Acceptance apparently tinged with a little remaining doubt. "A young black CI. The report mentioned just one cop, one stalker, one shot dog, and one plugged man toting a shotgun. Good job, but no mention in the report of any bait."

"I'll be damned if I'll expose my best resource. If I put him in the report, it won't be long before he's useless. Then you guys will have to do all the 'track down, shut down' yourselves."

"Isn't your bait too old to interest the kidnappers?"

"Not if he comes across as having an ax to grind with his parents, and with his school, and with everyone in his neighborhood. A boy with that large an ax just might know where some new babies are being hidden."

The commander took a deep breath and then slowly exhaled. "What's the boy's last name?"

Nick paused. Giving a last name would be instantly verified by an experienced Pop Police commander. From what he could tell, this commander was definitely experienced.

"Williams," the boy stated. "That's my last name, but Officer Nicholas and I agreed from the start not to use our last names."

Nick managed to keep any surprise from crossing his face. He had never given the boy his name.

The commander took another deep breath. He motioned to his two men to release the boy. "Before I let you go, tell me, please, what are some of the duties of bait?"

The boy paused and then gave Nick another grin. "Finding out names and occupations."

Nick felt a little chill at the base of his neck. He watched as the commander pursed his lips, his eyes focused on Nathan.

The commander narrowed his eyes. "Okay, Nathan. My occupation is obvious. My last name is not. What is it?"

"Frederick," Nathan replied without hesitation.

Commander Frederick was obviously caught off balance, his eyes wide with surprise. "How—"

"The two Pop cops who roughed me up and dragged me here used your name six times." Nathan swung his head around to glance at the two men. He paused and then chuckled. "Six times they said, 'Commander Frederick,' but only once favorably." Nathan returned his gaze to Commander Frederick as the two burly Pop Policemen betrayed the slightest hint of squirming.

Commander Frederick shifted his attention to his two men and chuckled. It was a soft chuckle portending many hours of extra duty. He shifted back to Nathan. "Well, young man, if you are of top-notch bait quality, you will be able to give me"—he swept a hand in the direction of the two now visibly unsettled Pop Police—"at least their first names. I would expect no less."

Nick prepared to intercede. He would claim high stalker-case priority.

"Jerome Fisher," Nathan announced, "and Charles Draco. Both sergeants."

Four jaws dropped in unison: Commander Frederick's, Nick's, and those of Jerome and Charles.

Commander Frederick was the first to recover. "And how did—"

"From their Population Police ID cards."

Each man dove into the nearest uniform pants pocket with his left hand and retrieved his ID card. The quick sigh of relief was cut short as each studied the card he held and then at the one the other held.

"Is there a problem?" Commander Frederick asked, his tone official, unforgiving.

Nathan was quick to offer an explanation. "Not sure, but I might have mixed up the cards when I put them back. They were jerking me around quite a bit, and I could have—"

"Understood!" Commander Frederick cut Nathan short. The two Pop cops were now shaking visibly. He looked back at Nick. "You and your bait get lost." He was quick to add one more thing as he contemplated his two quivering officers. "And, Detective, watch your own wallet."

Nick and Nathan marched off together.

Behind them, three seconds of silence was followed by rapid-fire shouting. Nick recognized the commander's voice. Nick chuckled and glanced back over his shoulder. The two officers who had grabbed Nathan were standing at rigid attention as their commander barked at them, alternating face-to-face with each man, each time nose almost touching nose.

Nick turned back to find Nathan just then turning right at the corner about ten feet in front of him. Nick quickened his pace and followed the boy around the corner.

He stopped in his tracks, the hairs on the back of his neck prickling furiously.

Now about thirty feet ahead, Nathan stood facing him from the center of a semicircle of about forty paracops.

Nick took a deep breath and swallowed hard.

CHAPTER 19

◆

"Detective Garvey." The towering black man standing immediately behind Nathan acknowledged Nick with a nod. "Welcome to our piece of Manhattan."

Nick could feel everyone's eyes on him. He nodded acceptance of the welcome, deciding it best to keep silent for the moment.

The man, at least six foot two with glasses and extremely close-cropped hair about the same length as his trimmed wraparound beard, placed his right hand on Nathan's shoulder. "I'm Howard Williams. My son tells me you're a fast talker, good at defusing a tricky situation."

Nick again nodded acceptance.

The man grinned. "And you're also wise to the value of silence."

"I try," Nick replied. "How does your son know my name? It was obvious how he got the names of the two officers."

"Several of us dissected your actions at Saint Vartan's two days ago. Nathan obviously heard your name then. He's got an excellent memory, so when Commander Frederick recounted the same events . . ." He gave Nick a "forces of nature need no explanation" shrug.

Bits and pieces were hitting Nick at peculiar angles. He blinked, trying to focus on just one peculiar bit at a time. He narrowed his concentration on Howard Williams. "You also overheard what the commander said."

Nathan's father nodded.

"You were nearby."

Another nod.

"And you were probably watching when I first spotted your son."

Nod and a shrug this time. "I'm the guardian of the surrounding thirty-plus square blocks."

Nick raised an eyebrow. "Guardian?"

Howard chuckled. "I prefer that title to chief, leader, king, or president. They all strike me as a bit self-centered. My job is to keep the people in our neighborhood safe. Guardian seemed appropriate. As you can see"—he waved both arms, indicating the circle of men—"I have lots of help."

"And," Nick offered, "a good guardian would keep his own son out of trouble."

"Most of the time. But the best guardian would teach his own son how to handle trouble."

"I would say you're one hell of a teacher," Nick offered, nodding at young Nathan.

Nathan looked up at his dad and said something while pointing at the building where he had first seen Nick.

Howard nodded at his son. "Nathan, being ever the student, asked that you enlighten him as to your interest in the old man."

"Wasn't interested in the old man, although he does appear to have a terrific garden—one of the best I've seen. Have you been up to see it? Looks like he's doing some special plant experiments." Nick could see that Guardian Howard was not going to respond on this subject with however long a pole Nick gave him. "I *was* interested in why, at 10:42 last night, federal construction truck no. 48 was parked in front of that particular building."

Howard Williams looked the tiniest bit perplexed. "Truck no. 48? I don't—"

One of the men, a reddish-blond six-foot-plus youth two paces behind Howard, stepped to his side, said a quiet few words, and then stepped back.

"Truck no. 48," Howard stated evenly, "it appears, has been seen parked in several locations in our area over the past two-plus weeks, each time for no more than an hour. We do not interfere with their business. They are responsible for erecting the grid, and we have no desire to slow them down." He chuckled and continued. "I assume you've heard that old-time battle cry, 'Power to the People'?" He extended both hands, again indicating those around him. "Same people."

"Different power," Nick added, completing the thought.

Howard flashed a broad smile. "Never imagined I'd say that I liked the way an NYC cop thought, but—"

"You'll make an exception this one time."

"That I will. This one time."

"I have what might be another exception."

Howard nodded to continue.

"Truck no. 48 doesn't belong to the federal crew responsible for building the grid. I've seen the master assignment list, and every truck working on the grid has a three-digit number. No exceptions."

The tall young man again stepped forward and this time said more than just a few words to Howard.

Howard pursed his lips after two or three seconds. After a few more seconds, he closed his eyes and took a deep breath. When he was finished, the man reclaimed his position.

"Let me guess," Nick said. "There were other trucks with just two digits."

"There were." Howard nodded, his face a sudden study in consternation.

Nick was well aware that every paracop he had ever dealt with, leader or not, was not disposed to trust NYC cops with anything beyond their own name. He decided to keep any interest he had about truck no. 48 and uneasiness about the Secret Service to himself. "Anything you can share?" he said, hoping his handling of Nathan's earlier problem might have bought just the smallest amount of goodwill. "Whatever you pass on stops with me."

Howard locked eyes with Nick. He sucked his lower lip between his teeth. "There was a truck no. 27 spotted twice in our area. Three others—no. 16, no. 52, and no. 71—were spotted within other areas, no. 27 both times less than an hour."

Nick nodded his thanks. "And the others, less than an hour?"

"Don't know. We keep moving when we're outside our neighborhood."

"Any way you can point me in the right directions? It *is* important."

Howard raised his left hand to beckon the tall youth forward for a third time. Words were again exchanged.

"You have access to a car?" Howard asked.

Nick nodded.

"Brian will go with you to get it. After that, an hour should do it. Please drop Brian back here."

"In one piece," Nick promised.

A redheaded tall man standing on Howard's right shook his head. "I don't think that's a good idea. We can't track them. We can't—"

Brian held up his hand, moved to the man's side, and whispered in his ear. The older man shook his head several times before nodding with what Nick took to be reluctant acceptance.

Brian then said something to Howard, who took something out of his pocket and replied, "Here. Take mine."

Brian nodded and stepped to Nick's side. "Ready when you are." Nick was surprised when the man extended his hand. "Brian McKenna."

Nick shook his hand.

As they headed toward Nick's car, Nick left a quick message on Tim's phone that he was following up on truck no. 48.

CHAPTER 20

◆

J ason had called ahead to let Bert know he would be stopping
by with some assignments. He found him sitting as usual in
front of his bank of seven oversized video monitors. He saw
that Salazar was resting on the ramp leading down to the far end of
the pit, with the female Komodo safe in the cage behind her mate.
He could see all was quiet, normal, and as it should be in the Freed
household.

Jason took the chair next to Bert. "I need you to resurrect those
old video taps you had set up to monitor the presidential residences
in Brazil and Argentina."

"Yes, Director," Bert replied. He pointed beyond the video
screens to his sleeping quarters. "I'll have to go back and retrieve the
appropriate satellite transponders."

Jason nodded and watched Bert motor off.

He turned his thoughts to Brazil and Argentina. A treaty could
be negotiated but not accepted and signed without council concurrence. They knew the treaty rules and had chosen to ignore them.
The video taps would be key in helping them learn their lesson.
Their lesson, unfortunately for them, would now have to be learned
the hard way. He would monitor high-level, backroom negotiations
for peace between them and then counter each such understanding,
calling on a multitude of troublemakers: mercenaries, insurrection-
ists, gangs, and whatever other groups would respond to thirty pieces
of silver. He'd keep the pressure on for about a year, enough for both
Brazil and Argentina to fully learn their lesson—and to finally learn
their place. Jason figured he'd pour just a little salt on the lesson,

arranging for Chile, Peru, and Ecuador to gain noticeable influence and energy allotments. He didn't want to congratulate himself in advance, but it was definitely a workable plan. Definitely.

He eased back in his chair and glanced up at the seven monitor screens. The three center monitors each displayed, full screen, a single street scene. The outlying monitors, two on each side, displayed four scenes split in quadrants. Every moment of every video was being recorded.

Jason bent forward to the left-center monitor. The screen showed a tall redbrick building. The coverage was distant enough to not reveal the grid overhead but close enough to show grid support no. 17-862 and, about ten feet to its left, just pulling to a stop over a manhole cover, federal construction truck no. 32. *Make that "supposed" federal construction truck,* Jason mused.

Jason, long ago, had sat still for Bert's tedious monologue about how he didn't have to press the marking key, since the movement of any vehicle into camera view qualified as a major variation and was automarked—a simple concept that took him three-plus minutes to communicate.

Jason pushed his chair back from the console when he heard Bert motoring back from his distant inner sanctum. He noticed, even from a distance of more than forty feet, that Bert was bringing more than the bag of transponders in his lap. Bert was steering his chair with his left hand while cradling a blond cocker spaniel puppy in his right. The puppy's tail was wagging wildly as it whined and strained toward Bert, licking his face repeatedly from right ear to mouth and back.

Jason had observed Bert's routine with the puppies enough times to appreciate its repetitive efficiency.

Bert dropped his bag at Jason's feet. "I'll hook these two into the network," Bert said, moving his head from side to side to accumulate a few more wet licks. "First, though, I have to take my little friend here to lunch."

"Is that so?" Jason asked, raising an eyebrow. "To whose lunch are you referring?"

Bert chortled and winked back at Jason.

Bert motored his chair halfway back around the periphery of the circular area, which was depressed, pitlike, for a depth of five feet. The severe negative slope of the pit's side walls produced a diameter at the bottom that was six feet larger than at the top. This negative slope was sufficient to keep Salazar and his companion contained to a predetermined area. To keep Salazar and friend where he wanted them, Bert had also fashioned each with embedded shock chips under their collars that worked wonders. The pit was almost thirty-five feet in diameter with, at the opposite side, a curved, water-slide-like ramp descending from a cage: the common sleeping area.

At the near side, where Bert stopped for a moment, was a four-foot-wide folding ramp he used to lower wheeled bowls of puppy food and, of course, puppies. The ramp was also strong enough to support the wheelchair on the rare occasions he needed to motor down into the pit to clean or retrieve something after he had used their embedded chips to move them back into their cages, which he would then close remotely.

Jason marveled at Bert's dexterity, at how, still cradling the blond puppy, he managed to maneuver a nearby bowl of dog treats over to the top of the ramp and then, using an eight-foot broom, guide the bowl down the ramp and out slightly into the pit.

Jason had witnessed Bert's puppy-for-lunch routine five times previously. Once the bowl was lowered, the puppy—a terrier, a lab, even a Rottweiler once—was released to make an eager dash to the wafting aroma of super treats.

Jason watched Bert accept two more loving licks and then reach down and point the puppy down to the waiting bowl. The little cocker spaniel loped down the ramp, almost slid past the bowl, and then corrected and started to chow down, tail wagging in rapid tiny arcs. It was obvious to Jason the puppy was aware only of the tasty morsels in the bowl.

As expected, Salazar did not break training. The male Komodo waited until Bert had motored back to the screens and, more importantly, had raised his hand as a signal that he would not activate the shock chips.

The little cocker spaniel was busy gobbling and munching and never saw Salazar's hip-swinging waddle of a charge. There was only one short, final yelp, followed by the faint crunching of bones.

A semismile crossed Bert's face, even though Jason knew the man was disappointed that it had all happened so quickly. Bert liked a much-longer pursuit: the lunch puppy catching sight of Salazar, running off, and trying every which way to escape—jumping up to reach the edge of the pit and falling far short; running to the opposite side of the pit from Salazar, who just kept wagging his whole body toward his future meal; darting back and forth, to and from Salazar; barking and yelping; and slowly losing energy until that final yelp, when Salazar used its gigantic jaws to chomp on the puppy's tail or one of its legs. That drama could take an hour or two and set Bert all atingle.

Jason shook his head. This time Bert would have to be content with the puppy licks on his face.

"Can we test the transponders now?" Jason asked.

Bert grabbed the bag, fished inside, pulled out an elbow-shaped piece of hardware, and started to connect it to the underside of the desktop. He then retrieved the second elbow and attached it.

"Connected," he announced.

"Working?" Jason's glare allowed no wiggle room.

Within seventeen minutes, both connections proved most acceptable.

"Full recording," Jason said. "Any and all conversations."

Bert nodded.

Jason, as he was leaving, wondered for just an instant if Salazar would find President Lenora Allison to be a tasty morsel.

CHAPTER 21

◆

Nick was the first out of the black sedan. They were parked a half block from a grid pillar. He slowly pivoted clockwise in a full circle, his gaze darting up, then down, then back up again. "Nothing stands out," he said, waving his hand about for Brian to see. "How long was the van parked here?"

"It was already here when I turned that corner," Brian said, motioning back to the corner of Seventy-Sixth Street and Third Avenue. "I watched it for just shy of forty minutes."

"But this is not your neighborhood."

"We have an arrangement with this one."

"How many men did you see?"

"Only one, about a minute before the van pulled away. He climbed down from the passenger door, walked to the back, seemed to tighten something, and climbed back in the same door, and the van left."

"Was he part of a Population Police patrol? I know they pass through most of the city several times a day."

Brian shook his head. "Different uniform. Besides, the Pop Police patrol through here every day at nine a.m., one p.m., and five p.m. Never off more than five minutes either way."

Nick shook his head, trying to make sense of a parked van and no worker activity. Six in the morning was a bit early for a forty-minute meal. Why would . . . His gaze stopped about ten feet in front of their sedan. There was a manhole cover.

He turned to Brian. "This car is about half as long as the work vans. Imagine the center of the sedan is the center of the van. Is it parked in the same spot?"

Brian gave a quick shrug and then crossed the street. After reaching the other sidewalk, he walked the twenty yards back to the corner from where he had first spotted the van. He turned back and studied the scene. He raised his right hand edgewise about ten inches from his nose. He slowly moved his hand ever so slightly from side to side. "Not quite!" he shouted to Nick. "Stand in front of the car and start walking ahead. I'll tell you when to stop."

Nick raised his arm in agreement and started walking. Two, four, six steps.

"That's it. Stop!"

Nick looked down. He was standing right on the manhole cover. He returned to the sedan, opened its trunk, and retrieved the tire jack and a flashlight with a large leather loop.

Even using the handle to the jack, which was a reasonable fit to the cutouts in the cover, it took both Nick and Brian the better part of five minutes to pry the heavy metal lid free of its support ring and up to where they could grab it and flip it onto the asphalt.

Nick sent a quick message to Tim: "Going sewer diving." He then told Brian that he was going down the metal ladder welded tightly to the north side of a five-foot-wide metal tube, which ran down from the manhole cover support ring to some water, its reflective surface barely visible in the sewer darkness.

"It looks to be about forty feet to the bottom." Nick put the flashlight loop over his head, stooped down, braced his hands on either side of the open manhole, and swung his legs forward and down onto the steel ladder.

From the first step down, he let the flashlight dangle free as he firmly grasped the steel ladder's side tubing. He preferred descending one rung at a time—the local—rather than taking the express, which would have meant grabbing just the outside the ladder with hands and feet, sliding straight down, and landing in a heap.

The first five feet down was reasonably visible from the overhead sky. Nothing struck him as being out of place.

During the next five or six feet, he paused every third rung and made quick sweeps with his light. Nothing on the damp, mold-covered brick walls caught his attention. There were no patches of freshly wiped brickwork, no chisel marks, no sign of anything—wires, paint, padding, drill holes—added anywhere on the ladder or on the walls.

The remaining ten feet or so was significantly slower going. Nick paused on each rung to inspect his illuminated surroundings. All the way to the bottom, which was covered with at least three inches of slowly moving water, he was unable to discover any obvious irregularities.

He moved the light to his wristwatch to see that almost fifteen minutes had passed since he'd first descended.

He was about to start sweeping his light around when he heard the first shouts from above, followed by gunfire.

He heard two voices, neither of them Brian's. Nick's policeman sense of time told him barely three seconds had passed between hearing the second voice and the first of five shots.

He was already looking up when Brian, in a controlled slide, his hands and feet pressed against either side of the ladder, plummeted to where Nick was standing. Nick stepped back just in time.

"Council guards!" Brian yelled. "Get us away—now!" He released the ladder and almost sank to the ground.

Nick caught him and felt the wetness at the back of his right shoulder. Nick immediately pulled Brian away from the ladder and from view of anyone up at street level.

Within two seconds, there were three light beams zigzagging around the foot of the ladder. Nick could partially make out what was being said above.

"Alarms . . ."

"Bastard crawled away."

"I'm going down."

"Finish him."

Nick probed the right front of Brian's shirt. Wet.

Brian took a labored breath. "Just the right shoulder."

"Good," Nick replied, draping the young man's left arm around his own shoulders and carefully lifting him more fully upright. "Can you—"

"Feet are okay."

"We're moving."

"There should be a bend to the right just ahead."

Nick swept his light from side to side along the tunnel, saw the curve about twenty yards ahead, and confirmed its existence to Brian.

"After that, I think there's a side sewer tunnel about fifty yards on the right. Take it, and it immediately branches into three." Brian's words sounded as if they were pushed through clenched teeth.

Nick didn't wait a second longer. He walked Brian as quickly as he could. There was not much water on the tunnel floor, so he didn't have to move slower to avoid splashing sounds. He could see the bend about five steps ahead. He hoped whoever was descending the ladder was at least six rungs from the bottom.

Apparently, he was.

Nick rounded the bend.

With the wetness increasing on the back of Brian's right shoulder, Nick knew he'd have to stop soon and try to devise some kind of pressure bandage. Otherwise, the young man would bleed out. He stopped and was about to lower Brian so he could tend to his wound.

"No!" Brian's voice was a growl. "Keep going. The third tunnel will be our cover. Keep going."

Nick shifted Brian back to traveling mode, such as it was. Shining his light ahead, he could make out the sewer opening on the right, now half the projected fifty yards. As he moved them slowly to the branching sewer tunnel, Nick kept his ears pinned on any sound, however small, that they were in someone's crosshairs.

As they reached the opening, he gently hefted Brian up over the six- or seven-inch elevation to the side tunnel. He was careful not to touch the side walls. They were of metal construction and were covered with mold and grime; any contact would wipe some small part clean and betray their passing.

As they entered, Nick saw two tunnel branches straight ahead. He looked to the immediate left then the immediate right. "There's no third tunnel," he whispered into Brian's left ear.

"In my pants." Brian's breath was labored. "Left pocket."

Nick retrieved the small square that Howard had tossed to Brian as they left.

"It's a light," Brian wheezed. "Black light. Squeeze both sides of the cover. The third tunnel is hidden. The light . . ." Another wheeze. "The light will reveal the handle."

Nick squeezed as instructed. After rotating the light ninety degrees, he swung the nearly invisible beam from his far left to his right, finally spotting a bright red arrow pointing to the left. Nick could barely make out a very faint red smudge, which, as he leaned forward and focused, he saw on a shallow indentation. He reached with his free left hand and pushed left in the indicated direction.

The metal wall slid open quietly and easily. Nick helped Brian inside and pointed at the edge of the metal door with the black light. A corresponding indent was visible. He pushed, again to his left, and the metal door slid closed.

Nick turned on his own flashlight and lowered Brian to a dry spot on the tunnel floor. He ripped off his own shirt and tore it in half, folding each half into a pad about four inches square. Next, he unbuttoned Brian's shirt and pointed his light to the entry wound. It was still bleeding, slowly but without letup. From the feel of the shirt's backside, the exit wound was losing blood at about the same rate. He slipped one of his shirt halves under Brian and, probing gently with his fingers, against the exit wound. He placed the remaining half atop the entry and rebuttoned the shirt.

As best Nick could tell, the shirt was tight enough to keep his makeshift bandages pressed against the wounds—hopefully enough to slow blood loss.

He was pleased to hear Brian moan as he lifted the young man again into his embrace. Any sound was a sign of life.

He was even more pleased when Brian took two shallow breaths and said, "Keep the black light on." Another breath. "Follow any blue arrow you see. Blue's our color; it will take us home."

Nick was about to take their first steps when he heard muffled shouts from the other side of the metal door, which he was now praying he had closed all the way. He didn't dare move. He could make out at least four voices but couldn't make out any words. Thirty seconds later, the shouting ceased and was followed by the sound of boots, which faded as the guards marched away.

Nick turned on his own light and risked a glance at his watch: 8:22 p.m. He had no idea how many blue arrows and how many minutes or hours it would take to get Brian "home."

He wrapped his right arm around Brian, making sure to press his upper arm and his hand against both the entrance and exit wounds as he started down the tunnel, sweeping the black light from side to side with his left hand.

CHAPTER 22

◆

Bert powered his chair back into his main room. On his lap rested his dessert plate of three Bartlett pears covered in still-warm milk chocolate.

As he motored toward his main console, Bert's gaze drifted from his dessert plate to Salazar resting atop his dirt mound at the opposite end of the pit. A quirky vision popped into Bert's head. The image of Salazar biting into a chocolate-covered dachshund brought an amused smile to his lips. He decided that next time—

The still-flashing alarm light brought him up short, blasting all thoughts of chocolate puppies from his mind. He glanced up at the big digital clock over his desk: 8:22 p.m.

He sped his chair to his desk. The alarm was being generated from screen seventeen. Bert checked his log screen: screen 17 monitored grid support no. 43-372 and had been serviced by truck no. 27 three days ago. He switched 17 to his main screen.

There were three vehicles: one sedan and two vans, all black. There were five—no, six—men standing around an open manhole.

"What the hell?"

Working the touch screen, Bert set playback to the previous automark point. He entered his usual thirty seconds prior to any video automark.

The scene was clear for twenty-five seconds. Then a black sedan pulled into view, forcing the automatic frame mark. The sedan stopped. Nothing alarm-worthy yet.

Bert frowned as two men stepped out. Lowering his head, he peered intently over his glasses at the screen as the two men talked

112

before one man crossed the street and then apparently directed the other to move atop a manhole cover. The last caused Bert to moan.

He froze the frame and zoomed in on the face of the man standing on the metal cover. He had to apply a good amount of sharpening to the frame but was able to coax from it a good, crisp image.

The man standing on the manhole cover motioned the other to come back and then went to the sedan, opened the trunk, and removed a jack handle.

When the two freed the cover, Bert stopped the playback. He wasted no time dialing the special emergency phone. Pickup was within two rings. Impressive for such a busy man.

"What is it?" someone asked on the other end.

"Remember yesterday that cop we looked at on the screen from a tape three days ago?"

CHAPTER 23

◆

After thirty minutes of sloshing from tunnel to sewer to tunnel, Nick was soaked up to his knees. He hoped the black light gizmo had long-life batteries. He reached his hand an inch farther across Brian's chest and found a heartbeat. It was there but faint. He worried that the batteries would outlast the young man.

The tunnel they were currently trudging through had next to no water. It did, however, have the occasional rat that, as they approached, squealed in defiance at their intrusion before scurrying to the other wall of the tunnel. The tunnel reeked of wet garbage and rat feces.

Nick was still on guard, straining for any sound or flash of light from their pursuers. There had been none since they'd moved deeper into that first hidden tunnel. He had to move slowly because he had decided to use the black light only, not wanting to miss any invisible color codes, not wanting to switch to his regular flashlight and risk Brian slipping from his grip.

He stopped suddenly, reacting to a distant clank of metal on metal. He turned off the black light. Nick had no doubt that, if their pursuers found them, they would both be killed. He moved quietly to the nearest tunnel wall and tried not to breathe.

Nick counted twenty faint heartbeats and decided he could wait no longer.

Ten steps. Twenty. Twenty-five. No further sounds. He turned the black light back on, wishing he had someone to work his flashlight.

His granddaughter and flashlights suddenly came to mind. When she was three, he remembered, she had been fascinated by holding a flashlight for his hand-generated shadow animals. Had she been with him now, she would have wanted the black light. Nick smiled. She was his little scientist, his little engineer, always fascinated by how things worked, reading every *Why Things Work* book she could find.

Another blue arrow.

Nick dropped the black light into his left pants pocket and, fishing around, pulled out the flashlight. After just two left-to-right sweeps, he spotted the slight indent. Holding the light between thumb and forefinger, he pushed with his remaining free fingers. Nothing. He opened his mouth wide, inserted the butt end of the light, and clamped it with his teeth. He used his full hand and pushed to the left. The panel slid open.

He stepped forward and gently lifted Brian over the metal saddle. Once safely inside, he reached back and gave the panel a shove. There was a sliding sound but no click of closure.

He reached back for another shove and was greeted by six clicks—clicks that Nick recognized as weapons being cocked. All Nick could see was the hand that reached in and removed the flashlight from his mouth.

CHAPTER 24

◆

Forced to kneel in the tunnel blackness, Nick felt his knees start to ache. Although an occasional flashlight beam would sweep across his face, his captors remained in the dark. They had removed Brian from his grip right after pulling the flashlight from his mouth.

"Slide the door all the way. Now!" had been the only nonwhispered exchange he'd heard since they'd been captured by what he guessed was a band of at least five men, probably more.

Since the capture—must have been at least three minutes, Nick figured—his mind spun round and round, trying to come up with any ploy to prevent them from both being shot. Any half-viable threat—or offer to help—would do. He guessed that abject pleading was out.

He thought of his daughter and granddaughter. He would never get the chance to convince Sandra he was not the evil man her mother had painted him to be. He would never get to see Nicole grow up and change the universe.

He thought of his job, relishing the old days when a cop's presence had made at least a little difference, regretting the present when "Do less with less" seemed the mantra. He thought of Tim, who at least had a home life and who was an honest cop, if just a bit too pliable. They worked together more often than not, shuffling papers back and forth across their half of the desk. Unable to suppress an involuntary chuckle, Nick projected that, if the situation ended as he expected, it would fall to Tim to clean up his deceased partner's cluttered half of their desk. Into each life—

"He's coming," someone announced in a louder-than-normal whisper.

Someone grabbed him under each armpit and pulled him to his feet. He was about to meet someone. He prayed it wasn't his maker.

He heard someone say, "This one has been shot and is in bad shape."

Nick could make out some rustling, followed by a sharp moan. He knew the moan came from Brian.

Suddenly a blinding light flooded his face, forcing his eyes shut.

"He's okay. One of the few on our side."

Nick immediately recognized Howard Williams's voice and opened his eyes as light flooded the tunnel. He could make out at least a dozen men wearing green fatigues, plus maybe twice as many in blue. Howard stood five feet in front of him, also in blue.

Howard smiled, gave Nick a slight "Follow me" wag of his head, and then stepped to him and put an arm around his shoulder. "Thanks," he said. "It looks like Brian will make it."

CHAPTER 25

$\blacklozenge$

efore stepping into the shower in Howard's apartment, Nick
sent a message to Tim's phone describing his activities over
the past twenty-four hours. He detailed how the two-digit
trucks were apparently involved with underground activities, adding
that he had no more details yet. He let Tim know where he was and
that he would contact him later.

The reply message greeted Nick as he was drying off. Tim was
scouring a wider net of video downloads, trying to find anything
pointing to how the vice president and four agents had met their end.

At Howard's request, Nick dropped most of his clothes in the
hamper and put on the fresh ones his host had provided.

Nick emerged barefoot from the bathroom. "You got any dry
socks?" he asked as he entered the breakfast alcove just off the spotless
kitchen. "I've been walking in these all day."

Howard grinned. "I think I can manage one." He looked quiz-
zically at Nick. "You need both? Left *and* right?"

Nick rolled his eyes. "How's Brian?"

"Not completely out of the woods yet. But he has stabilized and
is starting to gain strength."

Nick nodded slowly, reluctant to yield to any sense of relief.

"The doc did say, if he makes it, your patchwork saved his life."

Nick nodded again.

They mumbled "Thanks" at the same time.

Howard went down a short hall, turned into a room on the
left, returned with a pair of dry socks, and handed them to Nick.
He pulled out a chair at the breakfast table and sat across from Nick.

"We have to talk." He first hunched forward, then leaned back, the serious look on his face betraying some sort of inner turmoil.

"There's a problem," Nick said, seeing and suspecting the obvious.

Howard nodded slowly and leaned forward just enough to place his arms atop the table, his fingers tapping lightly on the plastic surface. "You're an official NYC cop. A pro cop."

"And that's not a good occupation around here," Nick offered, pulling on his second shoe.

"Better than some."

"But not many."

"Definitely not many."

Nick groped for the laces on his right shoe, all the while keeping his eyes locked on Howard's expression. "Are those 'not many' occupations shooting offenses?"

Howard chuckled. "Only when approved by neighborhood council."

Nick glanced down and checked that both socks were snug. "Many such approvals lately?"

"Not lately," Howard replied. "And none in the near future."

"It's a trust issue, right?"

"It is."

"All of you trust the regular cops about as much as we trust you."

"About as much," Howard acknowledged. Then, with a slight smile, he added, "And who are you to suggest you are a *regular* cop?"

Nick returned the smile. "I guess it comes down to your position and your viewpoint," he postulated, receiving a nod. "I swear I'll never reveal anything I've seen or where I've seen it that would in any way compromise your neighborhood."

"Not my neighborhood. The neighborhood belongs to every resident." Howard paused for a moment. "Make that every *accepted* resident."

"*Accepted* seems to be an often-used word in your neighborhood's vocabulary: accepted spokesman, accepted practice, accepted resident."

"It's the way we agreed to operate. I'm not the neighborhood's leader; I'm the spokesman. I'm the spokesman as long as I have the confidence of most of the residents."

"And how do you determine that confidence?"

"We have frequent meetings to make sure everyone knows what is happening in regard to any specific issue. No decision is reached until just about everyone agrees they are well informed."

Nick suppressed a chuckle. "Leaders from the dawn of history have touted the value of an informed citizenry. Then they turn around and pass five hundred pounds of paper containing single-spaced minute scribblings they claim the citizens need and must approve. Once the citizens give a thumbs-up, they find out where their thumbs really *did* end up."

"Not in this neighborhood. We don't allow any secrecy on any part of a proposal when voting on any issue. In our neighborhood, if the details of a proposal are kept secret—or just seem like they are—the proposal is voted down. If we find that, somehow, one part of a passed proposal was so buried that it was, for all intents and purposes, secret, that section—and probably the whole bill—is automatically deemed null and void."

"You make it sound like some kind of utopia."

"It ain't. Far from it. Significant problems can take hours of debate to resolve. You always have some people who are never well informed." Howard cupped a hand to his chin. "Come to think of it, even simple problems can take hours. Utopia it is not, but it works. So far."

"So far?"

"The World Council comes up with new rules, new laws, and new regulations that keep us busy trying to find out where trouble is lurking and how to steer clear of it. If we don't steer clear, we end up in one of the council's civil courts, where we're judged by a set of legal precedents from Ukraine, Morocco, Kenya, or whichever is best suited to the council's needs. The council gets us to do what they want not by shooting us in the head but by maneuvering us to where we have to choose between toeing the line or shooting ourselves in the foot. The council calls it 'international law,' but in reality it's just international handcuffs. Make that international, arbitrary, now-

and-forever handcuffs. Even before the World Council, politicians pushed more and more rules our way. Nothing really changes."

Nick agreed that international law was just a highfalutin way of tearing up the US Constitution. He was still intrigued by how Howard's neighborhood worked. "Do the other neighborhoods work by acceptance?"

"No. Of the fifteen Manhattan neighborhoods, maybe one other. For the past six months. You met them in the tunnels. The rest are mixed between militarily structured groups and 'brotherhood' types. All with rules and banishment for not following orders. Over the past few years, we've accepted nineteen 'banishees.'"

"Does your neighborhood ever banish anyone?"

"No. Some leave of their own accord, but we've never forced anyone to leave."

"Is there cooperation with the other neighborhoods, more than just the one that found Brian and me?"

Howard stared at Nick as if he were trying to burn through Nick's eyes and into the soul behind. "If I told you, I'd have to kill you."

"Seriously?"

"Not really." Howard smiled. "But the vote would probably resolve that I, and I alone, since I revealed the secret, should break your kneecaps and drop you on the steps of your precinct."

"Then please, don't tell me."

"Oh, I'll tell you."

"I think . . ." Nick wasn't sure what they were engaged in: banter, threats, or . . .

"I'll tell you when you pass 'acceptance.'" Howard cupped his chin again.

Nick frowned.

"In about an hour," Howard finished.

Nick's eyes didn't open as wide as saucers, but close.

Howard chuckled. "After dinner."

CHAPTER 26

———◆———

The meeting room was an old high school gym with tiered benches on all four sides of the basketball court. Nick sat where Howard indicated: half-court, behind the scorer's table, where Howard was shuffling some papers. There was the buzzing drone of what Nick estimated to be a thousand conversations.

The paper shuffling stopped, and Howard stood up, moved around the table, and strode partway to center court.

Without any buzzer, without any request, without waving of hands, without any flashing of overhead lights, the conversations tapered to a stop.

"Thank you," Howard said, holding two or three sheets of paper. "I see we've got at least double our usual attendance." He looked to his left for a moment then to his right. "If I didn't know better, I'd make a guess you were planning to vote on something tonight." This was met with a positive murmur of agreement. He chuckled and looked back toward Nick, then to the opposite side of center court. "We've got at least a couple of items to cover first then any new business. Following that, any items for vote." He glanced down at the top sheet. "The first: unwarranted searches by the Pop Police." He looked up to that part of the assembly directly opposite him. "Pop Police and unwarranted. Anybody want to comment?"

Nick saw at least fifty hands shoot up around the court.

Howard gestured with the papers in his hand to a man on the other side of the court who was just starting to stand. Nick recognized the redheaded tall man who had done his best to stop Brian and himself from driving off to become sewer rats. He introduced himself to Nick as Brian's father, Robert McKenna.

"The Population Police are stepping up their searches: searches of people, searches of homes, searches of . . . of even little kids. I'm a peace-loving man, but—"

Howard nodded. "But you'd like to punch them in the face."

"For starters," Robert confirmed, returning Howard's nod. "They present no warrant, give no reason, and brush aside any objection, and if you show the slightest resistance—"

"They haul you away and lock you up!" An elderly woman about six seats to Robert's left stood. "My husband was just trying to stop them from searching me so roughly. They hit him with their club-stick things and took him away. Three days later, he was dropped off at our park. He had a black eye, bruises all over his body, and a broken arm. That was a year ago. He hasn't gone outside since, refuses to even step out the door." She wavered for a moment as others reached up to steady her and then slumped back to the bench.

Robert waited until the woman caught her breath. He turned back to Howard. "Didn't we have something in our history that outlawed such searches, that made them downright illegal? Don't they have to have 'reasonable cause' to execute a search? Don't we have something called the Constitution?"

The auditorium was filled with rousing cries of agreement.

Howard looked back to the table and motioned to the man who had been sitting at his left. "Franklin?"

The man stood but did not move to Howard's side. "We still have the Constitution, but it requires that the federal government as well as each state abide by any treaty signed with any international entity." Franklin paused and cleared his throat. It was obvious he didn't like being the center of attention. "Our treaty with the World Council requires that we accept and"—Franklin stifled a second cough—"accept and embrace something called the Cairo Protocol, which bypasses pretty well most of what we would call 'reasonable' when it comes to searches. The Cairo Protocol—Cairo, Egypt, is the model the World Council has implemented throughout . . ." Franklin was caught short by a string of coughs.

Howard thanked him and turned back to Robert. "Franklin told you what we've all known for eighteen years. When you sign up to follow international laws, you find your own laws are chipped away."

Robert nodded and then shook his head and sat back down.

"I don't blame you," Howard said, "for blowing off steam. Personally, I'd like to blow off a few of their heads."

"I'll volunteer for that!" someone shouted.

"Count me in!" someone else said.

"Sign me up too!" another person in the crowd shouted.

Howard looked at the woman who had spoken earlier. "It's Margaret, isn't it?"

She nodded.

"Margaret, would it be okay with you if I stop over a few times a week? I would like to try to get your husband to reduce his fear and maybe even go for a walk outside with you and me. A walk in the park would probably not be a good idea, but there are enough other options."

Margaret nodded gratefully.

"However," Howard continued, "we'll have to coordinate our own patrols, paracop or otherwise, to coincide with our people moving about. I think many of us have noticed that, when they see a group of at least three of us, they tend to leave the less vulnerable alone. They may search us, but they leave these others alone." He took a deep breath and exhaled as he swept his gaze from one end of the auditorium to the other. "It adds another layer of complication to our lives but, I'm convinced, is worth it."

Nick watched as those listening either nodded their agreement, shrugged their acceptance, or shook their heads in resignation.

Howard jotted a few words on the sheet he'd been referring to and then slipped it to the bottom.

"Our second item, the one we always review: stalkers."

All background conversations halted.

"In the past week, there have been seven incidents, only one of which—and that's one too many—was successful. Four of the remaining six were interrupted prior to abduction, with the stalkers run out of the neighborhood and the other neighborhoods alerted.

The remaining two attempts were interrupted subsequent to abduction, the children freed, and a total of five stalkers beaten, bound and wrapped, bound again, and then thrown into the Hudson River."

Throughout the assembly, Nick saw at least a dozen fist pumps.

"This leads me to our second-to-last scheduled item: the first all-neighborhood meeting in three years. We're having less success deterring stalkers with each passing year. I know most of us—and I include myself—have little respect for how the other neighborhoods run things, but we do have at least this one major problem in common. In two nights, there will be a meeting of eleven of the fifteen neighborhoods in Central Park to see if there is any way we can increase our defenses. I'll need three others to attend with me."

Robert stood immediately.

Howard nodded and said, "Two more."

Slowly, two more stood up.

"Good. Now before our last scheduled item, I'm opening the floor to any new business."

Directly across midcourt, a portly man in what Nick guessed to be his early sixties stood up. "The city's Electric Control Board just notified me yesterday that my monthly allotment of electric power is being reduced to less than half of what it was. My clothing business will suffer. We take unwanted cloth—linen, cotton, silk, even old plastics—and we wash, press, and sew it into usable clothing for the neighborhood. I employ seventeen members of our community. I won't be able to keep them all after such a power cut. That and all the monthly regulation hoops to jump through will shut me down. Can you somehow get that message to the mayor?"

Before Howard could answer, seven people stood: five women and two men. Each related a similar cut in their electricity supply and projected similar impacts to their small businesses. As for all the regulations, the consensus was the mayor hated entrepreneurs.

Howard lifted a hand. "I'll raise the issue with the mayor's community relations commissioner. However . . ." He made a circle with his thumb and forefinger. ". . . I think we all know how much relief that will bring."

Various snorts, grunts, and groans from around the gym confirmed Howard's assessment.

Howard motioned across midcourt. "Robert, can we get a group together to explore any way of pooling our electricity allotments? We've done it with drinking water. Maybe—"

"No problem. We'll get it done," Robert said, not standing but nodding.

A young lady at the far right end of the court's near side stood. "I've got a three-year-old boy. I've been told that the microwaves that are not caught by the grid will sterilize young boys. Is that true?"

Robert raised a hand and was recognized by Howard.

"Not true, Nancy. The microwave intensity even atop the grid is nowhere sufficient to sterilize young men or . . ." He indicated himself with a shrug. "Or slightly older ones. Even atop the grid, the microwave intensity is one-twentieth of what the government considers borderline safe."

"Which government?" Nancy asked.

"You got me there, Nancy. The federal government."

"You mean President Allison's government."

Robert shrugged. "The World Council does back up those numbers."

"Small comfort," Nancy said as she slumped down.

Howard brought the microphone to his lips, but before he could speak, an elderly man at the opposite end of the court from Nancy stood. His left hand shook as it pressed down upon a cane.

"They're poisoning our water. I've seen them hovering around our tank reservoirs. They should be shot!"

Howard's shoulders slumped. Nick could see his eyes roll. "You say that at every meeting, Vernon."

"And every time they've been poisoning our water."

"Vernon, you're just being a nervous Nellie. You should know better."

Howard looked down at the papers in his hand, his manner dismissive.

The faint sound of singing started from those surrounding Vernon. "Ring around the rosie, a pocket full of posies. Ashes! Ashes! We all fall down."

It was repeated for a total of three verses, gathering singers from various spots.

After the third time, Howard nodded his head and smiled. "Vernon, we'll do the same as we do every time you bring your concern to our attention. We'll have the water in all six tanks tested."

"Thank you," Vernon said, and sat down.

"Anybody else have any new business?"

No one else raised a hand.

Howard cleared his throat. "Now our last scheduled item. I would like to propose Detective Nicholas Garvey be accepted into the neighborhood with full privileges."

Robert stood. "Are you sponsoring him?"

"No. I'm just proposing. Because of the position to which you have entrusted me, I feel it would be inappropriate for me to sponsor. I would like someone else to stand for him."

Robert sat back down. "I appreciate what he did for us—and for my son—but he's an NYC cop. No neighborhood has ever accepted an NYC cop."

"He might put a target on all our backs," a man suggested from under the basket on the right.

"One more target among many," Robert offered. "Could be he'd remove a target or two from our own backs while putting one on his."

"He did stop those stalkers in the red neighborhood," Margaret observed.

Nick smiled inwardly, thankful that Margaret didn't conclude her offering with "He can't be all bad."

There were four or five more comments ranging from wary to tentative. None was negative, but none concluded with sponsorship.

After everyone appeared to have their say, Howard turned back to Nick. He had a discouraged I-tried-my-best look on his face.

Not wanting to force Howard to state the obvious, Nick stood and took a deep breath. "I appreciate Mr. Williams's efforts on my behalf, but I can't—"

"I'll sponsor him!"

Nick turned to his left as eleven-year-old Nathan jumped to his feet and marched to Nick's side.

Nathan's action was greeted with shocked silence.

Remembering to exhale, Nick looked at Howard. Nathan's father looked frozen in surprise. Nick wondered if such a young boy was able to sponsor, if Nathan could—

"As will I." Margaret stood, bracing herself against the shoulder of the man sitting next to her. She took a breath and shivered. "I'll also sponsor Detective Garvey, that is."

Within a minute, everyone was standing. Applause started slowly and grew. Nathan grabbed Nick's hand and squeezed.

The squeeze was the same as the one Nicole gave him whenever he picked her up and whenever he dropped her back home. He gave himself a quick blink, holding back a single tear in each eye.

The applause continued. Nick nodded his thanks.

The blue neighborhood had a new citizen.

CHAPTER 27

◆

After what must have been at least a hundred welcoming backslaps, Howard, Nathan, Robert, and Nick retired to Howard's apartment to unwind.

Robert shook Nick's hand for the third time. "No hard feelings about my resistance to the acceptance. I wanted to make sure all views were heard." Still pumping his hand, Robert added, "Proud to have you in our neighborhood."

Howard and Nathan grinned, adding their own appreciation.

Nick looked at Howard. "Can I ask the reason for the nursery rhyme when you and Vernon were talking?"

Robert laughed at Howard's sheepish expression.

"It's a reminder," Howard said. "Whenever anyone—myself included, obviously—tries to cut discussion short by calling the other person a name, it is considered a tactic used by kindergartners, first-graders, second-graders, and retarded politicians to call someone a name without giving any reason for the name being used. Our neighborhood has the tradition of using a school-yard nursery rhyme to remind the name-caller that he's acting like a little schoolboy."

"Or schoolgirl," Nathan was quick to add.

Still chuckling, Robert smiled at Howard. "If Howard had ignored the 'ring around,' there are about fifteen more nursery rhymes available. The one tonight is always the first. Forty or fifty years ago, they could have come in handy when someone called another individual a racist or woman hater or denier without ever giving any sensible explanation. In those days, it was a tactic to shut down discussion that was uncomfortable to the individual calling out the names. We use the nursery rhymes to keep all of us honest and engaged in the discussions."

The three men raised their wine glasses as Howard said, "To all the ring around the rosies keeping us all on the up-and-up."

Nick gestured with his glass toward Robert. "Speaking of 'around,' you seemed quite confident the neighborhood would find a work-around for the power cutback."

"We will. No doubt about it. It's not like the World Council or the mayor deciding who gets what. Have you ever seen power poles in Africa or South America? People splice into them right and left, across the sidewalks, even across the streets. Half the power poles end up looking like they had a bad hair day. We're a community of individuals—individuals who are always willing to help anyone. Anyone, that is, who is a doer."

Puzzled, Nick tilted his head. "Anyone who is a doer?"

It was Howard's turn to chuckle. "You'll have to forgive Robert. He forgets you're new to the neighborhood and aren't acquainted with our guiding . . ." Howard squinted as if searching for the right word. "Our guiding *attitude*, for want of a better term. This attitude holds that there are three kinds of people in this world: those that do, those that cannot, and finally, those that will not. We find that those that do get things done; that those who cannot would like to help but are unable for some reason and are helped through life by those that do; finally, that those who will not will find every reason in the world to do nothing."

Nick nodded his understanding. "And do those that do and those who cannot give help to those who will not?"

"We'll help in many ways, especially if the individual is young and finding their way. We'll review all incentives. We'll provide assistance, guidance, and counseling."

"But if none of that works, do you continue giving help?"

"Not many of us," Howard answered. "A few may keep giving help to a persistent 'will not' because they're a relative, but no one in the neighborhood gives what is most important in life: respect. As a neighborhood, we extend ourselves to show everyone the merit of a contributing life. We do our best to make sure all of our incentives, be they planned or otherwise, lead in that direction. Should we find negatives in our schooling or in our administration of justice, we meet to explore avenues for correction. Eventually, most of the 'will not' souls get their act together or wander away. If they stay, they have to start becoming a doer, or ultimately, they lose their right to vote."

Robert chimed in. "And if they *do* wander away, it's no loss to the neighborhood. Of course, they may find a so-called benevolent group, some government, perhaps, who will sustain them through their life at our—"

"At our expense," Howard finished. "Robert is our resident, certified, tenured, PhD-level political economist who believes—"

"Who believes," Robert interrupted in return, "a market run by private enterprise operates by the proverbial invisible hand, while a market run by government—any government—wields a most visible middle finger. Also, I bet you didn't know all politicians and bureaucrats are, by choice, haberdashers."

Nick shook his head, confused. "Haberdashers?"

Robert grinned. "For the longest time, I didn't know they also ran a clothing business, until I found they've been getting into my pants since I wore diapers."

Howard wagged his head. "We only have all night, so please don't ask him how one dies under each form of government."

Robert smiled and took up the challenge. "Economics recognizes three forms of government and advises how one is likely to die under each. The three, and their form of likely death, are communism, execution; socialism, starvation; capitalism, old age."

Howard raised his wineglass. "To Robert. He has a million of them." He then turned to Nick. "I'm surprised you haven't asked us if our neighborhood or any other neighborhood was responsible for the murder of the vice president."

Howard's directness took Nick aback. "Are you responsible? Or any of the others?"

Howard smiled. "Speaking for this neighborhood, no. Speaking for the others, I doubt it."

"Why?"

"No neighborhood needs the pro cops or the federal cops or, possibly, the World Council Guard prying into our every move. Some government arm is always trying to squeeze us. None of the neighborhoods would want to entice any one of those arms to wrap themselves around their necks. We stay as far away from their business and activities as possible with the hope that we'll have at least half a life."

Nick was convinced of at least this neighborhood's innocence. "Do you have any thoughts as to who did murder the vice president?"

"None. Scuttlebutt has it that the five men were killed in a warehouse area and then dumped on the steps of city hall. From what I understand, four of the men were shot. There are more than just a few people living in that area. No one heard nor saw anything."

"A silencer could have been used."

Howard nodded in agreement. "But one elderly man and one not-so-frisky dog on a leash saw a limousine pull right into that area as they, the man and his dog, turned the corner. There were no bodies before he turned the corner, but there were five upon their return."

"Thanks for the information. It eliminates several possibilities."

"Glad to be of help to one of our own."

More subjects and stories were batted around for another half hour until Nathan, in his pajamas, walked up to the three men. "I forgot, Dad. Before I go to bed, can we tell Detective Nicholas about the Gardener?"

Howard shrugged his agreement. "We call him the Gardener. Don't know his real name. He supplies us with various plants and seeds for our own gardens. Gotta say, his stuff grows ten times better than what we used to have."

Nick, remembering the mental itch he had almost forgotten needed scratching, asked Howard, "How long has he lived in that building?"

"Don't know. We discovered his presence by accident almost twelve years ago. Could have lived there another ten or twelve before that. It was an abandoned health clinic before then. The Gardener started sharing plants and stuff with us about ten years ago. Periodically, he'd have some assistants help him out. They left us alone. We left them alone."

Nick stopped drinking the wine but remembered little of the conversation that followed, the resurrected mental itch becoming persistent.

When at last Howard suggested it was time to "close for the night," Nick knew where he had to go. He shook hands and headed out into the night.

CHAPTER 28

◆

Nick flashed his badge at the security guard just inside the doors of the main New York City Public Library. The guard's expression was impassive, much like that of the stone lions out front.

This was the best place Nick could think of for discovering the identity of the Gardener.

He checked his watch: 2:15 a.m. Almost six hours before the start of his Monday morning shift. He trotted down three flights to where the periodicals were stored and, hopefully, cataloged with some semblance of regularity.

At one time, every page of every US newspaper and of foreign capital newspapers was copied into a digital database. Unfortunately, lack of funding had killed that activity twelve to fifteen years ago with the computers and data hardware removed. Putting his itch to rest would require his scouring through years of newspapers.

Somehow he remembered the old man Howard had referred to as the Gardener. His flickering memory of a *New York Times* front-page photograph suggested where to look.

The *when* was still a problem.

Flipping a mental thirty-sided coin, Nick decided to check the *New York Times* starting thirty years ago with the oil terrorists. He made five trips to the archive shelves, retrieving three large boxes, each time placing them atop the one long table. He found he had retrieved not quite four years' worth of the *Times*.

Nick opened the first box marked 3Q2027 and noticed that the oldest issues were on the bottom, with the more recent filling the top.

He dug down for the issue dated Sunday, September 19, 2027, and placed it and those on top upside down on the far end of the table.

Nick flipped over that Sunday issue, straightened out the front page, and read the headline: "Terrorists Attack World's Oil."

The first paragraph noted how hundreds of working wells, both on land and offshore, and strategic storage holdings had simultaneously been attacked throughout the Middle East, Russia, South America, the North Sea, Alaska, Texas, and Oklahoma. Underground reserves in the United States, Europe, China, and others had also been compromised. Initial estimates were that at least twenty thousand terrorists had carried out the synchronized attacks.

There were pictures of seven heads of states. None was the Gardener.

Rummaging through the remainder of the 3Q2027 pages, Nick remembered how, by that Tuesday morning, September 21, 2027, the terrorists had, in the words of the *Times*, "sucked the lifeblood out of the West." A genetically engineered bio culture had been injected down each well and into each immense, government-built underground chamber containing veritable seas of crude. The culture was an exceptionally virulent variation of the ones that had been used since the early 1990s to "digest" oil spills polluting seawater.

No face appeared on that September 21 front page. Instead, the *Times* displayed a drawing of a double-helix DNA strand. The claim was that the 1990s bio culture had somehow been enhanced from a formula for digesting oil, then dying away, to a monster solution that would not die and would not rest until every drop of oil within its reach had been devoured.

Three days later, Friday, September 24, 2027, the *Times* front page showed a picture of an eight-year-old Arab boy who had been captured in a skiff while speeding away from an oil rig in the Gulf of Mexico. When the Coast Guard vessel had been spotted by the terrorists, the young boy, along with nine adults, tried to abandon the rig by jumping into their speedboat. The boy went second and broke a leg in the jump. The bio culture had been injected, but the eight terrorists still on the rig had been shot by the Coast Guard cruiser as they descended the center ladder and were preparing to jump. The ninth adult, trying to restart the stalled speedboat, had been wounded, fell into the water, and was rescued and put in chains. The young Arab boy was reportedly placed in a Houston juvenile detention facility. A doctor in that facility's infirmary reset the boy's leg with moderate success.

Nick vaguely remembered the boy being sent to some kind of school with a campus fenced on all sides and then, after a couple or so years, being sent back to the Middle East.

Box 3Q2028 contained the one-year anniversary issue in its Tuesday, September 19 issue. The headline read as follows: "Life in 1 AO!"

Nick remembered reporters referring to the anniversary as the first-year After Oil. The AO suffix survived for several years. There were five rows of six photographed faces pictured on the first page.

The reportage detailed how, within three months of the attacks, those 60 percent of the known world's oil fields and reserves that had been targeted were found to be barren. What was once oil had been reduced to a liquid black slag. Useless black slag.

The Wednesday, May 16, 2029, issue displayed six pictures. The largest was of the governor of Colorado, whose state had voted to institute a complete ban on genetic and DNA research. The margin of passage had been 78 percent for, 22 percent against. Four of the pictures were of various clergy, whose sermons and encyclicals, Nick remembered, had crisscrossed the airwaves as they called for an end to man's "renewed savaging of the Tree of Knowledge." The remaining picture was of a sweatshirt imprinted with the body and wings of a fly; the head, trunk, and tusks of an elephant; the feet of a duck; and the tail of a skunk. Enclosing the image was a red circle with a line through it and, just below, the slogan "If God wanted it, he would have made it." That particular sweatshirt became a worldwide best seller.

Nick noticed as he closed the 2Q2029 box that the *Times* had dwindled to a twelve-page daily newspaper. Twenty-four pages on Sunday.

At 3:46 a.m., he came to the second-anniversary edition of Wednesday, September 19, 2029. Its headline bemoaned, "2 AO! World Posts 'Going Out of Business' Signs."

Oil had been perceived as the main energy engine supporting civilization's dynamic growth. Alternative energy sources had been well into development, some even to market, but none ready to fill the tremendous gap left by the drop in oil reserves. Countries with as much as a third of their previous petroleum reserves became kings of the new oil hierarchy. A barrel of oil cost more than an ounce of gold for the first time in history. Industries that couldn't adapt died.

All fifty states had passed genetic research bans with prison sentences of up to twenty years for violations. Most of Europe, South America, Asia, and Africa passed similar laws, with, in two countries, death penalties a probability.

A second, smaller headline stated that severe hunger had become increasingly common throughout Africa and many parts of Asia. Its impact was starting to be felt throughout Europe, Russia, and the Americas.

The Tuesday, October 8, 2030, issue of the *Times* showed two pictures: one of Christopher Price and the other of Jason Beck. Severe hunger had become increasingly common throughout Africa and many parts of Asia. A week earlier, aid workers in Yemen had been trampled to death by almost a million starving souls. The incident had been captured on video and shown that evening in the United States. The article below the two pictures reported the formation of the World Council as a replacement to the United Nations, which had fallen into disarray almost two years before the terrorist attacks of 2027. Jason Beck would be the supreme director of the World Council, with Chris Price his second in command. It was noted that Chris's wife was one of the aid workers killed in the stampede incident. The organizing goal of the World Council was to coordinate food production and to steer a significant portion of it to villages, towns, and even countries where the need was overwhelming.

4:31 a.m.

Photographs of Jason and Chris again appeared on the Friday, September 19, 2031, (4 AO) issue. In response to pressure from thirty-six politically sovereign entities, the World Council passed an embargo on the number of children a couple could have—the number being one.

Nick remembered the riots that embargo had engendered, riots that persisted until the World Council agreed to the creation and trading of "birth vouchers." The Chicago Board of Trade had been chartered as the initial exchange to register the sale and purchase of any vouchers being exchanged.

4:43 a.m. brought Nick to the fifth-anniversary issue of Sunday, September 19, 2032.

The headline didn't mention 5 AO. Instead it read as follows: "World Council Buys World's Oil."

Jason Beck was again featured on the front page, along with six oil company executives and nine heads of states. The World Council had negotiated with those pictured to "purchase" what estimates described as 90 percent of the world's oil. The negotiations were prompted by warfare between many nations, which were trying to either acquire or keep oil resources.

5:19 a.m.

The issue of Monday, July 11, 2033, brought Nick's search to a screeching halt. The *Times* blared in two bold headlines,

The War Is Over!
All Drugs Now Legal!

That was one week after his brother-in-law had gone out on his July 4 "final run." Nick remembered the rationale presented: the money saved on not policing and not incarcerating drug sellers and buyers would be spent on rehab facilities and on education. There had been a two- or three-month, short-term increase in the number of addicts, who now purchased their stash from government stores. When the rehab and education programs were running full steam, the number of addicts dropped to 60 percent of the number before legalization. The politicians beamed over their success. Within two years, the funding for drug rehab and education had to be chopped down to 20 percent of promised levels due to other needs claiming the money. The drug lords returned, but not the redirected police. With the apparent return of old times, the number of addicts, new and returning, started to climb.

Nick reached the last papers of 2034. He repacked the box and trudged off to swap for another fifteen.

On Wednesday, February 20, 2036, the mayor and the police commissioner announced that the city would recognize various neighborhood groups as auxiliary NYPD squads. Neither the mayor nor the police commissioner displayed anything remotely suggesting they were pleased with the announcement. They had been pressured by the neighborhoods for six months. With the regular police force cut to a third of its 2026 level, the professional police had to have support. Hence, the pro cops were photographed shaking hands with the leaders of the newly nicknamed paracops. No men in the picture captioned "Welcome Aboard" were even close matches to the Gardener.

Nick breezed through the rest of 2036 and the first nine months of 2037. There were only five front-page photographs over those twenty-two months.

5:51 a.m.

Nick opened the thirteenth of the last fifteen boxes he had retrieved.

Again, no pictures in the first issue of the *Times*, now down to eight pages on the daily issues.

Monday, January 4, 2038, again had pictures of Jason Beck and Chris Price. The World Council, having by then solidified its hold on most of the world's resources, announced that it was only appropriate that a unified canon of international law apply to all countries. Nick remembered the hundreds of street protests against the trashing of the US Constitution. Within three months, the protests had dwindled to seven, disappearing completely within another two weeks. Nick recalled the previous night's meeting in the gym. International law was still drawing protests there.

What struck Nick as crafty on the World Council's part was the law's application to federal or national laws and courts: all federal regulations were henceforth null and void. Nonnationwide regional jurisdictions were granted some key exceptions, which had led to the creation of the seven associations within the United States. But that had resulted in an overall weakening of government at all levels.

Nick shook his head. He hadn't time for political analysis. More boxes were needed.

6:02 a.m.

The headline on Wednesday, November 7, 2040, alluded to the Conservative Party winning the presidency and Lenora Allison winning reelection and maintaining her position as majority leader of the Senate. About a dozen other individuals were pictured in head shots. Nothing again.

He plowed on.

He flattened the Friday, January 25, 2041, issue of the *Times* until it was a full, smooth sheet.

"Yes!" he shouted.

The Gardener. Full face on the front page. No doubt about it!

"Yes!" he shouted again, not quite as loud.

The Gardener looked at least forty years younger, while the issue spread out before Nick was less than twenty years old. Right under the picture was the subject's name—Owen Pendleton—and the date of the picture, 2019.

The story's lead just below the picture stated that a Dr. Owen Pendleton, world-renowned bioengineer, had been traveling in his car at a high rate of speed on a particularly icy section of road that had not been sanded. His car skidded into a bridge abutment and burst into flames, which consumed both the car and the driver. Dr. Pendleton was pronounced dead at the scene. An autopsy showed a complete absence of alcohol, prescription drugs, or any other type of drugs.

Nick shook his head. One itch had been scratched away only to be replaced by another.

Dr. Owen Pendleton had been burned to a toasty crisp sixteen years ago but had been tending to a bountiful rooftop garden just two days ago.

Nick checked his watch: 6:12 a.m. He had time. Time to learn about—Nick decided to give Dr. Pendleton a new nickname—Mr. Resurrection.

Nick pulled up a chair, took a seat, and started to read.

CHAPTER 29

◆

Nick moved the table lamp closer. The article under the picture of Dr. Pendleton was just four paragraphs in length.

Dr. Owen Pendleton was killed early yesterday morning when he lost control of his automobile on a patch of ice-covered roadway passing under the George Washington Bridge. Paramedics were dispatched and arrived at 1:17 a.m., just four minutes after the reporting call had been received. By the time they arrived, the car had already burst into flames, consuming the automobile as well as Dr. Pendleton. Dental records matched at the autopsy revealed the identity of the burned corpse. Tests also revealed that Dr. Pendleton's driving had not been impaired by any foreign substance. No trace was found of alcohol or prescription or recreational drugs. Since there were no relatives of record, Dr. Pendleton's interment will be provided for by the federal government.

Dr. Pendleton was the Nobel Prize–winning bioscientist who invented the bioremediation agent CP-42, a microbe-laden solution that was able to "eat" twenty times its own mass in crude oil. CP-42 had been used successfully twelve times from 2013 to 2022 to remediate small and large oil spills, both in salt water and bodies of freshwater. CP-42 was preferred over similar solutions because, immediately after its petroleum repast, it died.

Dr. Pendleton became a controversial figure when it was determined that a modified version of CP-42 had been used by the oil terrorists of 2027. Its primitive capability of destroying twenty times its weight and then dying had been modified by the terrorists so that "CP-42-M," as it was called, could digest at a minimum three hundred times its original personal best. This descendent of his invention made Dr. Pendleton an outcast for the last ten years of his life.

Since Dr. Pendleton left no will, living or otherwise, directing the disposal of his remains, his charred remains will be cremated with final disposition to be determined. No services have been scheduled.

"Can't even trust obituaries anymore," Nick muttered as he turned off the lamp and pushed it back. At least the "obituary" had been correct about one thing: final disposition of the remains were *still* "to be determined."

Nick slumped back in the chair and pondered how much, if any, tie-in Mr. Resurrection had to any plot on the president's life. It was just one of those "pain in the back of the neck" things that would bother him until he could resolve it. Was Dr. Pendleton up to his old gene-manipulation tricks, breaking hundreds of international and domestic laws? Who kept him sequestered and protected? Was he involved with truck no. 48? With the Secret Service? Did he know anything about the murder of the vice president? Did Howard know Pendleton's history?

Nick glanced at his watch: 6:12 a.m. Time to pack up and head out for his shift.

He shook his head as he gathered the last five boxes. He had scratched one uncertainty only to exchange it for at least three others. Hopefully, it would be a quiet day at the precinct.

CHAPTER 30

———◆———

"N ick!" Tim thundered, raising an open hand to the heavens. "Where the hell you been? I've been trying to call you for the past twenty minutes."

Nick shrugged. "My squawker was off."

"Well, turn it on, dammit!"

Nick glanced at his watch. He was only two minutes late. He certainly hadn't expected Tim, of all people, to be barking at him before he could even get to his desk. Tim was well-known throughout the precinct as mumble-quiet and bleary-eyed until his morning coffee.

Not today.

"What's got your ass all afire?" Nick asked, trying to tempt Tim's brow to unfurrow.

Tim gestured across the room to where the computer technicians, Glen and Fred, sat slumped over their desks, their heads resting atop folded arms. "We finally viewed one of the Secret Service agents some hours before he was shot."

"Great!"

Nick and Tim walked over to the computers and their attached video monitors.

After several keystrokes by a bleary-eyed Glen, his monitor snapped to life, showing a street scene. In the background was the old United Nations building. A black limousine pulled up to the curb in front of the building, and a well-dressed man stepped out. Glen paused the video when the man turned back to the limousine, apparently to say something. Glen zoomed the display in to where the man's facial features were on the verge of being blurred but still useful.

Tim gave a fist pump. "It took nine hours, but we got him. We matched him to the senior agent."

Nick was impressed with the team's success. "Now all we have to do is track his movements both before and after."

"The next twenty-eight seconds go a long way in that direction."

Glen restarted the video. In just a few seconds, another man exited from the front of the building and strode right up to the agent. Again, keystrokes and a frozen frame. Enlarged, the left side of the face was clear.

Nick leaned closer to the screen. "Looks like he was in a knife fight years ago. Any idea who he is?"

"We haven't been able to identify the second man, but it's clear from the badge on his lapel that he has some association with the World Council."

"Interesting," Nick said.

"As soon as Glen and Fred get some strong coffee, they'll try matching—"

Captain Gilmore burst out of his office. "We've got a killing!"

"Okay," Nick said. "We get ten, maybe fifteen killings a week. What's so special about this one?"

"It's probably a construction worker. A *grid* construction worker."

"You said 'probably'?"

"No one's been able to get close enough to see. All we know is it's a male body caught up underneath the grid. The mayor called down himself. What with the president's ceremonies in ten days, the mayor is a fine-tuned ball of panic."

"So one call from the mayor and we have to jump—"

"Not *one* call. *Three*."

"Three calls? Since when?"

"Since twenty minutes ago. I was going through the roster to see who was available to assign, but on the last call he insisted that, in his words, the 'A team' be assigned. I guess he's afraid President Allison's gonna kick his ass for real this time."

The barest trace of a smile tugged at Nick's lips. The captain was referring to a recent cartoon in the paper showing President Lenora Allison and Mayor Lyle Banner atop the grid. The president was depicted kicking Banner in the ass and over the edge. The balloon over the president's head had her saying, "This will bring power to the city, not to you!" President Allison's normally cropped just-above-the-shoulder dark brown hair had been converted into a couple dozen red, yellow, and orange lightning bolts radiating outward. The point: the mayor hadn't wanted the grid but needed the energy it would provide and had been given only one choice by the president.

"Has grid management been informed?"

Captain Gilmore shook his head. "Not to my knowledge."

Nick recognized a potential hot potato when he was hit with one. The grid, started just over three years ago, was funded by what passed for the federal government. The actual construction was manned exclusively by workers from the Pennsylvania-Jersey Association, and having a Penn-Jersey citizen killed in New York would be big trouble. Carter Johnson, the association's chief executive, would seal shut all bridges and tunnels into Manhattan until the perpetrators were convicted or hell froze over. Nick guessed conviction *and* hell freezing. The steel cable for the rectenna microwave wiring plus the stabilizing guy wires were made in Pennsylvania proper, and the high-strength plastic of the grid itself came from New Jersey. Having one of their own turn up dead on the city's doorstep could grind construction in the city to a halt.

As Nick and Tim put on their jackets, Nick rolled his eyes. "So the mayor is so edgy that he wants the two of us?"

"The mayor insisted. Seems you're the department's crack investigation team. Also, just a guess on my part, the chief is still concerned this may be connected in some way to the rumors about an attempt on the president's life."

"Well then, we better be going."

"I called down to requisition a car. It should be ready"—the captain checked his watch—"in about thirty-five minutes."

Nick put on a sad face and shook his head. "The mayor will be so very, very displeased with the delay, but we'll have to tell him that." Nick turned to Tim. "Is that grid-mobile thing I brought in three days ago still upstairs?"

"You used your handcuffs to lock it to the fire escape. No one told me it's been returned."

"Excellent. Our trusty steed awaits upstairs. You'll enjoy the ride. It's open air, and we'll be almost there when the car is ready."

Captain Gilmore chuckled and waved them on.

Tim rolled his eyes heavenward and shrugged as Nick grinned and turned, leading them to the building's only elevator. Nick hoped the precinct's elevator worked all the way to the twelfth floor. The chances were fifty-fifty at best.

It did.

"Isn't she a beauty?" Nick asked with mock pride as he unlocked the handcuffs. "Hop in. No waiting, no fuss. Ten times quicker than taking the bus."

"What isn't?" Tim said as he eased into the passenger seat.

Nick turned the key and watched the battery charge gauge swing to over 80 percent. "Almost a full tank of corn juice."

As Nick released the clutch, Tim reached for the roll bar.

Nick chuckled. "Expecting we'll break the sound barrier?"

Tim's grip relaxed as the speedometer inched up to, then steadied at twelve.

Unencumbered by competing bicycle traffic or by any need to secure their vehicle with the local paracops before having to walk six or seven blocks, they reached the body in twenty-two minutes.

Finding the location was no problem. The grid seldom if ever entertained a cluster of nine uniformed NYC Police, let alone a swarm of seventeen paracops and five hard-hat construction workers.

Nick turned the key to Off, and the grid tractor glided to a stop. Nick and Tim climbed out and carefully walked to a group of paracops. Their shoulder patches proclaimed they were from the Battery Battalion, the largest of the neighborhoods that ran the full width of Manhattan, from the tip at Battery Park up to Canal Street and the Manhattan Bridge. It was an area Nick almost never worked.

The oldest of the five hard-hats, the only one in yellow, had been staring at Nick and Tim since they had pulled up and parked next to the group. He looked at Nick and pointed at the grid tractor. "Where did you get that?" he demanded.

"Midtown Tunnel," Nick stated. "It was involved in a crime. You'll get it back in a few days."

Tim gave the hard-hat his card. "My number."

Leaving the two of them, Nick pushed his way through the crowd. He found two more construction workers and an NYPD lieutenant kneeling just before the edge of a large unfinished, open section of the grid. The two workers were rigging the finishing touches of a metal mesh sling draping down into the hole. The surrounding grid area had been covered with large sheets of thick, rigid plastic, its yellow color providing a visual safety clue that extended back to the old New York Stock Exchange building sixty feet away. The building itself, a victim of online trading, had been closed down in 2022, sold to a developer in 2023, and had seventeen floors of apartments constructed above it in 2027, just three weeks before the oil crisis. It had never had tenants.

Nick knelt and peered down. About eight feet below grid level and a bit to his left, he could make out the body hanging upside down, its left foot caught in the microwave cables. Another, larger mesh netting had been rigged to hang about three feet under the body.

"How was he discovered?" he asked the lieutenant.

The lieutenant stabbed a thumb back over his shoulder. "The paracops found him and called us."

"That's unusual," Tim said, joining them. Old yellow-hat was right behind.

"Not here it isn't," the lieutenant said. "You're used to the midtown and uptown paracop brigades. I'm sure they could strip a body like this in seven seconds. And that includes four seconds spent calculating profits. We have a slightly—and I mean *slightly*—better class here."

"Fine." Nick touched the shoulder of a construction worker who was preparing to lower himself into the mesh sling.

The worker looked up.

"Me too," Nick said. "Have to check the body before it's moved."

The young worker looked up at his supervisor.

Old yellow-hat nodded assent, adding, "There's room for two as long as you don't thrash around."

The remaining young hard-hats lowered the sling slowly below grid level. The surrounding view just below the grid was eerie. Viewed from such a small angle, the grid lost its transparency; a dull gray ceiling started just inches above them, stretching out in all directions. Visually confusing were the surrounding buildings, their gray and brown stonework splashed in broad swatches of brightness, giving the perception of light without a source. This perception was modified as they inched downward until, five minutes later, they had reached their chosen elevation and the source of light was the same as viewed from the ground.

The construction worker turned to Nick. "He wasn't one of us. Not with those shoes. No way!"

Nick shifted to move closer to the body. He found his footwork to be minimally productive. He felt as if he were marching in a pool of gelatin and marshmallow, his stepping motions resulting in precious little forward progress.

"Use your elbows, not your feet," the young hard-hat offered.

Nick nodded and elbowed his way to the edge of the sling, which tilted a bit as he traversed. They were still about five feet away from the body's backside. Nick decided to settle for visual inspection only until the body was hoisted above.

The question of whether the man's death was accidental was answered by the seven bullet holes in the back of his jacket. There were also more than a few holes in each leg. Nick concluded the man had been shot while out on the grid.

Nick tried to put himself in the shooter's shoes. *If I shot him from the Stock Exchange building, which was probable, I might want to cover my actions. If I did, I'd either pull the body back inside or I'd push it over the edge to the street below. Dropping it over would be easy: slip it over headfirst while keeping the legs straight so they wouldn't catch.*

Nick flashed a light across the cables around the body. It would be very difficult to drop a body over and have it get snagged like this one. Unless, Nick imagined, the body fell spread-eagle against the cables. At least ten cables crossed under each grid cutout. The cables were always installed first, then the grid squares. Here there were cables but no grid. A body falling that way could easily bounce and end up spinning somehow, catching its left foot in some spinning pinwheel motion that twisted one cable over the other, clamping the foot and thus the body out of reach of any retrieval. If he were the shooter, he wouldn't want to attempt pulling the body back up or freeing it to drop to the pavement.

Feeling increasingly uneasy in the swaying sling, Nick nodded to his copassenger.

The man stood and pulled two long ropes from his belt. He whipped one then the other around the body, tied slipknots in each, and cinched them tight.

Nick marveled at how the young man had secured the body without touching it, moving it, or spinning it.

Having successfully secured the body, the young man reached down in the mesh and retrieved two long, slender poles. Each pole ended in a Y-type branch. Nick was most impressed when the young man shoved each Y against each of the two cables ensnaring the body's foot and, with a quick twist of each pole, freed the body.

The young hard-hat waved to those atop the grid. "Up!"

The return trip took fifteen minutes. As the body's feet cleared the grid opening, the shift from being pulled by ropes only to several hands grabbing at the body caused a slight twisting of the body itself. Nick looked up as its face rotated into view. Although he was a couple of feet below the face and the face was upside down and sporting considerable facial hair, something about the features struck him as familiar.

Finally, with grasping hands and arms, the hard-hats pulled the body up and over the grid lip.

The sling containing Nick and the young worker was next to be hauled up. With the young hard-hat's hand on his elbow and another two hands lowered to his upraised hand, Nick scrambled onto the grid.

He looked down at the body and felt like he'd been hit in the stomach with a sledgehammer. He recognized Gerry Martin instantly, even though he was wearing what had to be a fake goatee and ridiculous wraparound sideburns. That much facial hair hadn't grown in the time since he'd last seen Gerry. Nothing else was required. It was obvious Gerry had been on some sort of undercover work.

"You okay?" Tim asked, his tone concerned. "You look as if you've seen the end of the world."

"Part of it, at least." Nick tried to swallow, but his mouth was suddenly dry. He pointed down at the body.

"You know him," Tim guessed.

Nick nodded. "He's my old partner, Gerry Martin. Several years after he left the department, he joined the World Council as assistant to Chris Price, the council's second in command."

"What's he doing up here?"

"Don't know. I hope I didn't get him killed."

"Why would you think that?"

"I called him out of the blue on Thursday. Captain Gilmore asked me to use a World Council contact he knew I had to follow up on the vice president's murder. I asked Gerry to let me know of any council plots against the president."

"Did he report back with any?"

"No. But I can't help thinking—"

"Wait till we get back. No thinking before then."

Nick nodded.

They enlisted the paracops to help them wrap Gerry's body in a construction tarp for transport to their precinct.

As they were placing the body in the back of the grid tractor, the chief hard-hat moved between Nick and Tim and the tractor, his hands raised high. "Before I'll let you take that tractor again, I want *your* card," he said, pointing at Nick.

"Don't have one," he told the man. "We have a dead body to get back to our precinct ASAP. You're welcome to accompany us. You got a choice: third seat or second bag."

Finally, the lieutenant stepped in and wrote a makeshift receipt for the tractor, which, after receiving a nod from Nick, he committed to have returned by the next day.

As Nick turned the key, the yellow hard-hat was intent upon getting the last word. "There's only twenty-four of these on the whole project. Special design. If it doesn't come back in one piece, I'll make sure it's your asses, not mine, that get ground up."

Nick nodded as the tractor began its acceleration to twelve miles per hour.

Tim, now an experienced passenger, didn't grip any handles.

CHAPTER 31

◆

Nick and Tim watched the four technicians strip the body and run through Gerry's clothing, wallet, pistol, money, keys, a crumpled gum wrapper, an ancient subway map—everything on his person with the possible exception of pocket lint. Everything was itemized, photographed, checked for prints, and then returned to them as each item completed its course.

Nick kept remembering his time with Gerry on the force. Gerry was the quickest learner he'd ever seen. Honest, loyal, brave: all the things a cop hoped for in a partner. A partner—Nick couldn't shake the feeling—that he'd set up to be killed.

He felt Tim's hand on his shoulder.

Upon returning to their desks, they were called into Captain Gilmore's office.

"Well?" he demanded, looking from one to the other.

"Nothing, Captain," Tim offered, turning toward Nick.

"Nothing much," Nick added.

"And what, may I ask, is nothing much?"

"Victim's name: Gerry Martin, staff manager and assistant to Christopher Price, vice director of the World Council. Finally: no motive, no witness, no clues, no leads."

Captain Gilmore nodded. "Nothing much," he agreed. "Other than he was your former partner and a high-level employee of the World Council. Other than that . . ." The captain threw up his arms, feigning alarm. "Holy shit!" He stood and moved out from behind his desk. He half sat, half leaned against the front. When he spoke, his voice was lower and had a hard edge. "I don't like this one. There's

152

too much pressure from the mayor's office. Too much pressure and too much panic. Solve this thing, gentlemen. Solve it yesterday." The chief pushed away from the desk, paced to the glass door, paused for a moment, and then turned back. "And watch each other's back and your own ass while doing it. Don't tell anybody anything. Not the feds, not anyone from Penn-Jersey, not the mayor. *Especially* not the mayor. I'll keep him up-to-speed. An appropriate speed. I don't want him going all SWAT on me. Anyone asks you a direct question, you refer them to me. Tell 'em all you know is what you read in the papers and that I canceled all your subscriptions."

Back at their desks, Nick and Tim spread Gerry's clothes and belongings out on the top of their adjoining desktops. A torn, faded subway map was the only item other than a wrinkled gum wrapper and a wallet. The wallet was abnormally bare—several bills, no receipts, no business cards, no jottings of important phone numbers, no pictures, no matchbook cover or cocktail napkin from some favorite hangout. The clothes had no labels and no unusual grease stains. The shirt's left sleeve hem was partially torn, but other than that, as far as they could determine, there were no wear patterns, abrasions, or thinned spots unusual for Gerry's work requirements.

"I gotta hit the head," Tim announced after forty minutes.

"Take your time. These aren't going anywhere."

"Don't tell the mayor anything while I'm gone," Tim said, mimicking the captain's baritone voice.

Nick grabbed Gerry's left boot from the top of his desk and feigned a high-arching death blow. Tim spun, crouching in faux evasive action.

Nick placed the boot back on his desktop and shook his head, trying to push back the leading edge of exhaustion. The subway map might be somewhat important. With the exception of just three or four lines running on nothing resembling a recognizable schedule, the subway had not been operational for almost eighteen years. His guess was that Gerry was using it for determining tunnel locations, but there were no markings of any kind on either side of the map.

He slumped back into his wood-back chair and stared at the boot. Made of mustard-yellow rawhide, the boot was what had kept Gerry in one piece; without that boot, there would have been no murder, because there would have been no body—just splatter that would have been picked clean by the local paracops and then dumped. Nick wondered if Gerry would have appreciated the job done by his left boot—his good, hardworking left boot. He could just barely make out the etched boot size.

He leaned forward and, propping his chin on his fists and his elbows on either side of the boot, peered down his nose into the boot to better determine the size of Gerry's foot for no good reason other than marking time until either a better idea or Tim arrived. His professional guesstimate would have been eleven and a half.

He squinted at the number: 12. Close.

Beneath the number 12 was the stock or SKU number. Below the stock number—

Nick sat bolt upright. Below the stock number were ten numbers scratched into the sole. He committed them to memory. If Gerry had scratched the numbers, they had to be important, but what they meant, he hadn't a clue.

He returned to the contents of Gerry's pockets. The money—three singles, one five, and one ten—showed no unusual markings. The wallet, folded and unfolded every which way, held no clue of why Gerry had been killed, much less of why he had been up on the grid outside the old Stock Exchange. Nick shook his head.

Gerry, fresh out of the academy, had been assigned as his partner more than nineteen years ago when both were beat cops in the old precincts. Gerry, six years younger than Nick, had good instincts right from the start. The best instinct was always keeping his partner in the loop. If they were ever sent out on different assignments, Gerry would, without fail, leave Nick a brief note of either his whereabouts or of his progress. The note was usually on Nick's desk. But sometimes, when in a bind, Gerry would . . .

Nick's arm shot past the wallet to the crumpled gum wrapper. Carefully, Nick opened the wrapper and spread it flat. No note. Not worth putting in your pocket, unless . . .

He scribbled a brief note to Tim, scooped up his jacket, and took the elevator to the roof and the grid tractor.

Fifteen minutes later, he was back at the Stock Exchange building. The murder scene was deserted now. A small floodlight was clamped near the grid opening to warn any casual evening grid strollers of the potential for disaster. Nick didn't figure there were too many casual strollers seven stories up, but what the heck—it was a pleasant evening, and risks were meant to be taken.

All windows were locked from the inside. Nick decided not to force anything and climbed down the construction ladder to the street level.

He gained entrance into the building, climbed seven flights until just even with the level of the grid, pushed open a window, and stepped out. On hands and knees, he scoured the surface of the grid between the opening and the Stock Exchange. Back at the precinct, Nick had remembered that twice in their seven years together Gerry had left some crucial information buried in a thick wad of bubble gum.

The first time, just after a year together, Gerry had been on a short solo undercover assignment and felt he had been spotted. To prevent any incriminating information being found on him, he had stuck the wad on a stair railing outside a brownstone. Gerry hadn't been spotted, retrieved the gum with its treasure, and joked about it with Nick.

The second time was after their five-year-partnership anniversary. He discovered Gerry's wad stuck to his—Nick's—own desk lamp. "What the hell?" Nick had demanded, pulling the still moist clump from his lamp. Smiling broadly, Gerry had told him to look at the tiny note inside. They had both made detective on the same day.

Nick was positive—hopeful, really—that there was a third wad of gum somewhere near.

After thirty minutes on his hands and knees, Nick bumped into the Stock Exchange building. Time to go inside.

While looking up another level, he spotted the broken window and decided to check that section first. On that floor just above the grid, there were three office suites facing the grid. Each was a multi-room suite. All three were vacant and empty of furniture of any kind.

After a slow perusal of each suite, Nick, on a hunch, chose the cleanest one to search first. The other two had a small layer of dust everywhere. The middle suite had a definite, very recently scrubbed-down look. He nodded and got to work. The suite had four rooms. The leftmost was the largest with many nooks and crannies. He checked each nook, passing up none of the crannies. A single twelve-inch blond hair with its root was all he found. He put the hair in a plastic evidence bag.

He stood still in the center of the room and slowly checked the flooring. There were slight scratch marks where at least a dozen chairs had been moved back and forth. Most peculiar to Nick was a smell that took him back almost six years to when Nicole had been a baby. The smell was the pungent aroma of a baby's diaper in need of a change. He inhaled deeply. Make that many diapers in need of change. Make that many *recent* changes. He was in a stalker warehouse.

The remaining three rooms consisted of two small office-type rooms with a larger room in the middle. The far-right room sported the smashed window to the outside.

Nick moved to that rightmost window and looked out and down. It was a fair leap, not one he would want to take unless forced. He suspected this was the window that Gerry, had he been here and under duress, would have used to jump down to the grid.

He looked around the room. There were no pipes behind which to hide a wad of gum. If there had been furniture in this room and Gerry had stashed gum anywhere, Nick was sure he would not have chosen furniture. That left doorknobs and window frames.

The doorknobs on either side of the one door hid no gum. He did notice two drops of blood just inside the door.

Nick moved to the open window. Disregarding for the moment the frame top, he curled and ran his hand down the left side, along the bottom and up the right. He repeated the sequence, reaching along the inside of the frame.

Nothing.

He moved left to the next window. It was locked. He repeated the inside sequence: left, bottom—

Pay dirt!

Nick pulled the wad free. He positioned his flashlight on the sill so its beam shone on his open hand. He started kneading the wad and immediately felt a small square object.

Bringing his penknife to bear, he worked the gum free of a small gray square. He turned it over several times in his hand before he noticed some etched marks on one side.

Wishing he had a magnifying glass, Nick squinted at it.

It showed three numbers, apparently etched by machine. He shook his head. Were they some combination? Were they some code sequence? He had no idea. They could be a phone number area code, for all he could—

Of course!

They didn't match any sequence in the ten numbers scratched into Gerry's boot, but ten numbers did match the length of a phone number with an area code.

He ran the ten numbers forward and then backward in his mind. Knowing Gerry, if the numbers were indeed a phone number, he would enter them backward.

What the hell, Nick thought. *It's never too late or too early to make a call.* He reached into his pocket, retrieved his cell phone, turned on the recording feature, and then dialed the ten numbers from the boot in reverse order.

There was silence for about five seconds. Finally, there was a connection, and he heard ringing.

After the tenth ring, he decided calling what he thought was a number was probably not the best idea he'd ever had. He had just decided to hang up when the other end of the line clicked active.

"Hello?" someone said in a woman's voice.

Impulse kept Nick from answering. Something told him to wait, to make her say something else. He counted off the seconds to himself. He got to seven.

"Hello?" the woman repeated. "Gerry, is that you?"

Nick thumbed his phone twice before he was able to stop recording. He'd recognized the voice and figured she wouldn't appreciate surreptitious recording.

"Who is this?" demanded President Lenora Allison.

CHAPTER 32

◆

Nick took a deep breath. He had no idea what Gerry had been up to, but if he'd had the president's private line, he must have had her trust.

"Nicholas Garvey, Madam President." He wondered for a moment if Madam was the proper salutation. "I was a friend of Gerry Martin's."

"Was? He spoke of you often. Has something happened?"

"He was murdered."

After a short silence: "Where is his body?"

"At my precinct's medical room."

"Is that where you are now?"

"No. I came back to where he was killed and pieced together your phone number."

"Where did you find it?" Her questions were coming rapid fire.

"It was in one of his boots—backward. I came back here and found a small gray chip with three numbers. Although they didn't match any sequence of those in his boot, they did make me think of area codes."

"You said you 'came back here.' Where is 'back here'?"

"The old New York Stock Exchange building."

"I need you to stay there. I'll have a Secret Service detail pick you up. I need to know what happened—but not over the phone. Can you be in front in about ten minutes?" A slight pause. "If, of course, you're willing."

What the hell, he thought. "Ten minutes," he agreed. "In front."

"Thank you, Nick."

Nick made one last, detailed survey of both rooms but found nothing except the spotless floors and chair scratch marks that had first caught his attention.

He made it to the front door just as a large dark limousine cruised to a stop at the curb. Two men in suits got out and waited for him.

Nick walked to the limousine, double-checked the two proffered credentials, and then ducked inside. As soon as he was settled, the limousine moved out.

Jason Beck had just completed his eulogy comments to be delivered tomorrow on behalf of Gerry Martin, "trusted and loyal World Council executive," when his Bert-only phone rang.

He decided an unanswered ring or two wouldn't hurt. He double-checked his opening to assure it had the proper amount of sincerity. "The World Council is a family of individuals each dedicated to serving people everywhere. Today we are gathered to remember a key member of our family. We should both rejoice and mourn. Rejoice that Gerry Martin accomplished so many positive things in life. Mourn that there will be no more such accomplishments."

Jason nodded. Definitely a reasonable amount of sincerity on behalf of a traitor.

He picked up the phone. "Yes, Bert?"

"The cop, Nicholas Garvey. Our tracking videos followed him all day. He made two trips to the old New York Stock Exchange building, the first time with a bunch of other cops checking out some kinda crime scene. After his second trip, this time alone, he spent an hour and three minutes inside before he was picked up outside the building by a black limousine. There were three other men inside, including the driver."

"And?"

"The limousine, with Nicholas aboard, drove into the Lincoln Tunnel."

Jason paused for a few seconds, turning over several scenarios in his mind. Behind each was either President Lenora Allison or Chief Executive Carter Johnson. Whichever one, he'd have to increase tensions between them. Worked before, he thought. It would work again.

"I see," he finally said. "You tracking on the other end?"

"Yes, sir. No problem there. However, there are only about a fifth of the cameras—but enough to keep both car and cop in our sights."

"Good. Keep me informed. And Bert—"

"I know. Anyone who is worth noting is worth tracking."

"Exactly."

CHAPTER 33

◆

The limousine pulled into the parking lot of a motel on the outskirts of Georgetown. The three agents asked Nick to follow them as they went into a sparsely furnished office. One of the agents went behind the counter and reached up to the board, where about a dozen keys were hung. He tugged downward on one of the key hooks.

The door at the far end on the counter clicked loudly.

The three men ushered Nick into the room.

President Lenora Allison was sitting behind a desk at the far end of the room. Her hair was a bit longer than shown in recent photos—slightly below shoulder length but still businesslike and still dark brown—and unlike the recent cartoon, no red, yellow, and orange lightning bolts shot out from her head. A few gray strands did show here and there.

She motioned for Nick to take a seat. "Thank you for agreeing to come."

"Gerry was a longtime friend."

"I know. He worked directly for me for about three years after both of you were reassigned in 2047."

Nick couldn't hide the surprise on his face.

The president continued, her own expression gaunt. "It was his own request, seven years ago, that he be inserted into the World Council."

Nick felt he should ask some question. He had many but wasn't sure which one would be respectful. She looked approachable, trusting. Hell, Gerry had trusted her. "What was his assignment?"

"To become valued, depended upon. To observe. To influence. To report."

"It seemed he was successful. Until last night."

"Exactly."

"What happened?"

"We don't know. His assignment was to observe, as best as was possible, Jason Beck's movements and to support and, when possible, influence Christopher Price."

"Which was he doing last night?" Nick tried not to sound as if he were interrogating the president. He wasn't sure if he was being anywhere near successful.

"As best we can determine, he was trying to infiltrate some neighborhood gang. For what reason we don't know."

"The mission, whatever it was, was unauthorized?"

"After inserting himself into the council, Gerry never worked under any kind of continuing authorization. He had broad discretion. Whenever he started any new activity, he usually gave us either details or general goals."

"Usually?"

The president nodded. "Usually. This time, not."

Nick grimaced. It seemed Gerry had spread very few bread crumbs on his trail. "I want to help. How?"

President Allison leaned forward over the desk. "You knew him better than anyone. Even us. You knew him well enough to find that gray chip you mentioned."

Nick dove a hand into his pocket and pulled out the chip.

The president accepted it but shook her head. "Hopefully, it's something we can access and decode. If the chip contains any answers, someone will let you know immediately."

"Maybe his apartment has the answer—or at least a hint."

"Maybe. Would you be willing to try to find the answer, or at least the hint, if there is one?"

Nick nodded. "Definitely!"

The president nodded her thanks. "It may be extremely dangerous."

Nick nodded back. "It may. And it may not. I'll do my best."

He started to stand and then paused. "Was the vice president on some assignment that got him killed?" He studied her face to read any reaction.

"No, he was not. He would make occasional diplomatic trips to the World Council but nothing that could be considered dangerous."

"Was five days ago one of those 'occasional diplomatic trips'?" Nick felt he was approaching some line of questioning marking the point of diminishing returns.

"Not to our knowledge." President Allison stood and extended her hand. "Thank you, Nick. Gerry, many times, mentioned that you were his role model, that, if anything ever happened to him, I should seek you out. That it was you who found him was Providence's doing."

The three agents walked Nick back to the limousine. A fourth agent was standing next to the driver's door, looking down at his cell phone. One of the three agents stepped to the driver's door and conferred with the fourth agent, still engrossed with his cell phone. The other two moved to the two rear doors, opened them, and motioned Nick to the middle seat. The two agents took positions in the third seat. The third agent slid into the driver's seat.

The standing agent pocketed his cell phone and stepped up to Nick's window, motioning him to lower it. "I'm Sam Kirby, President Allison's lead Secret Service agent." He handed Nick a single cell phone. "One of us will be assigned to you every hour, every day. Any problem, just press Send and we'll be at your side within minutes. We intend to give you considerable freedom—but also intend to keep you alive."

Nick nodded his understanding and accepted the phone. Then, as the agent turned away and started to raise the window, Nick froze.

Sam Kirby had been the key figure on the roof garden with Owen Pendleton.

Agent Kirby walked around the front of the limousine and took the passenger's seat next to the driver.

Nick's noggin was buzzing and itching full bore.

He squeezed his eyes shut and shook his head. Maybe Owen Pendleton was just a prolific and very successful gardener who used only natural growing techniques. Maybe Agent Kirby was only reviewing notations of planting dates and not records of gene manipulation. Maybe President Allison was not a behind-the-scenes puppet master growing forbidden fruit . . . and vegetables.

Maybe. Maybe he'd always have an itch. Maybe this time he didn't want to even *think* of scratching it.

CHAPTER 34

◆

Immediately after being returned to the Stock Exchange building, Nick motored the grid tractor back to the precinct, where he signed out a car and headed immediately to Gerry's apartment. Gerry had moved twelve or thirteen years ago, and Nick had never been to the new home. Gerry's old two-room flat had been spartanly furnished: a kitchen area, table, two straight-back chairs, cooking range, refrigerator, dresser, and a bed.

After only one wrong turn, Nick secured his vehicle in an alley behind Gerry's address.

The apartment was in shambles: dresser and night table drawers pulled out and strewn on the floor; three picture frames pulled off the living room wall; toilet tank pulled over; heating vents ripped out; the single police radio smashed; clothes pulled out of the two closets, many slashed and left on the floor; and refrigerator contents dumped in the sink and on the kitchen floor. Most interesting to Nick, a series of indents just above the floor-level wall molding and probably a hundred or more gouges all across the floorboards.

Nick reached two conclusions immediately. First, a group of thugs had been looking for something—something they didn't find in any drawer or in any toilet and had tried the floorboards as a last resort before coming up empty. Second, Gerry's apartment had been tossed *after* he was killed. Otherwise, the search would have been more selective, more secretive, more tidy.

Nick wasn't surprised the thugs had failed to find anything. Gerry, more than anyone he knew, was always one step or more ahead of any adversary, and by the look of the thorough mess in the apartment, this was one hell of an adversary.

Nick shook his head, trying to make some sense of the scene and of Gerry's murder. A determined adversary had searched for something Gerry Martin was believed to possess and had come up empty. If Gerry indeed had something of such importance, he would not have left it in his apartment.

Nick concluded that someone was convinced Gerry had a secret: something to hide, something that could harm that someone. If so, where? How had Gerry kept one step ahead this time?

Nick remembered Gerry several times saying "The way to keep steps ahead is to sometimes keep steps behind." It had never made any sense to Nick at those times and didn't make sense now. He scratched behind his right ear. The closest he could come was something like, "Keep ahead by remembering where you've been." Big deal. It still made no sense. It still—

Of course! Nick smiled. Had to be.

Gerry had told him all about this apartment when he moved. He had gone on about everything—the number of rooms, the neighborhood, the purchase price—as he gave Nick a copy of his new door key. Nick had never used that shiny new key like he had the old key to the old apartment. Gerry had never mentioned what he'd gotten for his old apartment. What if he'd never left it? There were many more apartments in New York City than people when he had moved. What if Gerry had kept his old apartment?

Nick remembered where he still had Gerry's old key. He needed eighteen minutes to return to his own apartment, then nine more to cover the six blocks to Gerry's old digs.

Nick spent another hour walking in random directions at each intersection, keeping a close eye to his left and to his right as well as behind. When he was confident that he was not being followed, he moved into an alley three blocks from Gerry's old building. Alleys were almost always shielded from any video surveillance.

The ease of entering the building suggested to Nick that few people still occupied its floors, which was fine by him.

Nick's old key worked smoothly. He stepped in and was surprised when he threw the switch and the lights came on. He noticed that every window was totally blacked out.

The apartment was still two rooms but was a bit more cramped than he had remembered. Nick saw only one chair but two tables. Both tables were covered with papers, files, and scribbled notes. Three cardboard boxes of manila files were pressed squarely against the wall just right of the door to the bedroom. He entered the bedroom. A small metal box rested slightly askew in the corner by the roughly made bed.

He would start with the metal box. It was closed and, he observed as he picked it up, locked. It was heavy for its size: about fourteen inches by eight and eight inches thick. An eagle with spread wings was embossed on the cover. He left the bedroom and cleared a spot at one of the tables with the chair, set the box down, and sat.

The metal box was thick and would be extremely difficult to force open. Just below the latch were three numbered wheels. A simple trial of one thousand combinations would suffice to get the box open—if, that was, Gerry had neglected to leave some form of self-destruct mechanism inside that would trigger if someone tugged on the latch after trying just a few bad combinations. Nick had never known Gerry to be a neglectful person. The box would have to wait.

Nick pulled the chair to the other table and started searching through loose papers, files, folders—anything to get a handle on what Gerry was doing in the Stock Exchange. He could tell at a glance that most of the loose papers were copies of World Council expense reports. A second glance revealed that none was Gerry's. There were accounts for at least ten different names. Nick smiled. Gerry had always had an eye for detail. He was obviously trying to track down someone. The dates ran from more than a year ago to as recently as a few days ago.

There were only four names on accounts submitted over the past six or seven weeks: Marie Garcia, Harvey Lauter, Duane Evers, and Benjamin Kinner. The four had submitted one expense statement at the end of each week. Duane Evers had the most reports with the most detailed entries. Nick couldn't find any form of marks or notes on any of the reports.

Nick remembered Gerry's long-ago habit of not writing directly on any document—even a copy he himself had made—when he had tracing paper available. He picked one of Duane's documents from three weeks ago and flipped it over and dragged his fingers across the surface. He felt pen impressions in several places. None of the other people's reports had any similar impressions. He guessed that Gerry had had tracing paper on hand and had used it to make a few notes. He lifted the paper toward the light. He could make out some cursive writing and a single arrow pointing to a time and location entry.

Gerry had obviously found something interesting about Duane Evers's entry for that day at 3:17 p.m., when he indicated he was at . . .

Nick blinked. The street intersection was in front of the Stock Exchange.

If this Duane Evers person was involved in Gerry's murder, it didn't seem logical he'd document a trip to the scene just four days before the shooting.

Nick found a pack of six no. 2 wood pencils in one of the cardboard boxes. He folded one of the non-Duane papers in half lengthwise, then in half widthwise, and then pulled out his pocketknife and started to cut and scrape at two pencils' worth of graphite. He pulled together all the Duane expense papers, clearing the table of all others save two blank sheets for his own note-taking. He pulled forward the Duane paper documenting a stop across from the Stock Exchange, flipped it over, felt for impressions, and having found some, pressed his right hand lightly into the graphite dust. He gently passed his darkened hand over several locations on the impressions. He flipped the paper back, held it to the light, and was able to make out, just barely, some written notations. He wrote the date and his own notes on his own, improvised log.

After forty-five minutes, he had found and transcribed seven vouchers with Gerry's tracings.

Looking down at his chronological notes, Nick saw that Gerry had been interested in Duane's movements over at least the past five weeks, with the last date of interest being four days before Gerry's death—the day before they met in the park.

Nick noted one paper from three weeks ago that was of particular interest. That paper had in its upper right corner the tracing impressions of two capital letters—VP—followed by an address with an apartment number. It took Nick several seconds to remember that, whenever Gerry had been involved in stakeouts, he'd always noted in his reports his stakeout position as VP, his vantage point.

Nick's guess was that Gerry had staked out Mr. Duane Evers.

He owed it to Gerry to do likewise. Owed it to Gerry and to the president.

He checked the address again and, realizing it was in a neighborhood with a somewhat-ragged reputation, decided he would be needing help from Howard for any long-term presence. Hopefully, his recent "acceptance" was worth something.

After deciding he would come back later for the three cardboard boxes, he stuffed all the Duane-related time sheets into a bag, rolled it, and tucked it in a jacket pocket. He pushed the chair back, grabbed the metal box, and left.

CHAPTER 35

◆

Jason Beck answered the phone on the third ring. He hadn't been expecting a call from Bert until his usual reporting time and had been wrapped up in drafting his speech to be given before the lighting ceremony in Manhattan. He had completed it and was ready to start drafting the words he would deliver after the lights failed to respond. "Hello, Bert."

"Big news, sir."

Jason rolled his eyes hopefully. "How so? Is this related to Detective Garvey?"

"In a way."

Bert always had to be hurried along. "In what way?"

"The limousine went to a motel in Georgetown, stayed for about thirty minutes, and then returned with the detective to Manhattan. He was dropped off at his own car, and the limo continued north."

"And where did Detective Garvey go then?"

"That's not important right now, sir. It's where the limousine went."

Jason exhaled deeply. "And where did the limo go?"

"It parked in front of a building with a roof garden. I had put an autotrack on one of the passengers in the limo. He was the only one of four who got out of the limo."

"And where"—another deep exhale—"did this passenger go?"

"Into the building and up to the roof."

"And out to the garden."

"Yes, sir."

"And how do you know there is a garden on the roof?"

"Pure luck, sir. I happened to locate a camera on the roof next door."

"Next to the building with the roof garden."

"Yes, sir." Bert's voice was getting a little excited. Jason could tell his wheelchair minion was nearing the point of his call. "Did I tell you I had the passenger on autotrack?"

"You did," Jason affirmed, his eyes shut.

"I was sleeping when the alarm went off."

Jason, eyes still shut, was starting to wonder if the point would be reached within the next twenty-four hours. "The alarm?"

"Yes, sir. Remember many years ago when you gave me a list of people you wanted tracked using our first facial-recognition algorithm?" Bert didn't continue, obviously waiting for an answer.

"Yes, I remember. That was over twenty-some years ago. I thought you had discontinued that specific tracking since it was unreliable."

"You never told me to discontinue it, sir."

Jason gritted his teeth. "Fine. I never told you. What triggered the alarm?"

"It wasn't a *what*, sir. It was a *who*."

"Fine. Who triggered the alarm?" Jason's right fist was clenched tight.

"I thought he was dead, sir."

"You thought *who* was dead?"

"Owen Pendleton, sir."

Jason's eyes flew wide open. "He *is* dead. Burned to a crisp. Sixteen years ago."

"No, sir. He's alive. It's him."

"How are you so sure? Wasn't it nighttime?"

"I double- and triple-checked. It was dark, but I was able to grab control of the roof camera next door so that, an hour ago, when the morning light was bright and he came out again into the garden, I was able to zoom closer and double-check again. It was him, sir. No doubt about it."

"Thank you, Bert."

"Do you want me to do anything, sir?"

"Thank you, but I'll take care of everything."

Jason hung up and immediately dialed a two-digit number.

Seven rings.

The line clicked open.

"Jeremiah?" Jason said, wasting no time.

"Yes, Mr. Director."

"I have a mission for you that may require quite a few of the Council Guards to carry out."

Details and timing were given and accepted.

Jason hung up. His right fist was still clenched.

He had been suspecting that Detective Nicholas Garvey had his box. A longtime partner and friend of Gerry's would be the logical handoff if Gerry was at all spooked. But if Owen Pendleton hadn't burned up almost twenty years ago, there was an excellent chance that the metal box with its eagle was in his apartment, that Gerry Martin had never had it.

Whatever. It wouldn't exist for long.

CHAPTER 36

◆

"It's a good thing you brought me into this," Howard said as Nick pulled close to the curb and turned off the motor. "The leaders here think city cops are good for one thing: dog food."

Nick turned toward him, eyebrows arched. "I wouldn't be wrong guessing they have big dogs?"

"And hungry too."

"And hungry too," Nick said, grinning as he echoed the words.

"Kidding aside," Howard said with a frown, "this is the harshest neighborhood in Manhattan. There's only a small group responsible for citizen safety, and I use the term *responsible* with reservation. They're months, if not years, away from being able to provide consistent street security. This neighborhood, as I'm sure you're aware, has been the responsibility of three different groups over the past five years. This last group, who we'll be meeting with shortly, has been the most positive, most beneficial, but still lacks a firm presence. They're still working out how to live with the World Council Police, who have two facilities within this neighborhood: one a training center, the other a detention building. They've agreed to the Treaty of Neighborhoods, but only reluctantly. They don't want to anger the Council Police, and at the same time, they don't want to offend the other neighborhoods. They're still finding their legs, their balance. As for city cops—"

"Dog food?" Nick offered.

"For starters. They're disorganized but can cause you big problems. I've been trying to work up a relationship with Alexander, their leader, but it's in its infancy."

"Does Alexander have a last name?"

"Not that I've heard from him or any of the others," Howard replied as he climbed out of the car. "Follow me." He motioned to the front door of Mama's Baked Goods and Noshery.

Inside were seven men, including one seated at the farthest of five in-line tables. Six men, split three and three, were standing along opposite walls of the room. The man at the table motioned for Howard and Nick to join him.

"Thanks for meeting with me, Alexander."

Howard received a questioning nod. While still staring at Howard, Alexander nodded toward Nick. "His name?"

"Nicholas Garvey," Howard replied before Nick had a chance to answer.

Alexander nodded, no longer questioning. "The cop and your newest citizen."

"You heard."

Still not looking at Nick, Alexander said, "What does he want?"

"He wants to spend some time in an apartment in your neighborhood."

"Why?" With that one-word question, Alexander shifted his gaze to Nick.

"A friend of mine was murdered farther uptown, and he had ties to an apartment in your neighborhood."

"And what are you going to be doing in the apartment?"

"Observing."

"Observing what?"

"I'm not sure. All I have is a name. I don't know where this man lives. I know he doesn't work in this neighborhood. Other than that, as I said, I'm not sure."

"Well, I'm sure. Sure of what you will *not* be observing. You will not be observing me or any of my men. You will not be observing any of our women. You will not be observing from any location other than that apartment."

Nick hastened to assure Alexander. "Agreed."

"I know you're the cop who shot that stalker and his dog. I know you saved an infant from being kidnapped. I would like to believe your heart is in the right place." Alexander's gaze was steady, his eyes burning into Nick's. "But if you pull any smartass stuff, I'll make very sure that heart stops beating. Understood?"

Nick nodded. "No problem."

"I'll be the judge of that."

CHAPTER 37

◆

The building itself was unlocked but not the apartment Gerry had chosen. Since he had not found a key, Nick was left to his own devices, realizing quickly that his lock-picking skills were significantly rusty when it took him almost three minutes to gain access to the apartment.

It was evening, almost seven, and dark.

Using just the downward-pointed beam from his flashlight, he made a quick tour of the three-room apartment and got a feel for the layout—a big room facing three windows, that room separated from a kitchen by a dust-covered peninsula, across from a door to a single bedroom—before retracing his path in methodical steps, double-checking each corner, each wall, each floorboard.

After almost two hours, it was the floorboards in the big room that caught his attention—three floorboards, to be exact. Three small scuffed areas—silver-dollar-sized—revealed where Gerry had set up a tripod. Nick nodded. Had to be a tripod. Its two back legs were close to parallel to the apartment's street-side windows, the front leg in line with the center of the group of three windows. Standing by where the back legs would have been, Nick estimated the distance to the window at about ten feet. He paced it off. Three strides made it between nine and ten feet.

Gerry had been using either binoculars or a video recorder to observe one of the apartments across the street. The distance from the window precluded all but three apartments, none having any window blinds, each in the same vertical line—one directly opposite, one above, and one below. He pulled out his own recording binoculars, scanned the three, and chose the lowest. Gerry would have the best unobstructed view into that apartment, the other two, with every window starting about four feet above floor level, presenting greater obstruction because of viewing angle.

Nick pulled up a straight-back chair, faced it away from the center window, spread his legs, and sat facing the window with his elbows braced along the top of its back, his hands holding the glasses to his eyes.

Hours passed, and Nick sat still. He checked his watch: 4:37 a.m.

Another hour dragged by. The start of his shift had to be much less than three hours away.

His back and legs were starting to get stiff when he muttered that he was getting too old for this. He checked the time again: 5:52 a.m.

He dropped his right hand to massage his thigh when a light went on in the apartment. He surveyed the room. There was a desk against the wall on the left and a sofa in the center farther back. Nothing else was visible. Slim pickings, but this was the view Gerry had chosen.

For several minutes, he saw just the light. For another few seconds, he caught a glimpse of a pair of trousered legs—a man's—as someone walked right to left, then back. Then he saw nothing for another ninety seconds until a young man sat down at the desk.

Nick pressed the binocular Record button and zoomed in for a reasonably clear view of the left side of the man's face.

"Damn!" Nick said half aloud. He recognized the scar. It was the man captured on video who had exchanged words with the soon-to-be-dead Secret Service agent.

He zoomed further in as the man started writing—left-handed—on a pad. The writing broke into blurred pixels, forcing Nick to zoom back to a sharper view. It was a pad of at least twenty pages, the top few of which might reveal what had interested Gerry and perhaps led to his murder.

The writing took a while, each line taking two to three minutes, with frequent checking of some source on the desk above the pad and just out of view. Arm motions when the man was not writing suggested to Nick that a book was being continually checked, pages being flipped back and forth. The writing and pausing and writing and pausing took almost a full hour and two sheets before the man stopped.

Nick watched him stand and then rip off the top two sheets, fold them twice, and stuff them into his trouser pocket, the right one. As Nick expected, the next four or five sheets were ripped off, as well, removing any possibility of tracing the entries. This Duane Evers, assuming that was his name, was no rookie.

The man stood, slid a book down from the top of the desk, picked it up, walked out of Nick's view, and turned off the light illuminating the desk. Some slight illumination, probably from a hall light, remained. Nick was willing to bet his reputation that the retrieved book was the man's information source book.

Nick checked his watch: 7:07 a.m. Go-to-work time. The remaining light was turned off. The scribe was leaving the apartment.

Nick put the chair back as he decided to leave his station as well and follow the man he assumed was one Mr. Duane Evers of the World Council.

His shift would have to wait.

CHAPTER 38

◆

Nick hurried to the ground floor and waited for his target to emerge and turn to Nick's left. Watching through the lobby windows, Nick waited until the man continued walking past the intersection before he moved out. Nick turned to his right, walked to the intersection, crossed the street, paused for several moments while he scrutinized the street layout ahead, and then crossed back to his target's side of the street, where he headed in the same direction at more or less the same speed. There was less chance for him to be spotted by the target, since he would have to stop and look behind him enough times to recognize a pattern.

The man he figured was Duane Evers was just a bit more than two blocks ahead. Between the two of them, Nick counted seven people moving with or against their flow just on their side of the street. Nick figured he could shorten the distance to about a block and a half without creating suspicion. He decided to cross to the opposite side every two or three blocks to vary Duane's background.

Seventeen blocks later, Duane crossed the street and entered a coffee shop. Nick, who had returned to the same side of the street as Duane, kept his pace constant, walking past the shop to just before the next intersection, where he found a store with a small alcove from where he could watch the shop without being spotted.

Nick was aware that the old Stock Exchange building was just two blocks farther on. He thought of Gerry and gritted his teeth. He didn't know the exact density of coffee shops in Manhattan, but there had to be several good ones within four or five blocks from Duane's apartment. There was something special about this particular coffee shop, and Nick figured it wasn't the coffee.

Nick eased up on his teeth-gritting just as he spotted Duane exiting the shop. He was holding a drink in his right hand and a partially wrapped item in his left. He took about ten steps back toward his apartment, hesitated for a moment in front of a trash can, and then turned toward it, lowered his drink to the sidewalk, unwrapped what Nick guessed was a donut, and stuffed it into his mouth. Nick shook his head. No donut, like no coffee, was worth seventeen blocks.

He couldn't see Duane's hand dip into his right pocket, but he did see it holding something as it moved up to his mouth in a dabbing motion. Nick watched as the napkin equivalent was then wrapped up inside the donut wrapper and flipped into the trash can.

Duane picked up his coffee and continued walking back in the direction of his apartment.

Nick knew he had to get to the trash can before anyone else did. He was confident that what Duane had wrapped in his wrapper were his notes written ninety minutes ago. How to see the notes, snap a picture of each, replace them, and not arouse suspicion?

The question was answered as he spotted a drunk trying to navigate the corner across the street. The drunk was one store down the side street, staggering from side to side as he slowly achieved an approximation of forward motion.

Nick decided to risk letting Duane get five or six blocks ahead as he slipped into a shuffle rather than a stagger. His clothes would suggest that he would not be super drunk, but his plan required he be only one drink shy.

He slowly approached the intersection, wrapped his left arm around the lamppost, circled it completely once, and then lurched into and partway across the intersection. Nick hesitated and then returned to the curb, his shoulders slumping slightly with each step. As he approached the curb, he fished his cell phone from his pocket, covering it with his right hand. He did a forward-then-back two-step while climbing atop the curb. Upon achieving his prior elevation, he executed a slow left face, then a right face, then a left face again.

Nick straightened up, took three measured steps toward the trash can, and then, still twenty feet away, let his shoulders slump back and allowed a little left-then-right motion creep into his shuffle.

At the trash can, finally, he braced himself with both hands, gripping the basket as if deciding whether this might be a good spot to empty his dinner from the night before. He saw the food wrapper atop the trash in the half-filled can.

Nick straightened up again and held his phone up about six inches in front of his face. Slowly, he moved his right hand and phone to his left, then back to his right. As his hand and phone were returning to his left, the phone slipped into the trash can.

Nick shook his head in a what-the-hell motion. He straightened for a moment and then lowered his head and both hands into the basket. He retrieved his phone, quickly opened the wrapper, and saw the expected yellow sheets. He flattened the two sheets as best he could, clicked off two flash pictures of each, and then rerumpled the sheets into the wrapper.

No more than ten seconds had elapsed. He made a show of wiping his phone on his right pants leg. He figured six or seven wipes would suffice to cleanse his phone of any fictional grime. His phone now clean, he saluted the trash can and shuffled off in the same direction taken by Duane, who by now was probably a good eight blocks ahead.

When he reached the corner, he repeated his left-arm wrap around its resident lamppost, paused, looked right, looked left, paused, looked right again, and then shuffled left and crossed the street. He continued shuffling straight ahead to the next corner, where, finding yet another lamppost, he did a slow, full 360-degree turn, checking for anyone tailing him. Satisfied, he crossed to the right, maintaining his shuffle for another two blocks.

He had to get back to Gerry's stakeout and check out his treasures, but first he had a shift to start somewhat late. He resumed a normal gait—and then some.

CHAPTER 39

◆

N ick made it to his desk just forty-five minutes after the start of his shift. Tim greeted him with a quick reference to "bankers' hours."

"Sorry," Nick said.

"Where the hell you been the past two days? And what was behind that message yesterday about the president?"

Nick motioned Tim into an empty office, closed the door, and brought his partner up-to-speed on everything: how he had discovered a living corpse named Owen Pendleton, how he had discovered Gerry Martin had been working off and on with the president, how he had met with the president, how she'd had very little reaction when asked about the vice president, how the Secret Service was somehow supporting and/or protecting Mr. Pendleton, how Gerry had been tracking a World Council employee named Duane Evers, and how that Mr. Evers was the second man in the video to greet the murdered Secret Service agent.

He didn't tell Tim about the two messages he had retrieved from a trash can and nothing about Gerry's old apartment. Some itches were too vague to share at the moment.

After Nick finished, Tim shook his head. "Better you than me."

"Anything new on the vice president?"

"We've backtracked just over a week, following his limo in reverse back to when he came into Manhattan via the Lincoln Tunnel. Nothing suspicious there, so we started tracking the guy you've now identified as Duane Evers."

"Anything pop up?"

"Nothing. He's quite adept at avoiding continuous video tracking. We'll be following his outside movements for a block or two, but then he'll turn a corner and we totally lose him. We've tried tracking him after the murders as well."

"And?"

"And nothing."

"What about the captain? What does he—"

"Mayor called him to his office. Captain says to continue the video search."

"How can I help?"

Tim suggested forming two teams to check different videos. Tim moved with Fred to a second monitor, while Glen and Nick took the first.

Six hours later, Tim called out, "Got him again—for a few moments, at least!"

The video was date-tagged four days before the vice president was murdered. Duane Evers emerged from a restaurant three blocks from the World Council building. He was accompanied by one fairly obese man. They paused for several moments on the sidewalk, exchanged some words, and then left in opposite directions, with Duane returning to the World Council. The time stamp indicated it had been almost four in the afternoon.

"Rather late for lunch," Tim mumbled.

"Maybe not," Nick offered. "Maybe they started at noon, and Duane's buddy weighed only a hundred pounds then but was really, really hungry."

Tim shook his head. "Maybe."

Captain Gilmore entered the precinct and marched right up to the video team. "Status?" he said in a tone just shy of barking.

"Not much," Tim said. "We've gone back three weeks before the murder and have not captured that senior agent even once. We did, however, capture the man he met with the day he was shot. We found him every day. By himself. The one exception, four days earlier, here meeting with one very fat man."

Captain Gilmore gritted his teeth and shook his head.

Nick stood up and stretched. "What did the mayor—"

"Off the deep end. All precincts have been put on extended-duty time—twelve-hour shifts—until all threats have been neutralized. He has decided to close all bridges and the two tunnels into Manhattan, with only federal grid workers allowed passage."

Nick sank back into his chair. "Twelve-hour shifts. Do we get credit for time served?"

Tim tried unsuccessfully to suppress a chuckle as Captain Gilmore first glowered at Nick and then rolled his eyes.

"Any current trace of those phony trucks?" the captain asked.

Nick and Tim shook their heads.

Nick stood again. "Not since I went down the rabbit hole."

Tim agreed. "That probably tipped them off."

"How far back in time can you retrieve video?"

Tim looked at Fred.

"A week to ten days," Fred said.

"Go back to the rabbit hole and before. See if you can find where those trucks go. I'll keep the mayor off our back—at least until tomorrow."

The two teams returned to their screens. After another three hours, they managed to get a video of one of the two-digit trucks in motion. Tim and Fred managed to review at least two hours of video before and after in many different directions. By eight in the evening, they had tracked one truck backward to the Yonkers border. Just before nine, they had tracked it forward to the same location.

Glen shook his head. "I can't access any video beyond that border. They appear to be using some unusual encryption. Long Island I could handle, but not Yonkers. Sorry."

Nick nodded. "We'll pass the location on to the closest precinct. Can you set up some sort of continuous video capture of that area?"

"Yes. It will take about an hour or less."

"Most likely nothing will show, but at least we'll have it covered. When you've finished, pack it in for the night. I'm sure the mayor will have new adventures for us in the morning."

Tim didn't even try suppressing a chuckle this time.

Before he left, Nick sent two cell-phone pictures to the lab printer. He folded the two printed sheets and slipped them into a pocket.

Nick returned to Gerry's vantage-point apartment immediately, the photos of the two messages burning a hole in his cell phone.

He locked the door behind him and moved across the dark room to the small table. After pulling out his flashlight, he spread the two sheets and started at the top of what he decided was the first page. There were twelve rows of sets, each set consisting of three numbers separated by dashes. Each number in a set ranged from one to four digits, with each number set on a row separated by a comma.

Nick scanned the rows of each page, counting sets per row. Three minimum, five max. He nodded. Obviously a book code. First number in a set pointed to a page; second, down to a line; third, across to a word.

One problem.

Many of the numbers for line count and word count were of the three- and four-digit variety. He doubted any book had 8,073 lines per page, let alone 459 words per line. As to the number of pages, he thought back to the view through the scope and surmised that the book itself couldn't have been more than 250 pages long—much less than the suggested. He moved the light to the second page and then down to the fifth line—much, much less than the noted 7,623 pages.

Nick retrieved his binoculars, remembering the book and its cover had been pulled down into view for just a moment before the lights were turned off. He scrolled backward through the footage until he came to a frame where the cover of the book, after zooming in, was visible in reasonable detail. The cover was a dull yellow and bore the World Council logo and the author's name: Christopher Price.

Interesting.

A book written by Gerry Martin's boss was being used to encode messages from Duane Evers, a World Council operative, employee, flunky, subdirector, or whatever, and that same Mr. Evers would eventually drop the messages into a garbage can two blocks from where Gerry had been murdered.

Damned interesting.

Nick made a quick trip to the bathroom, closed the door, and turned on the light. As he washed his hands, he looked in the mirror and shook his head. His thick dark eyebrows above his eyes were now matched by equally thick and dark bags below them.

He decided that immediately returning to his own digs was a good idea, one that would afford him about six hours' sleep before morning, when he would confront Gerry's boss at the World Council.

CHAPTER 40

Jason's Bert-only phone rang at 8:42 a.m. "Yes?" he answered.

"Detective Garvey just entered your lobby."

"And?"

"And yes, I'll train additional World Council hardware on him starting . . ." Jason thought he heard Bert's chair moving and a switch or two being thrown. "Starting now."

◆ ◆ ◆

After passing through two security checks just inside the old UN General Assembly building, Nick marched straight across forty feet of tile floor to the lobby desk stuffed right under an overhang that looked like the outside edge of a hundred-yard cement boomerang. That overhang was the second floor. There were two more floors with their own boomerangs.

"I need to talk with Christopher Price," he said, showing his shield.

The young man's face started to transform into a no-chance-in-hell expression.

Before it gained voice, Nick held up his right hand. "Call him and tell him I have information and questions about Gerry Martin."

The expression changed to "if one quick call will get this nut off my back" acceptance.

The call was placed.

Nick wasn't sure how he should work Director Price. He had been Gerry's boss, and from everything Gerry had mentioned about him during their too few meetings after Gerry had joined the World Council, Director Price had been a good and square shooter.

But that was his—Nick's—opinion of Gerry's opinion of Director Price. He now had to walk in blind. That meant that, for the time being, he should look out for and avoid walking on as many eggshells as possible.

Seven minutes later, Director Price appeared at the desk. "What information do you have about Gerry?" Price's eyes searched Nick's.

"I have more questions than information."

Price exhaled. "And they are?"

"My first question. Who is Duane Evers, and what is his position here?"

The director gave a slight flick of his head and led Nick over to the open stairway that went up for fifteen steps and then did nearly a 180 back for about forty more steps. Nick wondered if in the old days any adventurous youngster had ever skateboarded down to the ground floor.

After reaching the second floor, Director Price led him down three crossing hallways to an empty office. "Why do you want to know about Duane Evers?"

It was plain to Nick that he'd have to give information to get information. Ah, well. Screw the eggshells. "I have reason to believe he is somehow connected with Gerry's murder."

"What reason?"

"Gerry was surveilling his apartment, and yesterday Mr. Evers went seventeen blocks out of his neighborhood to leave a message just two blocks from where Gerry's body was found."

Director Price chewed at his lower lip for several seconds. "Duane Evers is Jason Beck's sole assistant, his go-to man, his—"

"His cleanup man?" Nick finished.

Price nodded. "Yes, but I don't think—"

"I do!" Nick said, his voice heavy.

Price took a slow breath. "The message. You said he left a message. What was it, and to whom did he give it?"

"It was a coded note left in a garbage bin, and I didn't stay around to see who retrieved it."

"Were you able to decode it?"

"No, but I know it is a book code: page, line, word. I've also seen the book but don't have a copy."

"Then you don't have much other than conjecture."

"I was hoping you might be in a position to help, might know the book."

Price suppressed a half chuckle. "How would I know the book?"

"I think it's a World Council book of some sort. It had the WC logo."

"We publish many books. I can take you to our store back off the lobby. There must be over a hundred different titles there. Would that help your investigation?"

"It didn't look like a typical souvenir book." Nick pulled out his cell phone and thumbed up the picture. "It also has a name on the cover. See?"

Price's eyes widened as he saw the book cover. His shoulders sagged, and to Nick's ears, his slow sigh sounded like a moan. Price took several deep breaths. "There are less than twenty copies of that book, and none are supposed to leave this building."

"Unless . . ." Nick prompted, watching the director's expression transition from confusion to concern and finally suspicion.

"Unless he has special permission."

"From . . ." Nick continued the prompt.

"From higher up."

Nick decided to prompt no further.

"Stay here," Price said. "I'll be back in about ten minutes."

Nick moved behind the one desk in the room and sat in its chair. There was no outside view, which was probably why the office looked barren and unused.

Director Price returned in nine minutes with a brown bag. "I'll have to walk you past security with this. It should help."

Price kept the bag under his arm as they walked back to the lobby.

"If I'm right," Price said as they walked, "Gerry mentioned a police officer he used to work with. He didn't mention a name, but—"

Nick nodded. "We did. Nine years."

Price accompanied Nick past both security stations and to the front doors. "Should you find anything, Detective Garvey, please let me know."

Nick shook Price's hand as he accepted the bag. "You'll be the first to know. The killers, second."

Price nodded his thanks.

Nick walked through the doors and turned right uptown, toward his precinct.

Price watched Nick go, started to turn back to the security stations, and then shook his head and walked out and to the small park across the street. He sat on a bench facing the World Council building for nearly half an hour, his attitude and demeanor one of a man contemplating one of the great mysteries of life.

Thirty years ago, there had been only one passion in his life: how to defeat starvation, the scourge killing millions each month in Africa, Asia, and South America. He had decided that would be his life's mission, his crusade, less than a year after graduating from Dartmouth.

He had clipped a few bond coupons and financed the graduation present to himself of a year's travel around the world. His plan afterward was to return to the States and become a lawyer, businessman, teacher—whatever. His plan was altered by the second hundred thousand swollen bellies, bone-thin arms and legs, and vacant eyes occupying the faces of dying three-month-old babies, their mottled lips unable to suck milk from their mother's shrunken breasts. Before he encountered a second hundred thousand, he had decided the salvation of his soul depended upon his doing something—doing *everything* to end the evil plague surrounding him, a plague previously always safely below his horizon.

First, his eyes were opened. Then his trust fund. He would defeat the evil in Ethiopia first. Then . . . then he met Gabrielle, an ebony-haired Christian aid worker attached to the regional Red Crescent. Her green eyes and her soft way with dying children captivated him. Apparently, he captivated her. She soon became one level more important to him than fighting starvation. They were married after just three months, just after they moved their operations to Yemen.

For two years they wrestled with local bureaucrats for medicine, food, and doctors. She would tackle local mayors, police chiefs, and warlords head on for food, water, and promises to stop fighting for as little as two hours so they could rescue injured children and their mothers. For two years they made love under mosquito netting. For two years he contacted bankers for donations, begged doctors with and without borders to staff their huts for at least a week, and bribed hospital officials to overorder and then redirect lifesaving medicines. For two years they were inseparable, working, sweating—she looked super in fatigue pants and a man's shirt—and saving lives together.

After two years, he had an opportunity to return to New York City to present to six different charity groups in the hopes that at least three of them would fund permanent hospitals and secure food distribution centers. He was reluctant to go without her, but she insisted, telling him with a kiss that, if he didn't go, there would be no mosquito-net time for a whole month.

He left for the planned two weeks.

Three days later, she was crushed to death when more than half a million starving men, women, and children converged on their food center.

He saw replays on CNN. Shot from a hovering helicopter, the footage showed what looked like a million iron shavings suddenly finding a magnet. Four food tents were the magnet. An unending sea of emaciated souls were the shavings. The tents were completely trampled. It took three days to count the dead: 17,512. The injured were twenty times that number. None of the aid workers survived.

Chris never returned.

Jason Beck contacted him within hours of the CNN broadcast. He refused to take no for an answer when offering to share his apartment with Chris. That half year with Jason saved him from drinking a full bottle of something and then going for a midnight swim in the Hudson.

Finally, he looked up, his eyes clear. He stood and walked back into the World Council building.

CHAPTER 41

◆

When the blue light flashed on his phone, Jason picked it up immediately. "Yes, Bert. I assume this second call is important."

Bert assured him that it was, that just a few minutes earlier Detective Garvey had met with Christopher Price in the lobby of the World Council building. He relayed everything his videos had captured, from them talking to the detective showing Director Price something on his phone, to their moving to a room on the second floor, to the director going alone to his own office and retrieving a small book with a yellow cover.

"He grabbed a rumpled lunch bag from his wastebasket and stuffed the book inside and returned to the second-floor office."

Jason could hear Bert pause to take a deep breath. He figured it best to wait out the pause in Bert's rush to deliver the news.

Finally, Bert got his wind back. "When I returned to the director going back into that lobby-floor room, it was no more than a minute when they both came out. The director turned back to the elevators, and Detective Garvey left the building."

"Who had the yellow book?" Jason asked.

"The detective, I think. His jacket pocket had a bulge about the right size. Oh, and the director didn't take an elevator. He left the building and crossed to the park across the street. He sat on a bench for twenty-eight minutes doing nothing, last I checked."

"Thank you, Bert."

"Do you want me to check back on Director Price?"

"No, but continue to keep tabs on Detective Garvey."

"Will do."

Jason was about to break the connection when Bert spoke again. "I'm running short of puppies."

Jason shook his head. "You'll get more by this evening."

He had just cradled the receiver when his secretary appeared on his screen, announcing, "Director Price to see you, sir."

Jason tapped the Admit button. Apparently, Christopher wasn't still in the park.

Christopher's demeanor, as he walked through the opening glass doors and right up to Jason's desk, was uncharacteristically casual and loose. Jason's second in command was always ramrod stiff, as if braced against the world lest something cut him down. But right now, standing across the desk, Christopher Price looked surprisingly relaxed.

"Please, Chris," Jason said, motioning to a chair, "take a seat."

"No, but I thank you. I just wanted to stop by . . ." Chris nodded, as if confirming a thought. "Just wanted to let you know I plan to leave the World Council." He smiled across at Jason. His eyes widened. "Immediately. I forgot to say *immediately*."

Jason motioned to the chair again. "Chris, please. Take a seat."

Chris sat.

"What?" Jason started. "Why? Did something happen?"

"No, nothing happened," Chris assured him. "I just realized I'm tired." Chris cocked his head slightly, as if calibrating something. "So very tired after so many years."

Jason seldom was caught off guard. This was one of those times. "Can I—" He corrected himself. "Can *we* change assignments around? Give you different responsibilities? Give you more assistants? Give you—"

Chris shook his head. "No. I'm just so tired."

"How about we arrange for you to take some time off. Six months or a year could refuel you, recharge your batteries. You could take time to write that book on overpopulation you've always talked about. "You could—"

"I no longer care about population. Over or under. Haven't for months. No, *years*."

193

"But remember, Chris. Remember what you told me after you recovered from that Yemen thing? You explained to me that all those humans were starving to death not because there wasn't enough food in the world; *they were starving because there were too many humans.* Remember?"

The corners of Chris's eyes constricted. "You're wrong, Jason. I never recovered from that 'Yemen thing.' You're right, though: I do remember saying the problem was too many humans. I also remember you, right after that, jumping up from your writing desk to prance around the coffee table, chanting, 'Footprints! Footprints! Of course, footprints!' You grabbed me and hugged me, announcing to the invisible world, 'It's not how large any one footprint is. It's the total *number* of footprints.' After that, you charged back to your desk, crumpled all the papers you'd been working on, and then pounded away on your laptop, creating a new mound of pamphlets."

"So you never believed population needed to be controlled?"

"In the beginning, I did. It seemed the most workable solution. But as growth turned into decline, innovation plummeted. I could see, of course, ever larger populations were only part of the problem causing poverty and starvation. For years after Yemen and the population restrictions, everywhere I looked there were dozens of new regulations each and every day: what you can and cannot do, how much you can do, where you can do it, and what hour—not hours—you can do it. Regulations killed not only the unseemly but progress in medicine, in food technology, in energy innovation, in—"

"Okay, okay." Jason waved a hand, hoping for silence.

"Not okay, Jason. Population growth was not the problem. It was tapering to a sustainable number, to where the world would be in balance."

"Balance?" Jason blurted out.

"Yes, balance. Balance with the environment. Balance with humankind's ability to provide sustenance. Balance with innovation, allowing manageable increases in population. Balance—"

"Enough. You sound . . ." Jason shook his head. "You sound . . . *unbalanced.* If you felt so strongly, why didn't you convey your misgivings to me?"

194

"Because the whole world was too far down the rabbit hole—a hole you were most invested in."

Jason gritted his teeth for just a moment and then reminded himself how that might look. "Chris, we need you. The council needs you. I need you. You have years of experience and knowledge that can't be replaced. That can't be—"

Chris raised an open hand. "The council doesn't need any one person. Well, other than you. You are the brains and the face of the World Council. I've just been fortunate enough to be along for the ride and to be able to contribute, in spite of my 'misgivings,' an occasional positive idea now and then."

Jason could see that Chris had made up his mind and wasn't about to change. "So maybe you'll write that memoir and dedicate it to Gabrielle."

Chris blinked, and his jaw tightened for a moment. He chuckled. "She would like that. But no, I've learned that writing is not my thing. All I want to do is retire and . . ."

"And what?"

"Retire and kick back. Maybe even buy a fishing rod." He stood.

Jason also stood and shook Chris's outstretched hand. "Take care, Chris. And if you need anything, anything at all . . ."

Chris nodded, turned, and left.

Jason watched Chris on his screen as his former partner walked down the hallway. As Chris turned left into his office, Jason alerted his secretary that he was not to be disturbed until he signaled.

Jason spun his chair 180 degrees and stared, unfocused, out the windows at buildings and ancient, virtual images—images of old-world kingdoms and empires.

Jason reflected on Chris's long association with the World Council. To the world outside, Chris was a key director with great responsibility and power exceeded only by Jason's. Through all the years, Chris had been critical to the favorable image the council projected into the world. Even in the halls of the World Council, Chris was respected and revered, all that regard being critical to the growth of the council.

Jason concluded he'd have to decide if the council was big enough to continue extending its reach without Chris Price. Chris inside the council was no problem. Chris outside the council could be an extreme danger ... a danger Jason was reluctant to tolerate.

He called Bert and instructed him to restore outside tracking of Chris, including tapping of all his phones.

He ended the call and resumed staring out the windows, turning various end-game scenarios over in his mind.

CHAPTER 42

◆

Nick had just returned from his lunchtime visit to Sandra's hospital bedside when Tim stopped him short.

"A call came in on your phone while you were out." Tim's expression was one of what-didn't-you-tell-me-this-time? "I've been instructed to tell you that the Gardener has been taken."

Nick answered with a grimace, which he sensed told Tim he was indeed short on some key information. Nick took a breath. "He's an old rooftop gardener up in Howard Williams's neighborhood. He's the living corpse I told you about yesterday. Was there anything else in the message?"

"Just a return number." Tim handed Nick a piece of paper. "Might this be part of the 'president's in danger' investigation?"

"Somewhere between definitely and remotely. I'll fill you in after I call this number."

Nick went into an empty office and dialed his cell.

"Hello." It was Howard Williams's voice. "Nick?"

"What's this I hear about the Gardener being taken?"

"He was pulled out of his building by a contingent of World Council Guards. They shoved him into a paneled van and took off south. I figured they'd be taking him to the council's Detention Center in Alexander's neighborhood. He confirmed it."

"Do you think Alexander would be open to our running a rescue operation on his turf?"

"As long as he can be far in the background. Same as I'd want in our neighborhood."

"I've been in that facility three times in the past eight years, and they ran things pretty tight. There's very little chance of success if we were to storm our way in. I think I need to be arrested, and I need to bring my partner, Detective Tim Branson, with me. To Alexander's, not to jail. I need him to help me plan my arrest."

"I think you're right about not forcing our way in. Alexander says the place is near impregnable."

"Can you lay your hands on some Council Guard uniforms?"

"We've got ten or twelve."

"Only need four, one of them a sergeant's."

Howard suggested they meet where they had met Alexander before. Nick hung up, rejoined Tim, filled him in on what had happened and on what passed for a plan, and told the captain they had an assassination lead and had to follow up immediately.

"I guess I would be advised to choose early retirement over this rather than being fired," Tim said as they took the stairs down to the garage.

Nick chuckled his agreement.

On the way, Nick filled Tim in on what had happened the past few days: meeting with the president, finding Gerry's notes, shadowing Duane Evers—pretty well everything except the real identity of the Gardener. That bit of information Nick decided to keep from Tim and from everyone else. For now.

Alexander met them in his alleyway. "Detective Garvey," he proclaimed, extending his right hand. "Howard said he has the uniforms. He also said—and I'm quoting him exactly"—he fixed his gaze on Tim—"that 'Detective Tim Branson is also trustworthy and should not be shot on sight.'"

Nick smiled and nodded. Tim thanked Alexander for following Howard's recommendation.

Alexander took them inside to his office. He motioned them both to sit. Then, looking at Nick, he said, "Howard said you think it best to get arrested to get inside. I think you're right. The best time for your 'arrest' would be third shift, about a half hour after midnight. That shift is covered by Council Police rookies and near rookies. The Council Guard whenever it is involved in an interrogation seldom stays that late."

"But will the Council Guard do something to the Gardener before third shift?"

"Definitely. He'll probably be interrogated. The intensity of said interrogation will depend on who ordered his arrest."

"Do you know how many Council Guards went in?"

"Yes. And we'll know how many come out before midnight. I assume you're going in, regardless."

"Regardless. I need to change my appearance in case there's an old-timer janitor who recognizes me. I was assigned there for three days the last time; don't want to be stopped at the door by the cleaning crew. I also need to ditch the phone in my jacket somewhere uptown. It's being used to keep track of my whereabouts."

"Gotcha. I'll take care of that, and I have someone who does makeup quite well."

"Big help. I'll need you—or a lawyer, if you have one—to work with Tim to concoct a believable arrest warrant stating why I'm being brought in and why, as an important capture, I should be locked up for later interrogation."

"Hopefully, locked up next to the Gardener."

"Hopefully, but doubtful. I just need to get inside the building."

"With luck, you'll just have newbies to deal with."

"Isn't there some type of commander? I thought all shifts anywhere in the Council Police had to have a senior officer with experience."

"This commander, one Lieutenant Marcus, has a sweet tooth that only a certain lady can satisfy. He steps out at least three times a week."

"Three times a week? Must have a large sweet tooth."

"Don't know the size of his tooth—or the size of anything else he has, for that matter." Alexander stood and headed for the door. "Back in ten," he said over his shoulder.

Nick huddled with Tim to discuss the crime he would be arrested for committing. "The grounds for arrest have to be obscure, but the implications possibly far-reaching—far-reaching enough for me to be interrogated for more than just five minutes. It might be worth weaving in the Stock Exchange building and, separately, construction truck no. 48."

By the time Alexander returned with a man and two women, Nick and Tim had worked up a broad and, hopefully, enticing set of warrant details. All that remained was to have them converted to legal jargon. To Nick's surprise, the two women were lawyers and sat down with Tim.

The man, with a large canvas purselike bag hanging from his left shoulder, shook Nick's hand and introduced himself as Dusty. He sat Nick before a mirror and started making spread-finger measurements of Nick's face.

"The eyebrows have to be thinned," Dusty said. "Drastically."

More finger measurements. "Your cheeks, forehead, and neck have a good weathered look. That stays." He looked up at Nick's hair. "Good luster. About 15 percent gray in the dark-brown mix. I'll up the gray to about fifty-fifty. You have some deep bags under your eyes. I'll leave them. Guess you haven't gotten much sleep lately." Dusty squinted at the top of Nick's nose before touching with his left forefinger. "Two pronounced creases running about an inch above the brow line. They fit with the weathered look but are too recognizable. I'll cover those, and I'll make your mouth fuller, less . . . less tight at the lips. Your chin is so firm and prominent I won't be able to soften its structure, but I can give you a dimple. When I'm finished, your own mother wouldn't recognize you."

Dusty retrieved a couple of small bottles from his canvas bag and started applying a foundation two shades darker than Nick's facial skin.

Alexander sat next to Nick and observed the transformation process. "If they lock you up, how are you going to escape?"

"With lock picks."

"Lock picks?"

Nick nodded. "Each of the three times I was inside that building, I was charged with springing a fellow NYPD officer or detective that the World Council Police or Guard had captured and stuck in a cell. I got all three out: the first two within hours, the last over the three days I made a pain of myself. The second time I took pictures of all the cell doors and exit doors. From the pictures, I could see which locks were involved. From that I was able to work up a set of lock picks I proved worked on identical locks."

"Okay. You made a set of lock picks. You'll never get them in. You'll be searched from head to toe."

"The picks are already hidden in the center. Seven copies, to be exact. One set for each cell."

"How could—"

"My third time in the center. I made sure they worked, then hid them in each cell. Several places in each cell. It's an old building, the Detention Center, and isn't in the best repair."

"I have a retired locksmith who can make picks that open anything. He works fast. I'll get him on something in case yours were found."

Nick shrugged and nodded. "Couldn't hurt."

"Okay. When you get out of the building, then what?"

"The Hudson River is right behind the building. A motorized raft would be quite handy."

Alexander grinned. "Howard said he was running one down."

Nick's chin was covered with a fake beard, and both of his ears enlarged and pulled closer to his head. The makeup was applied slowly and with care.

Around 10:30 p.m., Howard and four other men were shown into Alexander's office. They conferred with Alexander, and at 11:30 p.m. they started suiting up in the World Council Guard uniforms.

At 12:17 a.m., one of Alexander's men entered and gave his chief a folded sheet of paper. Alexander said that all Council Guards observed entering had since exited. Alexander chuckled when he reported that the Detention Center's lieutenant had been observed stepping out and heading in the usual direction.

"Man's gotta get his exercise. Looks like your adventure's a go— with minimum senior presence."

Howard and his four men and Nick hit the alley, climbed into a look-alike council van, and moved off, heading toward the Detention Center.

CHAPTER 43

◆

The five fake Council Guards hustled Nick into the Detention Center at 1:09 a.m.

Howard, dressed in his sergeant's uniform, marched up to the booking counter and dropped an official-looking folder on the granite top. "I have a prisoner delivery for Captain Marcus."

The young man with one stripe swallowed quickly. "Captain Marcus had a personal emergency and had to step out."

Howard suppressed a chuckle. Twenty minutes earlier, they had watched as Marcus left the center, walking briskly to his "personal emergency" five blocks away. They had given him ten minutes to let his emergency become intensely personal. Alexander had assured him that Marcus's trysts never lasted less than two hours.

"Who, then, is in charge?"

"Officer Pryor," the young man offered with another quick swallow.

"And is Officer Pryor available?" Howard asked sternly, knowing that council policeman second-grade Pryor had left the building seven minutes after Marcus's personal emergency. Alexander hadn't been able to provide a purpose for Pryor's excursions, but he assured Howard that they always lasted at least ninety minutes.

The young officer behind the counter was swallowing repeatedly at this point. "Officer Pryor is not available." Another quick swallow. "Perhaps I can help?"

Howard nodded. "Perhaps you can." He motioned one of his men to bring Nick forward. "See the handcuffs? Remember 'prisoner delivery'?" Looking to his left, Howard saw the positive answer to his next question. "Do you have an empty cell?"

Rapid eye-blinking replaced swallowing. "Yes. Yes, we have some just inside, and—and others downstairs."

"Just inside will be fine."

The eye-blinking slowed as the young man tapped several keys on a computer. Within thirty seconds, two other men appeared from the rear areas.

The young man looked up at Howard. "First, we'll have to strip him, search him, and lock him down."

"Thank you. We'll wait until your men have done that."

"Will you be interrogating him?"

"No. I'll be calling in one of our experts first thing in the morning." Howard looked at the three cells just inside. He could make out someone lying on a cot in the center cell. He motioned inside. "In the meantime, lock him up in one of those cells."

"Are we required to feed him? We had to give the elderly man in there two meals."

Howard tilted his head as if mulling over the question. "No. No food. In my experience, an empty stomach helps interrogations pull out more information."

The young man gave a relieved nod.

"Just leave him alone," Howard advised. "Let him stew. Let it sink in where he is and what's in store for him."

"No problem, sir."

Howard motioned his four men to leave as he took station, standing directly opposite the middle cell. He stood, looking official, for the ten minutes he figured it would take for Nick to be returned.

The elderly man in the middle cell eventually raised his head from his cot and looked over in Howard's direction, a quizzical expression on his face. He started to push himself to a sitting position.

"Plant yourself back in your bed," Howard whispered. "I know you know about putting plants into beds."

The man's brow furrowed and then eased as recognition started to take hold.

Howard shot him a quick wink, flicked a needlelike device onto the man's cot, and then returned to station.

"Sergeant Williams!" the booking desk officer called out. He was waving some papers at Howard.

Howard stepped back into the entry room and back to the counter, where he signed the second-to-the-bottom line on the transfer papers. He looked up. "It needs your signature too."

"Of course," the young man said and signed his name.

Howard ripped off his copy, returned to his station, and waited for Nick to be returned to his cell.

Owen Pendleton remained still on his cot, wondering what a man from his neighborhood was doing dressed up in a World Council Guard uniform and why he had thrown something on his cot. He looked on top of the blanket to the left of where he was sitting. He picked up the item, an L-shaped device with the longer leg having irregular bumps and indents. It wasn't metal—probably ceramic or something similar. He shook his head, deciding he was getting too old to wrestle with happenings beyond his control.

Owen was soon to learn some things were not beyond his control.

Nick, dressed in prison drab, was marched back to the cell area, and, with a healthy push, shoved toward the cot in the leftmost cell. The cell door was locked after him.

Howard stepped to that cell, grabbed the outside handle, and gave it several strong tugs. The cell door clanged and clicked but remained solidly locked. He indicated his approval.

The two men who had processed Nick returned to their stations somewhere in the bowels of the Detention Center.

Nick gave a slow tilt of his head to Howard, signaling all was okay. Howard left.

Nick checked that there were no council personnel in the room holding the cells. Satisfied, he went to the rear of his cell, where the wall joined the floor just short of where Owen's cell began.

Nick started scraping at the six-inch section where he remembered burying one of his lock picks.

He scraped off nothing but dirt. He tried harder but found that the section had been covered with new epoxy.

He stared into Owen's cell. It too had a more solid look than he remembered. Time for plan B: a trip to the bathroom, where he'd hidden yet another pick. Failing that, plan C.

Before Nick could search his memory for a possible plan D, Owen stood and walked to their common set of bars. He held an open hand. "The man that brought you in threw this onto my cot."

Although he'd never seen it before, Nick recognized the item immediately: the ivory lock pick Alexander's friend had rubbed into a freedom pass.

Nick grinned and took the pick. "Thanks, Owen."

Owen shuddered and then stood straight, defiant. "I don't know you. How do you know my name? No one knows my name."

"More than a lucky guess. I've watched you check your plant beds. I've watched Sam Kirby and two others review various plant data with you on your rooftop. I've heard Howard Williams relate how you provide various foods to his neighborhood. I've—"

"Who is Sam Kirby?" Owen asked, worry creeping into his tone. "I know Howard Williams, but . . . who are you?"

Nick's eyes widened. "Do you know Lenora Allison?"

Owen's eyes narrowed. "If you mean the president of the United States, no, not personally."

"I believe you," Nick replied, not really sure why he did.

Owen took a step back. "Who are you?"

"The man who's going to get you out of here."

Nick shot a glance at the front desk to see if he and Owen were relatively free of observation. He was satisfied and was about to turn to the task at hand when he caught sight of a tall Council Guard marching through the front door and stopping at the desk.

"Commander Jeremiah" were the muffled words Nick heard through the glass paneling.

The young council cop behind the desk nodded and waved the commander in as Nick eased back to his cot. He watched as this Commander Jeremiah, about six foot two and definitely athletic, strode purposefully up to Owen's cell, pulled a key from his right trouser pocket, and unlocked the door.

The man motioned impatiently at Owen. "We've got a few more questions to be asked and answered."

This Commander Jeremiah struck Nick as a no-nonsense Council Guard who knew how to handle himself in any situation. The way his eyes swept every corner of the hallway and of each cell when he approached told Nick this dark-haired tall officer was not to be trifled with.

Owen emerged slowly from his cell. He and the commander went into the back rooms.

From what Nick remembered, the nearest interrogation room was four offices down on the left. From the reference to "a few more questions," Nick guessed he had maybe five minutes to get ready. He checked the front desk again. The young cop was looking down at some papers.

Nick slowly rose and edged to his cell's door. He inserted the pick and started to work it side to side and front to back. After about thirty seconds, he heard an audible click as it released.

He checked the front desk again and saw that the desk cop was turning his back to the front desk, apparently looking for something.

Nick eased out of his cell. Trying to be as quiet as possible, he opened the door to the front area and started toward the desk.

The young man was still riffling through some papers. As Nick, avoiding casting any sound or shadow, moved around the far end of the desk, the officer started to turn back, having found what he was looking for.

Nick slammed the side of the man's head with the paperweight from the counter. The officer sank quickly and quietly. Nick checked for a pulse. Weak. He unsnapped the officer's holster and removed the pistol.

Nick stripped himself and the young man. He swapped clothes and, holding the pistol, draped the man's arm over his shoulder and hefted him into what had been his cell. Nick laid the man facedown on his cot and then returned to the front desk. He positioned a small mirror so he could view the cell area.

Another two minutes passed before he finally saw the door beyond the cells open. After glimpsing Owen and his interrogator, Jeremiah, Nick turned his back to them and began to shuffle papers, all the while watching the cell area through the mirror.

Jeremiah, holding Owen's right arm, opened the center cell and gave Owen a push inside and then locked the door. Nick watched as Jeremiah stepped to Nick's old cell for a moment and then turned toward the front desk. Nick kept to his paper shuffling.

He watched Jeremiah's reflection as he approached the desk. He could feel Jeremiah pause behind him.

"Officer Landstrom, I need to exit."

Nick turned and pointed the pistol between Jeremiah's eyes. "If you don't want a permanent exit," Nick said as he flipped a set of plastic handcuffs to Jeremiah, "you'll put these on behind your back and we'll go back to the cells."

Nick marched the compliant Jeremiah to Owen's cell and opened it. "Time to go, Owen. Double occupancy is not allowed."

Owen complied nervously.

Nick motioned Jeremiah to kneel on the cot facing the wall. Once Jeremiah assumed the position, Nick wrapped duct tape twice around his head, covering his mouth.

"Lie down," Nick commanded.

When Jeremiah was down, Nick wrapped duct tape around Jeremiah's feet and the right bedpost.

He turned to Owen. "Let's go. We haven't much time before someone will be missed or someone shows up."

Nick led Owen down the corridor past the interrogation rooms to the end of the hall, where they turned left and then right to the rear door.

Nick turned to Owen. "We'll have to run about fifty yards. The alarm will go off as soon as I open this door, but we should have more than enough time."

Owen nodded. "Thank you. I'm glad to get away from all those questions."

"Why did that Jeremiah officer come back? What did he want that he didn't get on the first interrogation?" Nick asked the questions offhandedly as he worked on the exit-door lock.

"He didn't interrogate me when I was brought in. I didn't even see him until just now. He wanted to know if I had some old metal box."

Nick's mind seized on the words *metal box*, but only for an instant. The lock clicked open, and the alarm started shrieking.

"We head for the river, Owen. A motorized raft awaits."

CHAPTER 44

◆

With the alarm wailing, Nick pushed hard against the door. It opened slowly. Nick took two steps out and checked every direction. Nothing. He reached back into where Owen was shrinking back in the dim inside light and pulled him forward.

"Gotta go, Owen." Nick pointed in the direction of the river. "Stay right behind me. We want to land in the raft, not the water."

Forty strides brought Nick to the edge. He looked down and spotted Alexander smiling up at him. Nick turned and helped Owen step down into the raft, after which he jumped in. Immediately, the electric motor, already running, kicked into high gear, and they were off.

The raft did a U-turn and headed south, contrary to Nick's expectations.

He leaned over toward Alexander. "I thought—"

"Council Guard boat. Headed here almost as soon as the alarm went off."

Nick nodded as Alexander kept the softly humming raft speeding south. Just before Battery Park, Alexander steered into a jetty, snuggling the raft under the overhanging boardwalk. Two minutes later, a council powerboat churned slowly by. Three men could be seen on the deck, scanning the shoreline with binoculars.

After the boat was well past them, Alexander cut the motor and stood. "I phoned for our pickup. We'll leave here and have to walk six blocks."

The three men climbed out: first Alexander, then Nick, and finally Owen, whom they helped gain stable ground.

"Follow me," Alexander said, waving over his shoulder.

Jason had been expecting a call from Jeremiah for the past two hours. When he saw the ID, he picked it up before the second ring.

"Jeremiah?"

"Yes, sir. I meant to call earlier, but the rescue was much earlier and a bit more violent than we planned for. One of our men is in the hospital."

"Was the rescue successful?"

"Yes, but not as expected."

"Explain."

"We had been monitoring unusual movements from Penn-Jersey into Manhattan, per your suggestion. The Secret Service agent you alerted us about never surfaced and was never a part of the rescue. The group was probably local. Council Guard impostors brought in an arrestee, who was locked into a cell adjacent to Pendleton's. I went there just before two a.m., per plan, for further interrogation."

"About the box?"

"Yes, sir. I grilled him for ten solid minutes about the box. I described it in detail, using your information: dimensions, ornamentation, etc. Nothing."

"Are you sure?"

"Yes, sir. I can spot lying at a hundred paces. Pendleton has never seen the box."

"Where is he now?"

"Walking north from the Battery Park area. They headed south from the Detention Center in a motorized raft. We lost them for about two minutes but doubled back and found their raft, abandoned."

"I see."

"Do you want us to intercept them? It would be no problem."

Jason thought for a moment. "No. Find where they go."

"I've got video of all who were in the center. I'm sending it to you now."

"Fine. Thank you, Jeremiah. Good job."

"Thank you, sir."

Alexander had several of his men join their march as they passed some of the intersecting streets. By the time they had eight blocks behind them, there were a dozen additional men in their group.

Nick turned to Alexander. "I thought we were planning on six blocks."

"We were. Change of plan. We're being followed."

"Are they grouping to attack?"

"They just seem to be watching our movement, not gathering strength. If they do attack, they are dead men. They've seen our numbers grow, so they'll keep their distance."

Alexander directed the group into a building on their left. As they approached the lobby, doors were opened, and the group moved through. The doors were closed, and the bulk of Alexander's men stayed near the doors. Nick, Owen, Alexander, and three others moved farther into the lobby, where they turned their flashlights on and entered into a stairwell and down two floors.

Alexander motioned to an office on the right. They entered, and all sat on the several couches arrayed against the walls of a room about fifteen by fifteen feet. "We'll stay here until I get the all-clear signal. No one's putting us in a box."

Nick sat next to the trembling Owen. "We'll be okay, Owen. Alexander here knows what he's doing. Like he says, he won't let anybody box us in."

Owen shuddered for a moment. "I know," he said, looking at Nick. "But everyone keeps talking about boxes."

"Sorry," Nick said, trying to reassure Owen.

"I know. I just hope there's no eagle on our boxes."

"I don't think—" Nick looked askance at Owen. "What eagle on our boxes?"

"The box that man interrogated me about. He said it had a raised eagle embossed on the lid."

Suddenly, Owen was the center of Nick's universe, the surrounding room blurring out of focus. "Did he say how big the box was? "

Owen nodded. "He said it was about the size of a shoebox. I told him I never saw it. Just like I said."

Nick leaned closer to Owen and was about to ask his own questions about the box when Alexander stood.

"Our followers have passed by. Time to go."

Jason called Bert as soon as the videos started downloading.

"They're clips from very early this morning, almost forty minutes ago. I need any identification markers you can use to tell me who these men are."

"No problem," Bert assured him. "I'll get you an answer, probably within a couple of hours."

CHAPTER 45

◆

Finally, after almost an hour, Alexander ushered Nick and Owen into a nondescript building and instructed them to have a seat.

"This is my safe house. We'll be secure here." He turned and started walking farther into the interior. "I'm making myself some breakfast. Anybody for scrambled?"

Nick and Owen raised their hands at the same moment.

Nick turned to Owen. "Had your interrogator asked you about a box before I was brought in?"

"No. Just that one man, and just at that one time."

"Did he ask about any people? Any names?"

"He did ask if Seth Morris was my nephew."

"Was he?"

"Yes. And I told him that he was."

Nick stopped for a moment and squinted his eyes at Owen. "The name Seth Morris is vaguely familiar."

"Saint Vartan Park. Almost twenty years ago. He was found dead, tied to a swing, shot in the head."

Nick remembered. He and Gerry, still patrolmen at the time, had found the body. The case had been turned over to some detectives but never solved.

"Did your interrogator say your nephew had the box?"

"No. He seemed to know he didn't. He asked who Seth's friends were. I only could think of a couple of names."

"Was Gerry Martin one of those names?"

"No. I don't remember any friend named—" Owen paused, his brow suddenly furrowed.

"Yes? What is it?"

"I think . . . I think I remember my nephew mentioned that name—or one a lot like it—a couple of times when he was in high school and visited me for a couple of days. I just remember the name, not if they were friends or anything."

Jason got Bert's return call fifteen minutes after giving him just one hour to identify the group who had dragged Owen Pendleton out of prison. He could almost see Bert smirking on the other end of the line. Jason knew Bert always tripled the time projections he gave.

"Results?" Jason asked.

"Yes, sir. Not all the men, just one."

"Which one?"

"The prisoner in the cell next to Pendleton: Detective Nicholas Garvey."

Jason sat silently as his mind raced. "Thank you," he finally mumbled, and broke the connection, then started drumming his fingers atop his desk. His jaw muscles tightened, grinding one set of teeth against the other.

The situation was far from out of control but did require some meaningful tinkering of trajectories. Owen Pendleton: freed from prison and on the run but, according to Jeremiah, knew nothing about the box. No problem at the moment. Not worth any action.

Sam Kirby: not observed at the jailbreak. President Allison's lead agent with some kind of involvement with a supposed dead man. Another reason against liquidating Pendleton.

Detective Nicholas Garvey: although a new factor, involved up to his eyeballs. Treading lightly here might pay dividends. He'd met Allison. Distract him enough, and he might lead to who had the box. Given the right plan, distraction of the meddling detective could be transformed into full control. Jason was confident he'd come up with the right plan for the detective.

Another name found its way into Jason's thoughts: Christopher Price. Detective Garvey had met with Chris and soon after Chris had resigned from the World Council. It was doubtful he knew anything damaging, but he'd been around long enough to learn how Jason did things.

Jason reached into his desk drawer, pulled out his thin cell phone, and sent a numeric text: "7.05."

Jason arrived at his location no. 7 more than ten minutes early. He allowed himself the extra time to review the situation.

Chris was leaving. He was now a loose end, and if there was anything Jason hated, it was that. Loose ends meant a loss of leverage, and if it turned out there was only one secret to universal power, leverage was that secret.

He wasn't worried about Chris over the short term. His twenty-seven-year second in command would, he had no doubt, kick back and relax for the next three or four months, recharging depleted batteries. It was the long term that concerned Jason. Chris's admission that he no longer cared about population control—hadn't for years—was his concern. Too much population for the earth was his major leverage with him. It was what kept him in the council's orbit.

Jason stared out at the Hudson River. Should he plan for the short term or long? Over the short term, he had President Allison and her damn energy grid. Over the long term, he had President Allison to bring back under his control. Carter Johnson would be a bit easier—but just as important. Each had an independent streak that had to be channeled.

He realized both the short and long term presented pretty well the same challenge: neutralizing two enemies that were enemies of each other. Once neutralized, they could be controlled. Maybe, Jason thought as he looked away from the main riverway to the crumbling concrete of the near seawall, "marginalize" was a better choice than "control."

Yes, *marginalize* was the right word. After her grid was shown to accomplish nothing, Allison would lose credibility and, most importantly, the mantle of hope. When her big project failed, people—and the associations—would see all glasses as half empty and leaking fast.

Jason nodded to himself as he spied the other man arriving, exactly on time. Both the short and long term were going to require high focus on his part—focus that the Chris situation could only disrupt.

Jason got out of his car and walked straight to the other man. "Christopher Price," he said, handing over the usual dossier with pictures and schedules. "Accidental." He paused momentarily as he handed over the folder. "Accidental and public."

"And the time frame you need is what?"

"As soon as possible." Jason turned to go and then spun back around. "By Monday," he said with an emphatic nod. "Since it's early Saturday, you've got almost the whole weekend to plan."

The other man gave a can-do nod and walked off as Jason returned to his car.

CHAPTER 46

◆

Nick was still wrestling with the image of the metal box with the eagle when Howard finally arrived. With bad news.

Howard turned to Owen. "Your roof garden is crawling with Council Guards, as expected. You cannot return. Our whole neighborhood is filled with regular Council Police, again, as expected. What wasn't expected is that they seem to be setting up permanent residence. They have moved furniture and material into three abandoned buildings in our neighborhood. Again, you cannot return."

Owen, sitting in an easy chair, nodded, his face somber

Alexander motioned for Howard and Nick to take a seat at the table. "What do you propose be done, Howard?" Alexander asked.

Howard curled his hands, currently resting on the table, into tight fists. "There's not much we can do. Our priority, first and last, should be to get Owen to somewhere safe."

"And where might that be?" Alexander prompted.

"God only knows." Howard slumped back in the straight-back chair, his expression more one of exhaustion than of defeat.

The three of them discussed alternatives for several more minutes.

Nick reached into his pocket. "I may know someone who can provide an answer."

He told them who that someone was. After some discussion, they finally agreed to let Nick make the contact.

Nick pulled out his regular phone and called President Allison.

There was a short pause before the line started ringing. Three rings passed before the line clicked open.

"Hello. Detective Garvey?"

Nick took a quick breath and exhaled. "Yes, Madam President."

"You had the phone we gave you dropped off in Central Park. We've been unable to contact you."

"Intentional, Madam President."

"And your reason?"

"I decided that it was the best way to keep your Secret Service from disrupting our rescue—our *successful* rescue—of Owen Pendleton from the World Council Guard."

Her silence was telling. As he counted off the seconds, Nick could almost sense President Allison's surprise.

"Madam President?" Nick prompted.

"Why exactly are you telling me this?"

"A week ago, I saw your Secret Service agent, Sam Kirby, walking with Owen through Owen's rooftop garden."

More silence.

Finally, she spoke. "Is Owen safe?"

"Yes, but we can't keep him here."

"Where are you located? I'm dispatching a detail to pick up Owen and protect him."

"Excellent, Madam President," Nick replied, giving the location for pickup after reading a note shoved in front of him by Alexander.

Alexander, Howard, Nick, and Owen were quickly relocated to a deli six blocks away. When three agents walked in less than ten minutes later, Nick figured President Allison had several Secret Service crew stationed throughout Manhattan. Kirby was not among the three, but Nick caught an expression on Owen's face that told him that Owen recognized at least one of the men.

The senior agent stepped in front of Nick and held out a small gray cloth bag tied shut with string. "The president told me to give this back to you. Scans revealed nothing's inside."

Nick opened the bag and overturned it. The gray chip tumbled out.

The agent watched as Nick turned it over several times in his hand. "I was told that it's slightly magnetic but nothing else."

Nick started to return the chip to the bag.

"I recognize that chip," Owen said, stepping closer.

Nick's eyes widened. "From where?"

"My nephew had one just like it in college. It was the fob on his key chain. It had his dormitory room number stamped on one side."

"What was your nephew's room number ?"

"Three oh five."

CHAPTER 47

◆

Nick finally got back to his apartment. He'd had a harrowing day but knew he probably had several hours of coffee and staying awake ahead of him.

The box Owen's interrogator had asked about—the very one Nick had brought back from Gerry's apartment—was lingering in the back of his mind. But for now he had some serious decoding to do. He pulled out the book Chris had given him and set to work.

The projected several hours stretched on. And on.

Nick stood up from his single table and stretched. He'd been struggling with the two sheet images and the World Council book for—he looked at his watch—five hours and had produced only meaningless word combinations. He had to stretch his legs.

He stood and started to pace his two-room apartment. His furnishings were intentionally minimal: a clock and lamp on the table next to the bed, a wastebasket next to the toilet and one under the kitchen sink, the table with one straight chair, one set of dishes, and one refrigerator with an energy storage box that sucked in extra electricity when available and pumped it out when not. He owned no video screens, no photographs. He did have a dozen or more drawings taped on the refrigerator and on several walls in his main room. The drawings had each been done by Nicole, and he treasured them all.

Nick returned to the table.

He had tried page counts starting forward and starting backward, line counts starting up the page and starting down, and word counts starting forward and starting backward. He had started with words at the edge of the page, then at the spine. He combined each with the other. Nothing made sense. Working with just the first ten of the forty-three sets on the two pages gave him nothing but gibberish. Stretching again, he glanced down at his first four ten-word attempts:

exempt dogs stream journey bar recent feet man shape less
bend city link fox help total beverage bounce drink point
keep illegal last liability energy vice empty radio yes tool
note lunch year muscle motion issue dive parameter up

Nick sighed. He was missing something. He didn't believe Mr. Duane Evers had employed a second-order code in which each word would itself point to . . .

Something about the third set screamed, "Look at me!" What about it was worth—

Yes!

The first letter of each word stopped screaming and started to whisper: *killeveryt*. What if he put a space between letters four and five? He'd have *kill everyt*. The message could be *kill everything* or *kill every t* . . . Whatever the message, he was certain it began with *kill every*.

Nick allowed himself one final stretch and sat back down. There were forty-three sets, so the message should have forty-three letters. He would continue with the third line's approach for the next ten sets and see how it worked out.

Fifteen minutes later, Nick had the additional ten words, which produced a twenty-letter string: *killeverytbfpctaaaof*.

Gibberish. Again!

Nick checked his watch: 3:52 p.m. He grabbed the bag he'd picked up at a deli on his way back. It looked like he'd need some nourishment, because it was beginning to look like he had a long night ahead.

He decided to stick with *killeveryt* or *killevery* and spin the next ten sets through his previous seven decode approaches as a separate group.

Nick pulled out a Greek salad wrap and started decoding, chomping almost in rhythm with each page flip. If he'd had a dozen more salad wraps, he would have been able to chomp his way almost to exhaustion.

Nick slapped the pencil down and looked at his watch. He had just decoded what he believed was the message.

It was just past 4:30 a.m.

The message, he was fairly certain, read thusly: *Kill every remaining connection to Nightshade.* What it meant he had no clue. The term Nightshade had never popped up during any precinct briefing, news story, or report. So he had a decoded instruction from one Duane Evers to some unknown person, or group, or organization, or . . . Nick had to admit that without further information, the decoded message was a dead end. He had to move on. To what?

To the box!

He had the box the council wanted. The box that had been in Gerry's possession. The box given to Gerry years ago by Seth Morris. The Seth Morris who'd had a college room with the number 305. The same number scratched into the gray chip, the number that had made him think of telephone area codes.

Nick retrieved the metal box from beneath the floorboards under his bed.

Once back at his kitchen table, he turned the box over several times and several ways. The slight thumping sounds with accompanying slight vibrations confirmed there was something—or some things—inside.

He thumbed the three combination wheels on the front to 305. Nothing happened when he pressed the release latch. He slouched back in the chair.

Damn! A code he could break but not understand. A box with possible clues inside, but a box he couldn't open.

He rubbed his hand across the embossed eagle on the top of the box and wished he could convince the bird of prey to reveal its secrets. Its wings spread almost the full length of the eighteen-inch top. Instead of sporting arrows in its claws like those on some old coins, the eagle's claws were splayed out and held a banner of five geometric shapes, each just slightly indented into the metal cover and each with tiny markings within.

Nick, straining to make sense of the markings, studied each shape. Starting from his left, he noted a circle, a triangle, a square, another triangle, and another circle.

The senior agent that had come for Owen and had returned the chip had commented that it was "slightly magnetized."

Nick grabbed the chip and placed it into the square indentation, room number facing up.

Perfect fit.

He held his breath and paused for an instant before pressing the release latch again.

Nothing.

He flipped the chip so the room number faced down and pressed again.

The box clicked open.

CHAPTER 48

◆

Nick took a deep breath, exhaled slowly, and then reached into the box and grabbed everything he could see.

He pulled out a couple of envelopes and a bulky package wrapped in an oily sheet of plastic, which was tightly wrapped, belt-like, with two passes of duct tape.

He reached for the two envelopes. The first had Director Christopher Price handwritten on its front. The second, Detective Nicholas Garvey.

Nick opened the envelope with his name. There was a group of folded papers and a small voice recorder. He counted seven sheets with various cryptic notations, which he recognized immediately as being the tracings he had already partially decoded.

He picked up the recorder and pressed the Play button. A second passed before Gerry's voice called his name.

"Nick, you're listening to this because you found the magnetic chip I left for you, either on my body or in a wad of chewing gum. Since you have it in your possession, they've killed me.

"I have three favors to ask of you, old friend. First, please give the envelope addressed to Director Price to him as soon as possible. The two remaining favors can wait.

"Second, the folded sheets document my research into the movements of Duane Evers, executive assistant to Director Jason Beck. I've suspected he's involved in the trafficking of infants and children captured by various stalker networks. This suspicion will soon be proven. Again, if you're hearing this, I haven't survived and am requesting you follow up in any way you can.

"Third, the thick bundle of documents wrapped in oilcloth was given to me, along with the box, years ago by Seth Morris, a friend since third grade. I'm sorry that I never told you that I knew him. He was killed because of its contents. I have added a few notes myself to his research. I need the contents given to an authority you trust, but no one inside the World Council should be the recipient, since there are assertions as well as confirmed facts of monumental evildoing by some within the World Council. You'll know the prime suspects when you read the material. I feel you should acquaint yourself with the contents but should take no direct action or investigations.

"You've been a most loyal, honest, and supportive friend, and I don't want you ending up like Seth Morris—or, if you're listening to this, like myself.

"In addition to being executive assistant to Director Price, I have been doing various investigative assignments for a third party in addition to my own, completely separate follow-up on Seth's compilation of evidence of many, many crimes he was convinced were perpetrated by the World Council. I trust this third party completely and have given them your contact information. Should they contact you, it will be up to you to decide if they should get the documents in the oilcloth. I trust you more than anyone.

"While undercover trying to nail down the infant trafficking group, I've recently encountered an operation tied to the World Council with the code name Nightshade. It has something to do with preventing any chance of President Allison's grid turning on even a single lightbulb. My initial evidence and suspicions on this matter are in the envelope for Director Price.

"I thank you for the many years we were partners. You took a young rookie and molded him into what I like to think was a top-notch professional. Let me rephrase that: top-notch means a half notch below you.

"Since I'm recording this the night of the day we met in the park, I've had no chance to unearth anything related to the vice president's murder. Likewise, if any council plan does exist to target President Allison, I wouldn't doubt there's a connection. My sense is that the president is more than capable of withstanding any direct attack. Should you not be playing this, I will keep both ears and both eyes wide-open.

"Looking forward to my erasing this and to us having a very cold beer together—soon.

"Take care."

Nick rewound and listened a second time, trying not to picture Gerry sitting down to dictate such a dismal projection of his future. Dismal and, unfortunately, accurate. He wondered how many previous such messages Gerry had recorded and then survived to erase.

He replaced the seven tracing sheets into his envelope and dropped it along with the recorder into the box. He lifted the wrapped package of documents and held it for several moments, gauging its heft and bulk. He shook his head. If evildoing was afoot, it was one hell of an afoot.

Every fiber of Nick's being screamed to open the package, but it was Monday and his shift started in less than three hours. He'd have to squeeze in an hour or two of sleep. President Allison was scheduled to throw the grid switch Thursday evening. Captain Gilmore would be insisting on overtime, not undertime.

He dropped the package into the box, locked it, and placed it carefully under the hinged section of floorboard, listening for the two barely audible clicks that indicated the two underside latches had locked the four-by-three-foot section in place. He visually checked the floorboard, making sure nothing appeared uneven or marked in any way. Two men killed nineteen years apart was good enough reason for caution.

Nick picked up the magnetic chip and surveyed the room for a safe hiding place. A small diorama taped to his refrigerator caught his eye. Nicole had made it in school and had given it to him over a month ago. It had twigs and small stones representing some type of forest scene.

He had no glue or chewing gum, so he opened an overhead cabinet, took out a jar of peanut butter, opened it, stuck in a finger, and put the small brown wad on the front of the chip, covering the number 305, and stuck it into the diorama.

Plain sight was sometimes the best hiding place.

He set his watch alarm, flopped down on his sofa, and closed his eyes.

The next time he opened his eyes, his watch read 7:12 a.m.

He picked up the envelope addressed to Director Price and went down to his car.

He pulled into the council's garage at 7:29, showed his credentials, parked, and reached the front desk at 7:36.

"I'd like to speak with Director Christopher Price. He said he would meet me here in the lobby anytime I needed."

The young man checked his screen as he punched in an entry. He shook his head. "Sorry, Detective Garvey. Director Price has not been in for the past two days. Can I take a message?"

Nick thought for a moment. "Thanks, but no."

He turned and headed out and up to the garage.

He would have preferred to head back to his apartment and open the oilcloth bundle, but he was going to be overdue at the precinct and decided he at least had to put in a short appearance.

Jason was not expecting a call from Bert, so it took him into the third ring to retrieve the phone from his lower right drawer. "Yes, Bert?"

"It's Detective Garvey again."

"What about him?"

"He was just in the lobby of your building, asking for Director Price."

"Is Detective Garvey still in the lobby?"

"He left less than a minute ago."

"Thank you, Bert. I'll follow up from here."

"There is one thing, Director Beck. I need—"

"More puppies?"

Bert grunted in the affirmative.

Jason realized he had to finalize a plan for handling Detective Garvey. He decided against having the detective killed. He needed him seriously distracted until after President Allison's satellite switch-throwing. If Garvey were killed, the mayor, always nervous as hell, just might get frozen-cold feet and call off the lighting ceremony. That would result in leverage being postponed.

Jason keyed into his terminal the access code for Bert's secret transcribed files on various individuals. After a quick check, he entered the code calling up Bert's file on Detective Garvey. In less than a minute of checking the detective's background, Jason knew the most effective gambit. He keyed a series of instructions into a small tablet computer that he could erase from anywhere in the world.

Jason closed the connection and wasted no time calling Duane into his office.

As Duane entered, Jason motioned him not to sit. "Detective Garvey, the older man in the video with Gerry Martin, has become a minor thorn in the council's side. He needs to have his attention focused in another direction."

"What can I do to help, Director?"

Jason handed the tablet to Duane. "The details are there."

Duane read the three screens' worth of detail and then handed the tablet back. "I'll get the ball rolling immediately." Duane gave Jason a no-problem wave and left.

Jason allowed a quick smile. Always being on top of things allowed supreme flexibility in dealing with any and all problems.

He decided it was also time to distract, or slow down, the grid workers. Their work was essentially finished, so what he had in mind would not impact President Allison's plans for lighting the grid. In fact, it would probably make her more determined to throw the switch.

Jason reached into his desk, retrieved his cell link to Reynolds, and dialed 2666, or BOOM, on the phone keypad, the agreed code for approving the Lincoln Tunnel bomb.

CHAPTER 49

◆

Upon signing in at the precinct, Nick was immediately cor-
ralled by Captain Gilmore, who sent him out to check on
three reports of suspicious activity. All three proved to be no
problem, and he returned and reported to the captain.

Once at his desk, Nick picked up a yellow sticky note. Louise
Braddock had called to tell him that at 3:00 p.m. they would have the
Patrick sisters watch Nicole while Louise took Henry to his annual
physical. Nick nodded to himself and started to read through the
morning and afternoon reports. He was startled when Tim tapped
him on a shoulder and, tilting his head slightly, motioned for him
to follow.

Since the interrogation rooms were all empty, Tim chose the
nearest one and closed the door after them. "I don't know if this has
any impact on your—our—investigation, but . . ." Tim took a deep
breath, exhaling slowly.

"What?"

"Director Christopher Price drowned this morning at 10:17."

Nick's eyes narrowed.

Tim placed his left hand on Nick's shoulder. "I know you
wanted to get to the bottom of your friend's murder and—"

"How did it happen?"

"He was walking north along the bank of the Hudson River,
between Forty-Second and Forty-Third Streets. From what neighbors say, it was a daily ritual before leaving for work."

Nick was trying to process the time frame. He wrinkled his
nose. "But his shift starts at least two hours earlier."

"Several neighbors did mention that. Apparently, he started his walk at about the same time the day before. They figured he was on vacation."

Nick unwrinkled his nose. "So how did he drown walking on the sidewalk along the Hudson River?"

"There was a video camera across the street, so we lucked out and didn't have to rely solely on eyewitness accounts. It seems that, as Director Price was passing a traffic gap in the concrete divider, a small boy was doing a cartwheel, lost his balance, yelled out, and fell into the river. Price and another man raced to the edge, knelt down, and tried to reach the boy. After several seconds, Price reaches down further, as if grasping for the boy—you can't tell from the video—and falls into the river."

"What did the other man do at that point?"

"He immediately lay flat down and stretched his right arm and his chest out over the seawall, his left hand clutching what that precinct's police describe as a two-inch depression in the sidewalk. When they questioned him, he described pretty well what the video eventually depicted. They said he kept berating himself for not being able to swim, damning himself over and over for letting them both drown."

"Sounds plausible, but I gotta see the video."

"Third Precinct has it. I had Glen review it."

It took twenty minutes to reach the Third Precinct.

Nick introduced himself to the desk sergeant, whose desk was so high it was more like a podium. The rest of the squad room was similar to Nick's. Nick guessed the sergeant preferred a high line of sight of any and all desks and their occupants.

The officer, his expression blank, studied Nick's face and then checked the standard screen below the counter ledge. He looked up, his demeanor more welcoming. "Your fellow detective, Tim Branson, called ahead and said you'd be wanting to review the Price video." The sergeant motioned to a young officer across the room. "Patrolman

Joshua Sydney will take you to the viewing room. The video has already been set up."

Nick dutifully followed Patrolman Sydney to a small office almost twice the size of a closet, where he took a seat in front of a screen no bigger than eight inches by twelve.

Patrolman Sydney appeared a bit flustered as he turned on the video machine. "Sergeant Proctor selected this size of screen because the image gets increasingly grainy as the screen becomes larger."

"No problem, Joshua. I just want to see the events myself."

The patrolman seemed startled and then relieved at Nick's use of just his first name.

Nick gave him a smiling nod. "Do you have the witness transcript? The one given by the second man? I'd like to read that first."

"I do. I can," Patrolman Sydney said, snapping almost to attention before leaving to retrieve the report.

It was three typed pages. The questions, answers, and descriptions were pretty much what Tim had said, only with a bit more detail: Director Price and the other man, a Mr. Donald Rupert, forty-two-year-old plumber for hire, had reached the edge within a second of each other. Mr. Rupert stated the young boy's shirtsleeve was snagged on a rough patch of the seawall. He said Director Price had a longer reach than he had and suggested he, Rupert, hold him by one arm while he reached forward to grab the boy's upraised hand. Director Price reached down farther and farther, ever closer to the boy. Suddenly, Price tipped too far, lost his balance, and fell forward, almost dragging Mr. Rupert with him.

Two pages. Nick sat upright, tapping his fingers on the tabletop. He found no fault in the questioning or in the answers. The description itself would have been verified by the video. There were no "red flag" type of comments indicating the interrogators felt the testimony did not match the events.

The third page contained descriptions by the interrogators as to the anguish Mr. Rupert had displayed after not being able to jump in after Director Price and save him and the boy.

Nick handed the folder back to Patrolman Sydney. "Thank you, Joshua," he said. "I'm ready for the video."

The time from the boy's cartwheel to Mr. Rupert pulling himself back and then rolling on his back and pounding the concrete in anguish took two minutes, seventeen seconds. Each action matched the report.

Nick turned to Joshua. "I noticed you set up the video toward the end of the stream. How many days does the video cover?"

"Five, Detective Garvey. It recycles so that the current day is always day 5."

Nick winced. Hopefully, it wasn't too large to transmit to his precinct. "Can you send the whole thing to my desk?" Nick pulled out one of his business cards and handed it to Joshua. "My e-mail is on there."

Patrolman Sydney paused in answering. Nick was positive Joshua was torn between following precinct protocol, which would have meant referring the request to Sergeant Proctor, and honoring the request of an amiable detective.

"Just between you and me, Joshua. No need to bother the sergeant."

The video was waiting by the time Nick returned.

"What did you find out?" Tim asked.

"Pretty well as you described. Two-plus minutes ending in the loss of two lives."

Tim wagged his head in sympathy.

Nick sat quietly at his desk. His fingers started drumming.

"What?" Tim asked.

"Watch the video with me. See if you catch anything."

Tim sat beside him as Nick started the video.

It wasn't until the end of the third viewing that the back of Nick's neck started raising a ruckus. Something was wrong.

Nick restarted the sequence, this time his finger poised over the single-frame advance button. He let the video run until both Price and Rupert reached the end of the seawall and knelt down. He advanced the sequence frame by frame to the moment when Rupert reached out with his left hand to hold Price's right arm. Still advancing one frame at a time but more rapidly, Nick and Tim watched as Rupert used his left hand to pull Price's arm toward Rupert while Rupert moved his right hand to provide additional support. It was at that point that Price moved forward and then over with a sudden jerk.

Nick glanced at Tim, who looked undecided.

Nick and the back of his neck were more than undecided. He restarted the sequence at the beginning, single-frame-stepping through the little boy's cartwheel. Although the image was slightly grainy, the boy's legs appeared much more muscular than those of a six-year-old boy. In fact, the boy's whole body was more muscular.

What froze Nick's mind in its track was the cartwheel itself. He felt the whole thing came across as too professional for a six-year-old. What allowed Nick to shift mental gears was remembering what gymnasts called the dismount. It looked squared off and rock steady. There was a frame-by-frame count of slightly more than a second before the "boy" suddenly staggered the two or three feet to the edge and fell over.

Just before staggering, the boy could be seen moving his head from right to left, as if making sure he was being observed.

Nick relayed his thoughts to Tim. They both agreed: Price's drowning was no accident.

"See if you can find anything else, Tim. I gotta check out the 'accident' site."

CHAPTER 50

$\blacklozenge$

After twenty-three minutes of stating his need to a glaring Sergeant Proctor and then filling out and signing four different forms in triplicate, Nick was reluctantly awarded the use—for one hour—of the precinct's powerboat.

It was obvious Proctor felt Nick was encroaching on his investigative territory.

Proctor rummaged through an area behind the counter, retrieving a three-inch fob in the shape of the USS *Intrepid* with a single key. "Good condition going out, same condition coming back," he said in a warning tone as he handed the key to Nick.

Patrolman Sydney was instructed to take Nick to the skiff and walked him to the boat shed. "The ignition's a bit temperamental. Needs three or more rips with the key."

Nick cracked a smile as Patrolman Sydney swung a leg over the gunwale. "Careful climbing in, Joshua. Ol' Proctor would never forgive you if you fell in and drowned."

Joshua grimaced as he turned back to Nick, just completing his climb into the inboard skiff. "He does come off as a bit extreme, but if you don't mind, Detective Garvey, I've—"

"You've been ordered to stick with me, take me wherever I ask, and to report my moves back to the sergeant. Of course I don't mind. In fact, it'll make my investigation much easier."

Joshua heaved a visible sigh of relief as Nick handed him the key. Nick unwound both the fore and aft mooring lines and took the seat opposite Joshua.

"Where do you want to go?" Joshua asked, cranking the key and depressing the ignition button for the second time, after which the engine chugged to life.

"Down the river to the end of West Forty-Third Street."

Joshua revved the engine and headed out into the river.

Nick stared the half-block distance to the *Intrepid* and shook his head. Even from this distance, he could see the immense patches of rust running along all levels of the great ship's hull. Nick remembered when he had first seen the warship. It had been well over fifty years ago, and his father had taken him to the *Intrepid* and its museum. To his eight-year-old eyes, the vast ship had gleamed bright and bold. Now, as he opened his eyes, releasing that distant memory, the shape was still there, but bright and bold had been replaced by dim and dingy. The key fob looked more majestic than the real *Intrepid*.

As they cleared Pier 86, Joshua turned the powerboat ninety degrees to port and headed south. The next pier would be 84, with his initial goal being a block after.

Pier 83, the old Circle Line facility, had been decommissioned after the sightseeing company's bankruptcy and eventually, twenty years ago, had been torn down. Nick wanted to start where it intersected with Forty-Third Street. It was just twenty-five feet on the Forty-Second Street side of that section where Director Price had fallen into the river.

Joshua maneuvered the boat gently against the seawall, exactly at the Forty-Third Street midpoint. Nick hoisted himself atop the seawall before Joshua could ask what was next.

"Wait here," Nick shouted down to Joshua and then marched straight to the Forty-Second Street marker, turned left, crossed Twelfth Avenue, and headed for Eleventh.

Nick stopped in front of no. 635, the entrance/exit to Price's apartment building. He wasn't sure whether the all-glass facades flanking the doorway were original or of recent vintage. He wasn't even sure what the building had been—a museum, bank, or other commercial structure—before being converted into condominiums.

What Nick did know was that Director Price every morning exited through these doors, turned right, walked along Forty-Second toward the river and across Twelfth Avenue, turned another right along the walkway that started about thirty feet from the seawall, and then angled away before he turned another right onto Forty-Third and walked all the way to Seventh Avenue and Times Square, where he would continue to the East River and then to the World Council.

Everyone questioned said Price walked the same route every weekday morning starting at exactly 7:35. For the past two days, however, he hadn't started until just after ten in the morning.

Something had changed.

Nick decided there was no need to duplicate Price's morning constitutional beyond the point where he had fallen into the Hudson while trying to rescue a little boy who looked more like a midget weightlifter. Nick took off at a brisk pace, his eyes constantly alert to anything, whatever it might be, that could have distracted Price. Nothing presented itself.

Ninety seconds took him to Twelfth Avenue, which, with zero traffic, allowed him to keep his pace as he crossed to the nearby seawall.

Nick slowed his pace, scanning all the structures to his right as he moved along the sidewalk. He stopped when he reached the point where the "accident" had occurred. He turned and looked up Forty-Third. He could see he hadn't reached the middle of Forty-Third, standing just in line with the rightmost curb.

He looked down at the concrete walkway and the concrete leading to the seawall. He reached down and touched both. Pretty much the same hardness and roughness.

If practiced in the art, a youngster could turn a cartwheel or two without getting too many scrapes or cuts on his hands. If anybody tried a cartwheel and fell, their knees or noggin would encounter hard, rough concrete and transmit excruciating pain to the athlete. The youngster on the video had done two cartwheels before sticking what had appeared to be a solid dismount. Nick walked to the point where his best estimate said the boy had landed. It was at least ten feet from the seawall—a rather long stretch for the boy to keep losing his balance before toppling into the Hudson.

Nick crossed to the other side of Forty-Third, moved to the seawall, and motioned to Joshua to hold the boat steady as he clambered down. "Move slowly about five feet ahead," he called out to Joshua, his left foot on the gunwale and his left hand moving up and down along the seawall.

Joshua nodded and moved the boat the requested distance. Nick quickly moved both of his hands up and down the seawall as the boat inched forward.

"What are you looking for, Detective Garvey?" Joshua asked as he responded to another request to move five feet ahead.

"The other man who ran to help with Director Price said that the little boy's shirt was snagged on the rough seawall and that he was just dangling when they got there."

"Are you looking for a piece of the shirt?"

Nick shook his head. "Just looking for a rough spot in the wall."

"I can go even slower if you need," Joshua offered as they reached the end of the second five-foot section.

Nick stepped down from the gunwale. "Thank you, Joshua. No. We've covered more than the spot where the boy fell over. There are no rough spots in the concrete wall that could possibly catch hold of the shirt of a falling body, even the body of a little boy. However, if you'll back up about three feet, there is something I do want to double-check."

Joshua complied and, per Nick's request, held the boat tight against the seawall as Nick placed both feet on the gunwale and stood up straight, the top of his head just barely over the wall's edge.

Nick brought his right hand up to his nose level, about five inches below street level, and stopped any movement for two or three seconds. He nodded to himself and stepped back into the boat.

Joshua waited for the next request as Nick sat in one of the cushioned seats at the stern. After several seconds, curiosity got the better of him. "What did you find, Detective Garvey?"

"A handhold. Freshly cut."

Joshua pursed his lips and nodded, obviously impressed.

Nick stood. "Take us straight out to about twenty, twenty-five feet. I want to get a wider view."

Joshua faced the boat toward the Penn-Jersey shore so as to allow Nick an unobstructed view of the wall. He guided the boat forward the requested distance and held steady at that position.

Nick studied the seawall spot where he had just been, trying to picture a sequence—any sequence—in his mind.

The video had shown six other individuals running up to the edge as soon as the surviving rescuer shouted out for others to help. If the whole thing was not an accident, there had to be someplace where the young boy—supposedly young—could hide before the others rushed to the edge. Remembering video of the supposed accident, Nick estimated the cartwheeling gymnast would have had, at most, twenty-five seconds after Director Price "fell" in.

Nick shifted his gaze to the left, way beyond where he had inspected the wall with his hand. Slowly, he scanned to the right, pausing for a moment at the point of the handhold. He then scanned to the right all the way to Pier 81. Nothing.

He had started a return sweep when he caught it. The choppiness of the river had caused him to miss it before.

"Joshua, bring the boat to the wall about thirty feet to the right of where we were before."

Joshua gave a short crank to the motor, piloting them to Nick's requested location.

Nick motioned to Joshua to cut the motor and join him at the stern. "What is that?" he asked, pointing to some type of metal arch about two feet wide and no more than four inches high at its midpoint.

"It's a drainage pipe. I'm told they were put in about twenty years ago. It's high tide now, and the exit is almost submerged."

"How far back does it go?"

"Maybe a block. Maybe. I'm not really sure."

"Do you know its diameter?"

Joshua scrunched his eyes for a moment. "Three feet at least. Maybe four."

"Thank you, Joshua." Nick smiled at the young man as he reached back and scratched the back of his neck.

"Is there somewhere else I can take you, Detective Garvey?"

"No, I think I have all I need. We can go back. I'll fill you in along the way."

Nick was reaching back for a satisfied scratch of his neck when a gigantic explosion and flames erupted on the other side of Pier 81.

"What was that?" Nick shouted.

"I don't—"

"The Lincoln Tunnel!"

The flames died down within seconds.

Nick beckoned Joshua back to the wheel. "Swing out and around. Gotta see if we can help."

CHAPTER 51

◆

As they rounded Pier 81, they could see that the explosion was not in or near the water, rather a block inland, at least, from the seawall. Flames, smoke, and rubble could be seen far down on the other side of Fortieth Street, somewhere on top of the entrances into the tunnels.

Joshua pulled the boat to the end of Fortieth Street. Nick climbed out and tethered the back end of the craft tight to a cleat. While heading toward the bow, he caught the rope thrown up by Joshua and secured it to a second cleat. Nick reached down and helped Joshua to the pavement.

They turned and started running east on Fortieth. After twenty-five seconds, they reached Eleventh Avenue, where they could see almost a block ahead on their right.

"Looks like it's the one open tunnel on Thirty-Eighth Street!" Joshua hollered next to him, huffing and puffing almost as much as Nick.

They continued on to Tenth Avenue, where they could see a small group of workers and tunnel police racing toward Ninth Avenue, away from the tunnel entrance.

Nick and Joshua stopped to catch their breath. Nick bent over, hands braced against his knees. After five deep breaths, he nodded he was ready.

They reduced their speed to slightly faster than a jog, passing Thirty-Ninth Street, where they got their first good look at the easternmost part of the explosion. Bricks and concrete chunks were scattered across the roadway. Smoke spewed from the tunnel mouth. A few men were still running out from the tunnel. Nick and Joshua continued east for a half block to where the rubble littering the roadway was manageable. They leaped down, landing safely.

"Contact your sergeant!" Nick shouted to Joshua. "Stay here and secure this area out to Ninth Avenue. I'm heading toward the tunnel."

Joshua nodded.

Nick turned toward the tunnel and surveyed the rubble and the few men now scrambling out of the tunnel's mouth. He picked a quick but careful path through and around the piles of jagged concrete and headed toward the tunnel.

By the time he reached the tunnel, the men emerging from it had dropped to zero. The last three men were trotting away, their faces covered in black soot the same color as the smoke still billowing out. There were no bodies outside, or injured slumped or standing. Nick shook his head. A miracle.

Nick was about to turn back to see what help he could offer Joshua when a lone figure emerged from the tunnel, thrashing his arms to wave away the smoke.

Nick started toward the man, planning to see if he could be of any help. When he closed to within twenty feet, he stopped, his eyes wide.

He recognized the man: Captain Charles Reynolds.

Nick raced to Reynolds's side. "Captain Reynolds, are you all right?"

"Huh? Who are you?" Reynolds's soot-soaked expression was impossible to read.

"Detective Nicolas Garvey. Two weeks ago you helped me capture the scumbag who beat up my daughter and tried to escape through your tunnel."

Reynolds started to shake his head no but stopped. "Yea-a-a-h . . . yeah. I remember. How is your daughter?"

"Still in the hospital? How are you? And your officers?"

Reynolds weaved slowly to the nearest pile of rubble and sat. "I got most of them moving out as soon as the fire started. A few were farther in the tunnel. Doubtful they made it." He turned back toward the tunnel. "Damn!" he muttered. "I gotta go back and see if I can—"

Nick stepped in front of him and pressed both hands on his shoulders. "No way. We don't know what's still in there."

"But—"

"Again, no way!"

Reynolds's shoulders sagged.

"You said a fire started?" Nick prompted.

Reynolds accepted the offered handkerchief and started wiping around his eyes and mouth. "One of the grid work trucks. We were at our usual station about to check cargo on the truck just ahead of it. The fire just—" Reynolds coughed suddenly, black spittle forming on his lips. He dabbed his mouth again with the handkerchief. "The fire just sprang up from under the hood. The drivers jumped down and ran up to the two drivers we were checking. Only about four or five words were exchanged before the four of them raced back to the burning truck." Reynolds coughed again. No black spittle. "The one word I caught was *explosives*. I immediately told my men to get out. I turned to see if I could help the four drivers only to see two of them waving violently for me to get out. I started. Made it about a quarter mile before the explosion knocked me down." He stood and looked down at the handkerchief in his right hand. "Guess you don't want this back," he said, opening his hand, revealing a square of cloth more black than white.

Nick chuckled and shook his head. "Right. I'd never find a laundry willing to take that one on." He looked toward Ninth Avenue at the gathering crowd of police, grid workers, and bystanders. He gave Reynolds a single pat on the shoulder. "Let's go to where your men are. Might be one or two ready to ask for a sick day."

"Maybe more than just one or two." Reynolds took the lead, moving strongly toward the crowd.

Nick stopped as he saw Tim emerge from the crowd and run in his direction. He arrived slightly out of breath and held his ancient video tablet aloft.

"We were right, Nick! We were right. Price's drowning was no accident. It was rehearsed."

"What do you have?"

Tim activated his screen. "What you'll see is from just before nine the previous evening. I decided to check all the video. Fortunately, I started one day earlier and lucked out." Tim tapped the start icon, and three men were observed walking into the area of the "accident." The men continued to the seawall. One man was very short, about four feet tall. The men appeared to converse for about a minute when the short man turned back toward the camera and walked a bunch of steps before stopping. He turned around, paused for a moment, and then sprang into two cartwheels, ending just short of the river wall. The men again appeared to talk together.

Nick grunted. "Our 'young boy' ended those cartwheels much closer to the edge."

Tim agreed.

The screen showed the three turn back to the camera, walk across the avenue, and turn to their right.

Nick stopped Tim from turning off the screen. "Play that part just before they turn downtown."

Tim backspaced the video past the requested point to where they were just turning away from the Hudson River.

Nick's itch was starting to act up. He suspended a forefinger over the screen. "When they near the point where they turn, I'll stop the video."

The three walked slowly toward the camera. Most of the way they were shrouded in dim light. Just before turning, they walked under a single streetlamp. Nick dropped his finger onto the screen. The images froze.

Nick bent close to the screen and squinted. Not close enough. He finger-spread the image.

Nick ignored the short cartwheeler—not a leader—and focused on the tallest man. Angular face. Mustache. Light beard. Hair color not distinguishable due to black-and-white video and poor lighting. All in all, enough for an arrest flyer.

Nick shifted his attention to the third man.

He froze.

He spun around to check the crowd for the third man, the killer of Director Price. As Nick expected, he was nowhere in sight. Captain Charles Reynolds was gone.

CHAPTER 52

◆

Nick and Tim raced to the crowd milling around Ninth Avenue. Nick collared Joshua and enlisted him in the search for Captain Reynolds.

The three of them split up, each heading in different directions to the periphery of the crowd. Several of Joshua's precinct mates arrived and were pressed into checking each person in the crowd.

Within five minutes, it was obvious Reynolds was nowhere in the area.

"Damn!" Nick muttered.

He rounded up Tim and Joshua, introduced them to each other, and suggested they return to their respective precincts to set up a full alert on Reynolds.

Tim agreed.

Joshua's expression was one of confusion. "Shouldn't we also alert the World Council? It was one of their directors that was murdered. They would have a strong motive to work *with* us for a change to nail the killer. They have the farthest reach, given their Council Police."

"No. Absolutely not," Nick insisted. "At least one official at the council has dirty hands. I don't know or trust anyone over there."

Tim patted Joshua's shoulder. "Good suggestion, though. You'd think something like this would have them charging out in all directions in ten-alarm mode." Tim stuck an open hand toward the sea-wall and then swept it upriver toward Forty-Third. "Did you see any Council Cops when you were there?"

"No," Joshua admitted, his perplexed expression not much different from his previous confusion.

Nick patted Joshua's other shoulder. "I agree. Good suggestion. Better yet, good police instincts."

The young patrolman's Adam's apple bobbed up and down as he muttered, "Thanks."

Nick assured Joshua they would keep him apprised of any progress as the two precincts would most probably have to coordinate on both the Price murder and the tunnel explosion. "Tell your Sergeant Proctor our precinct needs you as our liaison contact."

"Yes, sir," Joshua said, his expression now confident, purposeful.

Joshua returned to his powerboat and Tim and Nick to their car. Nick called their desk sergeant and told him that they were returning.

As Tim pulled them away, he turned to Nick. "You implied we'll be investigating two crimes. You don't believe the explosion is accidental?" The edge of sarcasm in Tim's voice told Nick he was in agreement with Nick's position even before it was stated.

"We proved that Director Price's drowning was no accident. And we found the man who planned it running out of the exploding Lincoln Tunnel and then disappearing into and away from the crowd. No, the tunnel explosion was planned."

"Why did you tell your young patrolman friend that we want him as our liaison?"

"His sergeant is by the book in triplicate. He'd take days to approve any action. I figure giving him the impression that there's a formal linkup just might speed him up if we do need investigative assistance."

They rehashed their reactions to the previous evening's video. They explored who, both inside and outside the World Council, might gain from Director Price's murder. Nick ruled out President Allison as having no motive or advantage. He and Tim agreed that that left only three other entities: Carter Johnson, the World Council, or someone else. They shook their heads. At least they had eliminated one candidate. Only untold thousands left.

Nick got behind the wheel of the cruiser. "I'll drop you off at the precinct. I have to make a quick stop and check on Nicole before her two 'sister nuns,' as she calls them, initiate her into their old convent."

As he dropped Tim off, Nick asked him to let Captain Gilmore know he'd be back in less than an hour. Tim nodded.

Twelve minutes later, he pulled up in front of the Braddocks' and Sandra's apartment building.

He always looked forward to seeing Nicole, even if only for a few minutes like today. She always sparkled with enthusiasm regarding whatever new project or drawing she had just completed. He never failed to remind himself how lucky he was to have people like the Braddocks and the sister nuns watching out for Sandra and Nicole.

He was feeling downcast because of what Sandra was going through, but to be spending just five or ten minutes with Nicole filled him with more than just a smidgen of positive anticipation.

He climbed the three floors, opened the hallway door, and turned toward the Braddocks'. It was open. Most unusual—and not good.

Anticipation faded. Apprehension drifted front and center.

Nick pushed the door and stepped inside.

The older nun, Sister Edna Patrick, was sitting in the easy chair, blood dripping from the bullet hole in her forehead. He had no doubt she was dead.

His stomach began churning like a washing machine on steroids. He barely succeeded in preventing both knees from buckling.

He turned to go to the hallway when he found Sister "Maria" Judy Patrick lying facedown on the gray carpet, two bullet holes in her back. He was bending down to check for a pulse when someone behind him let loose a loud, ghastly scream.

Nick jerked upright and spun around. Henry and Louise Braddock were in the doorway. Louise's hand covered her mouth.

Nick went to them and eased a trembling Louise to a straight-back chair. Henry grabbed a second chair.

Louise's first question matched Nick's own. "Where is Nicole?"

Together they searched every room, bathroom, and closet in the apartment. They looked under the two beds and behind the break-front positioned astride a living room corner.

No Nicole.

Nick's internal washing machine acknowledged a second, super dose of churning steroids. There was no question in his mind. "Nothing has been ripped apart. They got what they were after: Nicole." He felt the sudden wrenching in his heart. His breathing became uneven: exhaling slowly one moment, gulping air in staccato bursts the next.

Nick went to the master bedroom, retrieved two clean white sheets, and placed them over the bodies, moving neither. To get Nicole back, he had to keep a clear head. And heart.

"Louise, Henry, I need you to come with me. I'm returning to the precinct, and you should not be here for at least the next few hours."

The Braddocks nodded acceptance.

Nick made a quick call to Tim and apprised him of the murders and the kidnapping.

It took the three of them fifteen minutes to gather needed belongings and descend the three flights to Nick's car. It took only ten minutes with his foot pressed all the way to the floor for them to reach the precinct.

Captain Gilmore ushered Louise and Henry into his office and gave them the most comfortable seats. He then returned to Nick. "I've put the medical examiner on standby as you requested. What's your plan?"

Before Nick could answer, Tim stepped forward and handed Captain Gilmore a folder. "I think this is probably related. It was the top folder on my half of the desk."

Nick watched expectantly as the captain opened the folder and checked its contents. He looked up after a scant six seconds. "My God!" he bellowed, almost ripping the folder in half before handing it back to Tim, who passed it on to Nick.

Nick searched both men's eyes for reaction and then opened the folder. Inside was a single sheet with four lines of type:

Monday, August 20, 2057

To: Detective Tim Branson, Precinct 17
As submitting officer, you are hereby notified that, as of
8:00 a.m. today, Delmar Pillsbury has met bail and has been
released.

Nick and Tim looked at each other and nodded.

"Gotta be," Nick said.

Captain Gilmore looked at each of them. "What do we do now?
How can I help?"

Tim shrugged. "Get paracops from every neighborhood working overtime."

Nick was silent, half lost in thought. He looked at Tim.
"Neighborhoods, yes, but . . ." He fell silent again. Finally, he looked
directly at Captain Gilmore. "I decided on the way here that I need
another prisoner released."

"Another prisoner? Released?"

"Yes," Nick said, his eyes aflame. "I need Half-Penny. He knows
the kidnapper labyrinth better than any of us."

Captain Gilmore agreed. "I'll make the call."

CHAPTER 53

Nick and Tim watched through the captain's office door as he made two calls.

The captain turned after hanging up and gave a thumbs-up signal as he came out. "And you're convinced taking him out will get you the information you need?"

"Yes, Captain," Nick and Tim answered almost in unison.

"Where will you be taking Mr. Stalker?"

Nick took a deep breath. "First, the Braddocks' apartment to check it out from his perspective."

"After that?"

"If he has information, wherever it leads. If not, back here."

The captain nodded his permission. "If he gets away from you, you take his place in the cell," the captain said, wagging a forefinger. "Slight exaggeration," he added with a wink as he turned toward his office. He turned back. "Very slight."

◆

Half-Penny was startled into a "Who, me?" look when Nick opened the cell door and motioned for him to come out. That look soon faded to one of almost mortal terror.

"Why? I haven't done anything." He blinked, apparently realizing what he had just said. "I mean, not lately. Not since—"

Tim popped his head into view. "Relax, little man. We just need your help for an hour or two. We'll have you back in your Rikers room here by nightfall."

Half-Penny turned back to Nick, his gaze now reduced to mere everyday terror.

Nick chuckled and waved him out of the cell. "By nightfall. And in one piece. I promise."

Tim drove while Nick and Half-Penny sat in back.

Almost a minute passed before Half-Penny spoke. "Where are we going?" he asked Nick, the fingers on both hands twitching furiously.

"To a crime scene."

Half-Penny's thin eyebrows crinkled inward as he frowned. "Why me?"

"There was a kidnapping."

Half-Penny shivered. "I'll help you, but you probably know kidnapping better than me."

"Maybe, but the more eyes, the better."

Half-Penny remained silent for several minutes as the car wound its way toward the Hudson River side of Manhattan. Finally, looking not at Nick but straight ahead, he said, "I've promised God I will never kidnap again. He told me I have to pay for what I've done, but I promised."

Nick, also looking straight ahead, said, "Yeah, I hear you," in a flat, unconvinced tone.

"And I promise you."

"Yeah, thank you," Nick said, his tone still flat.

"No, really. I promised my grandmother too."

Nick turned to him. "Ah, yes, your grandmother. She's fine, by the way. And she told me the same thing God told you: you have to pay for what you've done."

At that, Half-Penny lowered his head and remained silent until Tim eased the car to a stop in front of the Patricks' apartment building.

Nick stepped out and ordered Half-Penny to do likewise.

The three of them started toward the building.

They got about two-thirds of the way into its enclosed court-yard when Half-Penny slowed his pace and shook his head. "Where was the child kidnapped? I don't see a clear escape path."

Nick reached out and pulled him by the arm. "Inside, Half-Penny. Inside."

The forward lurch seemed to catch Half-Penny off guard. "Inside? That's crazy."

Tim led the way up three flights of stairs. The remaining seven flights, like at least 60 percent of the city's apartment buildings, were blocked off by old, splintered sheets of plywood.

He waited in front of the door to no. 312 until the others caught up. Nick gave a nod. Tim went inside first. Nick nudged Half-Penny to follow and then brought up the rear.

Nick had arranged that the two bodies not be removed until he gave the okay. The two sheets still covered each body. Small blood-stains marked each sheet.

Half-Penny winced when he saw the outline of two bodies in the living room and the hall. Tim pulled both sheets free, revealing two gray-haired ladies with blood-soaked wounds.

Half-Penny yelped and turned to Nick. "I thought you said there was a kidnapping."

"There was."

"But look at all that blood. This was a murder." He turned away, obviously horrified.

"A murder," Nick agreed. "*And* a kidnapping."

"But we don't . . ." Half-Penny paused to correct himself. "*They* don't murder people." He shuddered. "And they never kidnap inside. There's no way to escape with the child."

"They did in this case." Nick felt the heaviness in his voice.

"How old was the child?"

"Six," Nick said and then corrected himself. "And a half."

"Never!" Half-Penny's tone was adamant. "Babies! Our team only stalks babies. Hardly any teams kidnap older children. It does them no good, not like . . ." He shook his head forcefully. "Babies! Our team only does babies."

"Not babies only here," Nick stated as Half-Penny, lips clenched, sucked in oxygen through his nose. "Definitely not babies only here."

Tim bent down to replace the sheets over the bodies.

Half-Penny suddenly stomped his right foot on the floor. "El Camino!" he shouted. "El Camino!" His eyes were wide open, and his forthright nods suggested he was convinced of something.

"What's an El Camino?" Nick asked. He remembered Gerry Martin mentioning the name. "*Who* is El Camino?"

Half-Penny, his eyes still wide, swallowed hard. "El Camino smokes Cuban cigars that have to be at least two hundred years old. They stink, and the smell lingers in a room for days. It was El Camino!"

"Again, who is El Camino?"

"One of the stalker bosses."

"So there's more than one boss?" Nick asked, knowing the answer but wanting to check Half-Penny's truthfulness.

"Yes. About six or seven."

"And have you stalked for each one?"

Half-Penny shook his head. "No. Only three."

"Including this El Camino, obviously, since you know the smell of his cigars."

"Yes. Mostly." Half-Penny's two words were drawn out.

"Mostly . . ." Nick also drew the word out, as if tasting its flavor. "So since you know the smell of his cigars, you're more than just a street worker, more than just a runner. You've even been in the same room with this El Camino. You share a smoke with him? Plan strategy over a brandy."

Half-Penny's eyes opened to their widest yet. "No. No! If I even touched one of his cigars, he'd chop off my hand. If he caught me smoking one, he'd have my throat slit."

"Not a nice guy," Nick suggested. Experience told him the higher up the stalker chain, the more ruthless the company. One thing did bother him, though. "Why did your employer boss let you be in the same room with him if you're just a street man?"

"He had us in the same room just once. Twelve of us. He had us stand in a line in the middle of a room facing a mirror."

It was Nick's turn for wide eyes. Half-Penny had been in a lineup.

"Do you know where this room is?"

"No. I was in a group of three taken there by car with hoods over our heads."

"Do you have an idea of how long you were in the car? Of what direction you were taken?"

Half-Penny closed his eyes. After a couple of measured breaths, he said, "A bit over a half hour. I was the last picked up. At Saint Vartan Park. We went south, many left and right turns, but always coming back to the East River. Always." Half-Penny started rocking and twisting in place, as if reacting to a car making turns. "Always heading south. I think we got to Battery Park—I could tell from the sounds—then headed north."

Nick nodded at Tim and turned to the door, motioning for Half-Penny to follow. "We have a car, and you're coming with us to Battery Park."

CHAPTER 54

◆

Nick pulled the car to a stop at Battery Park and turned to face Half-Penny in the backseat. "Close your eyes. Do you recognize any of the sounds from when you figure they turned for their final straight run?"

Half-Penny did as ordered. He cocked his head, straining to pick up on any clues. After about a minute, he said, "I think so. Sounds good. Sounds close." He opened his eyes.

Nick looked over at Tim, who said, "Close enough."

Nick nodded his agreement and started the car. As he looked in the rearview mirror, he asked Half-Penny, "Did you say they drove slow or fast?"

"Between twenty-five and thirty miles per hour, I think. Their car must have had a lumpy tire. I remember counting between thump sounds."

Nick put the car in gear and started off, reaching twenty-five by the middle of the block. They all heard the tire-to-road thumps Half-Penny had just described.

Nick chuckled. "Guess we have the same tire problem. Must be something on the road."

No sooner had Nick leveled the speed, Half-Penny told him a bit more speed. As Nick approached thirty-two miles per hour, Half-Penny opened his eyes and announced the speed was pretty close.

After five minutes, Half-Penny cleared his throat. "I think we're very close."

Nick pulled to a stop. They got out and looked around. Half-Penny had been blindfolded and couldn't help with building exteriors. He had described how his steps had echoed as if he'd been going into a tunnel before a door was opened and he was pushed inside. Half-Penny said he had counted twelve echoing steps. Nick figured twenty- to twenty-five blindfolded feet, depending on whether Half-Penny had been pushed, pulled, or marched in file.

Nick and Tim inched themselves around in a full circle, looking for likely building candidates. None had the entrance suggested by Half-Penny.

Nick started to shake his head when he remembered what building was only two blocks farther along. He directed the other two back into the car, got behind the wheel, and started up.

He pulled in front of the Stock Exchange building in less than forty-five seconds. "Let's try this building," he said.

Tim agreed that the street-level front of the building could well match Half-Penny's memory of his blindfolded trip.

Nick led the way into the lobby, where he turned to the right and started up the stairs.

Tim and Nick were puffing a bit after the seventh and last flight. They looked over at Half-Penny, who gave no indication of being winded. They looked at each other and rolled their eyes.

Nick led them into the large room from which Gerry Martin had probably been shot.

He looked at Half-Penny, whose eyes were darting from side to side in their sockets. "Familiar?"

A little more eye darting and one complete 180-degree turn yielded an answer. "Yes! Yes, this is the room." A quick shudder took hold of Half-Penny and then passed.

"Where did the twelve of you stand?" Tim asked.

Half-Penny turned back to the first wall, where two landscape prints bookended a four-by-six-foot mirror. He took two steps backward. "Here," he said.

Nick went to the wall, reached out, and grabbed both sides of the mirror. He gave a healthy tug. There was no movement. He tugged first the framed picture on the right, then the one on the left. Neither moved.

Nick shook his head and walked to the door. "Stay right where you are." He moved into the hall and took a right.

Less than a minute later, he returned. "Yup. Two-way mirror. Good view from the janitor closet." He turned to Half-Penny. "Did you ever see anyone go into or come out from the closet next door?"

Half-Penny thought for several seconds. "No, never."

"Shit," Nick mumbled under his breath.

"Although El Camino went out that door once or twice for a minute or so then came back and gave the other men orders." Half-Penny scrunched his face for another several seconds. "You called it a janitor closet. I do remember seeing a janitor once walking past the door to the hall, the one we entered through. The door was closed, but I could see him through the glass, carrying a mop or a broom."

Nick perked up. He pulled out his phone, thumbed to the picture of Duane Evers, and shoved the phone in front of Half-Penny. "Is this man the janitor you saw?"

Half-Penny lowered his head to about ten inches from the picture. He gave his head a very slight negative shake. "I can't tell from that angle. I only saw him sideways."

Nick gave his phone several swipes before thrusting it back in front of Half-Penny. "How about now?"

Half-Penny stared while chewing on the inside of his right cheek. His answer was slow, his tone revealing sixty-forty confidence. Sixty-forty at best. "Ye-e-e-s."

Nick looked up at the door. "Which way was the janitor walking?"

Half-Penny made a right-to-left sweep with his hand.

Nick nodded. "Left side of the face." He made quite a few swipes across the surface of his phone. "Any better?"

Half-Penny's eyes widened. "The scar! Yes! That's him!"

No sound came out, but Nick mouthed with his curled lips, "Son of a bitch!" Nick, fury building in his chest, vengeance searing the inside of his skull, clenched his fists and started for the door.

Tim jumped in front of him.

Nick's eyes were still ablaze as Tim raised his right hand. "Stop! Think! Before you run off and skin this man alive. Just tell me who he is. Then I'll let you go. Was it that Duane Evers we saw in the two videos, meeting with the Secret Service agent and then with that oversized—whatever he was?"

Nick took a deep breath. "Yes. He's the one Gerry Martin was tracking. He was the one who left a two-sheet coded message for someone near this building that I'm trying to decode. Chris Price told me that Duane was Jason Beck's right-hand man."

By the end of the few seconds it took to tell Tim, Nick knew Tim's instincts were right: he couldn't just grab a high-level council member and throttle him for information.

He walked back to Half-Penny. "Have you seen this janitor other times?" he asked, his voice now almost under control.

"No, just that one time. El Camino often left a room and came back with instructions." Half-Penny squinted, obviously searching his memory. "*Detailed* instructions," he added. "Always detailed."

Tim had a puzzled look. "You said 'often left *a* room.' This wasn't the only room El Camino operated from?"

"No. We met here maybe two or three times. Always blind-folded. He spread locations all around."

Tim followed up. "Each location two or three times?"

"No. A couple only once, but most two or three times."

"Were you always blindfolded?"

"Only here."

Nick joined the dialog. "Did El Camino always leave the room before giving the group detailed instructions?"

Half-Penny counted to himself. "Half the time," he finally said. "Maybe a bit more."

Nick's eyes narrowed. "Do you remember these locations? Can you take us back to each one?"

"Most of them."

"This El Camino," Tim said. "What's he like?"

"Over six feet, very strong, his—"

Tim shook his head. "No, is he . . . is he a . . . a team builder?" Tim shook his head, apparently unhappy with how he was asking the question. "Does he ever ask for anyone's opinion on how something should be done?" Tim shrugged, clearly still unhappy with his line of questioning.

Nick got right to the point. "From what you've told us, he's the big boss. What happens if someone crosses him?"

Half-Penny seemed surprised at the question. "Never would happen."

"I don't mean a major confrontation. What does he do if someone screws up in a little way?"

"I've never seen anything like that." Half-Penny furrowed his brow.

"Ever hear anything like that?"

"Once."

Nick leaned in. "Did you ever *hear* what happened to the one who screwed up?"

"I never saw the guy again." Half-Penny was visibly uneasy with the questions.

"How did the guy screw up?"

"He . . ." Half-Penny shivered. "He gave El Camino advice on how to run his business."

Nick backed away. "Did El Camino kill him or have him killed?"

Half-Penny was shaking, head to toe. "Maybe, but I wouldn't testify. He will—"

Nick put a reassuring hand on Half-Penny's shoulder. "We don't need you to testify. We just need to get an idea of what he's capable of doing. We'll never take him to court, and we'll never let him know what we talked about. We wouldn't even mention we ever met you outside of the day you were arrested." Nick gave Half-Penny's shoulder a pat and withdrew his hand. "Besides, if we follow your drift, I think we've got our answer."

Half-Penny relaxed a bit. His shaking tapered off to an occasional shudder.

Nick turned to Tim. "We have to visit these El Camino op centers."

"Just the three of us? We'll need some strong backup."

Nick nodded in agreement. "No time for proper channels. I think I know where we might be able to get some backup."

He motioned for them to follow him.

CHAPTER 55

◆

Duane spotted the poorly disguised El Camino exactly a block away. Not wanting anyone on the street to see them together, Duane stepped quickly up to and through the front doors of the Grand Central Terminal. He hurried down the steps to the almost-deserted main floor, where, slowing just a bit for El Camino to see where he was going, he headed for one of the many decommissioned tracks. Thirty years ago, there had been hundreds of trains moving in and out of the terminal each day. Now there were at most only two, occasionally just one, and most of the time none.

Twenty minutes later, they met a quarter mile down Track 27.

Duane could see El Camino was uneasy.

"Why the face-to-face?" El Camino asked.

"Just three days to the throwing of the big switch. I know you prefer coded notes, but there's no time for them now."

El Camino shrugged.

Duane decided to get right to the point. "Have you activated all the kill switches on the grid?"

"Only thirty-two left. Got three teams working on it."

"Fine. You know the trucks can't be used, but get your men to complete the rest by Wednesday noon."

El Camino nodded.

"Have you received the packages you're to secure under the platform?"

El Camino nodded again. "But I thought your boss was going to be right next to the president."

Duane shook his head. El Camino spent too much time worrying about things that were above his pay grade. Once President Allison and Jason Beck were history, he would need El Camino for several months to help him consolidate power. After that, El Camino would also be history.

Duane made sure his face presented confidence and reassurance. "Everything has been cleared. Not to worry. They're designed to be inserted into each of the pipe support stands. Have your men install them before midnight tomorrow, Tuesday. The final inspection is—"

El Camino held up a hand. "The final inspection is noon Thursday. After which the whole park will be closed and under guard. It'll be installed on time. I've got six men on the construction crew. The preliminary work is complete. Just waiting for the six packages."

"Fine. I'll have the Council Police clear and shadow your cars as they did your trucks before." Duane turned to leave.

"Wait!" El Camino thrust his arms out at his sides.

Duane turned back.

"What about the granddaughter?"

"What about her?"

"She's tying up four of my men."

Duane took a deep breath. "We discussed this before the operation. Absolutely nothing is to happen to her until *after* the switch is thrown."

El Camino shook his head. "I know. I know. You may need her later."

"No, *we* may need her later." Duane patted El Camino on the shoulder. "We're in this together. After the switch is thrown, you'll have access to *all* of Manhattan."

El Camino nodded, turned, and left first, back down Track 27.

Duane waited until El Camino climbed back onto the platform and disappeared before he headed in the same direction.

CHAPTER 56

◆———

Just seconds after receiving the news that Delmar's body had been found, Nick pulled the car to his chosen destination and told both Tim and Half-Penny to stay in the car. He then closed the driver's door, walked about twenty feet, and sat on the curb.

He figured it would take at least twenty minutes before he was confronted. He was surprised it took only six.

"Afternoon, Detective." Howard Williams gave Nick a friendly curl of a lip and sat beside him.

"My granddaughter has been kidnapped. We believe it was carried out by an El Camino character."

"We believe?" Howard glanced over his shoulder at the automobile.

"A fellow detective and—"

"And the young thug you put in jail."

Nick looked at Howard, surprised.

"We checked out the car before I showed myself."

Nick nodded. "*We* checked?"

Howard gave him a wide grin. Nick could see Nathan and others emerging from across the street. They lined the opposite curb and waited.

"We need your help."

"Okay." Howard's tone was curious, cautious. "How much help?"

"We need to check out eleven safe houses."

"By 'check out' you mean . . ."

"Half-Penny will tell us what to look for. Then we—"

"Your young thug has the name Half-Penny?"

Nick nodded. "He's had most of his thugness beaten out of him."

Howard's eyebrows arched upward. "I didn't think the NYPD was into police brutality."

"It was a surprise and unexpected subcontract job." Nick told him how Half-Penny's grandmother of sixty-eight, working with only an umbrella, had brought about a conversion.

Howard chuckled, stood, and rubbed his backside. "Grandmas can be very persuasive at times. I know mine was." Still chuckling, he rubbed his backside again. "No umbrella. Just one hell of a sturdy cane."

"Can your neighborhood help?" Nick stood.

"I assume these eleven safe houses are not all in our neighborhood?"

"Don't think so. Maybe none. Half-Penny can tell us."

"Fine. We all go to my house. Grandma's boy will tell us what he knows, and we'll make a plan. The plan will tell us how many men we need." Howard motioned Nick to get back into the car and follow him. "Let's go."

Nick had one concern. "Will Half-Penny be safe?"

Howard waved Nick to the car and chuckled. "As safe as if he were in his grandma's arms."

Howard displaced Tim in the passenger's seat, and Nathan squeezed in right beside Tim.

It took them four minutes to get to Howard's home and another four for the rest of the crew to arrive.

Howard directed Nick, Tim, and Half-Penny to the sofa at the far wall of his living room. The others drifted in by ones and twos until there were at least two dozen men getting folding chairs. The front door was closed and locked.

Howard took the lead explaining Nick's predicament and what he needed from the neighborhood. "What's needed is a plan, and"— he waved an arm at a nervous Half-Penny—"this young man will get us started in that direction."

Half-Penny's nervousness visibly doubled.

From the back row, a man without a chair raised his hand and pointed at Half-Penny. "This is the stalker our recently accepted Detective Garvey captured while trying to steal a baby. I was in front of the precinct when recently accepted Detective Garvey hauled him inside."

Every head in the room snapped from the speaker to Half-Penny.

The speaker continued. "You're telling us we should take direction from a stalker?"

Nick started to stand. Howard motioned for him to sit back down as he glared at the speaker. "Direction from a stalker? No. From an undercover cop, yes."

Half-Penny's eyes bulged.

Nick swallowed to prevent gagging.

Howard continued, pointing at the standing man. "You were present, Horatio, when we all accepted Detective Garvey. You expressed some reservations but did not vote against acceptance, which requires a hundred percent. Cancellation of acceptance only requires a two-thirds majority. If you want, we can convene a vote meeting within the hour."

The heads swung back to Horatio.

Horatio shook his head. "Nope. No time. We've got a six-year-old being held by some old scumbag."

Howard nodded and announced that he would ask the undercover cop questions. "I know *what* we can do. He knows *where* we have to do it."

Nick made a fist and gave Half-Penny a gentle tap on his shoulder. It didn't appear to help.

"The first thing to know," Howard said to everyone in the room, "is what kind of building should we be looking for? A tall building? Short? Isolated? With a clear view? One of a gang of buildings?" Howard turned to Half-Penny.

Half-Penny shifted his weight to stand, but Nick dropped a hand on his thigh, signaling him to stay put. If he stayed seated, his shaking knees would be less visible.

"Usually tall buildings," Half-Penny said quietly. "Top floor. Always above the grid. Harder to spot."

"Lookouts?" Howard asked.

"Six. Two on the street side of the roof. Two at corner windows just under the grid. Two below them at street level."

The question-answer dialogue continued for ten minutes, after which all in the room indicated they were satisfied with what to look for. Several minutes were spent on a strategy that yielded the formation of six teams. If any team found what they believed was the guarded stalker location, there would be no action taken until Nick's group arrived.

Quadrant search locations were laid out, with possible buildings marked. The six teams branched out.

Half-Penny stopped shaking.

CHAPTER 57

◆

El Camino and a large boxer dog took up the rear seat of his twelve-passenger limousine. Three lieutenants, his "key three" as he thought of them, sat facing him.

"You know what remains to be done," El Camino said, jabbing a forefinger in their direction. "We've got thirty-two grid struts to get ready for Thursday. Midnight tonight is our deadline. You each know what remains to be done in your territory. Do I have to ask if each of you have the required switches?"

"Got 'em," the three said almost in unison.

The three started to exit the limousine when the youngest, twenty-seven-year-old Marco, turned back. "You promised the Council Police would keep our areas clear."

El Camino nodded. "So?"

"So our first strut is in my territory just out there," Marco said, pointing a finger at the windshield and at a manhole cover twenty feet beyond.

"So?" The edge in El Camino's voice, although slight, prompted the two older lieutenants to roll their eyes as they quickly stepped out.

"So," Marco responded without caution, "I don't see them anywhere in the neighborhood. Not now, not as we drove up. I just want to make sure my team is safe and we can complete the job. We've got twelve of those thirty-two."

"Tell you what," El Camino said, his words measured and slow as he waved a hand at the other two standing outside to leave and get started. "I'll wait here while you install this first switch."

Marco started to exit, but El Camino placed his left hand on Marco's right shoulder. El Camino reached backward for one of the three portable video cameras in the limousine. Set up, supposedly, for security, they each sent a recording signal to a recorder in the trunk.

"Take this," he said, pulling free the video unit tucked in the back corner behind his head. He tugged the power cord and battery free, looping it several times. He handed it all to Marco. "Have one of your men record how your team installs the switch. Might be a good idea to have a record of a job well done."

Marco shrugged, accepted the camera unit, stepped out, and motioned to his team.

El Camino watched them and was impressed with the efficiency of Marco's team.

Marco and his men cut the electric seal on the manhole cover, after which the five men quickly descended the ladder inside. All five reached the tunnel floor within thirty seconds. With the lights already on, Marco handed the camera unit to the shortest member of his team.

Marco's team had previously installed ninety-six kill switches, each one under seven minutes, street level to street level. He figured assigning one man to video everything would maybe add another minute.

They moved to the base of the assigned grid strut, just thirty-seven feet from the ladder. Marco's tallest team member helped unpack the portable sawhorses and planks. After assembly at the strut base, the remaining two men kept the makeshift table stabilized with one hand as their tall team member climbed aboard. Each used his free hand to focus the lights on the section of the strut at eye level of their man. With the four feet of table elevation, eye level was ten feet and two inches.

They located the target wires on the strut's backside. They eased them forward and stripped the insulation on the two twenty-two gauge communication lines clear enough for temporary jumpers to be installed.

With the combination communication and alarm lines now bypassed, they cut the original lines; connected the kill switch, a box about the size of a man's empty wallet; cut the temporary jumpers; and returned the box to the strut backside, where it was putty-glued in place.

They played the lights up, down, and across the strut. Marco saw no visible trace of their modification.

Marco nodded his approval and checked his watch as the saw-horses and planks were disassembled and placed in the four back-packs. It looked like they'd suffer only a forty-second delay.

The return climb was orderly and efficient, with a total add of just thirty-eight seconds.

"See, Marco? No interference, no danger to you and your team," El Camino said as Marco opened the limo door and handed over the video camera unit. "I assured you that the Council Police would do their work. They do it by keeping back, out of the way. They're aware of our work locations and will keep them clear."

Marco nodded. "I guess so," he said and started to turn away.

"Whoa there." El Camino grabbed Marco's arm and held fast. "What's with this 'I guess so'? You still have a problem with what we're doing?"

"Not what we're doing now, but what we've been told to do the past two days and what those who gave us orders know about details. Details that put us in danger."

El Camino directed Marco to sit again beside him. Marco sat.

"You're referring to the kidnapping?"

"Yes."

"I know I've had to take a man or two from everyone's team to—"

"It's not the men! She has to be guarded. What bothers me is who knows where she's being kept. Does your contact know? Do his bosses know?"

"And if they do, what's your problem?" El Camino was growing tired of Marco's attitude.

"What if they want a fall guy? What if the bosses want to look like heroes? What if they raid where she's being held? What if they shoot the men? Shoot most of us? What if they put you in chains or worse? Do they know where she's being held? Do you trust them? With your life?"

Damn good points, El Camino thought as he unwrapped the power cord, wrapped it around his left hand, and then unwrapped it again. *Damn good points.* In a few years, a smart young man like Marco would rise quickly up the ranks, maybe right up to . . . "Excellent questions, Marco. Come with me right now, and we'll see what precautions should be taken." He continued to wrap and unwrap the cord.

Marco looked surprised but pleased that El Camino was considering his concerns. "I don't want to be a problem."

El Camino gave the driver a wave to depart. "You aren't a problem, and you never will be."

As the limousine picked up speed, its presets locked all doors. El Camino unwrapped the video cord one final time and pointed to a Council Police patrol a block past Marco's window. Marco turned to look. El Camino slipped the video unit power cord around Marco's neck and pulled it tight.

Five blocks later, the limousine stopped, and the doors unlocked.

Pushing with his feet, El Camino dumped Marco's body in the gutter. He waved the driver on, giving him a new destination.

Marco had had a point. El Camino decided to solve the granddaughter problem. Two solutions were obvious: relocate her or eliminate her.

He'd decide in about twenty minutes.

Right now, he had to promote Marco's second-in-command.

CHAPTER 58

Howard, Half-Penny, Nathan, and two others had finished casing their first assigned building and concluded that it was not an active stronghold.

Fifteen minutes later, they pulled to a stop two blocks from their second building.

Half-Penny pointed out four lookouts: two at street level, two just below grid level. "That's gotta be the one," he said.

Howard nodded in agreement. The building fit the profile. He pulled out his phone and called Nick and the four other teams. "We have a definite on our second building."

None of the other teams had found an "active" building. They called a rendezvous with two other teams.

Nick's team arrived within six minutes. Tim's within seven.

The discussion on how to get inside the building bounced back and forth for two more minutes, with no satisfactory solution.

Finally, Half-Penny took a deep breath and stepped forward. "Most of them know me," he said. "Enough for me to get inside."

Nick shook his head. "Only one inside can't do anything. You said there's usually ten to twenty of El Camino's men inside."

Half-Penny shrugged. "Only one of us inside is all it will take to see if your granddaughter is there. Most of them know me," he repeated. "If she's there, I can signal." He extended both hands, determined to convince them. "See? No shaking."

After a minute of back-and-forth discussion, Nick and the others reluctantly agreed with Half-Penny.

Yes, no, and emergency signals were agreed upon as well as a time limit, after which Half-Penny was to be assumed dead. After a minute, they chose an entry gambit and sent Half-Penny on his way.

The three teams were discreetly relocated on all sides of the building to await a signal. If positive, a stealth entry would be mounted. If the signal were the emergency sign, all teams would storm in from all sides.

Nick's team took the front and left side of the building, Tim's front and right side, Howard's the rear.

Half-Penny grabbed a bicycle from Tim's group and circled back one block, downtown for another two, and then back to the original avenue so he could be spotted from three blocks away.

He was already puffing as his distant target came into view. He increased his speed.

As he pedaled to within a block, he released the handlebars and waved both hands over his head. After coasting a moment, he dragged his shoes on the roadway and slowed to a stop in front of two unshaven men, both of whom, thank God, he recognized.

"Benny! Jorge! Thank God! I gotta get inside before the cops find me."

The mention of cops unnerved the two.

Half-Penny shook his head. "They don't know where I am or what direction I took. I broke free when they were transferring me to another precinct. This bike was just leaning against a post. Before I could be cuffed, my new cop sneezed and I jumped on the bike and was off." Half-Penny had to grimace to suppress a smile. He was thinking that for the first time his grandmother would be proud of him for telling a big lie.

Benny and Jorge traded glances, their concerned looks easing.

Half-Penny was still puffing. "Can we get this bike inside?"

Benny nodded.

Benny directed Half-Penny toward the building's front door. He turned to Jorge. "Stay there for a couple of minutes. Keep your eyes peeled in both directions. I'll be back in short order. It's important we get Half-Penny and the bike outta sight."

Jorge nodded. Then Benny escorted Half-Penny and the bike inside.

In every building El Camino used, no matter how infrequently, there was always to be one elevator that worked all the way to the top. It was this elevator that the two men and the bike rode seventeen floors to the penthouse.

When they reached seventeen, Benny stepped out first, waving okay to a standing group of five men as he pointed to Half-Penny easing the bike free of the elevator.

"A couple of you don't know Half-Penny. He was one of our best stalkers before he got caught by the cops two weeks ago. He just escaped during a transfer and needs shelter."

Half-Penny glanced quickly around. Not seeing El Camino, he scrunched his lips. "I need more than shelter," he said, turning back to Benny.

Benny shrugged. "Shelter will keep you safe until—"

"Until the cops mount an all-out press." Half-Penny forced his breathing into a heavy, nervous rhythm. "They were holding me for killing a cop. They don't believe I didn't do it. I need El Camino to give me cover, to hide me where those damn cops can't find me."

Benny turned to the others. "Is El Camino still here? Didn't he say something about leaving?"

One of the group pointed to the door to the rear hall. "He left about a minute ago. He took the girl with him."

"He was carrying her," another said, cradling his arms in front. "Said she had fainted and he was taking her somewhere."

Half-Penny's stomach churned. He started for the hall door. "Maybe I can get him before he leaves."

Benny shook his head. "I wouldn't chase after him if I were you. Even on happy days, we all know how El Camino can be. Give us a chance. We can keep you safe."

Half-Penny waved his thanks as he opened the door. Not pausing, he hollered back, "If he's gone, I'll be back for your offer."

Half-Penny raced down the hall. He checked the rear elevator's floor indicator. It read *G*. El Camino was already in the garage. Half-Penny went to the hall's end window and thrust his elbow into and through its glass. He gave a wild sweeping wave—not one of the agreed-upon signals—and pointed down to where he knew the garage was. Not knowing if the signal had been seen, he charged into the stairwell and took three and four steps at a time.

He reached the garage ninety seconds later, just in time to see the rear end of El Camino's limo as the car pulled away.

Gasping for breath, Half-Penny spun in a full circle and then, slowly, in another circle, searching for anything that might look like—or hide—a little girl's body.

Nothing!

After racing out of the garage, he looked left and then right, waving like a madman, as if that would make Howard's car suddenly appear.

It did!

The car slammed to a stop in front of Half-Penny. Nathan, in the front seat next to Howard, threw open his door.

"Get in!" Howard shouted.

Howard told Half-Penny he had been standing at the corner of the building across the alleyway when El Camino's limo had emerged from the garage and gunned its way down the alley. He had raced back the sixty feet to the car and was just starting to give chase when he saw Half-Penny waving.

Howard and Half-Penny exchanged information as they charged down the alley to the street. Nick pointed left—the direction the limo had taken. At Nick's signal, Tim's car had turned around and followed. The limo had a two-block head start.

"He's got your granddaughter!" Half-Penny left out the part of her being described as unconscious. He berated himself for not getting to the seventeenth floor while El Camino was still there. He also speculated that if he hadn't volunteered to go in, they might have stopped El Camino's escape and rescued Nick's granddaughter. He prayed that she was still alive.

Howard's car spun out of the alley and tore off in the indicated direction, followed at a very unsafe distance by Nick's car.

After three blocks with no turns and not one glimpse of El Camino's limousine, Half-Penny cleared his throat. "I think I know where he's going. He's got something like a fort up around Central Park. It's on this avenue, straight up. It's just a guess, but—"

"But it's better than what we got now," Howard shot back, pressing even harder on the accelerator.

Six blocks on, they spotted Tim's car a block and a half ahead.

Tim was standing next to it. "I lost him. One twist, one turn, and I lost him."

Half-Penny leaned forward. "He went east?"

Tim nodded. "And back downtown, I think."

Half-Penny disagreed. "No. North! Harlem. I've never been there, but I know within a block or two." He looked reluctantly at Nick. "He calls it his 'dumping ground.' Anything he wants to make disappear, including himself, goes there."

"Let's go!" Nick shouted and hopped into his car.

Twenty-three blocks and twelve minutes later, Half-Penny suggested a counterclockwise search. Half-Penny had barely made his proposal when they spotted, two more blocks to the east, El Camino's limo pull into a garage and the door close.

CHAPTER 59

◆

The garage door was not yet closed and the limousine barely stopped when El Camino shouted "Stop here!" to his driver and flung open his door.

He stepped out of the limo and looked around, frowning that he didn't see more than the one startled man working on a rusted boiler. He'd called ahead at least a minute ago. He shook his head, reached back inside the limo, and pulled out the barely conscious girl. He had to hold her up by one armpit.

She groaned something unintelligible, her eyelids half shut.

There was a clatter at the far end of the garage as nine of El Camino's crew spilled out of the stairwell.

There was no time to wait for the men to apologize for their tardiness. "I'm being followed," El Camino said, pointing at the garage door. "Stop them!"

As the nine men spread out to cover all the windows, El Camino, dragging the still-limp girl, moved to the man at the boiler. "Open it!" he commanded.

The grubby man jerked almost to attention before fully processing the order. He circled to the right rear of the boiler and, pulling down on a stain-free lever, opened the full front of the boiler.

El Camino stepped up into the boiler, stood on a ledge, and glanced down the stairwell to the tunnels. Still holding the girl by her armpit, he turned back to the man, who had returned to the front of the boiler.

"Now close it."

The man nodded.

"And"—El Camino made sure he saw fear in the man's eyes—"do not stand guard. It'll draw attention. Go upstairs."

El Camino pulled out a pocket light and turned it on and pointed it downward. To make his descent easier, he hoisted the girl over his left shoulder. By the time he reached the fifth step, the boiler door was slowly closing. Three more steps and he guessed it was half-closed. One additional step brought the muffled sound of gunfire. Another two steps and the boiler door clanged shut with the gunfire, now barely a whisper, still raging.

El Camino's crew would be shooting automatic rifles from every window.

Half-Penny and the rest of Howard's group covering the rear were pinned down immediately. Half-Penny, Nathan, and Howard were at the rear corner of the building's left side.

Howard called for the other three groups to join in "ASAP." Then, waving to his own group, he directed them to spread out along the rear.

Half-Penny saw Nick at the front corner wave for others to move along that part of the building.

One of Howard's men was taken down by the second or third burst.

Howard immediately turned to Nathan. "Get over there!" he commanded, pointing at a dumpster not forty feet away.

Half-Penny stood up, grabbed Nathan, and keeping his own body between Nathan and any windows, ran them to the dumpster.

Howard gave Half-Penny a thumbs-up.

Nathan peered around the far side of the Dumpster.

Half-Penny pulled him back and, tapping the metal frame, said, "You wait here and don't move. I'm going back."

Nathan grabbed Half-Penny's shirt. "No wait!" He pointed underneath the dumpster. "There's a way in."

Half-Penny peered back down to where Nathan was pointing. "So there's a metal slab. So?"

"So see the handle?"

Half-Penny could see a six- or seven-inch indentation in the middle of the slab near the edge away from the building. "It's a dent."

The young boy shook his head and smiled. "I guess you don't get around much." He lay down and reached under the dumpster, sliding his right hand along the slab. He made a downward grabbing motion with his hand, fingers curled, and slid his hand forward about two inches. "They're all around the city. If this dumpster wasn't on top, I could almost lift it by myself."

Half-Penny checked the slab again. It was about ten feet from the building. He looked back and saw gunfire coming only from the first window. Apparently, no one inside had paid attention to their move to the dumpster. He nodded to himself. *It might just work.*

"I'll push it forward. You keep the dumpster between you and the building."

They exchanged nods.

Even though the dumpster was less than half full, it still took a grunting and groaning Half-Penny almost a minute to completely uncover the slab. He glanced up, noted that no one was standing behind the windows directly opposite, and then stooped down and grabbed the slab's recessed handle.

It was far from light. He grunted a couple more times before pivoting the slab upright. He could see a series of cemented-in pipes serving as ladder rungs leading down into darkness.

"Get in quick," he said, turning to Nathan, but the boy was already clambering downward.

Half-Penny turned to look back to let Howard know where they were going. He was alarmed to see Nathan's father lying on his stomach, not moving. He was hopeful that Howard was just presenting a low profile to the shooters.

He followed Nathan down the makeshift ladder.

Nathan already had a small light illuminating the tunnel floor as Half-Penny stepped off the last rung.

Half-Penny turned to Nathan and saw the boy bring an index finger to his lips.

Half-Penny heard footsteps far ahead. They belonged to someone who wasn't running—more like walking quickly. With each third or fourth step came a muffled, low-register sound, which lasted for a step or two.

After just a quick glance at each other, Nathan and Half-Penny started racing toward the source of the sounds, their sneakers making little noise.

Half-Penny counted off thirty-seven running steps and then stopped suddenly. The low-register sound was a voice. He strained to listen. He recognized the voice: it belonged to El Camino.

He turned, bent down, and whispered the name to Nathan.

The sounds were much closer now.

Half-Penny had to decide how they would sneak up and how—

The steps and the voice stopped suddenly.

Half-Penny strained to hear anything else.

Nothing. Several seconds passed before Half-Penny heard a metallic clang.

"Come on," Nathan said. "He's gone into another tunnel."

The two ran ahead for about a hundred feet and then stopped. Nathan swept his light first at floor level along the tunnel's right side, then to the left.

"What are you looking for?" Half-Penny asked.

"Fresh scrapes. Dirt spread out in an arc. Footprints. They didn't sound much farther than here." Nathan shook his head.

They moved forward another twenty feet or so.

Nathan made another sweep with the light.

Another shake of the head.

Another twenty feet.

"Here!" Nathan whispered, pointing his light down to a thin film of dirt. There were no scrapes and no arc tracings. There was in the slight film of dirt, however, the faint trace of a shoe print—just the front, not the heel—that looked to have started facing ahead before rotating clockwise to where it was facing the wall.

Half-Penny shook his head in disbelief. His partner was only eleven years old and was already a master tracker.

It took only about ten seconds to find the handle indent. It took another thirty seconds of experimenting to discover the door had to be pushed in and then down before it would release some internal catch, allowing it to be pulled open.

They took pains to open the door as quietly as they could. A metallic clang would doom their cause as well as Nick's granddaughter. Half-Penny stopped pushing when there was just enough room for them to squeeze through.

Once inside, they moved forward as quickly and as quietly as possible.

They soon encountered a three-way branch of tunnels. They decided to explore the tunnels right to left.

CHAPTER 60

◆

Nick's group made short work of those guarding the front of the building. He stood, made a quick survey from behind the cars, and then raced, shoulder extended, to and through the front door.

He was just in time to see three men descending the inside of what looked like a huge boiler. An old man was about to pull a lever down. Nick waved him aside with his Glock. He motioned for the man to exit the front door. He raised his hands to the old man in a suggested "I surrender" sign and then followed the three men down the steps.

He didn't want to attract their attention, so he kept well behind, hoping against hope they'd lead him to Nicole.

By the time Nick reached the last step, the three thugs were about fifty yards ahead, turning right into a side tunnel. He held his gun at the ready and quickened his pace. At the juncture where they turned, he could see them taking another side tunnel, this time to the left. He kept up his quick pace and, again, checked his quarry's progress. They were about thirty yards ahead this time and moving away but at a slower pace.

He was deciding how much of a lead to allow them when some faint noises from farther down the tunnel caught his attention. He could see a crossing tunnel about fifteen yards ahead. Any noise was worth checking out.

Nick peered around the corner and saw, in the distance, a garbage bin with a man standing behind the far side. On top of the bin was something he thought looked like a small person propped partially against the tunnel wall.

Nicole?

If so, there was no clear firing line of sight that didn't put her in danger.

Half-Penny and Nathan finally entered the leftmost tunnel. They quickly encountered a main tunnel into which theirs branched at what Half-Penny guessed was a thirty-degree angle to the right. Nathan covered his light with his left palm, and with Half-Penny above him, both risked a peek around the corner.

Not more than twenty feet away were El Camino and Nick's granddaughter. El Camino, breathing heavily, was leaning against some sort of metal bin.

In his left arm, he held a sagging little girl: Nicole.

He braced her against the bin, shoved his right hand into his pants pocket, and whipped out a large folded knife. Along with the knife, a piece of paper fluttered out and fell to the ground.

"Okay, little bitch!" he said in a growl. "End of the road for you. El Camino is home free now. And guess what: El Camino doesn't need you anymore." He stood straight, stretched the girl out atop the bin, opened his knife, and wiped the blade on his pants. "Let dumbshit Duane explain *this* to his boss."

Half-Penny grabbed the light from Nathan's hand as El Camino took a step back and then switched his hold on the knife in preparation for a downward stroke.

Half-Penny flashed the light forward so only the beam was visible to El Camino.

Trying to keep the light from shaking, he took a quick breath. "Follow me, men!" he shouted in as deep a voice as he could manage. "He's gotta be along here somewhere!"

Half-Penny immediately raised his voice. "Ten-four, Captain. Grenades are ready."

"Deploy!" the fictitious captain commanded in a deep voice.

Nathan peered around the corner again. "He's running away!"

"The girl?"

"She's still on the bin."

"She okay?"

"Can't tell from here."

"El Camino?"

"I can just make him out. Still running away."

Half-Penny, still amazed he'd put the fear of God into El Camino, peered around and saw El Camino's barely visible large frame disappear into the darkness. He motioned Nathan to follow him.

Nick's granddaughter was groggy but unharmed. Her eyes were shut, but she was awake. Her feet, from calf to shoe, extended over the edge of the bin.

Half-Penny reached under her neck and, propping up her head with his fingers, bent her upright.

She struggled three times to keep her eyes open. She gave several muffled grunts. "Is . . . is the . . . fat . . . fat man here?" Her head nodded, then rose slowly as she tried to focus on Half-Penny.

"He ran far away," Nathan said.

Nicole squinted at Half-Penny and then frowned. "Did . . . did your lips move?" She stopped nodding and clenched her eyes shut. "I didn't see your lips—"

"There are two of us here. My lips didn't move."

Nicole opened her eyes. "Is the fat man here?"

Half-Penny turned to Nathan. "Let's get her back with her grandpa." He looked down at the girl, his hand behind her neck. He became aware that she was holding her head up with little or no support. "She may need medical care."

"Grandpa," Nicole said, her voice just a whisper. She smiled.

Half-Penny, still cradling Nicole, glanced down at the folded piece of paper that had fallen from El Camino's pocket. He stooped down and snagged the crumpled paper between two fingers. As he straightened up, he heard a vaguely familiar voice behind him.

"Hey, look what we have here, boys."

Half-Penny and Nathan turned.

Three armed men stood glaring down at them, rifles held casually, their mouths twisted in eager grins.

Half-Penny recognized only one of the three: Benny's older, more violent brother.

Benny's brother raised his automatic rifle. "Half-Penny, what are you doing down here? Interesting load you're carrying. Looks like the little princess that El Camino was guarding. If he doesn't have her, I guess she's no longer of value." He motioned to his comrades to raise their rifles. "Take them out."

Half-Penny tried to pull Nathan behind him. As the two men raised their rifles, he closed his eyes.

A barrage of automatic gunfire reverberated throughout the tunnel.

Feeling nothing, Half-Penny opened his eyes.

Benny's older brother and comrades were lying flat in front of him, one with only half a head.

Half-Penny looked up to see Detective Nicholas Garvey.

"Thanks, Half-Penny. Thanks, Nathan."

"Grandpa!" Nicole shouted, struggling to stand.

Nick spun his rifle behind him and reached out to Nicole. She hugged him with all her might.

Nick smiled, gave Half-Penny an approving wink, and pointed down at the three bodies. "I saw those three come down. Figured they were my best bet to find the fat man. I found him but couldn't get a shot off." He patted Half-Penny on the shoulder. "Interesting technique you have there for chasing off bad guys."

Half-Penny reached for Nathan's hand, and the four of them headed back to the hatch.

When Nathan's light revealed the series of cemented-in ladder rungs, Nick told Half-Penny to climb up first. Then he and Nathan would carry Nicole up.

"I'm okay," Nicole said. "I can stand. I think."

Nathan and Half-Penny nodded at each other, and Half-Penny started climbing. He tipped the grating up to where he could peer out toward the front of the building. The first thing he noticed was the absence of sound: no gunfire. The second: no movement, no cowering behind trash bins, no scurrying for cover.

He listened intently for another few seconds. No activity.

"Is it okay up there?" Nick shouted up.

"Far as I can tell."

Nick motioned for Nathan to start climbing.

Nick turned to Nicole, who appeared reasonably steady on her feet. Maybe so, but he wasn't going to assume her climbing ability was unimpaired.

"Come here," he told her. "I'm carrying you up."

With his right arm wrapped around Nicole, he ascended slowly, grunting with each step as he pulled them up.

Nathan and Half-Penny were focused on helping Nick. When he and Nicole were on firm ground, they all relaxed.

It was then that Nathan turned and saw Howard lying on the ground. He ran to him.

Tim and six others rushed to their side within seconds.

Half-Penny walked to Nick, handed him El Camino's crumpled note, and then headed to where Nathan was bent over Howard.

Nathan was sobbing.

CHAPTER 61

◆

El Camino heaved his shoulder against the heavy door and emerged onto a sheltered alleyway ten streets up from his safe house he now assumed was in ruins. He marched toward the open end of the alley. His target: the white seven-story building across the street.

Few people—none of his crew leaders or any of their men—knew of this hideaway. He surely relished long evenings of wanton lust shared with no less than six women wearing tear-away clothing, but not even one of them knew of this building. Duane was the only one who did know. He corrected himself. The only one still alive, that was.

Once inside, he would call Duane and request a conference. El Camino repeatedly clenched and unclenched his fingers. It would be a request that he would make sure Duane honored.

Marco's words still haunted him.

He took the elevator to the seventh floor and, after opening the apartment door, went directly to the wall phone.

Duane answered on the sixth ring. "You okay, man? I was waiting for your call."

El Camino was caught off guard. Why would his call be expected? "You were?"

"Of course. The police radio has been detailing what happened—everything about the shootout at what I believe is one of your places. From what the reports said, I thought you were dead. I'm relieved to hear your voice, to know you survived."

Was he really relieved? Best way to find out was face-to-face. "We gotta talk."

"Fine," Duane agreed. "Where?"

"Here," El Camino said, giving Duane the location.

"Be there in thirty minutes."

El Camino hung up, musing over the fact that Duane hadn't asked what the talk would be about. Interesting.

He decided to get ready for Mr. Duane Evers.

First he went to his chair at the conference table and checked under the table for the Luger pistol held by two light spring clamps. Once sitting, he pulled the pistol free without a problem and checked its load. Satisfied, he returned the weapon.

Next he moved to the tapestry hanging on the left wall. Among the more than three hundred loose threads was—he found it immediately—a four-foot garrote. He assured himself it could be removed quickly and without being noticed.

After moving to one of the two sofas, one on each end of the room, he slid his hand down the inside of the armrest nearest the windows, touching the Lugar stuffed down against the touching cushion. He repeated the check with the other sofa.

El Camino stepped into the hallway and crossed over to his "observation room." Inside were twelve video screens, which together covered all entrances into the building as well as stairways, the elevator, and surrounding streets.

Should anyone approach the building from any quarter, a small key case would vibrate. He dropped the case into his left pocket.

All activity around the building was recorded, with any alarms also recorded. Over the past nine days, there had been no alarms.

El Camino's final check was the metal detector panel just inside the observation room door. All the detectors were built into door-jambs at each and every access to the building.

He pulled up a chair in front of the video screens and waited.

Twenty minutes later, Duane arrived, parking just around the corner from El Camino's building.

The screens showed no heat sources other than Duane's body. As he entered the building, the associated metal detector indicated no metal object was on Duane's person. El Camino watched Duane stride to the elevator and press the Up button.

After double-checking that the body-heat sensors were on automatic alarm, El Camino walked back into the apartment's living room, stood behind his seat at the table, and waited.

Duane greeted him with a quick nod as he entered. El Camino nodded in return and took his seat.

Duane sat opposite. "What the hell happened?" His tone was inquisitive, not accusatory.

"Somehow the cops found us. Don't know how, but they found us."

"The radio calls made it sound like a bloodbath. Dead bodies on both sides."

"I wouldn't know. I saw their approach, figured something was wacky, and headed down into the tunnels."

Duane lowered his head and sighed.

The sigh seemed one of honest relief, but El Camino was not about to take chances. He stood and began to slowly pace, first to the sofa on his right, then back around his chair to the sofa on the left.

Duane twisted in his chair to watch.

El Camino stopped at the tapestry and, his body blocking the view, snagged the wire garrote and concealed it in his palm. He looked back at Duane. "They got the little girl." His eyes were fixed on Duane's.

"Don't sweat it," Duane assured him, returning the fixed gaze with a questioning one of his own. "The girl was ordered by Jason. It was a short-term need. Thursday is the grid dedication. He has other things on his mind."

El Camino repeatedly clenched and unclenched the deadly load in his left hand. "I'm convinced we were set up. Someone wanted us wiped out."

As if melting one into the other, Duane's gaze went from questioning to one of understanding. "I think you're right," he said, returning to a normal sitting position, his back to El Camino.

"You agree?" El Camino asked, his left hand suddenly frozen in mid squeeze.

"Figure this way. Jason's plans have to change in some direction, in some way, after tomorrow. In the past, he's always kept me in sync with his plans for weeks and even months into the future. But that was in the past. For the past few weeks, he's revealed nothing of his plans, nothing of what he plans after Thursday, only two days from now, when he's had us make sure the lights will never switch on." Duane shook his head and then turned to face El Camino. "I think he has no further use for me or for you."

El Camino felt confused. It seemed plausible. It seemed—

"Unless . . ." Duane stood suddenly and faced El Camino, who flinched at the movement. "Unless it's only *me* he has no use for. Maybe he figures I know too much."

The two men stood facing each other.

El Camino was frozen, unable to read Duane's state of mind.

Duane also looked to be frozen, not plotting some form of treachery.

Duane was the first to speak. "Maybe he figures I told you. Maybe that's why you were attacked today. Do you have a safe house that even *I* don't know about?"

El Camino nodded, a rising sense of relief melting his frozen wariness.

"You should get there as soon as you can. Tell only those men you take with you. Since I don't know where you are, Jason can't find you through me, whatever he does."

El Camino nodded again, feeling his normal calm returning.

Duane cupped his chin in his right hand, as if wrestling with a complex plan. "Give me a cell phone only you have the number for. I'll record a greeting. 'Hello' means everything's okay. 'Leave a message' means there may be a problem headed your way. No answer means I destroyed the phone and am either on the run or dead."

El Camino gave his third nod and retrieved a phone from the desk drawer and handed it to Duane. "What about the ceremony on Thursday?"

"We should be okay. You've had all the devices installed, right?"

Another nod.

"If you can, have one of your men, one you *trust*." Duane emphasized the last word—trust—as if it were to give El Camino a sense of security. It did. "Have him check the routes leading away from the Battery Pier. There's a remote chance one of the targets may be less than mortally wounded. We'll need to know where they're taken."

"I'll take care of that."

"You sure?"

"Definitely," El Camino assured Duane, projecting trust and confidence with his voice. "But we shouldn't have any concerns. The six devices should take care of everything and everybody on the platform."

"Okay," Duane said, shrugging his submission to El Camino's plan. "Just make sure you're safe. If I make it through tomorrow, I'll need you. You know my plans for the city, and you know they depend on you. Not on your men. On *you*!"

El Camino nodded, and Duane left.

CHAPTER 62

◆

At Nick's request, Tim took Nicole, Half-Penny, and Nathan to the safe house where they had sequestered the Braddocks. Louise Braddock had received Nick's alert call and greeted them as they entered.

As soon as she went through the door, Nicole spotted Louise and ran into her open arms.

Louise pointed to the kitchen table, where a plate of fresh cookies waited. She watched Half-Penny follow Nathan into the living room, where the younger boy sat quietly in a hardback chair, his facial expression a blank numbness. Louise again pointed to the kitchen table. Nicole grabbed two cookies and marched to the right side of Nathan's chair, where she sat cross-legged on the floor. She raised her left hand to him, offering one of the cookies. Nathan did not respond. She placed it on his right knee.

Half-Penny, who, according to Nick, had lost both parents at a young age, walked over to the grieving boy's left side and sat on the floor, opposite Nicole.

Louise, Henry, and Tim watched the three from across the room. The youthful angst brought tears to Louise's eyes.

Nick soon arrived with the book for decoding.

Louise waved an open hand at him, motioning him to not bother the three youngsters. She offered Nick a cookie as he sat at the table and pulled out the note. He shook his head and thanked her.

Nick wrestled with the decoding for a good half hour.

Midway through, Louise caught Nathan lifting the cookie off his knee and taking a bite. Nicole raised her left hand again for him to hold.

Nathan took a second bite from the cookie, the remaining half clenched fast by his teeth. "Thank you," he managed to mumble as he took her hand.

Nicole smiled, as did Half-Penny.

Louise watched as the three started talking to one another. She managed a little smile—just big enough to hold back her tears. Little Nicole, acting beyond her years, held Nathan's hand while, every once in a while, Half-Penny would pat Nathan on a still-sagging shoulder. Nathan did not smile but did become more interactive.

Nick finally completed the decoding. He waved Tim over.

"El Camino's note instructs him to place all the devices at least three days before the ceremony. My guess: they're going to blow up the president when she's in the spotlight."

Tim looked over Nick's shoulder. "The Secret Service had to have checked out the whole site."

Nick nodded. "You'd hope so." He grabbed his phone and punched in several numbers.

A good twenty seconds passed before he heard a click and someone say, "Hello."

"Nick Garvey here. I just—the president gave me your number. Yes, Sam, it's important. I just received information that some sort of bomb has been placed somewhere near or under the platform where, tomorrow afternoon, the president is going to activate the grid to supposedly light up Manhattan. The bomb was to be installed three days ago."

"There's been no suspicious nor unauthorized activity anywhere on or near the platform."

"I assume you checked under the platform."

"Found nothing. On top or underneath. Nothing. I'd have to go back to the logbook, but I've double-checked it. Maybe it refers to a different location."

Nick looked up at Tim and shook his head. "Thanks. Yes, I'll definitely call if I learn anything else." Nick closed his phone and pounded on the table with his fist.

Nicole, Nathan, and Half-Penny jumped at the sudden noise.

Nick's voice rose several decibels. "That slimy, fat El Camino planted a bomb somewhere, and it's gotta be near where the grid switch is going to be thrown. I know it. Damn it! I know it!"

Nicole ran to the kitchen table. "Are you talking about that bad man who took me?"

"Yes," Nick said, hissing through his teeth.

Nicole straightened. "I saw his lips through the door window to the hall. It looked like he could have said *bomb*. I'm sure he said *very wet* and then *inside*. I'm pretty sure the last thing he said was *cover* and *up*."

Nick turned those words over in his mind for a few seconds, winked at Tim, hugged Nicole, and then reopened his phone and dialed the same number as before.

"We gotta meet," Nick said. "I'll call you again about where and when."

Nick and Tim started for the door when Tim's cell phone buzzed.

"Yes . . . what did you find? How many times? No, tell the captain that we'll meet him there."

"What was that?" Nick asked.

"Fred said they found where the vice president was staying in Manhattan. Stayed there at least a dozen times in the past month. Captain says we both have to check it out for any connection to the president. It's pretty well on the way to the Battery. We stop. I'll stay. You follow up on the bombs."

Minutes later, as they entered the vice president's apartment, Nick was the first to notice a familiar smell. "El Camino's cigars. Guess we know who done the deeds."

Tim nodded agreement and motioned to Nick to get going. "Keep the president safe."

CHAPTER 63

◆

Nick emerged from the alleyway and was crossing the street when he spotted the motorized raft with five men dressed in black pull into view and head toward the old apartment's dock. He was in position to wave off the throwing of the tie-down rope. He sat down on the dock instead and eased himself down and into the inflated raft.

"Hug as close as you can to the seawall as we head down," he said. "Turn off any lights. We'll be able to see our way, no problem. The moon's not much more than a sliver, but there's enough light for us to stand out if we're not careful. We gotta take it slow."

Sam Kirby nodded.

"Why the change?" the man at the rear of the raft asked. "We're ten blocks from the platform. With no running lights, it will take us another twenty, twenty-five minutes." His tone wasn't accusing, just puzzled.

Sam motioned to the speaker. "Nick, Captain Zachary Warren. Captain, Detective Nicholas Garvey."

Nick nodded. "I parked five blocks up and went down to the gates about ten minutes before I called you. Starting two blocks away, I noticed several of El Camino's men—can't miss their neck tattoos—trying to look casual as they lurked and hovered about every half block. No question in my mind that they were keeping an eye on the site. Making like a night watchman, I walked the full gate, left to right. I caught sight of tattooed lurkers on all of the streets leading away. I checked as best I could and saw no tattoos inside the gates."

"Any along the seawalls?" Warren asked.

"I had to check the East River side. None."

"Got it." Sam chuckled. "Slither in. Defuse. Slither out."

Nick gave a thumbs-up.

Sam nodded at Warren, who eased the seventy-five-horsepower outboard to an acceptable speed. The motor made no noise.

They hugged the seawalls all the way.

The raft slowed as they approached the platform. Sam, Nick, and two of the other four scoured the visible area. No El Camino lookouts spotted.

Slowly, quietly, the raft's motor propelled them under the platform.

Once the raft was still, three of the men pulled on goggles and grabbed breathing masks with elongated tubes running down to a battery-operated air pump. They each popped their breathing mask over their nose and mouth and slid over into the water, barely visible in the near blackness. After double-checking their goggle-and-mask integrity, they sank out of sight.

The remaining man opened a small metal case, revealing a small screen under a shielding shroud. The man leaned into the shroud. After twenty seconds, he started speaking in low tones. Nick couldn't make out what he was saying, but it was obvious he was communicating with his three comrades.

After ten minutes, he turned to Nick. "All six pillars have been checked. Down to bedrock. Nothing."

Nick pursed his lips and looked over to the screen. Bombing the platform while the president stood center stage made terrific sense if you were a terrorist. Sam had said the platform itself had been thoroughly checked six times in the past week, so any bombs had to be underwater. He thought back to what Nicole had said she'd heard.

Very wet had to mean underwater. And didn't *cover* and *up* imply that the bombs were buried? What else could—

"Inside!" Nick looked back up. "As I remember, the pillars are made of steel. Right?"

"Stainless," Warren answered.

"Hollow?"

"With walls two inches thick."

"Could a bomb be placed inside?"

"With extreme difficulty. But there are no wires coming out from the pillars."

Sam chimed in. "You've been watching and talking to the three men fifteen feet underwater."

"Yes."

"How?" Sam looked at Nick.

"Wireless communication," Warren answered.

Nick nodded at Sam. "Could you set off a bomb with your wireless communication?"

Warren's brow furrowed suddenly. His sigh that followed was the sigh of a man who knew he had missed the obvious.

Nick lowered his voice. "Have them check each pillar from water level down through the mud until they hit bedrock. Have them look for any electronic receiving device leading into the pillar."

Sam nodded. "And looking for any device is defined as scraping all sides of the pillar, also checking any noticeable increases in pillar diameter, then checking—"

"Got it!" Warren was on the underwater phone giving instructions.

Ten minutes passed.

Twenty.

Twenty-six.

Warren pulled his head back from the screen. "We got a match!" He gave Nick and Sam one firm thumbs-up before barking a few commands into his headset.

"Two of the pillars each have a receiver-transmitter about five inches below the muck atop the bedrock and placed about two feet away. There's a second receiver inside each pillar connected to what appears to be C-4 packed tight inside for at least two feet. I told them to leave everything as is and check the other four pillars."

Sam looked first at Nick and then at Warren. "We'll have to disarm them."

"Eventually," Warren said. "I'd prefer that the scum that put them there don't know they've been neutered until they throw whatever switch they have."

Nick cleared his throat, shivering in the cold. "Can you do that now? Without—"

"Definitely." Warren pointed at the screen. "They've got everything they need." He cupped his hand over his earpiece. "We've got a third."

The fourth, fifth, and sixth receivers were announced at less than two-minute intervals.

"Could there be more bombs?" Nick asked.

Warren held up a finger. "A moment. Yes. Understood." He turned back to Nick and Sam. "The first pillar has enough packaged C-4 to send pillar and platform to the next county. If the other five have the same, no other bombs would be worthwhile."

Within ten minutes, word was passed up that all six were packed the same.

Warren passed down the order to remove the C-4 while leaving the receiver wiring untouched. He emphasized that *untouched* meant for the entire operation—no disconnects at any time.

It required a shade more than a half hour to disable the first bomb: nine minutes to fluoroscope the inside connections and the extent of the C-4, twelve minutes to drill and chip the receiver free, eight minutes to pull the seven-foot triple-wrapped boa of C-4, two minutes to parallel all connections and clip the C-4 free, and three minutes to replace the receiver and repack the opening.

They did a little better dismantling the remaining five bombs, timewise.

The three no-longer-submerged bomb experts clambered aboard the raft, removed their breathing masks and goggles, and gave one another and Warren high fives.

A call was put in for another group of men to stand watch.

After twenty minutes, six armed men arrived in a second raft and took up position.

Nick and Sam's raft slithered out eighteen minutes before sunrise.

CHAPTER 64

◆

Duane, arriving at his office suite at his usual 7:30 a.m. time, found Jason's note.

My office as soon as you get in.
J

Duane unlocked a desk drawer, dropped the note inside, and relocked the drawer. He turned to go to Jason's office but paused for several moments. What did Jason want? There was no way he could have tracked El Camino's crew. Not even Jason's tracking guru could have without access to the underground. No, he told himself, all plans were safe. He headed off to Jason's office.

Duane noticed the blinds on Jason's windows were open. Unusual. He opened the door and stepped inside. Before he could ask anything, Jason motioned to him to close the door.

Jason directed Duane to sit. "I'm thinking of not attending the lighting ceremony with the president."

"What prompted that decision?" Duane did his best to suppress any facial expression, either of surprise or of concern.

"Last night, I realized that my presence might dilute the public's perception of the president's failure. When the lights don't go on, she should be the one standing alone to take ownership. My sharing the stage might defuse the blow."

Duane swallowed quickly. He had to come up with a convincing counterargument. "Might let her off the hook."

"Exactly," Jason said with a nod.

"Or at least keep the hook from sinking in deep enough."

"Again, exactly. I know the hook will catch to some degree, but I feel it better that everyone watching see her without me."

"But you accepted her invitation over a month ago."

Jason nodded. "So?"

"So do you remember our rationale for your agreeing to join her?"

"To have the world see that I was not her enemy; that, if her efforts proved successful, I would be projected as ready to work with her in growing the energy pie."

"True," Duane said, mentally casting about for an angle to reverse Jason's unexpected decision. "And what was your plan should the grid lighting fail . . . as we know it will?"

"Not just *my* plan. It was *our* plan. Actually, *your* proposal, as I remember. I would be seen as sympathetic with her plight, perhaps even supportive, all the while letting the media decide that the grid was a terrible idea to begin with. With that assessment, her office and her plans to counter the policies of the World Council would be wounded. Mortally."

Duane nodded, still searching for that angle. "And—"

"And?" Jason said, tapping his left forefinger on his desk. "And her prestige will drop like a rock while the World Council will be viewed as the down-to-earth alternative." Jason stopped tapping. "No pun intended."

Alternative! That was the angle Duane needed. "I agree: her prestige will plummet. That was our plan. What we might not have explored sufficiently is the concept you just mentioned: the World Council would be viewed as the alternative. If you are not by her side when she throws the switch, they won't see any alternative at first. They might see it as the World Council, but—"

"But who?" Jason's brow furrowed. "Who else could be viewed as an alternative?"

"Carter Johnson."

"Carter Johnson?"

Duane was not supposed to be aware of Jason's secret plan that allowed Carter's people to blow up the Lincoln Tunnel, but the city was filled with dozens of rumors. Time to use one. The right one. "There's a lot of buzz on the streets that it was Carter Johnson's thugs who blew up the tunnel to hammer the president. There are other rumors, many rumors, but what if this one is more than a rumor? Could Johnson be viewed as an alternative?"

Jason's furrow deepened. "Carter has stated many times that the grid is a most stupid idea."

Duane just shrugged and waited.

Jason stood, strolled to the giant window behind his desk, and looked out at the East River, brightening in the morning sun. The view included Brooklyn, Queens, and almost ninety degrees to his left, the easternmost edge of the grid.

He turned back to face Duane and nodded. "We must be seen as the *only* alternative. I'll join the president."

Nick figured returning to the precinct would be the best place to strategize their next moves. Before he could formulate the outline of a plan, Tim waved him into the captain's office. The room was empty save for themselves.

Tim closed the door behind them. "The captain's still at the apartment. He sent me back to work with you."

"Was it the vice president's apartment?"

Tim nodded. "Surrounded by apartments for the four Secret Service agents."

"Any clues to why he was murdered?"

"Neighbors in two apartments below stated there were frequent loud parties."

"Loud enough to kill over?"

"Doubtful. All the apartments were clean as a whistle, except one. The apartment of one of the agents has gunshot residue on the bathroom doorframe, suggesting he was killed there. The captain is gathering any and all artifacts and statements. He told me to come back and help you."

Nick and Tim rejoined Sam, who was adamant that they should press hard on El Camino's gang, rounding up every last one. Tim countered that they should call off the ceremony. Nick, undecided, believed neither hitting El Camino nor shutting down the ceremony would prove workable. Of one thing Nick was certain: the president, whatever the risk, would not cancel the ceremony. He put it into words, and Sam reluctantly agreed.

Nick walked to the whiteboard and wrote down three bullet points:

*Uniformed and plainclothes police, with only 10 percent in uniform.

*No stopping El Camino's men unless arrest viewed as by the book.

*Second ring of plainclothes around uniformed guard at the barrier.

Sam and Tim held back any comments, allowing Nick to add four more:

*Maintain raft patrol throughout ceremony.

*Plainclothes on all line-of-sight rooftops.

*Two separate com lines. One, standard info. Second, actual & encrypted.

*All police and Secret Service security: by the book.

Nick paused and looked at the other two. "I understand Jason Beck will be attending and on the platform with President Allison. True?"

Sam nodded and held up his cell phone. "I received confirmation a few minutes ago that he will be attending a breakfast meeting with the president to review protocols, stage position, etc."

"I assume you review with Beck's security team all your plans?"

"Definitely."

Nick listed another bullet point.

*Normal interfacing with Beck security team. Protect, but no alert.

Nick put down the marker. "Any major point I've missed?"

Tim and Sam silently reviewed the eight bullet points. As professionals familiar with the ins and outs of security and protection, they knew what detail each bullet point entailed.

Sam nodded. "Think you got it covered."

Tim shook his head. "Nope. You've got nine plainclothes for each uniform. What about patrols in the rest of the city?"

Sam nodded again. Both looked to Nick, who had to think for more than just a few seconds.

"We'll have to enlist some paracop help."

Sam let loose a loud guffaw. "*Enlist* paracops? Since when do they do favors for the 'poor-lice'?"

Nick winked at Tim. "I'll have you know, Mr. Secret Service Man, I'm a registered, bona fide, true-blue, accepted—well, just call me a multicop."

"Multicop?" Sam said with a chuckle.

Nick explained the backstory.

Sam chuckled again.

Tim looked almost convinced. "With Howard Williams dead, will the neighborhood agree?"

"I'm pretty sure, but we'll find out."

"You won't have to give them the details of why we need their help? The bombs, I mean."

"I think I can work up a story that will bring them aboard. The story doesn't have to be super convincing; neighborhoods always figure cops are liars, anyway."

Sam chuckled one last time. "Don't we all lie? Sunrise to sunset."

They shook hands, agreed on the plan, and left to set their various parts into motion.

CHAPTER 65

◆

Nick made it to Robert McKenna's apartment office by 8:30 a.m.

"Detective Garvey—Nick—what can we do for you?" Robert stood, walked from behind his desk, and shook Nick's hand.

"The NYPD needs a lot of patrol help this evening from at least fifty squads of paracops. We've been—"

"Fifty squads! What are you all doing? Is the entire NYPD retiring at noon?" Robert returned to his chair and sat.

"Not quite. Almost the entire department has been ordered to provide security for the president's grid lighting, and the commissioner will have only a skeleton crew patrolling the rest of the city."

"And your commissioner needs some flesh on the bones?"

Nick nodded.

Robert paused for several moments, rubbing the underside of his chin with the back of his right hand. "We could field about ten squads. For fifty squads, you'd need four other neighborhoods—at the least—to buy in."

"So I can count on you?"

"Yes, Detective Garvey. How are you going to round up another four or five neighborhoods?"

Nick gave Robert an exaggerated shrug and, for punctuation, an elevated left eyebrow.

Robert chuckled, bowed, and shook his head. "Are you twisting my arm, Detective?"

Nick offered another shrug.

Robert looked up and smiled. "Once accepted, always accepted. What time?"

"The grid-lighting security starts at four o'clock."

"Have your skeleton leaders in front of this building an hour earlier. With their neighborhood responsibilities."

"In triplicate."

"By the way, Detective, Half-Penny is—excuse me—your 'undercover cop' is super okay. Nathan talks about him a lot. Almost about as much as he talks about you. In fact, Nathan wants Half-Penny and Nicole to be by his side at his father's funeral on Saturday. Your Mr. Braddock set it up to be at the same time and place where he is giving the eulogy for the two nuns. Nathan would like you to say something on behalf of his father."

"Certainly," Nick said, surprised that anyone would honor him with such a request.

As Nick pulled away from the curb, he checked his watch: 8:52 a.m., just more than seven hours before he had to report back to the Battery Park location. He decided he could spare at least four, maybe five hours, with the box.

He called Tim and asked him to have the captain direct the skeleton team leaders to meet with Robert McKenna at Battery Park.

Nick got to his apartment at 9:27 and headed straight for the floorboards, sliding a thin putty knife along two separate side joints. Each movement was accompanied by a muffled click as a hidden latch released. He pulled the box up and carried it to his kitchen table. He stepped to his refrigerator and removed the magnetic chip from Nicole's three-dimensional artwork.

It was time to remove the oilcloth.

Nick grabbed an old pair of scissors from the silverware drawer and cut the oilcloth from top to bottom. He placed the package to his right on the table and unrolled it to his left. He shifted the now-flat oilcloth to his right, bringing to rest in front of him the rolled-up collection of various-sized papers, which were held together tightly by two thick rubber bands.

Nick looked down at the papers. Some were obviously old, judging from their moldy edges. Others looked crisp and relatively new. He picked up the roll in his left hand, managing to get his grip just halfway around, and removed the rubber bands. He wrapped it tightly in the opposite direction, replaced the two rubber bands, placed it back on the table, balanced two heavy books across the top, and got up to make himself a coffee.

Nick had planned to let the mess uncurl for ten minutes, but his impatience got the better of him. After just four minutes, he removed the books and, grabbing the whole collection in a choke-hold, removed the rubber bands. After squeezing one more time, tightly, he uncurled the papers.

There was some improvement—enough for him to discern handwritten papers from official-looking documents and copies of some twenty or more photographs. A few of the photographs were recent and others much older, with a couple, he mused to himself, older than his own baby pictures, which his mother had kept prom-inently displayed on her refrigerator for many years, taking them down only upon his pleading on his twenty-seventh birthday.

His attention was drawn to a seven-by-ten-inch manila enve-lope with a hand-printed legend on the cover. The print, in all-up-percase lettering, declared, "JASON BECK'S JOURNAL."

Nick picked up the envelope and gave it a couple more reverse curls. The sealing flap had been removed, making removing the con-tents quite easy.

The pages appeared to be sheared from an actual journal-type book. Nick counted thirty-two single-sided pages stapled twice along the left edge. Each page had a large handwritten two-digit page number on its top left, about two inches above the top staple. He quickly thumbed through, finding that the first fifteen were of the same paper and had left edges that looked stripped from their larger collection, probably by a ruler. He placed the set of pages atop his table, pressing the edges flat with his coffee mug on the middle of the left edge and applying his left hand to the center and his right to the bottom-right corner.

The first page displayed, in black ink, the handwritten heading:

USEFUL OBSERVATIONS
* Ownership—What Politicians Avoid to Remain Electable.
* Universities—Teach **What** to Think, Not **How** to Think.
* Privileged Class—Souls for Rent. Do Anything to Remain Privileged
* Soldiers—Must Be Paid—No Money, No Army.
* Laws—Enough of Them Can Make Everyone a Criminal.

The bottom of the page was dated 1/1/2019 boldly in the center. Nick guessed that Jason Beck preferred New Year's "observations" to old-fashioned resolutions. He ran his fingers lightly across the page and noticed indents caused by entries from preceding pages.

Nick bent the first page over, raising then lowering his coffee mug, and again pressed the edges flat.

The next page, dated 11/3/2020 and followed by the all-caps heading "CONTRIBUTIONS," showed more than two dozen names scribbled down two columns, with dollar amounts after each name. Nick blinked at several of the amounts. Each blink occurred when he encountered a thirty-seven-year-old figure greater than five times his current yearly salary. Apparently, it took a lot of cash to become a politician. Of twenty-seven names, Nick counted fifteen preceded by a green check mark, four by a red.

The next pages, two of them, made brief mention of how, on Tuesday, July 4, 2023, he had finagled his way, professionally, into the United Nations, securing prominent employment in its treasury arm. He resigned his Senate seat the next day.

On the same page, mention was made of two senators elected in 2022, eight months earlier: Lenora Allison and Carter Johnson. Nick didn't know if the accepted honorific title was supposed to be senator, the honorable, or something else. It was plain the journal writer didn't feel any honor should be attached to those two individuals.

Their names appeared each time without any form of title, five times for Carter and four for Lenora,.

Toward the middle of the page, mention was again made, via a newspaper clipping, of the same two Senate freshmen, who had broken from their respective political bases to lay out a plan to privatize Social Security. Made-up middle names had been inserted in the margin: Carter "Liberal" Johnson and Lenora "Conservative" Allison. The three paragraphs detailed proclaimed benefits and proposed time frames. In the margins were arrows pointing to various claims, their tails circling written comments such as *loonies, morons,* and *never be reelected.* Jason Beck had noted at the bottom of the page that neither had attended college in their home state. Allison had earned an electrical engineering degree from MIT in Cambridge, Massachusetts, followed by a master's in space technology from Stevens Tech in Hoboken, New Jersey. Johnson had received his bachelor's in history from Rice University in Houston, Texas, after which he moved on to Georgetown in DC, where he completed his masters in political science. "OF ABSOLUTELY NO USE!" was written in harsh red strokes with red slashes through the name of each of the four noted institutions. Nick wasn't sure whether the comment was intended to describe the senators or their college institutions. He dimly remembered that, years later, when the World Council was in full swing, a sweeping new law forced all university endowments to be transferred to the council with assurances, short-lived and bogus, that all future university expenses would be met by the council's newly formed education arm. Nick clearly remembered hundreds of colleges and universities shutting their doors from lack of funding, while others, like the four crisscrossed above, received continuing "aid" in the form of swarms of council-provided instructors to replace their errant, high-salaried professors.

The next page, dated 10/12/2023, contained a single column of nineteen names, all of which appeared Arabic, some with up to seven names. Each name was followed by a country: Egypt, Qatar, Oman, and Yemen. Two countries, Afghanistan and Pakistan, followed several names. All but two of the names were preceded by green checks. The remaining two names, from Afghanistan, had been marked with green question marks instead. All names included a circled number following its country. No red markings were anywhere on the page.

The paged dated 9/18/2024 started with a short paragraph noting Jason's promotion to director of UN Finance following the death of the previous director in a plane crash. Mention was made in an attached news clipping of that investigation, which concluded that the pilot, Patrick Farnsworth, had been "impaired" and at fault.

That news clipping was not easy to read, because a box had been drawn around the item in red ink with a big, slashing *X* through it. Also in red was the single word *LIES* in all capital letters, repeated, Nick counted, seventeen times. The handwriting was noticeably different.

Below that paragraph, untouched by any of the above red markings, was the three-word heading "PLANNED EXPENDITURE REDIRECTIONS," which was followed by a column of circled numbers from one to nineteen, obviously related to the nineteen Arabic names from the previous page. Eighteen numbers were followed by one or more dollar amounts. The remaining number had a red *X* through it. Nick flipped back to the previous page and noted the lone exception matched one of the two Afghani names with the green question marks. All dollar amounts were more than fifty and ran as high as 275, each followed with the single letter *M*. Nick shook his head, wondering how the lone fifty-million-dollar man, warlord, or whatever felt about receiving as much as five times less than the others in "expenditure redirections."

The 10/17/25 entry was devoted exclusively to senators Allison and Johnson and their successful shepherding of the Social Security Privatization Bill to a successful veto-proof passage into law. The sheet, with its handwriting devolving into scribbles, was filled with characterizations far worse than the *loonies* and *morons* Jason had used two years previous. Each of the two was a natural leader, Jason noted, and if they ever joined forces again, a new paradigm would blossom that would be extremely hard to control. Nick noticed that one line was quite legible, bold, and in all caps:

THESE TWO MUST BE KEPT AT
EACH OTHER'S THROATS!!!

Three exclamation points. Nick was impressed.

The next two pages were each subdivided into dated subsections. The dates ran from 11/1/25 through 7/12/27 and briefly explained how Jason was continuing to direct significant UN funds to various Arab states, the stated reason being to "encourage self-sufficiency." That self-sufficiency came to a head as noted on the almost-empty page headed with the infamous date 09/19/27. The page featured two hand-printed lines of three words each:

DEATH OF OIL
RISE OF CONTROL

Nick thought the second line spoke volumes when it came to Jason Beck's approach to the world.

The 9/19/29 page was primarily self-congratulatory, Jason having been promoted to deputy secretary general of the United Nations. One entry caught Nick's attention. It was the "goal" of having each sovereign nation "sell" all rights to its oil to the UN, the stated aim being to establish "energy equality" across all nations. People were starving around the globe. Energy equality, dispensed by the UN, would alleviate hunger and prevent millions from dying. Twelve target countries, representing 70 percent of the world's remaining production and reserves, were listed, with all but three checked off as complying. The three footdraggers were the United States, China, and Russia.

Nick remembered Russia having caved about two or three months later, its population plummeting, its old far outnumbering its young. With that unfavorable condition, its fiscal condition was teetering at the cliff's edge.

A half page was devoted to the moment when Chris Price joined with Jason on 10/08/30 to form what would become the World Council, supplanting the withered United Nations. Jason noted his intent to keep Chris focused on population control, using his devastation over his beloved Gabrielle's death as a motivational *CONTROL*. There was that word again—in all caps.

On the bottom half of the same page, dated 9/19/31, Jason gave himself a handwritten pat on the back after the World Council convinced all major countries to join a binding international embargo on the number of children permitted per married couple. One couple, one child became the law of all lands. A small note observed that a voucher system had been set up for childless couples to sell the right to have one child to another couple. From the harsh slant to the writing of that last sentence, Nick guessed that Jason was not very enthused about vouchers.

The full-page entry for 9/19/32 started with what read like another pat on Jason's back as the World Council reached agreement with the United States to join the Energy Equality Program after exactly three years of the program's initiation. The only major country still refusing to sell its oil and other fossil fuel rights to the World Council was China. The words *China rejects all overtures* were even more harshly slanted than those indicating Jason's reaction to child vouchers.

The 9/19/32 page concluded with some quick math that calculated that the World Council controlled 87 percent of the world's fossil fuels. The 2/25/33 page caused Nick to shake his head. Extensive references were made to old research, pre-death-of-oil research, into infectious diseases, their sources, their methods of spreading, their incubation times, and mortality rates. Nothing on the rest of the page fit with Jason's driving interest in controlling world politics. They were notations Nick might have encountered while perusing a med student's lecture notes.

The creation of paracops in New York City merited a single page dated 2/20/36. A short newspaper clipping was taped to the page. Underlined in red was the following sentence: "NYPD falls to 33% of 2026 levels, needing rescue by city neighborhoods." Nick remembered taking pains to be unavailable for the initial welcome aboard meeting between the NYPD brass and the neighborhood leaders.

The 1/4/38 page had notes scrawled all over it. Three separate clippings were taped to it, each proclaiming the same event: *International Law Replaces US Constitution.* The handwritten notes, again in red, ranged from *TRASHES Constitution, doesn't REPLACE it* to *Take that, Founding OBSOLETE Fathers.* Most ominous: *First Amendment, first to go!!!* Three exclamation points again. Nick figured that, in addition to loathing President Allison and Carter Johnson, Jason had little love for Messrs. Jefferson, Adams, and Washington.

The next page was of different texture and slightly larger. The handwriting was tight but neat and obviously didn't belong to the journal's original record keeper. Jason had used a pinch-writer. The ink was dark blue and, following the journal's original template, displayed the date 1/21/38 in bold across the top. The first paragraph was short, noting that a close friend, Margaret Farnsworth, had been murdered less than ten hours after handing the previous journal pages for safekeeping the day before. The current writer closed the paragraph by identifying himself: Seth Morris.

The remaining paragraphs detailed how Margaret, the stepdaughter of Patrick Farnsworth, had been convinced from day 1 that her stepdad was in no way at fault for the plane crash that had resulted in the elevation of Jason Beck. Seth wrote down how Margaret, going under her unchanged legal last name of Brittleman, had spent the previous thirteen and a half years working her way up the ladder at the World Council Headquarters. Her extreme and discreet professionalism had gained her the awareness of Jason Beck himself. After several interviews, he had appointed her to be his executive secretary in January 2036.

Seth described how she had gained Jason's full trust; how she had noted each appointment and contact; how she had passed along any of Jason's out-of-the-ordinary meetings to him, Seth; how he had repeatedly warned her to be careful and not press her luck; how, after one such warning, she had just smiled and handed him some repair documents showing replacement of several cockpit indicators and controls in the doomed plane within a day of the crash; how, as she had handed over those specific documents, she had asserted that no request for replacement had ever been filed.

The next page, dated 4/12/38, charged Jason with an obscene crime:

In June of 2035, China suffered a deadly plague that took 37% of its people, mostly young, working-age men and women. Children not having reached puberty were uninfected, as were the elderly. Those few infected who did not die spent months in rehab. China's industries were brought to their knees, and less than a year later, China agreed to the Energy Equality Treaty.

The page ended with Seth claiming he had proof that Jason Beck, via selected subordinates at the World Council, had introduced the plague in China, a plague whose infection parameters Jason had researched per his notes entered on the 2/25/33 page. The final two lines explained why Owen Pendleton's nephew, Seth Morris, if he indeed had possessed such evidence, had been murdered three weeks later: "I will safeguard the following evidence, add to it, and turn it over to the world. Jason Beck will rot alive in hell!"

The next four pages detailed the creation, packaging, shipment to China, and exposure of six "Patient Zeros." The pages proved the plague was planned but failed to tie it to Jason.

Another three pages, each covering one week, revealed Seth's investigations until he was found in Saint Vartan's Park with a bullet in his head. Low-level street thugs—thugs who had no direct contact with the World Council but were "acquaintances" of council employees—had confessed to the crimes.

Jason Beck was a prime suspect in the murder of at least 420 million Chinese people. What was missing was a smoking gun. One gun *was* mentioned. Seth wrote that he felt in danger and therefore had "acquired" a pistol for self-defense.

In his last entry, Seth wrote that he had removed from his apartment the metal box of evidence he had collected. He explained that, the night before, he had surprised a burglar ransacking his apartment and shot him dead. He had decided he would hide the box where a good friend would be sure to find it. The date at the bottom of this last page was 4/30/38, two days before Nick and Gerry had found Seth lashed to the park swing.

Nick spread out and uncurled seven more pages. Four were in Gerry Martin's handwriting. Three were accounting-type financial-entry sheets. The dates noted beside each significant entry started at 5/22/38 and ran through 8/10/57, one day after Gerry had met with Nick in the park.

Gerry was good. Damn good! There were at least four smoking guns: three on paper and one on voice crystal. Two photographs showed Jason meeting late at night with some man in nondescript clothes. Neither photo revealed the man's features.

Gerry, or Seth, had also included photographs of dead Chinese teenagers—*many* dead teenagers. One of the photographs showed a middle-aged Chinese man, lines of grief etched across his face, looking down at a corpse of a young man in his twenties. Nick recognized the photo and the middle-aged man from his long night at the library, poring over the front pages of the *New York Times*. The middle-aged man was then the premier of China. Now, twenty-two years later, he was elderly but still the premier.

Twenty-two years ago, that middle-aged Chinese man had thanked Jason and the World Council for developing a vaccine that was credited with stopping the plague in its tracks. Now, were he to learn what was in these documents, the still-spry premier would, doubtless, settle for Seth Morris's promise that "Jason Beck will rot alive in hell." Nick figured the premier would consider that just the starting point. In a just world, the whole World Council would join Jason in hell.

The sixth of Gerry's seven sheets tied in a neat, legal bow Jason's collusion with Middle Eastern rebel and terrorist groups. Three ledger pages were taped to that sheet, one atop the other. The ledger sheets spelled out in detail how Jason had helped fund the Arabic groups that had poisoned more than half of the world's oil. Gerry noted where he had hidden six additional ledger sheets.

Gerry's last sheet granted Jason Beck one thumbs-up, summarizing how, long after the World Council had "bought" 90-plus percent of the world's remaining oil, Jason had cajoled, threatened, bluffed, and bought off all major powers to begin programs to convert high-grade nuclear fuel, much of it installed in warheads atop rockets, into forms suitable for feeding into electricity-generating plants. Gerry complimented Jason's successful results but gave him a thumbs-down for hijacking about a hundred such warheads so he could hold any part of the world hostage at any time in the future for any reason or whim that possessed him at the moment. Gerry detailed the locations of twenty-seven still-active warheads, twelve of which had been reinstalled atop new missiles. He noted there were at least forty-two warheads he had been unable to trace.

Nick connected the voice crystal to his earpiece. Gerry's voice, hurried and in a whisper, stated he was closing in on a key operation in the nationwide kidnapping operation. This undercover assignment, Gerry whispered, was of his own doing, and its progress, even its existence, was unknown by anyone. Mention was made of his infiltration of a high-level kidnapping group operating out of Manhattan. He planned to wrap up his investigation shortly and would let some important people see his evidence. He said that Jason was involved in the evil trade up to his eyeballs and that the proof of the supreme director's complicity was also hidden in the ledger sheets.

Nick pieced together the time frame of Gerry's investigation and concluded the voice crystal had been recorded and dropped into the box just hours before Gerry's murder.

Nick wanted to delve deeper into the details of what Gerry had unearthed so he could construct a timeline to help President Allison and others understand the extent of the Jason Beck threat, but one glance at his watch, which read 2:09 p.m., told him it was past time to pack up and go.

CHAPTER 66

◆

Jason walked alone into the Waldorf's executive dining room just after one o'clock as the waiters were starting to clear the tables and headed toward where President Allison, her back to the entrance, stood. An aide motioned toward Jason, and she turned and nodded.

Jason strode directly to her and extended his right hand.

President Allison took it and gave it her usual firm shake. "I didn't expect to see you until the ceremony," she said. "I'm glad you could make it. Sorry you missed the food. It was excellent. The chefs in your city surely know how to do it up right."

"That they do." Jason decided to match banality with banality.

President Allison gestured with her left hand toward the projection screen at the center of the stage. "During breakfast we had a short presentation highlighting the sequence of events during the ceremony. There weren't many questions at all," she said, shrugging.

"Just compliments to the chef?"

"A few," she said with a chuckle. "Fewer than one would expect."

Jason surveyed the room, mentally ticking off each foreign head of state. He counted seventeen. China, Russia, Mexico, and most of the Arab states were present. He nodded to the half dozen who waved to him.

Jason took leave of President Allison and sauntered over to a group of three presidents and one premier, each of whom had waved. They appeared a bit uneasy as he closed in.

They shook hands and, where appropriate, bowed slightly while exchanging greetings and pleasantries. Intermixed were what Jason mentally labeled excuses.

"My energy minister told me I simply had to attend."

"Had plans to be here in a couple of weeks. Decided to move the trip up to see the great unveiling."

Jason's favorite: "My grandson insisted I come and bring him. He assured me it would help his science project."

Closest to the truth: "Wanted to check out energy alternatives. Maybe a grid in every country will help everyone when you have a supply constraint." Not so truthful, the second part.

"Jason's World Council anticipated that possibility," said President Allison, suddenly at Jason's left elbow. "That's why he's supportive of this effort."

Those words from the president raised the eyebrows of all four heads of state.

President Allison turned to face Jason with a slight smile.

The eyebrows of the four heads of state switched from raised to quizzical as each studied Jason.

Jason nodded. "True."

He and President Allison drifted off together. They stopped at the side table with five coffeepots.

Jason reached for the decaf. "That was all in the spirit of inclusion, I take it."

President Allison poured herself a large cup of espresso. "They looked like they needed something or someone to put them at ease."

Jason chuckled. "That they did."

"They looked very worried that you would cut their oil allotment to zero just for them attending the ceremony."

Another chuckle. "They did look that way, didn't they? I would never cancel their allotment just for being here."

President Allison finished a swig of her espresso and winked. "Never cancel, but review, maybe?"

"Can't afford to alienate well-paying customers."

It was President Allison's turn to chuckle. "'Can't afford to alienate.' I assume that's your story and you're sticking to it."

Jason offered a touché tilt of his head. "In that vein, if the grid is successful this evening, what will you do for an encore? Only one grid. Not enough power even for all of the city."

"A start."

"But only one grid."

"At a time."

"How much did this one grid set you back?"

"A pretty penny."

Another Jason chuckle. "How about 6.2 billion dollars in 'pretty' pennies?"

Mock amazement crossed the president's face. "You do have your sources. Who knew?"

Jason nodded, his hands spread outward in a gesture of generosity.

President Allison brought her hands together in mock applause. "All along you've refrained from commenting, but many know, myself included, that you're not rooting for success. On the contrary . . ." She tipped her head at Jason and took another sip of her espresso. "At seven thirty this evening, you'll be surprised how well the grid will work."

Jason nodded. "I agree. Everyone will be surprised at seven thirty."

He had to admit that President Allison was one cool cucumber. He allowed the smallest trace of a smile as he conjured up the image of Chef Jason Beck slicing and dicing one Allison Cucumber for an empty plate of grid salad.

Barbs and banalities done, they parted ways.

CHAPTER 67

◆

I t was three minutes shy of 2:40 p.m. when Nick returned to Area Sunrise, the code name the Secret Service honchos had settled on that morning for the Battery Park platform.

"Area Sunrise?" Nick said. "Who's the original thinker?"

Sam just shrugged and shook his head. "The mayor decided it would be appropriate," he said, checking his watch and pressing a button. "Let's see: September 6, sunset at 7:21 p.m. The switch-throwing ceremony is scheduled to start at 7:30. My guess is 7:35 for when it's actually thrown—enough time for any lights to stand out."

"For the history books, no doubt," Tim added, chuckling.

Sam shrugged again and stared straight at Nick. "What's the story with your paracops?"

"Robert McKenna is the director now. Elected last night."

"Isn't he the fellow who was against your selection—or approval or whatever?" Tim asked before Nick could complete what he was saying.

Nick nodded. "Yes, he was the one who held out the longest against my acceptance, but he accepts me now. He said his men are all in. I assume he's a poker player from long ago. He and a couple others will be here in about two hours after he gets his men stationed around the city as best as he can."

Sam pursed his lips. "Do you trust him? We'll have given him free range. Instead of preventing looting, he could, with no real police around, grab everything in sight."

"I trust him."

Sam looked at Tim, his eyes silently asking him the same question.

"If Nick trusts him, I trust him."

"Fine with you two, fine with me." Sam paused for a moment. "I'm not completely fine with the platform, though. I'm going back under to make a modification to the switch."

Nick's brow furrowed. "Modification?"

"I'm going to cut the line between the switch and the grid." Sam paused for a moment.

"And?" Nick prompted.

"And work up some way for me to throw a switch of my own that will prevent the switch the president will be closing from completing any circuit. What I still have to figure out is getting my switch to do the closing without using anything connected to the president's switch. I gotta keep the lines separate but throw my switch close to the same instant."

"Seems like you've got a lot to do," Nick said, recognizing the logic behind Sam's plan as well as the difficulty in execution. "Do you need us?"

"No, thanks. I know what to do and how to do it. I just have to figure out where."

"Tim and I will stay here. How long do you figure you'll need?"

"If I come back before the ceremony, it will be to *stop* the ceremony. I'll call your cell when I've replaced the switch. No call, *you* stop the ceremony."

Nick tipped his head in agreement. "Call when you first get down by the switch so I know we've got a connection."

Sam chuckled. "Will do, Mom." He shook hands with Nick and Tim and headed uptown.

Nick and Tim went across the street to the Secret Service command center. For almost an hour, they reviewed plans and real-time communications.

At 3:30 in the afternoon, Nick and Tim split up to check side streets, each with two Secret Service agents.

Ten minutes later, Robert McKenna hailed Nick, who crossed back to the entrance gate.

"Any problems?" Nick asked.

"None. We have seventeen units of our own men, plus thirty-six units from three other neighborhoods patrolling most of Manhattan. No serious activity."

"Thanks. I'll pass the word on up. I've already made it clear in no uncertain terms that your men and the others have free rein and must be left alone—within reason."

Robert grunted. "I know. We can spit on the sidewalk, but no breaking windows."

They both chuckled. Robert turned and left.

Nick and Tim rejoined the undercover details. No suspicious activity had been noted anywhere near Battery Park.

The first dignitaries, low level, started arriving at 3:45. Each was funneled into a credential checkpoint and then seated in a pre-determined seat with the admonition that no one could move about without an escort—the old kindergarten "raise your hand" rule.

Jason Beck arrived at 5:14 and had his credentials checked. Since he was to be seated next to the president, he was taken to the tented speaker-holding area.

Nick, now knowing what was in the metal box, decided to keep close tabs on Mr. Beck.

Over the next forty-five minutes, Nick entered the holding area three times. Each time he caught Jason watching his every move. Obviously, the CEO of the World Council was interested in him. Nick decided to make his own show of interest more obvious.

Sam called Nick with the go-ahead at 5:52.

President Allison arrived at six o'clock.

Nick was in the center of the holding area when the president entered. Although the entrance was thirty feet from Nick, she bowed her head in recognition. She was then ushered off to meet with some key dignitaries.

Twenty minutes later, as Nick was about to head out to the plat-form gate, President Allison's voice immediately to his left startled him. "How is Nicole?"

"She's fine," Nick replied, appreciating the president's concern. "Treats the whole kidnapping and rescue as a grand adventure."

"Good for her." President Allison smiled and gave Nick's left shoulder a quick squeeze. "You'll have to let me meet her sometime." She smiled again before being whisked away.

The Secret Service started their final preceremony surveillance dry run. Nick conferred with them just long enough to be assured that all rooftops and side streets were secure. He backed away, letting the Secret Service do what they did best, and returned to Tim at the gate.

At 7:10, the president, Jason, and six other officials were marched from the tent straight to the podium. By 7:20, everyone was settled.

The Secret Service relinquished only the tiniest bit of authority to the television director in charge of capturing the ceremony. Once made aware of the limits of his leash, he gave directions primarily to the Secret Service agent second in command. Through this chain of command, people and microphones were moved into place.

At 7:28, President Allison went to the podium. A Secret Service man approached and whispered something to her. She nodded, and he retreated.

At 7:29, the stage was flooded with light, and a video monitor to Nick's left flashed on.

At 7:30, the monitor displayed the president at the podium.

"Good evening, citizens of these United States," she said, slowly moving her gaze from left to right, as if including everyone in the viewing audience. "You all know why we're here this evening: to restore power to this great city; to restore energy; to restore pride, commitment, determination; to restore our destiny." President Allison paused and looked at the seat next to the one she had recently left. She extended her right hand in that direction. "Many of you may wonder why the supreme director of the World Council is here for this ceremony. Some of you may wonder if the grid has his approval." She paused again.

Nick watched the TV camera swing slightly stage right, zooming in as it did. On the monitor, Jason Beck's poker face was framed, throat to full head of hair.

President Allison pulled her arm back. The camera remained on Beck's face. "The World Council has not approved the grid, nor has it disapproved. Jason Beck has allowed us to go forth with this great experiment, has allowed us to, hopefully, pull free of our bondage to diminished resources." The president extended her right hand again. "I would like to ask Director Beck to join me here at the podium so that I may personally thank him for the World Council's position."

Nick noticed just the slightest ripple of surprise cross Beck's face. Jason Beck nodded, stood, and joined the president.

"Thank you, Director Beck, for allowing this mighty enterprise to move forward." She shifted slightly to her left, allowing Beck access to the microphone, should he be so disposed.

The camera, which had zoomed out as he moved to the podium, zoomed back in. Beck projected the assurance of a man possessing supreme confidence.

"Thank you, President Allison, for the opportunity." As the president had, Jason paused and moved his gaze slowly from left to right. "Thank you for the opportunity to share this stage with you on this momentous occasion. As President Allison has said, we neither approved nor disapproved of the solar satellite connection to this grid. We did not have the expertise. President Allison herself is the first of her team to have the background and the education to fully understand all the myriad ins and outs of this terribly complex technical challenge. She is the first, the foremost on her team, to know this project and the potential benefits it will bring. In a few minutes, when the city lights return to their former glory, it will be President Allison's dream embracing reality. The World Council just didn't have the insight to risk the billions spent to relight the world." Jason Beck started to turn back toward his seat, hesitated, and then returned to the microphone. He looked straight at President Allison, who stood just three feet to his left. "I salute you, President Allison, for your vision and your daring. Not only this city, but the world needs more light, and forgive the pun, throwing that switch"—he waved his left hand at the foot-long lever—"will be the highlight of your administration, the beacon of your engineering foresight, from which we will all benefit."

Jason gave the president a formal head bow and returned to his seat.

"Thank you for your kind words, Director Beck," President Allison said, reclaiming the microphone.

Nick watched with increasing anticipation as President Allison wrapped her right hand around the lever. The action reminded Nick of the bygone era of slot machines: pull and hope. Pull and hope.

President Allison faced the camera. "This switch and these lights are for all of you. They will bring power back to New York City. Back to the United States of America. Back, as you heard Supreme Director Beck just say, to the world. With the throwing of this switch, the world will reacquire cheap power, the engine that will propel us again onto and along the road to tremendous growth."

The camera zoomed in closer so that just President Allison, the top of the podium, and the switch lever were visible.

President Allison winked at the camera and pulled down on the lever.

CHAPTER 68

◆

After a full second, no city lights came on.

Another second, no streetlights came on.

After three seconds, the screen image changed to a shot of lower Manhattan, still dark, with a small square of the president in the upper left.

Four seconds passed, and Nick frowned. Without any prompting by an itch, he turned to Beck.

After five seconds, Jason's lips curled into a satisfied smirk.

At twelve seconds, with no shining city lights, Nick concluded Sam had been unable to reconnect all the circuits. He turned from the screen to the podium. President Allison wore a puzzled expression. Murmurs from the crowd started to build, floating to the podium.

Jason's smirk had turned into a broad grin at fifteen seconds.

At sixteen seconds, streetlights blinked on throughout the neighborhood. The screen image showed lights rippling on throughout Manhattan, from Battery Park up to the Empire State Building.

Nick saw relief sweep across President Allison's features. He turned back to Jason and saw an expression somewhere between stupefaction and seething fury.

Sporadic, low-level applause rose from the front row outside the gate. The applause built as it was joined from all quarters in the park. Horns and drums and gongs from the far reaches of the neighborhood joined in as windows were thrown open and people cheered.

Nick saw Sam pull himself up over the far edge of the platform. Sam stood and waved to Nick. Sam's body shook for a moment in the cool evening, and then he walked toward Nick.

The president watched as Sam crossed the stage in front of her. Guessing his destination, she stepped from the podium and approached Nick.

Sam was huffing and puffing as he stopped in front of Nick. "Damned feeder cable pulled loose just as I threw my switch."

Jason stood and joined the three.

Nick raised his left hand. "No sweat, big man. You finally did turn all the lights on. No one really noticed that it took ten or fifteen seconds."

President Allison gave Sam a stern look. "You had a second switch? Why?"

Sam shifted his gaze from the president to Jason and then back. His expression was a big question mark.

"No secrets," President Allison said, her tone controlled.

Sam nodded. "We had to disconnect your switch because of six bombs."

President Allison and Jason blinked several times.

"Bombs?" Jason asked a half second ahead of the president.

Sam paused again.

"No secrets," President Allison repeated.

"The six pillars holding up this platform were packed with C-4 explosive. Enough to blow the whole platform at least fifty feet in the air—if any piece of it survived the first two inches. The explosive was packed inside each pillar with igniter leads connected to your switch to blow when you brought it down. I installed the second switch using a separate power source after Nick and myself found the explosives early this morning."

"This morning?" President Allison asked, trying to piece things together.

"It wasn't just Sam and myself," Nick said, interrupting. "We had a raft of demolition experts with us checking the pillars from top to bottom. They were the ones who found the stuff inside each pillar, using some type of underwater x-ray machine. Took a while to find the first one, but then the rest were easy."

"Thank you, both," the president said.

"Yes. Thank you," Jason added. "I do have one question. How did you know where to look?"

Sam deferred to Nick with a nod.

"I pieced together something my granddaughter overheard about bombs being in the water."

Both Jason and President Allison looked puzzled.

"Who did she overhear, and where did she hear it?" Jason asked, his voice tinged with suspicion.

"She heard it while she was kidnapped. Actually, she didn't really hear it. She read lips through a door window."

"So it was one of her kidnappers?" Jason's mouth was tight, his lips almost invisible.

"A real fat one, she said. The one giving everyone orders."

Jason's eyes were steady, unblinking.

Well, Nick mused while watching Jason's unnatural calm, *at least one of the four of us knows who did it.*

CHAPTER 69

A cold sweat gripped Duane. The screen images were clear, very clear. Clear not only in resolution, but also in what had not happened. Clear in where the police were pointing: the six pillars. Clear in Jason's facial reactions and clear in who he believed responsible.

Duane knew Jason well enough to know that he must go into hiding. He immediately set about making a few "adjustments" to his apartment before retrieving his on-the-run kit.

◆

Jason, as soon as he closed the limousine door, pulled out his cell phone. He didn't know how the president had pulled it off, but the lighting of New York City had just brought her a wellspring of public support. He was determined to bring that support down by restoring balance in the political world.

A voice crackled over the phone.

"Jeremiah," Jason said, "I have immediate need of you and your men."

A time and location were quickly agreed upon. Jason pocketed the phone and gave the driver directions.

As the limousine sped north, Jason pondered how to restore the balance between himself and the president. She had captured the attention of all New York City. She had—no! Not just New York City. The whole country. The whole world. He must remove her from the picture while appearing to be her supporter. Jason smiled.

She had, before throwing the switch, shared ownership with the World Council. Being her supporter was now a given.

It hit him. The whole country knew President Allison had a political adversary. Time to turn that adversary into an enemy—a deranged but deadly enemy. Jason knew now what had to be done.

Carter Johnson. He chuckled to himself. *Stand up and take a bow.* Once he got Jeremiah moving, Duane was next on his list.

Duane descended into the basement and then into a tunnel air vent he had converted years ago. His first mission had to be the "blinding" of Jason. He had no doubt Jason would want him dead. Even with all the resources Duane had at his disposal, Jason's secret weapon would be able to track him down. He had to silence that weapon. *Now!*

He grabbed his survival folder with its list of names, placed it into a shoulder bag, and entered the tunnel.

CHAPTER 70

◆

While Sam talked with one of the young Secret Service agents, Nick called Robert McKenna to update him and get any status. No problems on his end.

"I hope it stays that way," Nick said, and hung up.

Sam joined Nick and told him they'd be on hand for a few more minutes while the president met with her newfound admirers.

Nick nodded. "I guess Jason Beck doesn't fall into that 'admirer' category."

"Guess not," Sam said, chuckling. "He sure left in one hell of a hurry."

"Rumor has it he couldn't stand the light," Nick said with a grin.

Sam feigned a painful grimace and grinned back.

President Allison made the rounds among all the dignitaries, foreign and domestic, shaking hands and assuring each and every one that the technology they just witnessed would be made available to all.

Each person she engaged was eager to hear her words. Their demeanor, in almost each case, was energized, almost excited—most unusual for dignitaries, statesmen, stateswomen, and senators, Nick thought. Several knots of people gravitated slowly toward President Allison, each eager for its group's turn to congratulate, applaud, receive commitments, and to simply bask in her success. Each group took up at least five minutes of the president's time.

After the third or fourth group, Captain Nelson Mooney, Sam's boss, drifted over. "Great work, you two," he said, shaking hands with both men. "The president told me you have an idea who planted the bombs," he said, looking at Nick.

"A tubby scumbag of a gang leader who goes by the name of an antique automobile: El Camino."

"That's it?"

"That, and the eighteen thugs I counted on the various side and spoke streets, each covered with his gang's neck tattoos."

"How did you recognize the tattoos?"

"I shot and killed seven of them. Yesterday."

"Oh," Captain Mooney said, clearly taken aback.

Mooney's cell phone rang. He excused himself and answered it.

CHAPTER 71

Jason was pleased with Jeremiah's preparation and the detail of his plan. "You're sure that's the best place for the capture?"

Jeremiah nodded. "It will assure minimum bloodshed—at least on our side and, if well behaved, theirs. Tell your man we'll be ready in less than twenty minutes."

"I've already alerted him," Jason said as he pulled out his cell and speed-dialed again. As he waited for the ring, he started to think of how he was going to dispose of Duane.

◆◆◆

Duane emerged from the subway tunnel into an abandoned building directly across the street from Bert Freed's apartment. This particular exit had served him well since he had broken it through almost two years ago after six arduous months tracking Chet Bolling's every after-work move. Duane could never figure out why Jason kept him as a council vice chair. Six weeks of tracking revealed why: Bolling took small dogs, two at a time, to the apartment Duane later determined belonged to one Bert Freed.

Duane climbed the stairs to the building's second floor and, starting at the leftmost corner office and working his way to the right corner office, checked out the front exterior of Mr. Freed's ground-floor apartment from all angles. Satisfied, he changed into a suit identical to the one Bolling frequently wore on his "dog deliveries."

Duane slipped in some sculpted foam around his stomach to approximate Bolling's girth. No harm in attention to detail. He'd need the visuals to gain entrance since he didn't have the password.

The six months had been spent befriending Bolling and then inviting him to several wild parties. In the process, Duane had learned Freed's name and that he had "one hell of a lot of computer screens." When he had asked Bolling about the dogs, after urging him to "bottoms up" his fourth beer during one of the parties, the hammered vice chair had mumbled that he just put them in cages in the rear of the apartment—and that on subsequent visits he never saw the dogs he had delivered the time before. He also revealed, halfway through his fifth beer, that Mr. Freed was strapped into a wheelchair and had a couple of weird giant lizards as pets.

It had been the many computer screens that had interested Duane. He had had his suspicions of Mr. Freed's role in the organization, which he later confirmed by staging several political "events" directed against the World Council, only to learn they had either been neutralized or destroyed. The confirmation was that Mr. Bert Freed was Jason's secret information guru. When, on a very few occasions, he had witnessed Jason entering the apartment, suspicion had given way to double confirmation.

As he buttoned up his overcoat that resembled Chet Bolling's, Duane knew his short-term safety depended on eliminating tracking guru Bertram Freed. He returned to the first floor and picked up the carrying cage with two sedated cocker spaniels he had brought with him.

While holding the dog cage in his right hand and a pocketed Glock 9 mm in his left, Duane emerged, crossed the street, and seeing no one around, released his handgun in his pocket and pressed the door buzzer.

Duane broke into a coughing fit, which he hoped would gain him entrance without the password.

After several seconds, the small speaker on his left crackled to life. "Password?"

Duane, coughing, muttered something that didn't sound like anything. Without prompting, he took a couple of deep breaths, raised his head only slightly toward the camera he knew was above his right shoulder, took one more deep breath as if ready to say the password, and then broke again into his best coughing jag. After about ten or twelve hacks, he backed away slightly and raised his left hand and the cage for the camera's view. He then tried to stretch out the word "dogs," interspersed with new coughs.

A buzzer sounded, and the door opened.

CHAPTER 72

Nick and Sam were checking in with the NYPD posted near the platform when Captain Mooney tapped Sam on the shoulder.

Sam turned. "Yes, Captain. Are we ready to move the president?"

The captain nodded. "We are. But I want you to stay behind."

Sam arched his eyebrows. "Why? Your phone call a minute ago have anything to do with my staying behind?"

"From the director. You and Detective Garvey discovered the bombs. A team from Homeland Security is on their way. The director has requested that you debrief them."

"All right," Sam agreed in a reluctant tone.

Jason, satisfied that his phone call had started the capture sequence, now had to decide the best way to handle the Duane situation. There was no question it had to be handled outside the council. He would need access to the recordings of every video camera in New York City so he could backtrack his underling's traitorous movements in the remote chance there was any blowback.

Jason clicked his teeth. Time to bring in his magic wand. He dug back into his pocket for his cell phone.

Duane reached behind to close the door but found it closing itself. Bolling had mumbled a description of the long hallway emptying into the large room containing a "shitload" of computer screens.

Underestimated, Duane thought as he emerged from the hallway. The main room was immense, reminding him of a roller rink he had skated in as a child. "A triple shitload of computer screens" seemed to Duane only a *slight* understatement.

Bert leaned toward the oversized screen in front of him, which, even from the distance of thirty feet, Duane could tell contained the image of him carrying the dog cage.

Bert swiveled his wheelchair to face Duane. "You're not Chet Bolling."

Duane coughed a few times. "He's sick. He probably—" Duane let loose with a string of coughs, covering his mouth with his free hand. "He probably gave it to me."

Bert said nothing as he sat and stared at Duane.

A couple more coughs. Duane lifted the cage slightly. "Chet asked me to get these over here as soon as I could. He said the schedule be damned." Duane waited for a reaction. Nothing. He motioned toward where Bolling had said the kennel was. "If I can get these pooches in their cages, I'll be on my way." Three more coughs. "Gotta get back and take my medicine."

Bert waved him on.

After forcing additional coughs, Duane lugged the cage toward the kennel door. As he passed the center of the room, he looked at the immense pit on his left. At the far side was a Komodo dragon resting on a ramp that led down into the pit. Several small bones scattered around the middle of the depression answered one question he had about what happened to the pups.

Duane opened the kennel door, closed it, and placed his cage on the floor. There was no need to place each of the spaniels into one of the kennel cages lining both sides of the passageway. Time was somewhat of a premium. After spotting some treats in a small bin, he tossed several into the small cage. He then slid his left hand into the pocket with his Glock, turned, and headed back.

Up ahead, Bert was on the phone, his back to Duane, who walked silently but swiftly toward the wheelchair. The words "dead man wheeling," a bastardization of an old phrase, flitted through his mind.

He had closed about half the distance when Bert dropped the phone and wheeled around to face Duane. He held a pistol. Pointed at Duane.

CHAPTER 73

◆

Jason's limousine, already covering its chosen route, pulled to a stop in front of Bert's building.

As the driver turned off the motor, Jason keyed Bert's number on his phone. There was no answer on the first ring. Expected.

Nor the second. Nor the third. By the fourth ring, Jason became concerned. He got out, marched to the entrance, and entered the nine-digit code he'd used before. The door did not open.

After about five seconds, he entered it again. Nothing.

More than a minute passed before Jason returned to the limousine. After motioning to the driver that they were staying put, he pressed a release button on the seat back in front of him. A flat tray with a laptop computer on it eased down into a horizontal position.

Bert had set up several programs in the laptop that could access a few control applications within Bert's mainframe. Jason vaguely remembered Bert saying something about a control routine for the front door. He started keying it in. After just two minutes, he knew it would resemble an electronic treasure hunt. Hopefully, a quick treasure hunt.

Jason stumbled on the control routine entitled "Delock" after just five minutes. He remembered its purpose as well as the required password. He keyed the fourteen characters and looked out at the building.

An overhead spotlight turned on. Jason got out and headed to the front door. There was no resistance as he pushed the door inward. He had a critical video to pick up.

All was quiet inside. The hallway was lit as usual, but no sounds of activity echoed inside. Far from usual.

Jason's mental antennae were already up as he entered the main room and found Bert's usual perch empty. The video screens were all lit. He moved to Bert's control station and checked for any clues of why all his calls had been ignored.

Upon finding nothing, Jason headed to the kennel area, Bert's second-most-used sanctuary. As he passed the screens, he saw immediately why his calls had not been answered.

Spread-eagled in the center of the pit was the upper half of Bert. Salazar and Samantha each chewed on a leg. Jason whipped out his revolver and then checked to see if the lizards were still chained. The chains were still in place, but he kept his handgun at the ready.

Bert's wheelchair was just inside the pit. Jason could see that the strap Bert always used had been cut in the middle. Intentional. Bert had many psychological problems. Being suicidal was not on the list.

Pistol at the ready, Jason continued into the kennel area. Six dogs. No killer.

He went back to Bert's control station. The video he needed would have been captured automatically. He had set up the location where all the details of the president's kidnapping could be captured. Now he had to retrieve the video that would point to both the identity of President Allison's kidnappers and their needless brutality.

Having watched Bert many times in the past, Jason knew there were only five recorders wired to capture "assigned events," an overhead view of Bert's own work space being one of them. Jason found what he needed on the third recorder. He dumped it to his minicrystal.

Before leaving, Jason decided to review the remaining two recorders. He believed he knew who had killed Bert, but there was no substitute for proof. Hopefully, proof was on one of the two remaining recorders.

The last recorder held the evidence: clear and incontrovertible.

The video showed a medium-wide view of Bert's control desk. The camera was mounted on the opposite wall facing Bert's workstation and all the screens. Bert, his back to the camera, was in his chair, working his keyboard. His two Komodo dragons could be seen sleeping in the background.

Jason wiggled the controller, jumping to the time he had called Bert. No change. Bert was still in his chair at the console, this time holding his phone to his ear. Jason searched for the sound control and flipped it on. He recognized the tail end of Bert's earlier comments to him over the phone.

Bert was starting to replace his phone when he suddenly dropped it, reached into his chair's side bag, and spun his chair a full 180. The action on the screen startled Jason, but then he saw the reason.

Duane Evers had just stopped approaching Bert. Duane had a pistol. So did Bert, who raised his pistol and fired. Duane feinted to his left and fired back, hitting Bert in the right thigh.

Bert screamed in pain. Across the pit, Salazar's head snapped to full attention.

Jason clenched his teeth as he watched Duane dig his knife high into Bert's other thigh, digging a trench down from hip to knee. While Bert continued to scream, Duane slid his knife under the wheelchair's seat strap and sliced it in two. Duane then pulled the chair and Bert back to the wall facing the near side of the pit. He braced his right foot against the wall and pushed off. In the twenty feet, he got the chair up to a good speed, jerking the chair to a stop at the edge, the front wheels dropping over.

The bleeding and screaming Bert was flung, rolling, almost to the center of the pit.

Jason watched in unison with the Duane on the screen as Salazar noticed the pit's addition and waddled over. Two minutes passed before the screams stopped. The chewing continued as Duane headed for the front door.

Jason was about to turn off the video replay when Duane reappeared on the screen and faced the camera.

"What's that little bastard going to do now?" Jason muttered aloud.

Duane tilted his head and then, slowly, took an exaggerated bow and exited again stage left.

"Okay, you little shit," Jason snarled at the video. "I've got a million ways to shred your traitorous ass."

CHAPTER 74

◆

Together, Nick and Sam talked with various bodyguards and security heads of many of the dignitaries, comparing impressions with their own.

After ten minutes, Sam turned to Nick. "They're not here yet."

"Who?"

"Homeland Security. They have a major office less than a three-minute walk from here." Sam frowned. "Something's screwy."

"Maybe—"

Sam waved off any suggestions. He pulled out his phone, punched one digit, and waited. And waited.

Nick figured at least twenty seconds had elapsed before Sam frowned again, stabbed at the screen, and lowered the phone.

"Not answering," he said.

"Who's not answering?"

"Captain Mooney. It's not like him. He's a stickler for detail. *Every* detail."

"Maybe they had to turn off their phones so they can't be located."

"Our phones can't be located. None of them. No need to turn them off." Sam's frown deepened and was joined by his pursed lips. He pulled the phone up and stabbed at it again, multiple touches this time. "I'm calling Billy," he mumbled.

"Who?" Nick asked.

"Will Prior. Youngest man on the team. Know his uncle. Promised I'd show his nephew the ropes. He'll answer."

Sam's frown started to deepen and then disappear. "Billy, Sam. The captain is not answering his phone. Is everything normal to plan?" Sam punched the phone into speaker mode.

"Not to plan, Sam." Will's voice was slightly tinny but clear.

Nick bent in to hear better.

"Not to plan, how?" Sam asked, his tone insistent.

"About three minutes ago, we turned left for six blocks then right again to continue uptown. I think I can see the Hudson River in the distance."

"Had you encountered a problem? Were you forced into evasive maneuvers?"

"Negative. I didn't see anything, and there were no communications from the captain other than the two course changes. We're still in a tight grouping. We're in the last car. The president's limousine is two ahead of ours, in the middle, and the captain's is in the lead."

Sam shook his head. "What street are you passing?"

"We just passed Fifty-Third. There's been no alert as to when we head back to the plan route. It should be soon because—"

Gunfire crackled from the phone's speaker.

"Holy shit!" Will shouted.

More gunfire.

An explosion.

"The limo just ahead of us blew up! The gas tank must have—"

Two distinct screams issued forth from the speaker before the phone went silent.

CHAPTER 75

◆

N ick slammed the brakes hard. Cars and bodies were strewn
everywhere for almost a full block.

He and Sam bolted from the car.

Two uniformed NYPD officers met them as they reached the
first body. Nick and Sam flashed their badges.

"Sorry, Agent Kirby," the older policeman said to Sam. "All of
your men have been killed—either from rocket grenades or from
gunshots."

"The president?"

Both policemen shook their heads.

"Couldn't find her," the younger policeman said. "She's not in
the immediate area."

Sam raised a finger to interject something, but the younger officer wasn't finished.

"We've got men spreading out to find her. My guess is that she
was riding in the third car."

"You're right. Why?"

"That's the only car not damaged. The five agents inside have
all been shot in the head, but no president. Again, my guess is that
they didn't want to blow up that middle car so they could capture
her and—"

"Kidnap her," Sam said, finishing his sentence.

The older policeman nodded.

"What's the body count?" Nick asked.

"Twenty-six," the younger policeman said.

Sam turned to him. "Twenty-six? Are you sure?"

"We're sure," the older policeman concurred.

"There were twenty-seven agents."

It took less than two minutes for Sam, with Nick right behind him, to verify the identity of each of the twenty-six.

Sam turned to Nick. "Captain Mooney isn't here. They must have taken him too."

Nick pursed his lips before asking the question to which he had a hunch he already knew the answer. "Was the captain in the president's car?"

"No."

CHAPTER 76

Nick watched as Sam paced back and forth along the driver's side of the unbombed limousine. It was obvious that a hundred alternate scenarios were bouncing around the agent's head.

"Mooney is with them," Sam finally accepted, reluctantly. "Either as a victim or as a perpetrator." From the scowl on Sam's face, it was obvious to Nick which scenario rang truest to Sam.

Jason stepped back into his limousine and pulled out his phone. After three rings, someone picked up on the other end. There were confusing sounds on the other end but no answer.

"Jeremiah?" Jason asked after several seconds. "Jeremiah. Are you there?"

Several more seconds of static passed before an answer came. "Yes, sir. Here, sir. Sorry, I was giving assignments when you called."

"Has the president been secured?"

"She has. Awaiting further instructions."

"Get her to the Jersey side. Keep her in safe house number 7. I'll have my man come there and . . ." Jason paused for a moment. "And finalize the operation. You are to keep her safe and hidden until he gets there. At that time, he'll finalize the remaining details, after which you and your men will carry out the termination. Once completed, you and your men will disperse quickly and quietly."

"Got it."

"And you and the men have worn only Penn-Jersey uniforms from the start?"

"From the start, sir."

"How soon can you get to Jersey undetected?"

"About two hours."

Jason did a quick mental calculation. "Fine. Call me back when you're on the other side. I have a video that needs to make the late news."

"Definitely, sir."

Jason turned the various times over in his mind for almost a minute. Finally satisfied, he keyed in the simple text: "14.15."

Less than a minute later, he received the confirming text.

Nick and Sam divided up the fifteen uniformed police into two groups, each leading their group on a flashlight search, grid-pattern style, of the area surrounding the massacre. Each of the men was responsible for an approximately six-foot-wide section as the teams trudged forward. The six feet overlapped slightly neighbor to neighbor. Traversing the asphalt road, they covered ten forward feet in about a minute. Crossing through grass, almost grass, and plain dirt limited each man to only two feet at best per minute.

After twenty minutes, Sam's team found a torn footlong dark-green uniform sleeve that had several burn holes and tears along its length. No patch or stitching indicated its owner's affiliation. It was, however, heavily soaked in blood at the ragged end. Its owner's arm had obviously been hacked off at the elbow; it was that drenched.

Sam shook his head in frustration and then handed it to Nick, who rubbed his hand across the fabric and then turned it inside out.

"Beats me," he said. "It's not New York City." He turned it outside out. "Definitely not any World Council cops that I know."

One of the policemen in Nick's group reached for it, prompting Nick to hand over the sleeve.

The man rotated it around its missing arm twice. "I'm not a hundred percent, but—"

"But what?" Sam and Nick asked in unison.

"Penn-Jersey," the officer said, handing the sleeve back to Nick.

Sam turned to Nick. "What's the next crossing to Jersey without a bridge?"

"Any place without a seawall."

Sam rolled his eyes. "We gotta cover them all."

Nick nodded in agreement.

Sam turned to the fifteen cops. "Consider yourselves deputized to the Secret Service. We've got three miles to the GW Bridge, and we have to scour every foot along the way."

The men received start-point assignments and then raced to their cars. Nick decided to call for help from his neighborhood. He placed the call and received a commitment of at least thirty men.

Nick turned to Sam. "I'll go right up to the Yonkers line and meet up with my group. We'll work down toward you. We gotta find her before they cross over."

Sam nodded and joined the last cop in his car. Nick got behind the wheel of his and charged off, heading north.

Jason had been parked at location no. 14 for fifteen minutes when his man showed up exactly ninety minutes from when he had placed the call. Reynolds got out of his car, and Jason motioned for him to get into his.

"I've got a critical assignment," Jason said as Reynolds pulled the passenger's door closed. "It's a termination, and I want only you to handle it."

"The termination should look like what? And proof you'll need how?"

"It must be captured for television. I don't want you to do the actual termination. I'll have about twenty men there who will carry that out."

"You have twenty men for a termination you don't want me to carry out. You want me there why? And there is where?"

"New Jersey. I need you there to make sure everything looks convincing. Convincing that a heavy force of Penn-Jersey Police killed President Allison in a most brutal and bloody manner."

"And your plan is to have this shown on TV? Why?"

"Not your concern," Jason replied evenly. "You're not to be seen when it happens. You're familiar with Penn-Jersey Police. The clothes are authentic, but I need you to assure the group's actions, in detail, match Penn-Jersey protocol exactly. There must be no doubt in any quarter that the president was assassinated by association forces, rogue or otherwise."

Jason received the man's nod of confirmation, bringing his comfort level almost to the 100 percent level. Reynolds had completed thirty-plus contracts over the past ten years, each executed with precision and devoid of any traceability. That success ratio would allow Jason to focus on other critical plan components.

Jason gave the details of the Jersey-side safe house where the president would be found. "It's opposite Yonkers."

Reynolds nodded again, exited the car, walked to his own, climbed in, and drove off.

Jason mentally rubbed his hands together. His right-hand man was on the job. He nodded and smiled. Why an eight-year-old Arab terrorist who had broken his leg thirty years ago would choose the name Charles Reynolds and return to the United States after twenty of those years was—Jason reached for the right word—*destiny.*

The boy had been held incommunicado by the Federal Bureau of Prisons for three years before being released to his home country. When he did return, intent on righting what he saw as old wrongs, he met with Jason immediately. Right off the boat, so to speak.

Jason's phone rang. It was Jeremiah calling from Jersey. President Allison must have traded Air Force One for Safe House One, Jason thought.

CHAPTER 77

◆

As Nick was nearing his destination, his phone rang.

"Hello?"

"Tim here. There's—"

"What is it, Tim? I'm driving to Yonkers to meet up with the neighborhood. Then we will—"

"There's a video of the massacre. It showed the five cars suddenly stopping. Now there are explosions all around. There are—"

"What about the third car? Has it been bombed?"

Tim focused intently. "Not yet. The second and the fourth have been blown up, but not the middle one."

"Has anyone gotten out of—"

"The first car just blew up. Jesus!"

"Has anyone gotten out of the middle car?"

"I can't tell. If anyone did, it had to be on the other side of—damn!"

"What?"

"The last car just blew up. A bunch of men in uniforms—not ours, fifteen or twenty of them—are surrounding the middle car. Shots are being fired. A lot of shots. Two men are pulling open the rear driver-side door." Tim stopped talking for several seconds.

"What's happening? What do you see?"

"They're pulling someone out. They're pulling out—I can't see. The person is facing the other way. Maybe if they just turned the person around and . . . it's President Allison!"

"How does she look?"

"Unharmed. She looks unharmed."

"We found four bodies in the car. Two in front. Two in back."

"Nobody else was pulled out as far as I can see. Is Sam with you?"

"He's taken the police that were on-site, and they're working their way up to the GW bridge. I'm meeting my neighborhood at the Yonkers line, where we'll work our way down to the GW. In fact, I'm pulling to a stop right now. My crew should be along in two or three minutes. When they get here, I'll keep you—" Nick spotted something up ahead.

"What is it?"

"Two figures down by the water's edge. Looks like they're tugging on a raft or something. I'll call you back in a minute or two."

Nick clicked off, pocketed the phone, pulled out his revolver, and slipped quietly out of the car. He moved to his left, where there was some waist-high brush to provide cover. He decided not to wait for any backup. If these were any of the kidnappers, any seconds wasted could be crucial.

Stooping, he maneuvered closer to about thirty feet.

From the edge of the brush, he saw two men, uniformed, their backs to him, wrestling with a rubber raft apparently caught on something underwater.

Nick checked his surroundings before he stood and moved toward the men, stopping about ten feet away.

"You two need a helping hand?" Nick asked, his sarcasm as steady as the barrel of his revolver.

The two jerked upright and spun around.

"I've heard that those Penn-Jersey rafts suck."

Nick shifted the barrel of his Glock from one to the other. "Hands behind your head, and sit on the edge of the raft, facing me."

The two men sat as instructed.

"Nice uniforms," Nick said, the compliment dripping with mock sincerity. "Unusual this side of the Hudson. Get them at the local costume store?"

"Not exactly," someone said in a deep voice behind Nick. "They're not real, but the gun I'm pointing at your back is."

CHAPTER 78

◆

Nick lowered his pistol, turned, and faced a six-foot-tall uniformed man pointing an assault rifle at him.

The man smiled at Nick. "Oops," he said, echoing Nick's own thoughts.

Nick's hands were cuffed behind him.

"Why don't we just shoot him and throw him in the bushes?" one of the raft wrestlers behind him asked.

"He's a cop," the man with the rifle said. "The fact that he's here, with gun drawn, may mean we've got problems. Our job is to get him across to Jeremiah so *he* can make the call."

The raft wrestler offered a reluctant grunt and pulled Nick around by his cuffed hands to face the raft, which had been untangled. Nick was shoved and pushed to the raft and then bumped headlong into the middle and down onto his back.

The men started the outboard and backed the raft off the bank. Once turned around, they headed toward what Nick assumed was the Jersey side of the Hudson. He had no view because the rifleman's left foot was pressing against his chest. All he could see was the rifle barrel pointed between his eyes.

No one spoke during the crossing.

The raft was met by two more uniformed men.

One of them looked first at Nick and then at the grumbling raft wrestler. "Gee, and I thought you were having trouble with your raft. All the while you were waiting on a passenger."

The words were greeted with more grumbles and grunts.

"To the truck," Mr. Rifleman said, pointing with his weapon. "Before we're spotted."

They carried the raft to a gray pickup, threw it in back, and tied it down, after which Nick and the rifleman got into the raft and sat facing each other, the rifle again pointed at Nick's forehead.

The pickup lurched forward.

With each turn, Nick closed a finger either on his left hand or on his right, corresponding to which way the truck turned.

The man with the rifle smiled. "Twelve and seven."

Nick frowned. "I beg your pardon."

"Twelve right turns mixed in with seven left turns."

"Was I that obvious?"

The man shook his head. "Nope. Not at all. It's just what I would do."

Nick gave the man a mock smile in return and kept counting.

After nineteen total turns, the truck clutched to a jerky stop.

Nick was rifle-waved to a standing position as the tailgate was dropped. He and his guard stepped out of the raft and back to the cabin side of the truck bed, against the cab, as the raft was pulled out and onto a gravel road.

Nick was directed off with the advice "Don't trip. That first step's a bitch."

A good-sized log house loomed at the end of at least sixty feet of driveway.

The grumpy wrestler grabbed Nick's left arm and pushed him step by step right up to the front steps, where he was brought to a sudden stop.

His rifle-bearing guard mounted the steps and knocked on the door.

After about ten seconds, someone opened the door. An athletic-looking man stepped out. He looked about forty and stood about six foot four. Nick recognized him as Owen's interrogator.

"What's this?" the man asked, pointing to Nick.

"A cop who tried to capture Charlie and Herman," the rifleman answered.

"Why didn't you put him down on the other side?"

"I didn't want to leave any trace, Jeremiah. I figured anything done with him is best done here."

Jeremiah paused and then nodded. "Good thinking. Bring him inside."

Grumpy Wrestler shoved Nick up the seven steps and into the log house, where he was stopped in the center of the large living room. Soft chairs, each containing a uniformed man, ringed an area to the far left, beyond which a door opened out onto some type of deck.

The man called Jeremiah confronted Nick. "I recognize you from our little encounter at the Detention Center, Detective Nicholas Garvey."

"It struck me as more than just a 'little encounter,'" Nick countered.

"Whatever you'd like it to be," Jeremiah said, and smiled. He looked past Nick to Grumpy Wrestler and tilted his head to Nick's right. "Put him in the room."

Grumpy Wrestler started to protest. "But—"

"In the room!" Jeremiah's tone and glare allowed nothing other than immediate obedience.

Grumpy Wrestler shoved Nick toward a massive door with two dead-bolt locks. Another uniform clicked both locks and pulled the door open. Nick was propelled forward, and the door slammed shut behind him.

Sitting comfortably in yet another soft chair was President Lenora Allison.

CHAPTER 79

◆

"Good evening, Detective," President Allison said, rising and extending her hand.

"Madam President," Nick said with a nod, his gaze darting left, right, up, down.

President Allison smiled. "Two doors: one locked, one to the bathroom. Three windows—none in the bathroom—all with bars. No loose floorboards. All furniture bolted to the floor. No phone. No TV. Room service only if you pound on the door."

"Looks like we're here for the duration," Nick agreed, plopping down into the other soft chair.

"I'm sorry you got caught up in this, Detective Garvey."

"Was there any warning? Did any of the drivers try to veer off, leave the column?"

"No. No warning. Everything was going well until the lead vehicle blew up. I was immediately shoved to the floor and held down. I heard and felt an explosion from somewhere behind. Then, soon after, another ahead. Then, behind, another."

"Is that when the shots came? My partner said the shots came after three explosions, killing most of the men not blown up."

"Yes. Then. I lost count of how many shots. How did your partner know about the gunfire? Was he nearby?"

"No, he saw it on video."

"It was televised?" The president's tone betrayed just a hint of confusion. "Why?"

"The best Tim and I could figure is that the Penn-Jersey boys wanted to show their muscles being flexed."

"Penn-Jersey?" The confusion was gone, replaced by incredulity. "Your partner said it was Penn-Jersey blowing up the cars and shooting?"

"Yes."

"What led him to believe that?"

"The uniforms. All the attackers wore Penn-Jersey uniforms. Tim has seen them before, and so have I. In fact, I was caught and brought here by three men wearing Penn-Jersey uniforms."

President Allison shook her head in disbelief. "Can't be."

"Why not?"

"Granted, I didn't see the attack, held down as I was on the floor. The shooting got closer, even into our limousine, which was when I felt the foot holding me down replaced by a full body. When the shooting stopped just after the fourth explosion, I was blindfolded as I was pulled up. I didn't see any uniforms or any of the attackers until I was brought into this room. I've seen only three men, and they were not wearing Penn-Jersey."

"The three who brought me *were*. So were two or three others on the other side of that door."

President Allison shook her head again—but with conviction. "Then they're fake."

"Fake?" Nick shook his own head right back.

"Forget it. It doesn't matter, one way or another."

Nick was aghast. "Of course it matters!"

"No." The tone was even. "One way or another, they plan to do us harm."

"You think?" Nick didn't bother to hide the sarcasm in his tone. He narrowed his eyes. "There's something you're not telling me."

"There are many things I'm not telling a lot of people." The president exhaled slowly. "Like I said, I'm sorry you got caught up in this."

"Got caught up in what? Tonight? Some of the other 'many things' you're 'not telling a lot of people'?"

"Yes. And yes."

"Hell, Madam President," Nick said, his voice rising on each word, "they probably will 'do us harm.' Great harm. And you want to keep secrets. I get it: dead men tell no tales."

"No, not dead men. That may well be both of us. I want to make sure live men tell *all* the tales."

Nick gritted his teeth, exasperation getting the better of him. "Like the tale, Madam President, that Owen Pendleton has returned from the dead after twenty years and is now growing unusual plants with, possibly, unusual chemicals. Is that one of the tales?"

President Allison held her head and expression steady.

Nick decided if he was in for a dime, it might as well be for a dollar. "Is one of the tales being that one of your senior Secret Service men act like Pendleton's right arm? Is that a tale you're not telling Sam? Or does he already know because he's the one bringing the supplies? Is that what Dr. Pendleton is doing? Creating new foods to supposedly help the world?"

President Allison let out a short sigh. "Yes, to help the world. And not just supposedly. And he's working on something else to help the world."

"Wow, a twofer! Two dead-men tales for the price of one?"

President Allison nodded. "Yes. Two tales. Minor ones."

"Minor ones? Minor like your vice president being murdered? Minor like the luxury apartment he and each of his Secret Service agents had? Are they part of yet another tale whose time has not yet come? My partner and I have been chasing down leads for the past two weeks and have come to only two conclusions: either Jason Beck had him killed for some unknown reason, or . . ." Nick looked sharply at President Allison.

"Or?" she said.

"Or you manipulated Jason Beck to have him killed for some unknown reason."

"Jason did it on his own. I liked Vice President Wellsley but didn't trust him. We knew he was aligning with the World Council and therefore excluded him from any loop involving critical information. He was a lost soul, basically."

"Did you 'like' the four Secret Service agents each shot in their head?"

"All four were longtime bodyguards from his days as governor of Colorado. He insisted they be granted agent status. I'm sorry they were murdered."

"At least you don't call those murders 'minor.'" Nick shook his head. So few things were what they seemed. His itch reappeared. "The Lincoln Tunnel!"

President Allison's eyes widened.

"Everyone believes Penn-Jersey blew it up to slow you down and to stop the grid. But now I would bet you *don't* believe it."

The president's expression was back to steady and noncommittal.

Nick wondered if Howard's neighborhood had a nursery rhyme for someone who keeps secrets at the wrong time. "Ring around the Rosie" just didn't seem to fit what President Allison was doing.

"Well, tell you what, Madam President," Nick said, giving up all semblance of holding back exasperation as he sat in the lone, stiff chair at the far end of the room, "I can do quite well without any tales to take to my grave. I just got through reading thirty-two pages from Jason Beck's journal as well as backup notes written by Margaret Farnsworth, Seth Morris, and Gerry Martin. If it wasn't Penn-Jersey, my second nomination would be Jason Beck himself. One of his journal entries described how he was going to keep you and Carter Johnson at each other's throats. When we're dead and buried, my partner knows where I keep secret stuff, and there'll be one hell of a bunch of stories that will—"

"You found the eagle box!" President Allison sat upright and leaned forward, her eyes wide, excited. "I don't know how much time we have left before we're put six feet under, but tell me all you remember."

Why not? Nick mused. Why not one final bedtime story about the Big Bad Wolf?

Nick too leaned forward. "Gerry had it hidden in his old apartment, which he never sold."

Nick began with the pages ripped from Jason Beck's journals and then covered the details of the notes written by Seth Morris and Gerry Martin.

President Allison's eyes opened wider with each revelation.

CHAPTER 80

◆

A single muffled gunshot brought Nick's metal box recitation to a sudden halt.

"Sounds like it came from outside," he said. "Not loud enough for the other room."

President Allison nodded.

Nick stood and headed for the door.

Before he got halfway, someone opened the door.

"Relax, Detective," Jeremiah said. "We just had a case of a guard almost shooting himself in the foot when an expected guest arrived early. He'll need a little bit more training in aiming first then shooting." He stepped in and directed both prisoners out with a flip of his left hand. He was unarmed.

Nick exited first, scanning quickly for any drawn guns.

None.

He stepped forward, allowing President Allison to follow.

Jeremiah motioned for them to take two straight-back chairs at the table in the center of the room, both facing the front door. "You can relax for the next few minutes. We're not going to shoot you."

"Not here," someone behind them said.

Nick and President Allison turned in their chairs. Nick recognized Reynolds right away.

"Madam President," Reynolds said, proffering an exaggerated bow. He turned his gaze to Nick. "Delmar is doing how these days?"

Nick gritted his teeth. "The same, I believe, as Christopher Price, whose 'accident' you orchestrated."

Reynolds pursed his lips and blinked four or five times in rapid succession.

President Allison coughed, and when Nick looked at her, she shook her head quickly, suggesting he be quiet.

Reynolds chuckled. "The president is shaking her head at you for what reason? Could it be she wants you to drop it, else we shoot you here and now?" Reynolds turned to Jeremiah. "Seems I have a fan here of professional thoroughness." He turned back to Nick. "My guess is you scoured the video record from the day before Director Price's 'accident.' Good work. Even for a pro cop."

Nick remained silent.

Reynolds shifted his gaze to President Allison. "One thought is to have Mr. Pro Cop here, Detective Nicholas Garvey, as I remember, collect videos of . . ." He paused and gave them an exaggerated wink. "Videos of my greatest hits. I have to admit, I've had quite a few, including Director Price." He winked at Nick. "I'm quite good at my job. Sometimes, though, I have to delegate, as you'll soon see." Reynolds turned to Jeremiah. "I was told there would be seventeen men in all. I count only fifteen. The missing men are where?"

Jeremiah shifted his feet and exhaled slowly. "One of our men got his arm completely blown off when he mishandled one of the RPG launchers. We picked him up and brought him with us, but he died. Also, Captain Mooney's not here. I told him to leave." The words were clipped, uneven.

"And why was that?" Reynolds's stare conveyed an intense warning that the answer had better be damned good.

Jeremiah cleared his throat. "He kept mumbling that he had been promised money for his service. I told him that the Council Guard always honors their commitments and his 'service payment' was waiting back at the World Council Building. I said I'd have him escorted back so he could collect. He accepted. I figured since he was not able to participate in your—in *our*—event, he was of no further use here."

"And?"

"And I had Walter, there"—Jeremiah pointed to his shoot-then-aim guard—"volunteer to drive him back to the city. He escorted Mooney to a van, where he cut the captain's throat."

Reynolds smiled. "I'm impressed."

Jeremiah appeared to breathe easier.

"And the body is where?" Reynolds asked, turning in Walter's direction.

Walter stepped forward from behind his two comrades. "Wrapped, tied, and dropped down a well by a farmhouse."

"Again, impressed," Reynolds said.

Nick figured Sam would applaud Captain Mooney's "disposition."

Jeremiah appeared fully at ease. He looked at Reynolds with a bit more confidence in his demeanor. "I was told we are to be at your disposal. Something about you directing how we finish . . ." He paused to stare at President Allison and Nick. "Finish things off."

Reynolds nodded. "I've picked a spot near an abandoned gas station less than three miles from here and have two men setting up lights and a high-definition video camera."

"We're ready," Jeremiah assured him.

Reynolds gave a quick visual sweep of the other men in the room. "About half of you are ready for a video debut. The other half aren't dressed for casual Friday. Each Penn-Jersey uniform must be per regulations. Have the men double-check each other."

After ten minutes, all uniforms were judged A-OK.

Reynolds nodded his approval to Jeremiah. "Get everyone ready to move out. We've got a video to make." He pointed back to the president and Nick. "Oh, and bring along our honored stars."

Reynolds and Jeremiah stood aside as four men pulled President Allison and Nick up from their chairs and out the front door. Jeremiah exited first. Then Reynolds followed them out.

Nick and the president were placed in the middle seat of the middle row of separate vans, second and third in line respectively. Nick had his arms spread out and hands cuffed to bars on the back of the left and right seats in front of him. He assumed President Allison was similarly stretched and cuffed.

Reynolds paused by the open left window on Nick's van. "It's just a short ride, pro cop. Just a short ride."

"Screw you, you piece of shit!" Nick snarled, tugging violently at his handcuffs.

Reynolds shook his head. "Careful, Pro Cop Garvey. Wouldn't do to hurt yourself before the curtain goes up."

Reynolds moved on and, without looking back, waved his right hand back at Nick. He crossed in front of the van, moved up along the right side of the van just in front, and climbed into the front seat next to Jeremiah.

Within a few seconds, all four vans moved out.

CHAPTER 81

◆

"This is the spot," Reynolds said to Jeremiah.

All four of the vans came to a stop halfway around a half-circular field about 150 feet in diameter. The road they had been traveling continued on, completing the equivalent of a giant U-turn before returning to forest cover. As Reynolds and Jeremiah stepped out of the first van, Jeremiah made a continuous circular motion with his right hand, indicating to the next three vans to keep their motors running. Near the center of the far end of the field, two men could be seen struggling with two dim floodlights atop towering pipe stands. Occupants of the other three vans, just now getting out of their vehicles, moved halfway toward the two men who were stretching out and tying down guy wires to the floodlight posts. A large video camera was perched atop a tripod between the two posts. The floodlights and the camera were pointed at the farthest part of the field from the vans, away from where Reynolds and Jeremiah stood.

Jeremiah pointed at the two men. "Who are they? What are they doing?"

"Electricians, setting up two floodlights," Reynolds replied. "Jason wants the assassination to be taped. Can't do that at night without some lights."

"As you stated." Jeremiah looked left and then right. "Why here?"

"Secluded. No chance of being seen. No possibility of interruption."

Jeremiah frowned for a moment and then called four of his men to his side. "Two of you," he said, motioning to the two nearest on his right, "frisk those two electricians for weapons. I see some type of

box near one of the poles. Have them open it for your inspection."
He then turned to the last two. "Keep your rifles trained on the electricians until they're cleared. Then check out the trees on all sides.
Just a moment." He waved another four men to his side. "Check
beyond the trees on all sides for at least a hundred yards." He signaled
the men to get started and then turned back to Reynolds. "Okay
with you?" His eyes were fixed and hard.

"Most assuredly. I'd have been surprised if you hadn't checked
everything out."

Neither Reynolds nor Jeremiah said anything as they watched
the two electrical workers being frisked. Jeremiah's men finally waved
okay and then rummaged through the black box before giving a
thumbs-up.

Jeremiah held the others back until five minutes later, when his
six men with rifles returned from deep beyond the trees and reported
that there was nothing in that area that could pose any threat.

Reynolds searched Jeremiah's face. "Are you comfortable with this
setup? If not, I can reschedule. Jason wants it done within twenty-four
hours. Worse case, we run the president back to the cabin while we set
up in another place. The detective, of course, we can just—"

"This will do."

Reynolds nodded. Jeremiah didn't strike him as being fully on
board.

Jeremiah turned to one of the two men who had frisked the
electricians. "What was in the box?"

"A car battery and a slider for each floodlight. There was also a
cable running to the video camera."

The second man spoke up. "I had them turn on the camera, and
I looked in the viewfinder while I zoomed it in, then out. Zoomed
out, you can see the highway on our right—or the left, if you're facing the camera."

Jeremiah paused for several moments before giving the first
man an additional instruction. "Go back and move the sliders both
up to their limit. I want to see how bright the floods get." The man
turned to go, but Jeremiah put a hand on his shoulder. "Move the
sliders yourself."

The man trotted to the floodlight towers and opened the slider box. After he knelt down and reached inside it, suddenly the flood-lights went from dim to bright, providing a sufficient level for video recording without forcing anyone to squint.

Reynolds watched Jeremiah walk beyond the lights to where the president would end up. He shielded his eyes and looked back up at the pole on his left and then the pole on his right.

He rejoined Reynolds. "Let's get on with it." He motioned for the six riflemen.

Reynolds double-checked the riflemen's uniforms. "As the execution squad, two each of the six should be shown emerging from the three vans: one right in front of the van holding the president, one right behind, and one from the president's van itself. They should position themselves so they are seen guarding, with their rifles, the emergence of the president and that detective. The two prisoners should each be held by two more of your men, each gripping an arm, with a third immediately behind the prisoner. The four remaining men should just step out of each van and stand as if guarding the vehicle."

"Who is to have hardware?" Jeremiah asked.

"The six men." Reynolds stared at Jeremiah. "I assume you'll be giving orders with a pistol in hand?"

Jeremiah nodded that he would. "Where will each prisoner be taken?"

"A little bit farther than you just went. The six with rifles should then take positions between the camera and the prisoners."

Jeremiah nodded his agreement to the location. "What is to happen then?"

"Tell the prisoners to kneel, facing the camera. Give it about to the count of ten. Then tell your six men to shoot. After that, the three men assigned to hustle them into position should check for vitals and visibly shake their heads, indicating there are none. At that point, the floods will dim."

"What do we do with the bodies?"

"Put them back in their same van. We take them back to the cabin, where Jason will have some others pick up the bodies for transport back to the city."

"Are we to call Jason after they're shot?" Jeremiah's tone suggested to Reynolds the question was some form of a test.

Reynolds gave a slight shrug. "I think it might be better if you call him just before the two are brought out of their van—just in case Jason has a last-minute change in plan."

"He seldom, if ever, makes changes," Jeremiah said, his tone now indicating the probability of a passing test grade. "But in this case, excellent idea."

"Good," Reynolds replied, not making any show of accepting the sliver of trust just offered. "Let's rehearse once so everyone knows their positions at each stage. We want to see the backs of the six riflemen and the kneeling president and detective. We don't want it to look staged, but we want to be sure the camera captures what Jason needs."

For the next ten minutes, all the men were slowly taken through each step with the lights set at their full brightness. At each stage, Reynolds and Jeremiah checked the camera's field of coverage and then moved everyone to the next checkpoint.

CHAPTER 82

◆

Nick watched the rehearsal as best he could. His outstretched, cuffed hands did not allow him to press his nose to the window, but he could see the action if not facial expressions.

The guy named Jeremiah was busy checking his fellow Penn-Jersey men as they went through marching two men to the far end of the field, made them kneel, backed away about twenty or thirty feet, formed a line, and raised their rifles. Jeremiah held a pistol and appeared to count off until the two kneeling men fell over sideways. Two other men marched to the fallen men and pretended to check them for breathing, after which they stood and shook their heads. They returned to the light poles, followed by the two fallen stand-ins.

After each major sequence in the process, Nick noticed Jeremiah checking with Reynolds as if verifying acceptable procedure.

Nick shook his head. There was no doubt in his mind who the two kneeling men were pretending to be.

He noticed that, after the last check with Reynolds, Jeremiah pulled out his cell phone, pressed its screen several times, held a brief conversation, hung up, and gave all present a thumbs-up.

Nick couldn't hear, but when Reynolds made a show of pointing to each van, raising his right hand over his head, and then making a sweeping counterclockwise motion, Nick concluded the vans were to back up some distance. The exaggerated motion suggested to him they were to return to just before the point where the forest gave way to the clearing.

He was right.

The floodlights were left on as all the men returned to their vans. Each vehicle backed up to the edge of the clearing until the video setup was no longer visible. Reynolds and the two video guys stayed behind.

Nick heard the radio crackle, followed by the single word *return*. Once all the vans had cleared the forest, they stopped. Nick could see Jeremiah emerge from the van just ahead of the one he was in and, using exaggerated hand gestures, direct his men out of their vans.

Nick was uncuffed and pulled out by two of his copassengers. His arms were pulled behind him and his wrists cuffed with a plastic strip and pulled tight.

He glanced over his shoulder and saw President Allison receiving the same treatment.

Jeremiah waved the two prisoners and their guards to the front, followed by six men with rifles.

The group moved slowly toward the spot chosen by Reynolds and Jeremiah. Once there, they stopped and were released. Neither the president nor Nick moved. The six men guarding them retreated behind the riflemen, moved to each side, and stopped.

Jeremiah stepped up to the center of the six riflemen as they faced the prisoners. He held his pistol in the general direction of Nick and the president. "Kneel."

Both remained standing.

Jeremiah waved his pistol at the six guards. who immediately stepped forward and forced both subjects into a kneeling position, with both legs then wrapped together several times in duct tape. The guards stepped back.

The lights, pointing downward, were elevated enough that Nick could make out what was happening in front of him. He saw six rifles raised into position.

Jeremiah pointed his pistol in the air as if about to start a race. He started his count. "Ten!"

Nick glanced to his left. President Allison had a defiant look on her face.

He heard Jeremiah call out "Nine!" and pinched thumb against forefinger in an attempt to match cadence. He fixed his gaze on Jeremiah and figured he would mirror the president's defiant glare.

"Eight!" Pinch.

He gritted his teeth. An image of Nicole with a broken barrette flashed before him. He blinked.

"Seven!" Pinch.

Nick refused to take his eyes off Jeremiah, imagining the son of a bitch drowning in his own blood.

Pinch. There was no *six*.

Nick caught a glimmer of confusion in Jeremiah's demeanor. The pistol was still elevated, but the man's head was tilted slightly, and he seemed to squint.

Time for another pinch, but no *six* or *five*.

Jeremiah suddenly burst into a fit of coughing. His pistol arm dropped, the barrel pointing to the ground. The coughing increased in frequency and intensity. Jeremiah turned and, coughing and hacking, walked back to where Reynolds and the group stood by the lights. He handed his pistol to one of the other Penn-Jersey uniforms and, still coughing, headed for the lead van.

Nick noticed that at no time did Jeremiah say anything to Reynolds. Nor did he acknowledge him in any way.

The man now holding the pistol conferred with Reynolds for several moments and then walked forward, taking Jeremiah's countdown position.

Nick wondered for an instant what number would be the new countdown start.

"Ten!"

Nick again pinched thumb against forefinger. He saw Jeremiah climb into the distant van. He couldn't see if he was still coughing. He wondered what the problem—

"Nine!" Pinch.

A swirling vision of Nicole replaced Reynolds and Jeremiah. Nick felt the tear behind each eye. He would never see Nicole again. And he would never get Sandra to believe he loved her.

"Eight!" Slight delay. Pinch.

The Patrick sisters, Nicole's two sister nuns, had sympathized with his Sandra problem, telling him often that time would heal—

"Seven!" Pinch.

There would be no time. No healing. Jason and his thugs would steal that. The two nuns had once said that when the end came, a blinding light embraced the dying. Maybe—

"Six!" Pinch.

Nick clenched both fists. He shot a quick glance at President Allison. Still defiant. No, not really defiant. At ease with—

"Five!" Pinch.

Why would anyone be at ease when about to be executed. Why—

"Four!" Pinch.

Nick was gripped by the image of Reynolds staggering out of the smoking Lincoln Tunnel. President Allison had reacted strangely when he had mentioned the explosion. Maybe—

"Three!"

His itch returned. Returned and cleared his eyes. President Allison's demeanor had changed when Reynolds had come into the room. Changed from deathwatch—

"Two!"

Someone was playing a game. Several someones. He'd be damned if he'd be a kneeling pawn. They'd have to shoot him standing up.

"One!"

Nick pushed hard against the ground. He rose to a teetering position and howled his hatred at those standing below the lights. "This is all bullshit!"

He knew the command "Fire!" would be next, but his brain only registered "Fi—"

Shots rang out.

The blinding light did embrace him.

He fell forward. He felt a quick pain and then nothing. Except floating. To earth.

CHAPTER 83

◆

Jason checked the time. *Yup,* he thought. *President Allison should be history about now.* After Jeremiah's confirmation, it would be time for Carter Johnson to place his head on the chopping block. Jason awarded himself a satisfied smile—a smile for World Council–class deeds. Deeds done and deeds soon to be. The world would be a much-more-manageable place with those two gone.

He checked his watch again.

Those two were well past their usefulness. They were—

Jason's Jeremiah-only phone rang.

"Right on time, Jeremiah," Jason said, still sporting the satisfied smile.

"Not quite, Director."

"What do you mean?" The smile gave way to gritted teeth and a frown.

"I'm not sure, Director."

"Is there anything of which you *are* sure?"

"I'm sure the president's execution was a setup—a scripted sequence to set her free and to set us up to be attacked."

Jason's breath caught in his throat. Then he managed to say, "What leads you—"

"I spotted men creeping up through the woods behind the kneeling president. I halted the countdown, handed the pistol to my lieutenant, went to a van, and took off. As I was leaving, I saw our firing squad gunned down."

"On your last phone call, you said Detective Garvey was also to be executed."

"Yes, he was. As I was driving off, I saw him stand up just before the shots were fired. He may have been killed by the other side."

Jason had to make some sense of the events. "I want you to come directly to my office so we can review—"

"Not safe, Director. If your orders regarding the president's execution were ignored—no! Make that subverted. If they did that, it's not the beginning of something. It's—"

"It's the end of something." *Or of everything,* Jason thought.

"I suggest, Director, that we regroup in one of your safe houses. I'm waiting to power a skiff across the Hudson River. There are tons more federal boats patrolling the waters than usual. I've got their patrol cycles almost calculated. They don't have as many up here."

"The increase was called up after the shootings. I agree. We'll meet. Call this number when you make it across the Hudson, and I'll give you directions. Let's shoot for one hour after your call."

"Will do, Director."

CHAPTER 84

◆

The field medic finally completed tying off the compression bandage on Nick's left shoulder.

"Sure you're not Irish?" the medic asked. "The bullet missed everything: heart, lungs, arteries, nerves, and everything else of importance."

Nick took a deep breath. "Thanks. Definitely not Irish, but I don't mind borrowing a bit of luck from a little green man." He tried lifting his left arm and winced at the broad shock of pain. "How long do I give my arm a rest? Is my southpaw pitching career over?"

The medic chuckled. "For the season, for sure."

Reynolds joined them. "What the hell possessed you to stand? It's a miracle you weren't killed."

Nick winked at the medic. "I was looking for a leprechaun."

"Seriously."

"I seriously thought you and President Allison were playing some kind of game. Since I wasn't included, I wasn't going to take any darkness—past or future—lying down."

"That's *kneeling* down, Detective," President Allison said, joining the three men.

Nick nodded. "Kneeling. Fine. I told you everything I found in Jason Beck's journal. Enough to bury him for his lifetime. You and"—he pointed at Reynolds—"your double agent play it so close neither of you even *need* a vest."

Reynolds placed his hand on Nick's right shoulder. "You sound pissed."

"He is," President Allison said. "Rightfully so. I should have given you some detail, at least."

"At least." Nick nodded again. He sneezed and then winced at the shoulder pain.

"But I suspect you figured I and my 'double agent,' as you refer to him, were working together when he showed up to run the assassination."

"After several seconds," Nick said as he successfully suppressed a second sneeze.

"As you said, Detective Garvey, we have enough evidence in Jason Beck's own words to 'bury him for his lifetime.' Only my plan is to make his lifetime extremely short by burying him as soon as we find him."

Nick shook his head. "A young man, Seth Morris, who uncovered much of the evidence and paid for it with his life, had an opinion on an appropriate punishment for Supreme Director Beck. I agree with him."

A uniformed FBI agent carrying an automatic rifle walked up to the group before President Allison could ask Nick to elaborate on Seth Morris's specific punishment.

"Time to leave," the agent informed the president. "We've contacted one Captain Gilmore, and he has agreed that we should rendezvous at his precinct." The agent cleared his throat. "Captain Gilmore also said that, if he's still alive, Detective Nicholas Garvey has a pile of paperwork to 'polish off.'"

Nick stood. He looked at the president. "I'll tell you on the way why I agree with Seth Morris."

President Allison offered Nick a pragmatic nod. "And I'll fill you in on most of my scams."

CHAPTER 85

Jason walked the two blocks of abandoned subway tunnel to his James Madison safe house. When he reached the rusted steel wall with faded graffiti of a giant octopus, he reached up and across, placing his left palm against the third sucker of the seventh arm.

The steel wall slid open without a sound.

Jason stepped inside and placed his right palm against a backlit screen to his right.

The door closed.

He walked up to the first floor and into the study, where he poured himself a glass of his favorite brandy, 1872 Janneau Armagnac. He held up the bottle. Only a third left.

He decided that, while he waited for Jeremiah's call, it was time to plan for the elimination of Mr. Duane Evers, which would solve a short-term problem—destroying the metal box being the solution to the long-term one.

◆

Nick was in the first van to arrive at the precinct. Captain Gilmore shook his hand and waved the rest of the caravan inside.

Coffee was ready for those who wanted it. Sam Kirby took a cup to President Allison.

Captain Gilmore took Nick aside. "We checked out the World Council building. Beck is not there. We have no idea where he's hiding out."

Nick mulled over the situation for several seconds. "He may be hiding, but he's got resources. Let's get Glen and Fred to work up a search pattern. We might just get lucky."

"Worth a try. But don't hold out too much hope."

Nick called Tim, and both went to explain to Glen and Fred what was needed.

Reynolds joined them. He explained what type of hiding spots would be suitable to Jason. "He would have a large multistory building, probably in Manhattan, with access both aboveground and below. He would have full electronic surveillance. He would have eliminated all construction records—probably most of the workers too. He would have installed an underground power system capable of supplying all his needs without drawing from the city system."

Nick tapped his right thumb and forefinger atop his desk. "What you're saying is that Beck has an invisible *and* opaque wall surrounding him that we cannot penetrate."

"Not a hundred percent." Reynolds pulled up a chair, took out his cell phone, and handed it to Nick. "Beck, if he plans on giving any orders or receiving any information, has only two methods of communicating: face-to-face or mobile phones. He had my phone modified so it would receive and transmit outside normal frequencies."

Fred grabbed the phone from Nick's hand and raced off. "On it," he hollered over his shoulder.

"Meanwhile," Glen said, "we'll check all videos leading out of the World Council."

CHAPTER 86

Sam Kirby was brought into the video search team, joining Nick, Tim, and Glen.

Fred and Reynolds took the cell phone into the precinct's transmission-shielded laboratory and very carefully opened its cover. Fred commented that he did recognize several of the chips and was comfortable that they could trace signal paths throughout most of the circuitry without activating communication to the world outside the lab.

Captain Gilmore sent most of his officers out on patrol while he monitored their progress and made notes on a city map taped to his office window.

President Allison kept everyone's coffee fresh.

◆◆◆

Jason answered Jeremiah's call and gave directions and evasion requirements. He met Jeremiah just outside the rusted octopus wall forty-seven minutes later. Neither man said anything until they reached the first-floor study with its electronic shield.

"What the hell happened?" Jason asked.

"My men on the firing line were killed. The others, possibly."

"Did you recognize any of them?"

"No. But nothing could have happened without the approval of Reynolds." Jeremiah collapsed into a stuffed easy chair. "He positioned everyone. He told me to count loudly—for the audio supposedly—from ten down to one and then say 'Fire.' As I drove off, he was still standing. If he hadn't planned it, he would have been the first to be shot."

"You said you saw Detective Garvey shot?"

"He sort of jerked as the shots were fired. Yes, he was shot. Dead? I don't know."

"Slight change of subject. The metal box."

"It wasn't anywhere in Gerry Martin's apartment, and I'm positive a lie detector will back me up when I say Owen Pendleton never saw the box."

If that's correct, Jason thought, *there's only one person who could possibly have it.* Detective Garvey had been stepping out onstage too much lately. It was time for his curtain call. The *final* curtain.

Nick's cell phone buzzed. It was Robert McKenna.

"Half-Penny said you'd want to know Duane Evers is in a car heading south on the old FDR Drive. He's currently . . ." Nick could hear McKenna talking into a second phone. "I'm told he's currently passing 106th Street. Half-Penny insisted I let you know." McKenna described the vehicle Duane was driving.

"Thanks for the information, Robert. And thank Half-Penny for me." Nick approached Sam. "I need you and your car. Duane Evers has been spotted."

Captain Gilmore filled in for Sam as the agent and Nick hurried to the garage. Sam got behind the wheel, and they headed off, first to the FDR Drive, then north.

Around Sixty-First Street, they spotted what had to be Duane's car racing south on York Avenue, a block to their left.

"Keep going," Nick said. "There's construction at Sixty-Third. We can get off there."

Sam took the turn at Sixty-Third almost on two wheels. Nick's phone rang just as they were settling back onto a solid four-wheel footing.

"Yes, Robert," Nick said, putting the call on speaker. "We're on his tail."

Sam interrupted. "He's getting back on the FDR at Fifty-Eighth."

Nick had missed what Robert had just said. "What did you say?"

"Just want you to know you've got one less scumbag to worry about. El Camino is dead. Mr. Duane Scumbag shot him."

"You certain?"

"The neighborhood up by 135th spotted Duane Evers originally. Their leader called us and then split his team up, two men following Duane's car, twenty breaking into the apartment building he left. They found what they described as a large, two-footed whale shot dead with one bullet to the head. From their description, we figure—"

"El Camino."

"Yes, El Camino. Half-Penny asked if the apartment smelled like a cigar factory."

Nick chuckled.

"There was a video room," Robert continued. "Seems Mr. El Camino recorded every room in his apartment round-the-clock. My caller said the main room's video shows that they got into a discussion that escalated. El Camino went to fidget with some big designer rug stuck on his wall. While he was doing that, Duane reached down at the end of a sofa, pulled out a gun, and in my phone buddy's words, 'shot the blubbery whale square in the forehead.'"

Sam broke in. "He's slowing down a bit. He's taking the exit ramp at Fifty-Third."

"He's going for the Queens Tunnel," Nick said. "The feds required the New England Association to reopen it and enlarge the entrance."

Duane cut right toward First Avenue, still shaking his head over El Camino's stupidity. *Massively stupid: stupid that he refused to lay low until things cooled off; stupid that he blamed me for allowing the lights to go on; stupid for suggesting he'd tell Jason about the failed bombs; stupid that, while he was fishing the garrote from the tapestry, he didn't imagine I knew each and every place he'd hidden a revolver.*

Duane turned left onto First.

His plan was to take the recently reopened Queens Midtown Tunnel first to Queens and then to Long Island. His World Council credentials would guarantee passage. He had a hideout and weapons stash just outside Smithtown. Most importantly, he had his survival kit with him: the folder with more than 2,700 names—names that would pay many thousands of dollars for his silence. Actually, a million dollars and more in several cases. He would disappear for a year or so, watch the new powers that be screw up everything they touched, and then return with new recruits to restore the World Council to world domination. This time he would be in control. This time—

As he turned left onto First, Duane glanced at his mirror and saw he was being followed. He slammed the accelerator to the floor. Of one thing he was sure: no car in Manhattan could keep up with his.

The streets blurred past. Fiftieth. Forty-Seventh. Forty-Fifth. The car following him was now more than two blocks behind.

He touched the brakes so as to navigate the left at Forty-Second as fast as possible.

Then he slammed on the brakes. Concrete barriers completely closed off the tunnel entrance.

"Shit!" he shouted, pounding his fist on the steering wheel. He'd have to make it through the tunnel on foot. He climbed out of the car and ran toward the continuous seven-foot-high barrier.

Screeching tires behind him turned him around just in time to see that damned detective jump out of his car and point a pistol in his direction. The sound had saved his life.

He vaulted over the barrier and crouched down. He knew running through the tunnel was now out of the question. There had to be another—

Just to his right was an elevator up to the grid. He knew every grid elevator had grid tractors parked nearby.

Still crouching, Duane raced to the elevator, opened the fence-wire door, slipped in, closed the door, pushed Up, and lay flat on the metal floor.

The elevator surged upward before Nick was able to clear the barrier. The half-second glimpse he got confirmed his suspicion he was chasing Duane Evers.

"Damn!" Nick said. "This is getting to be a habit." Only this time the other guy had gotten the elevator.

Nick moved to the rusted and rickety ladder and started climbing. He figured his quarry would have almost a minute lead on him, assuming there was more than one tractor. Assuming, also, that Duane didn't shoot out the tires. Assuming, finally, that Nick didn't reopen his wound and bleed to death.

When Nick was halfway up the ladder, an overhead shadow shaded him for a full second. He looked up and saw a grid tractor pull away and circle north. Nick increased his climbing speed, concentrating like a demon on each hand and foothold. Thirty seconds later, he cleared the ladder.

"Thank God!" he said after spotting two tractors with inflated tires.

He hopped into the first one, turned the key, heard the motor, and charged off in high-speed, twelve-mile-per-hour pursuit. He could see Duane about a quarter mile ahead.

One great disadvantage of chasing a grid tractor was that there were no fancy shortcuts. One advantage was there were no nearby buildings for the tractor being chased to hide behind.

Nick was minimally encouraged after five minutes to estimate he was now only about three hundred yards behind. Just ten or fifteen more minutes might bring him face-to-face.

His calculations were cut short by his phone ringing. While keeping at full throttle, he tapped the phone on.

"Detective, sir." It was Half-Penny.

"What is it, Half-Penny? I'm busy."

"The neighborhoods demand you stop chasing Duane Evers."

"What the hell? Why? I'll have him in a few minutes, and I'll bring him in."

"That's just it, sir. They don't want him brought in."

"That makes no sense whatso—"

Nick released the hand throttle, and the tractor glided to a quick halt.

About two hundred yards ahead, Duane's tractor was heading back toward him. Closing in from all directions save on the East River edge of the grid were hordes of neighborhood men. A few were driving grid tractors, and at least ten were piloting some sort of grid surfing boards with a single mast and a canvas sail, which moved twice as fast as the tractors did.

Duane turned to Nick's right toward the river.

Two of the men on the sailing boards pulled to within twenty feet of Nick, where they stopped and raised their hands in a stay-back gesture.

What happened next wasn't played out in super slow motion, wasn't staged like a chorus-line ballet, wasn't accomplished without sound of any sort, and wasn't devoid of all color like an old black-and-white movie. It just seemed that way to Nick as the tractors caught up with the sailboards, which pulled back to clear a path to Duane, who was still hugging the riverside edge of the grid as he struggled to continue south.

Three of the neighborhood tractors charged in: one to where Duane had been, one to where he was at the moment, and the third to where he was headed.

Duane's vehicle turned in toward the third tractor, apparently trying to crash through. That maneuver slowed him sufficiently for the first two tractors, along with the third, to pin his unit and drive him to the grid edge.

To the edge and over.

Nick looked down through the grid and watched Duane and his tractor crash onto a concrete roadway and burst into flames. Duane's body was thrown, limp and crumpled, ten feet away.

Some neighborhood men approached the body and retrieved belongings.

The neighborhood tractors began retreating. The two on the sailing boards saluted Nick and then turned and followed suit.

Nick's phone rang again.

It was Half-Penny. "Detective Garvey, sir."

"Yes, Half-Penny?"

"Some of the neighborhood men said they retrieved various papers and documents from the accident. They told me they will deliver them to you at your precinct."

CHAPTER 87

◆

Nick returned to the precinct by way of the grid tractor. As he locked it up, he gave the machine a quick pat and chuckled as he imagined one grumpy "yellow hat" lodging a complaint with Captain Gilmore.

The captain was the first to greet Nick. "No luck with the videos. No hide nor hair of Jason Beck."

Sam, who had beaten Nick back to the precinct, shook his head in agreement.

President Allison suggested everyone take a break for a few minutes. "Coffee's ready, and I had some donuts brought in. Sometimes, good solutions discover themselves when you sit back and ease up."

Everyone was way past agreement. Coffee was dispensed and the two pots refilled and set to heating.

Glen recounted for the group how the video searches had come up empty so far. "We'll keep looking, but the most likely ones have been of no use."

Reynolds took a sip from his cup. "We'll find him. The supreme director has to eventually hold court again."

"What about real estate records?" Sam asked. "You know. Titles. Who owns what?"

"No," Reynolds said, shaking his head. "Beck would never operate anything traceable."

"*He's* the one that likes to do the tracing," Fred said between mouthfuls. He looked at Reynolds. "Did you know your phone has a feature that can be activated remotely that allows some other specific phone to capture any nearby conversation?"

The surprised look on Reynolds's face told Nick that Jason Beck trusted hardly anyone.

Nick nodded. *Hardly anyone equals none in Jason Beck's world.*

Captain Gilmore presented his tally. "We can't track him retroactively by video. And property records won't work. The men I have out in the field will never be enough." He sighed and then looked at Nick. "Does our ex-con Half-Penny have any memory of any hideout?"

"I asked him," Nick said. "No leads."

President Allison sipped the last dregs in her cup. "Too bad we can't entice Beck."

Nick chuckled. "Like a cheese-filled trap for a rat."

The president also chuckled. "Yes. Like that."

Nick's eyebrows suddenly arched. He turned to Fred. "You said Reynolds's phone can be remotely triggered to capture conversations and send them to Jason Beck's phone?"

"Close," Fred allowed. "Conversations will be sent to *some* phone. I don't know whose phone it's linked to."

"Let's make an assumption. Can we trigger the capture and transmission from this end?"

Fred paused, frowning as he stared straight down into his coffee cup. "I guess we could. I'd have to check. I don't see why not."

"What do you have in mind?" President Allison asked.

Nick smiled and drained his coffee. "We all know who's the rat. I think I can come up with an enticing chunk of cheese." He stood and motioned for Fred to follow him. "Review the circuitry for me."

Nick and Fred returned with the phone two minutes later. It was placed on the table next to Nick.

"It will work. No guarantee, of course, that our rat will be listening on the other end. We will have to come up with a script before we activate the trigger."

Jason Beck pushed Duane Evers to the end of his retribution list. Nicholas Garvey had just made the coveted first position. Fortunately, he had plenty of Garvey background from when he had ordered his granddaughter's kidnapping.

Jason inserted his portable crystal into his computer and spent the next five minutes exploring several alternatives. To Detective Garvey, career was secondary to his family of two. Rekidnapping Nick's granddaughter would have a low chance of success. After a few more seconds searching through Detective Garvey's personal file, Jason settled on the new pressure point: Sandra Blanding, Nick's daughter. Languishing in a coma, she would be guarded primarily by medical personnel. An easy target. Impossible for Detective Garvey to ignore.

Jason decided to have Jeremiah get a small group and capture Sandra. He called Jeremiah and gave the order.

He stood and started for the door when something in his desk buzzed. Annoyed, he stepped back and opened the offending drawer. His "listening phone" was lit up. *How is that possible?* he wondered. He sat back down, retrieved the phone, placed it on his desk, and hit the On button.

Several seconds of silence were followed by background noise— the kind a person might hear in an office.

Nick counted to five after the phone's transmission circuitry was activated. He nodded to those standing or sitting around the table. Along with Nick, the standing four included President Allison, Tim, and Captain Gilmore. Like Fred, who was seated, they each had a handwritten script in front of them.

Nick raised his hand and pointed at Fred.

"This is one strange cell phone," Fred said, a slight tinge of awe in his voice.

Captain Gilmore noisily walked in place, mimicking the sound of someone approaching the table. "You talking to yourself again?"

"The wiring in this thing is nothing like any I've seen."

"How do you know? You just opened it a few seconds ago."

"I had a look-see in the lab, but I wanted you all to watch as I pointed out the unique circuitry inside."

"Forget the phone," Gilmore said with his usual tough SOB thunder. "What about the shooting in New Jersey? What the hell happened, and who the hell ordered it?"

"Don't know, Captain," Nick answered, sounding like he also had just joined the conversation at the table. "They captured President Allison and myself separately. They took us out in the woods to shoot us, when all hell broke loose. The firing squad were all shot and killed. Ditto for Charles Reynolds. A bunch of men jumped out of the woods behind the president and me and captured the remaining World Council Police."

"What's with this cell phone?" Gilmore asked.

"It belonged to Charles Reynolds," President Allison said. "We figured we could use it to trace it back to whoever ordered us killed."

"Don't we all have a good idea who ordered the executions?" Tim said. "Jason Beck."

"Probably the prime suspect," Nick agreed, "but he's nowhere to be found. As far as using the phone to track where our prime suspect is now, no success so far. We had Fred here open it up. What he found . . ." Nick pointed at Fred.

"What I found is interesting. The phone has two unusual features: it uses frequencies outside the normal communication band, and it transmits false outward transmissions with ghosting that force use of a fluctuating set of microwave towers to obscure the location of send and receive signals."

"Are you telling me," Captain Gilmore said, his tone suggesting more than just minor confusion, "if I order one pizza, the order goes out to three different stores, and they may each be delivered to a different location, none of which are my dinner table?"

"Uh, no," Fred said. "If you order a pizza, you'll get your pizza delivered to the address you gave. If I could eavesdrop, the address would be enough to find you—or at least the place where you said to have the pizza delivered. If you're not ordering something to be delivered, and if you never mention an address, the ghosting transmissions prevent us from triangulating your location. Instead of getting down to two blocks, we get it down, maybe, to two boroughs. Did I . . . make myself clear?"

Gilmore's voice still conveyed confusion. "As clear as thick Sicilian pizza."

"Is there anything we can do?" President Allison asked.

Nick cleared his throat. "Not at the moment. Other than Beck himself, the one thing I'd really like to find is the metal box with the eagle. Gerry left me a message that it had some, in his words, 'most interesting revelations about Jason Beck.'"

"You mentioned that box when we were held hostage," President Allison said. "No success?"

"No. I checked both his new and his old apartments. The new apartment had been turned upside down. No metal box. I double-checked. His old apartment, which I discovered he'd never given up, had some notes about a certain Duane Evers but no box."

"Is that the same Duane Evers who was chased off the grid and crashed and burned?" Gilmore asked. "That report came in fifteen minutes ago."

"Probably."

"So we can't find Jason Beck," President Allison said. "And we can't find a metal box with . . .'"

"With an eagle, according to Gerry," Nick said. "He did say he put it in something he called the 'Gabrielle Lockbox.'"

"Any idea what that is?" President Allison asked. "Or *where* it is?"

"Not a one," Nick said.

Captain Gilmore slapped the table with his hand. "Let's get back to work. If we can find any worthwhile clues, I'll order the pizza."

Everyone stood and walked away in different directions. Reynolds's cell phone was left transmitting room noises.

Jason got up slowly. He was stunned—but filled with renewed confidence. He'd have the metal box in his own hands within the hour.

He called Jeremiah. "Forget snatching Sandra Blanding. I have a different assignment."

"How many men?"

"Two hundred, at least. Fully armed."

"No problem, Director."

CHAPTER 88

◆

It took Jason less than thirty minutes to get to his remote entrance to the World Council building. He figured it would take him another fifteen to walk the six blocks of underground tunnels.

He checked his watch. Jeremiah was probably getting into position just about now. It never hurt to be doubly cautious.

The basement floors were deserted, as was the lobby.

Jason took the elevator to his floor and strode confidently to his office. He went to his desk, grabbed a master key and a small notebook from a drawer, and then headed out and down the hall to Chris Price's office.

He opened the door to Chris's office and from the doorway was able to see the framed photograph of Chris and his long-dead Gabrielle resting on the second level of the bookshelf. The two of them were smiling as they stood with arms around each other in an open field in Yemen, surrounded by at least three dozen grinning children. Directly below the picture was a small safe, which Chris had named Gabrielle Lockbox.

The combination to each executive's safe was kept contractually secret. Jason opened his notebook, skipped through several pages, nodded to himself, and started to dial the combination. The tumblers released on the last number. *So much for contracts.*

Jason pulled the door open.

The box was there, in all its dented and dinged glory. He pulled out the box, closed the safe's door, and hefted the box several times. Satisfied with the weight, he walked out with the box after closing the door.

He headed back down the hall to his own office, grinning all the way.

Jason's grin melted away when he opened his door and found Detective Nicholas Garvey sitting in his chair. *His* chair! With his feet atop the desk!

Ah, well, Jason thought. *A setup. Good thing I planned for it.* "Detective Garvey," he said with a nod. "Glad to see you again. I assume you didn't come alone."

Detective Garvey smiled at him, pulled his feet down, and stood. "Correct. I must say, though, I can't say too much about your chair and desk. Chair's lumpy and squeaky. Desk has too many drawers with too many buttons and gizmos inside. But then, I don't have delusions that I rule the world."

Jason smiled at Nick. "You don't rule anything. And never will." *But you do have delusions.*

Nick stepped from behind the desk and made a sweeping motion with his right arm. "In that case, you should take this seat."

Jason brushed past Nick and sat. "So when are the others joining us?"

"Soon," Nick said, sitting opposite Jason. He fished for something in a pants pocket. "But before anyone comes in, I thought you might want this." Nick opened his hand, revealing a small gray square. "It's magnetic and, used with a three-digit code, will open that box you're holding." He flipped the chip to Jason.

Jason reflexively caught the chip.

"The code is on the chip," Nick said. "Flip it number-side down, place it in the square indent below the eagle, thumb in the code, and—"

"And have it blow up in my face?"

"Hey, I'll sit beside you. Hell, I'll even open it while you stand here."

Jason smiled. "No, thank you. There are some things I do myself."

"Unlike murder."

Jason ignored him and opened the box as instructed. He pulled out a heavily wrapped package and held it up. He squeezed it several times. "These aren't journal pages."

Nick chuckled. "President Allison wanted to load the box with those big springy things that jump right out at you. The others were on her side, but—"

"But what?"

"But since I found the box, my choice prevailed."

"Your choice being . . ."

"Three pounds of Limburger cheese. A smelly cheese for a very smelly rat."

"Funny, Detective Garvey. Funny."

Nick shrugged. "I thought so."

"When do those who voted for the springy things join us?"

The office door opened, and a middle-aged man with a video camera entered. President Allison followed a second later.

"I did lose the vote," she said. "But upon reflection, Limburger cheese is a perfect match."

To Jason's surprise, President Allison stepped forward and, in a totally unexpected—and from his point of view, mocking—manner, shook his hand. Out of the corner of his eye, Jason glimpsed the man with the camera pointing it in their direction. The camera's recording light was blinking red.

"Rest in peace, Director Beck." President Allison held Jason's hand prisoner in a tight grip. "Your reign is over."

Jason yanked his hand free and stood. "Sorry, Madam President. It's your paltry reign that's over. You may have survived for the moment, thanks at least partially to a traitor, but I have the world at my command. You, Madam President, command precious little loyalty in your fractured country. Whereas, Madam President, I am the supreme director of the World Council. No matter what confrontation you plan to initiate, I can count on support from China, Russia, the Arab world—from wherever I beckon, support will rush to my side. If you plan to kill me, even dead, I'll still outlive you. Agreements reached long ago will bring the wrath of all these countries down upon your head. Only the supreme director can command such overwhelming support."

Nick took a couple of steps forward. "Perhaps we'll just have to replace you as supreme director."

Jason chuckled. "Good luck with that. No one else would be accepted."

Nick mimicked Jason's chuckle as he moved back to the door. "Maybe I can propose a candidate."

Nick opened the door, and Christopher Price entered.

Jason shuddered and sank back into his chair.

Price walked up to Beck, reached over, smiled, and shook his hand.

"So Reynolds didn't kill you," Jason said, hissing the words through clenched teeth. "So I've had two traitors."

Nick said nothing for several seconds, clearly basking in Jason's furious glare. "I think, Jason, we've found your replacement. Reynolds apparently set up a quick swimming lesson for Christopher: how to fall into the Hudson River while semiconscious and then swim to and into a drainage pipe within fifteen seconds. No need to worry, though. President Allison says you're not to be killed, just taken away. Away from any and all power."

Chris sat down at the desk, opposite Jason. "The president and I have laid out a long-term plan for the World Council. Eventually, each and every country will return to a state of political and economic sovereignty. Oh, and throw in legal sovereignty, as well. Each country will be disconnected from the coercion of World Council law. Each—"

"Never happen!" Jason hissed. "The president and, if not handled properly, even the World Council will be brought to their knees under the barrage of the six associations. There is supreme animosity . . ." Jason shook his head. "Make that *hatred* of the president and of the council. The Penn-Jersey Association would be the first to chew up and spit out the president. After her"—he stabbed a finger at Chris—"it'll be your turn."

Chris smiled and shook his head. "You're right, Jason. That scenario would guarantee certain disaster, were it to be true."

"It's true!" Jason snapped, his fists clenched.

Nick gave a slight shrug. "Well, not *exactly* true. The 'hatred' thing, I mean." He nodded at his partner, standing by the door.

The detective opened the door.

For a second or two, nobody was there. Finally, Carter Johnson stepped into the room, paused for a moment, waved to those around the desk, and then hurried over and around the desk to where he was able to pat Jason on his right shoulder.

"I never had any animosity toward Lenny," Johnson said. "Sorry, I meant to say President Lenora Allison." He turned and shook President Allison's outstretched hand.

Jason, gritting his teeth, bolted upright again. "What the hell is going on here? What is all this happy crap?" He turned to the man with the video camera. "And what the hell is he doing?"

"Recording our happy reunion," President Allison said. "Our happy reunion, which we will show at your memorial service."

"So I *am* to be killed, after all." Jason, almost sagging, reclaimed his seat.

"No." President Allison shook her head. "You're going to be locked up where nobody will see you. Detective Garvey convinced me that keeping you alive was best. He convinced me that Seth Morris had the right idea when he wrote that you should 'rot *alive* in hell.' Nick said killing you would be letting you off much too easy."

Nick stepped forward, smiling at Jason. "By staying alive, you'll be able to witness all the good and caring things that will be done in your name. I'm sure it will warm your heart. One little hitch: you'll see all, but none will see you."

"Because," President Allison chimed in, "they won't even look for you when they assume you're dead."

A sudden knock on the door caught everyone's attention.

Nick moved again to the door and opened it. "Come in," he said, smiling.

Reynolds stepped in, nodded at Nick, and walked to President Allison's side. "Contained." His one word was heard by all in the room.

"So," Jason snarled. "Traitor number 2 isn't dead, after all."

Nick stepped directly opposite Jason. Only the desk separated them. He reached over and patted the metal box. "Notice the eagle on top? I think you've killed a few people to get it back." He leaned partway over the desk. "Tell you what. Since we've emptied it of all its papers for review and appropriate actions, you're welcome to keep the empty box. Oh, and we'll toss in the cheese. President Allison and I discussed the contents while we were awaiting our executions, and we concluded that any combination of your journal entries would preclude any form of support you would hope to receive from the aforementioned China, Russia, Arab states, or any of the dozens of other regimes you've corrupted over the past thirty years." Nick straightened and offered a snappy salute.

Jason could feel venomous hatred erupt across his face. He didn't care.

Nick glared right back. "Tell me, O Great Supreme Leader and Director of Planet Earth, tell me why you had El Camino kill Vice President Jerome Wellsley. I know that he came over to your camp. Why did you kill him? Was he betraying you? Was he planning to cut you down to size?"

"He couldn't cut anything down to size. He was always small potatoes."

"Potatoes?"

"A small potato versus a large social plan."

Nick shook his head. "More like a large misplaced ego. What's the benefit in killing a small potato and four others?"

President Allison stepped forward. "He wanted me to be distracted."

"Close," Jason said. "You will be seen as a president who couldn't even protect your second in command. He was a simpleton."

"It doesn't matter how I will be seen. What does matter is what happens to each individual in this country. Hell, make that the world. Again, it doesn't matter how I will be seen, because you will never be seen again."

Nick gave Jason a dismissive wave of his hand. "And your butcher, El Camino, will also never be seen again. Seems your traitor number 1 shot him in the forehead."

Jason managed a chuckle. "He was Duane Evers's right hand, not mine. I have many right hands."

President Allison shook her head. "From what Captain Charles Reynolds announced a few minutes ago, most, if not all, of your right hands have been contained by four different Manhattan neighborhoods."

Jason stared first at President Allison and then at Nicholas. He imagined them pleading for mercy as they burned at the stake.

Chris Price stood up. "Time to go, Jason. President Allison has assured me that you will be well taken care of and want for nothing. Nothing except—"

"Except what?" Jason snarled.

"Except contact."

As Jason, led by Nick and Chris, stepped to the door, Reynolds, holding a phone to his ear, looked up at President Allison. "They still haven't found Jeremiah."

Jason's lips curled into a smile. "There will always be someone you can't find." *And,* he thought, *that someone will always find you.*

CHAPTER 89

◆

Nick held up a hand as President Allison started for the door. "We shouldn't discount Jeremiah and what he's capable of doing."

President Allison paused for several moments before nodding. "We proceed with the broad outlines of our plan. We take Jason to a remote and quite secure location. Then . . ." She paused for a moment. "Contact Sam. Have him double security and scour our route. We'll go normal speed at first, then faster, slower, or by different routes, per his recommendations."

Nick and Reynolds led the way as the group hurried to the first-floor rear exit of the World Council building. It took only a couple of minutes to reach the rear fire door. Reynolds waved Nick back and, pistol raised, stepped out into the back parking lot. Nick watched as Reynolds walked about forty feet to the right, returned, and slowly paced off the sixty feet to the left corner of the building, where he peered around the corner. He gave a thumbs-up to Nick, who stepped out and motioned for the others to follow.

Two Secret Service men stepped out first, one moving right and the other left. Upon reaching double Reynolds's distance on the right and the corner on the left, both made an elevated 360-degree sweep with special detectors. After about thirty seconds, they signaled to Nick that it was safe for all others to move out.

President Allison and Carter Johnson were the first out, followed immediately by Christopher Price. They headed toward the left corner.

The video man emerged next. He stepped about twenty feet from the building, turned, raised his camera, and started recording as the remaining four Secret Service men led a shackled and double-cuffed Jason Beck out and toward the corner.

Nick closed the door and followed the videographer, who was jogging sideways to the corner, taping all the way.

As the last group turned the corner, Nick could see the president, Johnson, and Price each stepping into a separate limousine, the first three of six. The fourth had three Secret Service agents outside the left-side doors, all three of which were closed. The fifth limousine had twice the number of agents, with the two rear left-side doors open. The last limo had, again, three agents outside closed doors.

Jason Beck was being hustled to the fifth limousine with open doors. The videographer was hustling twice as fast, getting ahead, taping all the time.

The videographer was the first to be shot. The camera hadn't fallen from his hand more than two or three inches when more shots rang out, taking down the four agents holding Beck. Beck was left standing not three feet from the rear bumper of the fifth limo. Nick knew immediately that the gunfire originated from atop the nine-story building just beyond a four-story brick job next to the parking lot.

The first three limos raced off. The twelve remaining agents crouched behind the remaining limousines and started to return fire.

Out of the corner of his eye, Nick saw Reynolds racing behind the last limo and along the seawall toward the building from where the shots were originating.

Tracer rounds started to come from the roof. Suddenly the flaming trail of an RPG arced into the fourth limousine. It burst into flames, taking the three agents with it.

Jason Beck turned to run back toward Nick just as a second RPG hit the fifth limousine. It, too, burst into flames, catching Beck in its inferno.

Nick, propelled by instinct, raced to Beck, now writhing on the ground. He whipped off his jacket and beat the flames down as best he could. Within seconds, he was joined by three agents who worked quickly to smother the flames and pull Beck out of range of fire.

The tracers continued for at least thirty more seconds, with the remaining five agents returning fire.

Suddenly the shots stopped. Nick hazarded a glance up at the building and saw Reynolds waving down at them.

"There were three of them," Reynolds recounted when he rejoined the group. "It looked like there was a fourth, but I only found the three. Jeremiah was most probably the one that managed to get away."

One of the agents came up to them and relayed a message from President Allison. "We gotta do our best to keep Beck alive."

Both Nick and Reynolds looked down at the still-writhing Beck and shrugged. "Tell her we'll do our best."

"Already did," the agent said. "Told her that he looked like a charbroiled pig. She just said to try our best. She told me what hospital to take him to if he can make it. She also told me to get the video camera and bring it with us."

Reynolds nodded at Nick to carry Beck to the last limo. "We'll get him there."

"It's not the closest hospital," the agent said, his tone and expression puzzled.

"The president has her reasons," Reynolds said, grunting as he and Nick carried Beck to the limo.

Nick had to adjust his grip three times as patches of burnt skin slipped from Beck's ankles.

The rear seats were lowered flat to provide the closest-possible approximation of a stretcher.

The agent, video camera in hand, answered his phone. Saying nothing, he listened for a short ten seconds and then lowered his phone. "The president said she'll meet us there."

"Then we go," Reynolds said, double-checking that he and Nick had Beck confined and braced enough to prevent any rolling. "He's ready. We're ready."

Suddenly Reynolds shoved his door open, startling Nick.

"Jeremiah!" Reynolds pointed at a car just pulling out from behind the adjacent building.

"How do you—" Nick didn't bother finishing as Reynolds jumped into one of the Secret Service vehicles and raced off after the fleeing car.

Nick gave a go-ahead signal to the driver.

All doors were closed. The limo pulled out and away from the two other burning limousines.

Reynolds caught up to Jeremiah's car between Second and First Avenues. He lowered the passenger window as he pulled even with the black vehicle. Positioning his automatic on the window ledge, he emptied thirty rounds into the car as they passed First Avenue.

Jeremiah's car didn't explode or veer to the side and crash into anything. It kept going straight through the barriers along the FDR Drive, raced across the FDR, and plunged into the Harlem River.

Reynolds pulled to a stop on the FDR and waited ten minutes, watching for any sign of life: a floating body, bubbles. Nothing. He turned around and headed to Mount Sinai.

CHAPTER 90

◆

As the limousine carrying Nick and Jason Beck pulled into the emergency entrance of Mount Sinai Hospital, three medical technicians in gowns wheeled a gurney out the door. President Allison was right behind.

The three technicians opened the tailgate and slid in a board stretcher on the limo deck along Beck's immediate right. With the help of Nick, they raised Beck's limp form several inches, centered him over the board, and gently lowered him.

"Is he alive?" President Allison asked.

Nick affirmed with a quick nod that he was. "He fainted about two minutes ago."

One of the technicians had his hand on Beck's neck. "The pulse is steady and not weak. Not strong either." Crooking his head toward the door, he said to the other two techs, "Let's get him inside."

As Jason was wheeled through the emergency entrance, President Allison motioned Nick to her side. "I gave a false name for Beck. If asked, refer to him as Peter Chekoff, the videographer."

Nick nodded and followed President Allison along the long hall into a private room that was now to serve as the presidential command center. Six Secret Service agents brought in a television and some special scrambler phones. They explained several operational quirks to Nick. To everyone's relief, they took food orders to be filled from a local diner. Reynolds came into the room in time to add his order.

After twenty minutes, a doctor entered the room. "Mr. . . ." He glanced down at the clipboard he was holding. "Mr. Chekoff is in stable condition." He looked up at President Allison.

"Will he recover?" the president asked.

"Eventually."

"And 'eventually' means what?"

"Three to four weeks to be able to leave in a wheelchair. After that, an additional three to four weeks to recover to where he can walk and talk. His burns, however, are severe and extensive. Both eyes have miraculously survived almost unharmed, but . . ." The doctor paused, pursed his lips, and glanced down at his clipboard.

"But what?" President Allison asked, pushing.

"Both sides of his face look like they melted."

The doctor's pager buzzed. He apologized and left.

President Allison nodded and turned back to Nick, who was walking over to the one monitoring phone that had started its red lamp to flashing.

"Any communication from the video broadcast team?" she asked.

"Not yet," Nick replied. "We did get word from the field team. Apparently, our chopper has crashed into the helipad, the event captured start to finish on video. The handshake videos are ready to broadcast at your command."

Reynolds stepped over. "You still want to broadcast them *after* the helicopter video?"

"It'll heighten the interest and the number of people viewing," President Allison said. "The first viewing will be treated as a news alert. We'll release the handshake segments fifteen to twenty minutes after. Later news cycles will sequence them as they wish. What will be repeated and repeated again is that Director Chris Price was on a secret assignment for Director Jason Beck—an assignment to pull the associations and the federal government into negotiations. It will come across that Beck wanted to expedite full association participation himself by flying first to Philadelphia and then to other association capitals."

"And to everyone's dismay," Nick said, shaking his head in mock sorrow, "Director Beck's hopeful mission ended in tragedy."

One of the Secret Service agents handed President Allison a note, which she glanced at and then held aloft. "The helicopter video is about to be transmitted to the two networks. We will be tapping in."

Two of the Secret Service agents pulled the curtains across the hall-side room windows and closed the door.

The screen sprang to full color. The view was of the World Council helipad, viewed from just aside the World Council building's side exit. The backs of four men were seen as they emerged from the exit. Three were uniformed Council Police. The fourth was a tall man dressed in a well-tailored business suit. As the group neared the waiting helicopter, the businessman turned back and waved, presumably at people still at the exit door. The businessman was clearly Jason Beck or, as the president observed, possibly an excellent stand-in.

Jason Beck was recorded climbing aboard the helicopter's side door, turning toward the camera for another wave, and then pulling the door closed.

About fifteen seconds elapsed as the copter's engines were revved to a higher speed. Finally, the bright green helicopter rose almost three hundred feet and then arched toward the New Jersey side.

Suddenly, out of nowhere, a flock of at least two hundred small birds appeared from the left side of the camera's view window. The flock was caught up in both of the helicopter's rotors. The copter was seen trying to curl back to the New York side and away from the birds. The central part of the flock was chewed to bits as the blades spun erratically.

The helicopter, struggling to maintain altitude but drifting lower, headed back over the helipad. Suddenly, about two hundred feet up, the chopper shuddered, stalled, seemed to hang suspended for a moment, and then plunged to the concrete landing pad. The crash and the burst of flames were awesome and all-consuming.

The World Council Fire and Security Departments were on the scene within twenty-five seconds, but nothing could be done. The video showed the three-and-a-half-minute effort to douse the flames.

In the end, two horribly charred bodies, Jason Beck and the pilot, were pulled free and zipped in large black bags.

"Impressive!" Carter Johnson said, shaking President Allison's hand. "When I beat you in the next election, you can always start a career in old Hollywood as—I think they called them 'moguls.' You did yourself proud, Lenny."

They both laughed, still shaking hands.

"I assume your stand-in rolled out the far side to safety as the engines were reaching speed."

President Allison smiled.

"And that you never had a pilot aboard."

Another smile.

"The bird animation was particularly impressive. I assume you're not going to include the warning that claims 'no birds were hurt or killed in the making of this video.'"

They chuckled like the old friends they were, shaking their heads in enjoyment of a mission partially accomplished.

Someone knocked on the closed door.

The TV was turned off and the door opened.

It was the doctor again.

"Agent Chekoff's condition?" President Allison asked.

"As expected. Maybe even a bit better. He may be able to leave in just two weeks, not four."

"Excellent news!" the president said with enthusiasm.

The doctor frowned slightly. "Does Agent Chekoff have a family? Wife? Kids?"

"Why do you ask?"

The doctor pulled out two eight-by-ten-inch photographs and handed them to President Allison, whose eyes suddenly widened.

"If he does have a wife and children, you might want to prepare them. Keep the photographs. They might help." The doctor turned and left.

Everyone in the room crowded around to see the photographs. Every pair of eyes shot full open.

Several seconds passed with no one saying anything.

Finally, Nick cleared his throat. "Doesn't look to me like you'll have to worry about hiding him. You've got your own real-life version of *The Man in the Iron Mask*. Only in this case it's the man in the *melted* mask."

President Allison glanced back down at the pictures again and studied them closely. From her expression, it was obvious a plan was spinning in her head and starting to form.

She looked back up at Nick. "You're right, Detective. Alexandre Dumas had need of an iron mask. We don't."

CHAPTER 91

◆

C hris Price was not used to having makeup applied, nor was he used to having a political aide rehearse talking points for at least the tenth time. He was used to speaking to TV cameras on occasion—but always *with* Jason Beck, not *about* Jason Beck.

They had all decided he was the one individual that everyone wanted to hear explain the past sixteen hours. The broadcast was set for prime time. Chris was seated behind a nondescript desk with the World Council flag on his right and the United States flag on his left. Missing was the flag of the Unified Associations.

The red light on the single video camera flashed on—Chris's cue.

"Good evening, ladies, gentlemen, citizens of all corners of the world. On this sad day, the day that witnessed the tragic death of World Council Supreme Director Jason Beck, I feel it is my duty to inform you of the many initiatives the council has undertaken over the past five weeks.

"As has been suggested on the snippets of video you have seen, which surfaced after Jason Beck's helicopter was hit by a flock of birds and, in a grisly spin, plunged onto the helipad, bursting into flames . . ." Chris paused and then, feigning a distraught look, reached for his glass of water and took a sip. "As has been hinted, Director Jason Beck sent me on a secret mission to broker, if not a peace, at least an understanding between President Lenora Allison and Association Chief Executive Carter Johnson. Since it was a secret mission, Director Beck arranged for me to appear to drown, removing any expectation for me to attend official functions, thereby avoiding any questions of where I was and what I was doing.

"I am supremely happy to inform you that the first part of Director Jason Beck's grand plan has come to fruition. As you saw in those video clips, and as you see on my right, POTUS and ACE have moved far beyond just an understanding and on to where they have committed to normalizing relations between the United States and the associations." Chris paused again for another sip of water. "Supreme Director Beck was overjoyed with the success of his plan."

Video clips first of the president and then of Carter Johnson shaking hands with Jason Beck popped into motion at the upper left quadrant of the video screen.

"As you can see, again, from these clips, Director Beck greeted both parties, opening his office for them to explore productive alternatives to the existing stasis. The following meetings were closed to video, but I can assure you that dynamic plans were proposed and, to Director Beck's delight, accepted. The three leaders realized that their proposals and action plans could serve as templates for the rest of the world. Director Beck decided the initial agreements reached yesterday evening had to be made public. He decided he would make the announcement in the great city of Philadelphia, the city where the United States Constitution was agreed upon and signed. It seemed a positive sign to Director Beck that a second great agreement should be announced from the same, exact site. He had called for his helicopter to take him to Philadelphia." Chris paused again, lowered his gaze, and let out an almost-inaudible sigh. "He was excited for what he envisioned in our future—more excited than I've seen him be in years." Another sigh, slightly more audible this time. "His vision must not die with him. Both President Allison and association chief executive Johnson have insisted that we must accomplish his vision for this country and must flesh out his initial plans for the rest of humanity." Chris lowered his head slightly and then raised it again, adopting a gaze of sad determination. "I have acceded to President Allison's and Chief Executive Johnson's demand that I assume temporary directorship of the World Council until the time that a permanent supreme director can be chosen." He pushed his chair back and stood.

The camera zoomed out to reveal President Allison and Carter Johnson standing just to the right of the desk.

Chris glanced quickly at them both. Finally, he stared directly at the camera, his look stern, purposeful. "We have hard work ahead of us, and to get it started, much less completed, we must work together." He glanced again at the two leaders. "Not just the three of us, but you, as well. All of you. All of us. Director Beck's vision was to move the world forward from the stability the World Council achieved in thirty years to a new growth, a new respect for each other, a new world for each of us." Chris turned and shook hands with President Allison and Chief Executive Johnson.

The lights slowly dimmed to black.

CHAPTER 92

◆

N ick and Reynolds formed a friendship. Reynolds let slip that he was heading home in a couple of weeks. When it turned out Reynolds had no permanent home, Nick offered the extra room in his apartment. Reynolds, after encouragement from President Allison, finally accepted.

Nick spent the allowed six hours each day in his daughter's hospital room, at her bedside. Reynolds accompanied him several times, noting, along with Nick, the incremental but perceptible improvement in her vitals. She was still in an induced coma, and Nick read to her frequently. When Reynolds was there, Nick talked about her incessantly.

"She rode her first two-wheeler on her fifth birthday," Nick mused aloud, smiling. "She must have passed it on to her daughter, who beat her record by a full year."

Nick only reminisced about the few good years, not the ones when Sandra had viewed him as the devil incarnate.

"What about you, Reynolds? You have any family?"

"Not still alive."

The matter-of-fact tone of the answer surprised Nick. "You're relatively young. What happened?"

"Jihad."

Nick's head snapped up, and he looked at Reynolds. "Jihad."

"Yes. Extremists killed my family and made me join their jihad."

Nick was dumbfounded. "How did you get away? You're here now, in this country."

"President Allison rescued me. Although she was not yet president at the time."

Like a fish hooked on a line, Nick couldn't let go. "When did she rescue you? How?"

"Your Coast Guard captured me and shot eight others just after we poisoned an oil rig in the Gulf of Mexico about thirty years ago. I was eight years old and suffered a broken right leg."

Over the next hour, Reynolds filled in many blanks.

Then-congressman Lenora Allison had intervened on behalf of the young boy the media had labeled "boy terrorist." Everything she did on his behalf was kept hush-hush, with no involvement with the media. While maintaining the fiction that he was incarcerated in a federal prison, she had cajoled the board of trustees of a Houston hospital to treat the boy's injuries. Upon his release and after verifying his background, she had him admitted to a local Muslim school.

After four years, a distant uncle, a Yemeni veteran, was located and, after his service record was vetted, was allowed to come to the United States. Over six months he met frequently with the boy and, separately, with then-senator Allison. It was decided by the Texas Supreme Court that the uncle would—and could—provide a stable environment and a positive upbringing.

"He and I returned to Yemen, where he taught me many things, especially the *whole* Qur'an, not just the parts favored by empty-headed, infantile murderers for more than a thousand years."

Nick saw Reynolds's clenched teeth and the rapid pulsing at his right temple and decided to try changing the topic. "Thanks for having everyone's back. You must really—"

"Sorry I couldn't get to Gerry Martin first."

"What? What do you mean?"

"Jason ordered me to take him out. He'd still be alive if I'd gotten to him before El Camino."

"I know. President Allison told me."

"Did she also tell you that my first death staging was that of Dr. Owen Pendleton?"

Nick's jaw dropped.

"True. I was twenty-two. My uncle had recently died, and I was given permission to return to the United States for a year. Toward the end of that year, I spent several weeks with Lenora, who had just been reelected Senate majority leader. I became aware that she was engaged in a secret effort with Senator Carter Johnson to somehow shield Dr. Pendleton from a whole onslaught of death threats. I overheard one such evening session, which was heading nowhere, and said my uncle had saved several neighbors in Yemen by orchestrating their fake deaths. They mulled over that approach for several hours, asking how my uncle would have carried out the operation. I gave them several options.

"By morning, they gave me my first 'death' assignment. Both Allison and Johnson required that nothing point to their involvement. Pendleton was contacted by a nonexistent international group offering to provide protection. Worn down from all the threats, he agreed. Sam Kirby has been the liaison from the first, assuring Dr. Pendleton that he had the protection of that international group."

"Wow!" was all Nick could manage.

"After Pendleton's car crash, I returned to Yemen. Ten years ago, Lenora and Carter, then vice president, asked if I would return and go undercover for them. I agreed."

"Damn good you did."

Reynolds glanced down to his side, where Nicole snoozed in a chair. "Your six-year-old granddaughter has problem-solving skills undreamed of by those in my country who use religion to justify murder."

"Really? How do you figure that?"

"Yesterday, when she and I went out to the cafeteria for a tea and an orange juice, she told me that she had been getting her mother to ease up on you. 'Mom used to hate Grandpa,' she said. 'But because she sees me laughing and hugging when he's around, she now tolerates him. Maybe, before one of them dies, I can get them to hug each other.' Big words for a young lady." Reynolds chuckled, his grim tension eased. "Big words and a big plan. Most men in my country don't believe in hugs. Only guns and machetes. Hugs solve problems. Guns and machetes *create* them."

Nick glanced over at the sleeping Nicole and fought back a tear.

Reynolds took a deep breath and continued. "But if all that is aimed at you are guns and machetes, you have to put hugs aside for a while and get the biggest and baddest gun and the sharpest and meanest machete ever seen. An extremist that relies on the end of a gun has no faith in his religion. Allah has a trash bin where he sets fire to all such hollow souls."

Nick looked back at Reynolds. "Amen to that."

Nick accompanied Reynolds to the military plane chartered by Sam Kirby to take Reynolds back to Yemen.

President Allison arrived an hour before departure. She and Reynolds hugged each other and talked up a storm, reminiscing non-stop until the boarding call.

When Reynolds climbed aboard, President Allison approached Nick. "Detective Garvey," she said, cupping his left hand in both of hers, "I've been getting daily updates on your daughter's condition. I was glad to hear that she's progressing better than anticipated."

"Thank you, Madam President."

"I have a suggestion. There is a hospital in Houston to which I have had your daughter's records sent. The doctors there, in concert with the doctors here, have reviewed all options and have concluded that her progress would probably accelerate if she were transferred. We'll be leaving in nine days for California, where we have a meeting with leaders from China and Japan. We will, however, be making a stop in Houston." She still held his hand, a questioning look on her face.

Nick paused for several seconds. He bit his lower lip. "Okay. If the doctors agree, so do I." He squeezed, then retrieved his hand. "Thank you."

Nick, with Tim's help, was overseeing the preparations for the transfer of his daughter to the president's plane, scheduled to depart in twenty-six hours. Nick was inside the suite where Sandra would be monitored. He was checking the stowed medications when he heard Half-Penny approach Tim just outside the suite door.

"Detective Branson, can I ask you for a favor?"

"Certainly, Half-Penny."

"For several days, Nathan has mentioned to me that he really wants to go with Detective Garvey—actually, to stay with him and with Nicole."

"That would require a boatload of approvals. Approvals not only from Nathan's neighborhood leaders but from Nick himself, and from—"

"This morning I talked with Robert McKenna, their leader, and he said Nathan had requested just that and the neighborhood council agreed to his petition. When he was two, his mom died after a long illness. A proven and previously approved lifesaving drug had been outlawed by, in Mr. McKenna's words, 'faceless bureaucrats.' Nathan, after his father was killed, and not having any kinfolk, was eligible to request attachment within the neighborhood. Detective Garvey, being an inducted citizen and all, was considered an acceptable choice."

Nick almost dropped one of the medications he was checking.

Tim also must have been taken by surprise, because his response took several seconds. "Are you sure that's what Nathan wants?"

"Yes," Half-Penny said several times. "For weeks, ever since his father died, it's been, 'Detective Garvey did this. Detective Garvey did that.' Nathan looks up to him."

Tim took another few seconds to react. "What about you? Maybe not in words, but you've expressed a bonding with Detective Garvey."

It was Half-Penny's turn, apparently, to be caught off guard for more than a couple of seconds. "I like Detective Garvey, even respect him, but I have responsibilities here. Can't do." Nick heard Half-Penny start walking to the front of the plane and then stop and return to Tim. "And I like and respect you too," he added.

Tim chuckled. "I'll see what I can do. Quite a few clearances and approvals will be required. I'll see what I can do."

Nick decided he also had to see what he could do.

Sandra had just been secured in the forward cabin suite and Nick was walking back when President Allison motioned to him to take the seat next to her.

"She will be fine, Detective. The Mount Sinai doctors assured me that she's in super shape to travel and that the doctors in Houston will have her up and around within weeks. Carter Johnson's younger brother is chief of surgery there. He doesn't feel surgery is required but will oversee every step taken."

Nick tried to muster a relieved look and achieved about 10 percent success. "I didn't know Carter Johnson had a brother."

"Morton," she said with a smile. "But he prefers M. Charles Johnson. Their parents were killed in an auto crash when Carter was twelve and Morton was seven. An aunt, their dad's sister, did her best to provide a home for them, but her parenting skills being quite spotty, Carter and Morton matured quickly and provided as much stability for her as she did for them. The two brothers learned that family is not only the genesis of life but also of character, of empathy, of receiving guidance in finding your unique path in life." President Allison, perhaps sensing Nick's unease, placed a reassuring hand on his arm. "Whatever fractures they have suffered, families can find ways to heal. Time and effort are two of the prescriptions. There are others. You are a wise man, Nicholas Garvey. You will find your family's way."

Nick thanked the president again. "I guess you and Carter Johnson haven't been the mortal enemies portrayed by everyone."

"Not by a long shot. Oh, we've had our disagreements, but we've been able to work out about 80 percent of the issues." She smiled. "Most in my favor," she added with a theatrical wink. "We both have an evidence-based view of the world. My engineering background sets off alarms when some politician tries to buy votes by shouting to the masses the rhetorical equivalent of claiming that Sir Isaac Newton was wrong and that he or she, having superior insight, will legislate that, when any apple disconnects from any tree, it will fall upward. Engineering principles dictate that you cannot just say something is so;

you must demonstrate with data and facts. Most politicians who claim they know the way to a better future just claim apples *will* fall upward and insist their words are truth. Carter has the same world view from his specialty in history. His view is that if something hasn't worked for half a century, it never will, regardless of the backroom wizards who say, 'This time is *the* time. Just close your eyes, believe, and trust us.'"

"I'm glad for that," Nick said.

Her voice softened. "We met between our junior and senior years at different colleges. We were on a six-day rafting trip down the Colorado River through the Grand Canyon. It didn't take long for us to discover the other's political leanings. What did take a little time around the campfire was to realize that, as far as solutions were concerned, there were many areas of potential agreement. One just had to put in the effort to see the opportunities.

"When we both entered politics, we met again and soon committed to have each other's political back, if not the other's programs. When it came to doing the right thing, we ignored the claims of our peers that we were each traitors to our respective alliances. We found that, by searching out common ground, we could work wonders."

Nick chuckled. "So you used your political friendship to ensnare Jason Beck."

Lenora nodded. "We both wanted to eliminate Jason Beck and his World Council. We both wanted to return to our own Constitution, shredding all the other international, restrictive crap. We even suckered him into declaring null and void all federal regulations pertaining to individuals and corporations. With those millions of confusing pages gone, we can now slowly develop new regulations only where absolutely needed—and only where they don't control people's lives and don't conflict with the Constitution. We both figured the grid would be our best chance to accomplish those goals."

"But . . ." Nick's voice trailed off momentarily. "But Carter Johnson told me just this morning that—"

"That my cherished rectenna grid can never pay for itself? And for all practical purposes, it's as useful as donkey dung?"

Nick nodded. "Pretty well his exact words. Only he substituted a horse for the donkey and—"

"And a more colorful synonym for dung?"

Nick smiled sheepishly and nodded again.

President Allison chuckled. "I've heard him use that synonym quite frequently when discussing the grid. And he's dead-on."

Nick blinked in surprise.

"Carter and I worked out the grid scam together. We—"

"Scam?" Nick couldn't believe *he* was the one interrupting this time.

"Yes, *scam*. It works in the engineering sense, but in the world of economics, it fails miserably in New York City."

"Then why build it at all?"

"We decided we needed a world-class large project to attract everyone's attention, including Supreme Director Jason Beck. We hoped, correctly it turned out, he would so enjoy Carter and me fighting over the project that he would let it proceed to completion. Carter and I figured Jason would do whatever was required to assure that the grid would not light the city."

"But it *did* light the city."

"Only because we cheated."

"Cheated? How in hell . . ."

The president gave Nick a self-satisfied grin. "We knew he was cutting most, if not all, grid power-feed connections. Knowing that, we convinced him to allow Carter to order the blowing up of the Lincoln Tunnel. Once the tunnel was off-limits, we brought in power-feed lines from New Jersey and, making use of old subway tunnels and hundreds of basements of unoccupied buildings, spread them out to already-prepared distribution points not on any schematics. Once we cheated the lights on, we had to go back and repair most of the cut connections. We also removed several software blocks we had put in to prevent any of his people from grabbing control of the satellite. For the past five days, the grid has operated as advertised."

Nick shook his head in wonder and admiration. "You had him no matter what he did. I guess it was key to have Reynolds as your inside man."

"It was."

"What are you going to do with the grid now?"

"Dismantle it."

Nick's eyes shot wide open. "Dismantle? As in take it down?"

"Exactly. It served both its purposes."

"Both purposes? Pulling down Jason Beck, I see. But what—"

"Jason stood on the sidelines as the grid was built, convinced, as were we, that gigantic government projects rarely, if ever, end up as anything more than that donkey dung Carter keeps talking about. We needed a fascinating circus show to keep Jason's attention away from our other effort: purpose number 2."

Nick was lost. "Purpose number 2? Your *other* effort?"

"Twelve private businessmen, willing to risk their fortunes and—if the World Council found out—their freedom, produced all of the hardware required to build the grid while, at the same time, building an alternative to the grid."

Nick was hooked. "What alternative?"

President Allison smiled. "A space elevator. Keep that to yourself. I don't want to jinx it. The whole world, including Jason Beck, will find out in less than six months."

The mention of Jason Beck still struck several chords of concern in Nick. "What do you think Jason Beck will do when the news hits?"

"There's not much he will be able to do."

"Yeah, you're right."

"I put his situation in the category of achieving balance. I firmly believe nature eventually assures a balance in most everything. Sometimes the balance can strike you as somewhat perverse. As you grow older and save your earnings, you eventually have much more money to pay the barber, but by then you have much less hair to be cut."

Nick chuckled, rubbing a hand through his own thinning hair. "Tell me about it."

"Another example of balance, Nick, is the list of names you retrieved from Duane Evers's knapsack."

"The list of 2,732 kidnapped children and their recipients?"

"Yes. Since you gave me that list, we've been able to identify the current approximate locations of 827 of those children and have effected the return of another 406 to their biological parents. Carter

Johnson and I will not rest until all of them have been located and those still alive returned to their parents. In all cases, criminal indictments are proceeding—and will proceed—against the receiving adults. By the way, that young police officer, Joshua Sydney, you sent to me for liaison has been most helpful. Helpful and eager."

Nick smiled and then suppressed a tear when he thought of kidnappers taking Nicole or Sandra from him.

President Allison peered out her window. "Right now, Detective Garvey, it appears you have yet another guest arriving."

Nick, holding Nicole by the hand, descended the plane's mobile steps. They reached the tarmac as Tim's limousine came to a stop about twenty yards away. "All out!" he heard Tim say to the two passengers in the seat behind him.

Nathan scrambled out first, followed slowly—after Tim forcefully nodded for him to exit—by Half-Penny.

Nathan looked up at Tim. "Thank you."

As Nathan turned—and before he could say another word—Nicole ran up to him and grabbed hold of his left hand.

Nick grinned. "Go along, young man. You're cleared for takeoff. Nicole will show you your seat."

Not needing a second invitation, the two of them raced up the stairs.

"Good job," Half-Penny said, glancing sideways at Tim.

"Last chance, slightly older young man." Tim turned to Half-Penny. "Wouldn't you really like to go along, as well?"

Half-Penny shook his head. "Told you, Detective Branson. I can't go."

Nick decided to butt in. "And pray tell, why not?"

Half-Penny's expression told Nick that he would rather have a tooth pulled than give up the answer to that question.

Nick decided an extra push wouldn't hurt. "Maybe I'll have to put you back behind bars until you come up with an answer."

Nick could hear Half-Penny's teeth grinding.

"Well, Julian?" Nick insisted, figuring his use of Half-Penny's given name would jog the answer loose.

"I can't leave my grandmother. She needs me!" Half-Penny's eyes were aflame.

"Got ya," Nick said, stepping forward and draping his right hand over Half-Penny's trembling shoulder. "I had a grandmother too. I understand."

"Good. You understand. So now you know why I can't go."

Nick tilted his head. "You didn't say you can't go. You said you can't leave your grandmother. There's a difference."

Half-Penny stomped on the tarmac with his left foot. "There *is* *no* difference!"

"Do me a favor, Half-Penny. Tell me again there's no difference after you look up at the plane's door."

His expression defiant, Half-Penny did as requested.

Half-Penny's grandmother, framed in the open door, waved down at him.

Half-Penny lurched toward the plane, took three running steps, broke to a sudden stop, turned, dashed back, and hugged Nick and then Tim, tears in his eyes. Not quite as fast as Nathan, Half-Penny raced up the steps.

His grandmother hugged him for what seemed like half a minute. Finally, the two of them waved down at Nick and Tim.

Nick shook Tim's hand. "I'll be back."

"I sure as hell hope so. If you think I'm going to clean out your half of the desk, you're crazy."

Nick and Tim chuckled.

Nick walked up the stairs. He stopped at the top and waved back.

Tim returned the wave and gave a thumbs-up.

CHAPTER 93

◆

C hristopher Price appeared on the World Council video channel each day over the following two weeks. At the end of those two weeks, a majority of the council's client states approved naming Price the new supreme director of the council.

"There can be only one supreme director, and he's no longer with us," Price stated during a televised press conference. "I've held the title *director* for over twenty years. I feel comfortable with that title and will keep it. I will humbly accept the additional responsibilities of fulfilling the vision of Supreme Director Jason Beck. He filled me in on most of his goals. He also kept a diary covering the ones he shared—plus others that I will digest and share with all of you. I ask for your patience and your prayers."

Another two weeks followed, with Price being seen with President Allison, Chief Executive Johnson, and various world leaders. New energy contracts were signed and old restrictions relaxed. Most notable among these relaxed restrictions were two policy reversals. The first reversal: zero population growth. Any family could have as many children as they could afford. The second reversal: genetic/DNA research restrictions. They were relaxed in crop-yield enhancements, both quality and quantity, when proven safe.

"I wasn't the first," Chris said, "not the first to have his death faked on the orders of Supreme Director Jason Beck. Sixteen years ago, Jason orchestrated the apparent death of Owen Pendleton. He hoped that Dr. Pendleton would continue his research on crop yields. Dr. Pendleton did and has improved yields by a factor of twenty-seven. Another of Jason Beck's visions has been realized."

Chris threw a switch, starting a two-minute video of Dr. Owen Pendleton showing off his rooftop garden to several heads of state. In the video, Dr. Pendleton referred to his DNA modification technique as the Seth Morris Process.

Chris also announced the dismantling of the Manhattan Grid. "The grid will be relocated where there is more consistent sunshine. It did okay in Manhattan but will do so much better elsewhere. Many more elsewheres. Many more grids. Like Supreme Director Jason Beck said several times, 'If you can make it in New York, you can make it anywhere.'" Chris chuckled. "Jason did like show tunes."

The speeches and reversals were applauded throughout the world. Germany: crowds in Berlin and Munich flowed cheering into the streets. Moscow: Red Square was crammed with jubilation. Beijing: orderly crowds chanted in unison. Sicily: hugs all around. Rome: slaps on each other's backs. Florence: handshakes. Paris: accordion music and raised wineglasses. Mecca: many extra prayers thanking Allah.

Every report from every part of the globe revealed unbounded joy on one extreme to earnest and thankful prayers on the other. Nowhere was there discontent. Except . . .

Far up on a hill about sixty miles west of Boston sat a psychiatric hospital. In room 417, a single disfigured man screamed at his in-room video screen.

"I never had those visions! Never those plans! Seth Morris was a little worm who died lashed to a swing. They're all lying! They say I'm dead. Liars! Liars! They're all liars!" The man shook his fist at the screen. His hands were charred and disfigured, as was his face. "I never kept any planning diaries! They are all liars! I hated show tunes! Hated them! Hated them!" As the man jumped up and down in place, his loose facial skin, almost black as coal, seemed as if it would slide off. "Christopher Price can rot in hell! In *hell!* In *hell!* Lenora Allison can rot in hell! No. Worse than hell! Double hell!" The man stopped jumping and stomped a foot. "Triple hell. Triple!"

Outside room 417, two orderlies watched the man's antics through a mesh screen and one-way mirror, their expressions each of amused and bemused concern.

They had watched Mr. 417, as they called him, react violently whenever global news came on his screen. They had once suggested to the head doctor that the video screen be removed from that room. They were told it would stay, for the committing doctor had made it a cardinal requirement, claiming eliciting such a reaction was the only way in this specific case that a cure could be wrought, which would probably require years of such treatment.

After the first few times Mr. 417 had claimed he was Jason Beck, supreme director of the World Council, they had relayed the claims to the head doctor. They were told that that specific delusion was what had caused him to be committed. To ease their concern, the doctor had shown them the report detailing the results of a DNA sample taken from the subject while he was under the care of the committing doctor. The report revealed that the man in room 417 was related to a group of backwoods farmers in lower Argentina and not to the Jason Beck DNA registered for over the past twenty-five years with over two dozen medical institutions worldwide. Closer identification of Mr. 417 proved impossible.

Even though Mr. 417's rants were almost an every-other-day occurrence, the two orderlies felt it their responsibility to observe and, if needed, intervene to protect. His video screen had just a week ago been hardened so that throwing his empty metal shoebox, which he frequently did, wouldn't damage any of the electronics.

Neither orderly could decide if Mr. 417 hated or treasured his metal box with its embossed eagle. When not thrown at the video screen, it was often flung at the nearest wall, but at night he cuddled it next to his pillow.

Mr. 417 was still marching around in circles, shaking his fist and stomping his feet on the floor. "I am Jason Beck! They cannot destroy the World Council! Small people need big government. Can't live without it! Big government needs big people to rule. I am the biggest of all!" Mr. 417 leaped onto his bed and began to jump up and down. "I am Jason Beck! I am Jason Beck, supreme director of the World Council! I am Jason—"

The older of the two orderlies turned off the sound feed. "Let's go," he said to the other. "Back in pattern. Mr. 417 is slipping into his own little world, where he can't hurt anyone. Even himself."

ABOUT THE AUTHOR

◆

Photo by Milan Rose

Carl H. Mitchell has an engineering and computer background and lives in Hillsborough, New Jersey, with his wife. They winter in Tarpon Springs, Florida. Along with downhill skiing, he counts among his hobbies the keeping of koi, of which he currently owns more than one hundred. Auditing a year's worth of bills for fish food and pond maintenance has led to the more accurate conclusion that the koi own him. He was drawn into the world of fiction as a young teenager by Victor Hugo's *The Hunchback of Notre-Dame*. Isaac Asimov and Ernest Hemingway completed his capture. He writes to entertain and challenge his readers. Visit his website, CarlHMitchell. com.

CPSIA information can be obtained
at www.ICGtesting.com
Printed in the USA
FFOW03n0125121117
43411857-42036FF